VIA FOLIOS 119

MISS ROLLINS IN LOVE

by GARIBALDI M. LAPOLLA

Library of Congress Control Number: 2015959107

Cover: https://commons.wikimedia.org/wiki/File:Report_of_Committee_on_
school_inquiry,_Board_of_estimate_an_apportionment,_city_of_New_York_
(1913)_(14763316472).jpg

The Chronology and parts of the Introduction reprinted from the reprint of *The Grand Gennaro*, Rutgers University Press, 2009.

Printed in the United States.

Published by
BORDIGHERA PRESS
John D. Calandra Italian American Institute
25 W. 43rd Street, 17th Floor
New York, NY 10036

VIA Folios 119
ISBN 978–1–59954–105–1

MISS ROLLINS IN LOVE

by

GARIBALDI M. LAPOLLA

with
Chronology, Introduction, and Bibliography by
STEVEN J. BELLUSCIO

BORDIGHERA PRESS

ACKNOLWEDGEMENTS

I would like to thank Borough of Manhattan Community College/ CUNY for awarding me the sabbatical that allowed the completion of this reprint. I would also like to thank Carmine Pizzirusso and Dean Anthony J. Tamburri of the John D. Calandra Italian American Institute and Deborah Starewich of Bordighera Press for invaluable assistance with the preparation of the manuscript. Many thanks are extended to Paul M. Lapolla for his permission to reprint *Miss Rollins in Love* and for the hours he has spent talking to me about his father. I would like to show appreciation for the support of my colleagues at Borough of Manhattan Community College/CUNY, especially Professors Maria Enrico, Frank Elmi, and Joyce Harte. Also, I would like to thank Bordighera Press for its interest in this project and for all it does for Italian American studies. Finally, I would like to thank my wife and children.

CONTENTS

Chronology 11

Introduction 15

Bibliography 27

Table of Contents, *Miss Rollins in Love* 33

Miss Rollins in Love, by Garibaldi M. Lapolla 35

About Steven Belluscio 267

CHRONOLOGY

1888   Garibaldi Mario Lapolla is born April 5 in Rapolla, Basilicata, province of Potenza, Italy, to Biagio Oreste Lapolla and Marie Nicola Buonvicino. In honor of his grandfather's Italian nationalism, he is named after Giuseppe Garibaldi (1807–1882), the George Washington of the modern Italian nation.

1890   Immigrates to New York City with his parents. Over the next decade, over 650,000 of his fellow Italians would follow suit.

1891   Eleven Italians are lynched in New Orleans in connection with the unsolved murder of Police Chief David Hennessy.

1898   Spanish-American War.

1910   Earns A.B. at Columbia University. Begins his public school career teaching English at DeWitt Clinton High School, Manhattan, New York, where he remains for more than a decade, with an interruption for World War I military service.

1912   Earns A.M. at Columbia University after writing a thesis on British romanticist Percy Bysshe Shelley (1792–1822) entitled "Shelley and the Political Parties of His Day."

1914–1918   World War I. Italian immigration stopped.

1917–1918   Enlists in the U.S. Army and is stationed at Fort Ontario, Oswego, New York. Mess sergeant for the hospital. Meets Nurse Margaret McCormick, whom he marries soon after. Signs a letter published in the New Republic on May 26, 1917, arguing that conscientious objectors be allowed to serve non-combat roles in the military. Is transferred to Washington, D.C. Promoted to sergeant first class.

1918   Marries Margaret McCormick.

1919   Son Paul McCormick is born February 11.

1921   Emergency Quota Act severely limits immigration from southern and eastern European countries.

1922   Summoned by the Advisory Council on the Qualification of Teachers, formed by Frank Graves, state commissioner of education, to determine the patriotism of teachers in New York State. Lapolla is questioned about the 1917 New Republic letter he signed. Son Mark Orestes is born February 17.

1924 Immigration Act of 1924 enacted, an even harsher version of the 1921 law. It prohibits Asian immigration entirely.

1925 Publication of F. Scott Fitzgerald novel, *The Great Gatsby*.

1926–1930 Chairman of Thomas Jefferson High School English Department.

1927 On August 23, Ferdinando Nicola Sacco (b. 1891) and Bartolomeo Vanzetti (b. 1888), two Italian anarchists, are executed for the 1920 murder of two pay clerks in South Braintree, Massachusetts. Given the antiradical sentiment of the court, many argue they did not receive a fair trial.

1927–1932 Principal of Thomas Jefferson Summer High School.

1928 Serves as judge in a Brooklyn Borough high school finals for the National Oratorical Contest on the Constitution.

1929 Publishes *Better High School English through Tests and Drills* with Kenneth W. Wright at Noble & Noble. Edits with poet and literary critic Mark Van Doren *A Junior Anthology of World Poetry*, published by Albert & Charles Boni, and praised highly in the *New York Times*. Divorces Margaret McCormick.

1930–1934 Principal of New York Public School 112.

1930 Exchanges letters with famed teacher and educational theorist Leonard Covello, refusing to allow the latter to use the as yet unpublished *The Fire and the Flesh* (then with the working title "La Dantone") as a sociological document for a study of Italian Americans because "it ain't no such beast."

1931 Publishes *The Fire in the Flesh* at the Vanguard Press to generally positive reviews in *Books* and the *New York Times*.

1932 Publishes *Miss Rollins in Love* at the Vanguard Press. Receives lukewarm review from the *New York Times*.

1934 Marries Priscilla Sherman. Is featured (with other Italian American authors) in *Gazzetta del Popolo*.

1935–1953 Principal of New York Public School 174.

1935 Publishes *The Grand Gennaro* at the Vanguard Press to acclaim in the *New Republic*, the *New York Times*, *Books*, the *Boston Transcript*, *Review of Reviews*, and the *Saturday Review of Literature*.

1937   Publishes *Required Grammar in the New York City Public School* at Noble
             & Noble. Interviewed on WEVD New York for a radio program about
             overcrowding in city schools.

1938   Speaks on June 29 at the conference of the National Council of Teach-
             ers of English and criticizes tendency to insist upon a "puritanical
             type of speech" no one actually uses and to reinforce it through teach-
             ing of grammar and usage.

1939   Publication of Pietro di Donato novel *Christ in Concrete.*

1939–1945 World War II. Over one million Italian Americans serve in the armed
             forces. About 250 Italian Americans, 11,000 German Americans, and
             100,000 Japanese Americans are interned for reasons of "national se-
             curity."

1945   In February, son Mark Orestes, trained as an Army Air Corps flight
             officer reported missing in action over Brod, Yugoslavia, after com-
             pleting eighteen missions and receiving the Air Medal. His death was
             confirmed eleven months later.

1946   Serves on a Teacher-Author Committee of New York City school and
             college instructors to protest Board of Education bylaw requiring text-
             book authors to turn over royalties.

1950   Unsuccessfully brings action against the New York City Board of Edu-
             cation in favor of uniform pay for principals of all city schools, el-
             ementary, junior, and senior.

1953   Publishes and illustrates *Italian Cooking for the American Kitchen* and
             The Mushroom Cookbook at W. Funk. The former is praised and widely
             publicized by reviews and interviews in publications such as the *New
             York Times,* the *San Francisco News, Il Progresso Italo-Americano,* the *Chi-
             cago American,* and the *Sunday Herald.*

1954   Dies in his sixty-fifth year on January 13 at Mount Sinai Hospital af-
             ter a massive stroke. His death is mourned and career celebrated by
             colleagues, administrators, students, and parents. The Parent Teacher
             Association donates to Public School 174 a plaque lauding Lapolla as
             "Educator, Leader, and Friend."

1965   Immigration Act of 1965 overturns Immigration Act of 1924.

INTRODUCTION

When Thomas J. Ferraro declared Italian-American writing "one of the better kept literary secrets of [the twentieth] century," he had in mind Garibaldi M. Lapolla, among other authors.[1] In their detailed and sensitive treatment of everyday life in early twentieth-century Italian Harlem, Lapolla's three published novels — *The Fire in the Flesh* (1931), *Miss Rollins in Love* (1932), and *The Grand Gennaro* (1935) — form a cornerstone of early Italian-American fiction for readers familiar with the likes of Silvio Villa, Giuseppe Cautela, Louis Forgione, Frances Winwar, John Fante, Mari Tomasi, Pietro di Donato, Guido d'Agostino, and Jerre Mangione. However, Garibaldi M. Lapolla's writing has not garnered nearly the attention it deserves despite his renown among scholars of Italian-American literature, the similarity of his fiction to that of canonical ethnic writers such as Abraham Cahan and Anzia Yezierska, and the recent entry into the canon of other Italian-American fiction writers (such as Pietro di Donato and John Fante). To be sure, one obvious reason is unavailability. While Lapolla's novels were generally well reviewed — especially *The Grand Gennaro,* considered to be his best work — they soon went out of print. And despite an Arno Press resurrection of his first and last novels in 1975, Garibaldi M. Lapolla's name continues to remain in underserved obscurity; he could very well be the best kept secret of Italian-American literature.

TEACHER, SOLDIER, WRITER

Born April 5, 1888, in Rapolla, Basilicata, Province of Potenza, Italy, to Biagio Oreste Lapolla and Marie Nicola Lapolla (née Buonvicino), Garibaldi Mario Lapolla (his given name reflecting the Italian patriotism of his paternal grandfather) left Italy and immigrated to New York City with his parents in 1890 before age two. He would lose his mother at age nine.[2] An exceptional student in public school as a child, Lapolla attended Columbia University, earning a B.A. in 1910 and an M.A. in 1912, after completing a thesis on British romantic poet Percy Bysshe Shelley.[3] In 1910, Lapolla began teaching English at DeWitt Clinton High School, then located in Manhattan, where he left a great impression on his students, including Mortimer Adler, who would become one of America's most celebrated

---

[1]Thomas J. Ferraro, "Ethnicity in the Marketplace" 398.
[2]Maria Luisa, "Conversazioni del Giovedì" 1; Olga Peragallo, *Italian-American Authors and Their Contribution to American Literature* 138; Martino Marazzi, "King of Harlem: Garibaldi Lapolla and Gennaro Accuci 'Il Grande'" 190, 207.
[3]Lawrence J. Oliver, "'Beyond Ethnicity': Portraits of the Italian-American Artist in Garibaldi Lapolla's Novels" 6; Robert Hornsby, e-mail message to Belluscio, 2 Oct. 2007. Lapolla's degrees were granted by Columbia College, not Columbia Teachers College, as has been erroneously assumed.

philosophers and public intellectuals of the twentieth century.[4] Thus began Lapolla's rich, productive, and lifelong career as an educator and educational theorist — a career interrupted only by military service during World War I in which he "held every position from buck private to cook to lecturer on personal prophylaxis to sergeant to lieutenant of artillery."[5]

From 1917 to 1918, Lapolla was stationed at Fort Ontario, Oswego, New York, where, after an "early [. . .] career [. . .] underscored by black marks" in which "he seemed temperamentally incapable of complying with regulations," "he disciplined himself to become a good soldier."[6] As mess sergeant, he nurtured what would become a lifelong passion and what had been a family tradition of sorts: his father had owned restaurants in Montreal, Quebec, and New York, and was known to claim descent from "a long line of cooks" dating back to Ancient Rome.[7] While a soldier in Flower Unit N, Post Hospital No. 5, Fort Ontario, Lapolla met his future wife, Nurse Margaret McCormick, whom he married in 1918 and with whom he conceived two sons: Paul McCormick (born February 11, 1919) and Mark Oreste (born Feburary 17, 1922).[8] Lapolla also served on the Associate Board of the *Ontario Post* newspaper and wrote for it, taught in the fort's school, played guard and tackle for its football team, and worked as a chaplain's assistant before he was transferred to Washington and eventually promoted to Sergeant First Class.[9]

After his successful tenure at DeWitt Clinton High School, where he taught on the faculty alongside famed educational theorist and Italian-American activist Leonard Covello, Lapolla served as chairman of the Thomas Jefferson High School English Department from 1926 to 1930 and principal of the Thomas Jefferson Summer High School from 1927 to 1932. In 1929, Lapolla's first marriage ended in divorce; in 1934, he married Priscilla Sherman, a fellow faculty member. From 1930 to 1934, Lapolla was principal of Public School 112, and from 1934 to his death in 1954, principal of Public School 174.[10]

Lapolla fought for social justice throughout his life, even running "for every office from Alderman to Congressman on the Socialist ticket" be-

---

[4]Mortimer J. Adler, *Philosopher at Large: An Intellectual Biography* 29.

[5]From the book jacket of the Vanguard Press edition of *The Fire in the Flesh* (1931), Oversized Folder 1, MSS 64, Garibaldi M. Lapolla Papers, Historical Society of Pennsylvania, Philadelphia (these papers are hereafter cited as GMLP).

[6]"Editor's Notebook," *Sunday Herald* 21 June 1953, newspaper clipping, box 4, folder 12, GMLP.

[7]Garibaldi M. Lapolla, *Italian Food for the American Kitchen* ix.

[8]Paul Lear, e-mail message to Belluscio, 1 Oct. 2007; www.ancestry.com; Paul Lapolla, telephone interview by Belluscio, 25 June 2007.

[9]*Ontario Post* 22 Sept. 1917, 29 Sept. 1917, 8 Dec. 1917, 20 Apr. 1918, 25 May 1918, and 1 June 1918.

[10]Marc K. Blackburn, "Register of the Garibaldi M. Lapolla Papers," GMLP, 1–2; *New York Times* 14 Jan. 1954: 29.

fore World War I.[11] Unwilling to sell short immigrant students, he campaigned endlessly for more intelligent, student-centered pedagogical practices in the tradition of John Dewey and a more pragmatic approach to teaching English grammar, rankling school administrators but advocating what would eventually become educational orthodoxy. In keeping with his democratic educational vision, Lapolla also challenged Board of Education by-laws requiring textbook authors to turn over royalties to the school district and fought for uniform pay for principals of all city schools.[12] This fighting spirit often got him into trouble. For example, in 1922, he was interrogated by the Advisory Council on the Qualification of Teachers — a by-product of the 1919 Joint Legislative Committee to Investigate Seditious Activities (also known as the Lusk Committee) — about his co-signed letter printed in the May 26, 1917, issue of the *New Republic,* which argued that conscientious objectors ought to be allowed to serve non-combat roles in the military during World War I and, more broadly, that there ought to be "a social setting within America sufficiently hospitable to all conscientious objectors."[13] Upton Sinclair would later relish the irony of Lapolla, "an artillery officer" during the war, "now . . . sitting on the bench, humbly waiting his turn to be browbeaten."[14] While Lapolla escaped the investigation unscathed, he would be unable to avoid similar controversy in the future. As principal of Public School 174 in Brooklyn in the early 1950s, Lapolla vigorously defended teachers persecuted by the House Un-American Activities Committee, arguing that they should be judged not for their beliefs but, rather, their ability in the classroom. "Aren't we, in fact," Lapolla wrote, "chasing a phantom that, in a more reasonable period, we would recognize and admit as such?"[15] Throughout his educational career, Lapolla remained aggressively committed to winning justice for students, teachers, and administrators and maintaining quality in education.

As an English specialist, Lapolla taught "grammar, American literature, English literature, poetry, Shakespeare, and remedial English."[16] Frequently dissatisfied with the status quo of English pedagogy, Lapolla published textbooks designed to teach English grammar more practically and to deliver an appreciation of literature to young students. During his career, he penned *Better High School English* (1929) and *Required Grammar*

---

[11]This quotation, taken from the book jacket of *The Fire in the Flesh* (1931), is qtd. in Blackburn, "Register" 2.

[12]"Teachers Oppose Loss of Royalties," *New York Times* 17 Sept. 1946: 7; "Principals Lose Pay Case," *New York Times* 2 June 1950: 12.

[13]"Teachers Secretly Quizzed on Loyalty," *New York Times* 17 May 1922: 18; Norman Thomas, et al., "The Religion of Free Men," letter to the editor, *New Republic* 16 May 1917: 109.

[14]Upton Sinclair, *The Goslings: A Study of the American Schools* 84.

[15]Garibaldi M. Lapolla, "Letter in Answer to Dr. Lefkowitz about So-Called Communist Teachers," GMLP, Box 1, Folder 2, 3–5.

[16]Marc K. Blackburn, "Register" 2.

in the New York Public Schools (1937) to serve the former purpose and co-edited with Mark Van Doren *The Junior Anthology of World Poetry* (1929) to serve the latter. Lapolla was also interested in educating the general public about the delights of the Italian cuisine he had grown up enjoying and masterfully learning to prepare. In 1953, he published *Italian Cooking for the American Kitchen,* designed to help Americans learn the variety of Italian cooking; that same year, he also published *The Mushroom Cookbook.* Lapolla also left behind a wealth of unpublished writings — essays, poems, plays, short stories, a novel titled "Jerry," and other unfinished manuscripts.

The unifying thread of most of Lapolla's written work — his textbooks, his cookbooks, and his novels — is the continuous negotiation between Italian and American cultures. His textbooks were designed with the Italian immigrant student in mind and the concern of how best to serve them in the American public school system. His cookbooks attempted to teach an American audience about Italian food and thereby provide an entrée into Italian history, culture, and geography: as Americans learned to prepare and appreciate Italian cuisine, these so-called foreigners in their midst would come to seem less foreign. Finally, his novels used turn-of-the-century East Harlem as a fictional staging ground for the oft-troubled coexistence of Italian ancestry and American dreams. All the while, *Professore* Lapolla is the patient and compassionate pedagogue, challenging his student — the reader — to grow beyond the limitations of prior experience.

Lapolla traveled widely during his lifetime throughout North America, South America, and Europe, including his native Italy. Lapolla was an avid artist; many of his pencil sketches, pen and ink drawings, and water colors — mostly urban scenes, rural pastorals, portraits, and still lifes — serve as a record of the people and places he encountered at home and abroad. Lapolla even supplied the pen and ink drawings of various foods for *Italian Cooking for the American Kitchen.* An expert letter writer, Lapolla infused his correspondence with wry humor and keen wit, both high- and lowbrow. He would regale his reader with evocative accounts of his New York surroundings before matter-of-factly addressing the main subject matter of the letter. His letters to younger son Mark Oreste Lapolla while the latter served in Foggia, Italy, as an Army Air Forces flight officer during World War II are ample evidence of this. In these letters to "Oreste," Lapolla discourses about Italian language, geography, and culture; the progress of the war; and the mood of Americans back on the homefront. Of themselves, these letters are little gems of geopolitics, cultural criticism, and homespun wisdom.[17] Some of the best of these letters were returned, for Mark Lapolla went missing in action over Brod, Yugoslavia, while flying a mission during February 1945. On January 5, 1946, he was

---

[17]Garibaldi Lapolla to Mark O. Lapolla, returned letters, 25 Dec. 1944; 7 Jan. 1945; 15 Jan. 1945; 31 Jan. 1945; 6 Feb. 1945, box 1, folder 3, GMLP.

reported to have been killed there.[18] An emotional man, Lapolla took his son's death very hard, and during his 1953 trip to Italy, he visited Oreste's gravesite with his wife Priscilla, writing in his trip diary, "I couldn't have come here and not done it."[19]

When Garibaldi M. Lapolla died of a massive stroke on January 13, 1954, at the age of sixty-five, Priscilla received an outpouring of condolences for "Gari," as he was affectionately known, from colleagues and friends throughout his life and career praising his qualities as an educator, intellectual, artist, and fellow human. The Parent Teacher Association donated a plaque to New York Public School 174 lauding Lapolla as an "Educator, Leader, and Friend." Although he died much too young, he had the great fortune of being remembered, and celebrated, by friends and acquaintances for all the many things he had accomplished.

"METHOD REALISTIC, BUT INTENT ROMANTIC"

Garibaldi M. Lapolla's reputation as a novelist, however, would be neglected until the 1980s, when scholarship began to recognize his talent and importance as "East Harlem's novelist"[20] — or, at least, Italian Harlem's novelist. Critics have rightly attributed Lapolla's obscurity in part to his refusal to accede to the aesthetic trends of the 1930s: high modernism and proletarian literature.[21] In course lecture notes, it is clear that while Lapolla was by no means opposed to the literary experimentation of the early twentieth century, he disliked the use of "pyrotechnical coloring and devices" for their own sake; and while Lapolla was himself a socialist, he dismissively refers to proletarian literature as "propaganda" "mainly concerned with revealing the life of worker-classes as they are allegedly developing a historic class-consciousness."[22] Furthermore, Lapolla celebrated what he called the "newer romanticis[m]" of contemporary authors who "have held to the notion that the novel was made to please, that factual scenes immediate to the readers' experience are not the inevitable material of the novel, that readers are still interested in the carefully organized plot, in remote peoples and times, in themes that have no bearing on modern conditions save in a large way, that propaganda for any cause

---

[18]"Missing Flight Officer Now Is Reported Killed," *New York Times* 6 Jan. 1946: 30.

[19]Paul Lapolla, telephone interview by Belluscio, 11 Nov. 2007. Lapolla, European trip diary, 1953, Box 1, Folder 9, GMLP.

[20]Robert Anthony Orsi, *The Madonna of 115th Street: Faith and Community in Italian Harlem, 1880–1950* 22. Richard A. Meckel considers Lapolla to be "as good as many of the better known ethnic/immigrant social realists of the 1930s and 1940s" ("A Reconsideration: The Not So Fundamental Ideology of Garibaldi Marto Lapolla" 127); and Lawrence J. Oliver claims, "outside of Puzo and Pietro di Donato, no writer has so skillfully portrayed the marble beneath the mud, to use Nathaniel Hawthorne's expression, of the Italian-American immigrant experience ("'Great Equalizer' or 'Cruel Stepmother'?": 116).

[21]Martino Marazzi, "King of Harlem" 191; Richard A. Meckel, "A Reconsideration" 128.

[22]Garibaldi Lapolla, "The American Novel" box 2, folder 3, GMLP.

is not the purpose of fiction." Lapolla admired Pearl Buck's writing for providing "pictures which please by their combination of the familiar in human nature against a background of the unfamiliar," her "method realistic, but intent romantic."[23]

This description goes a long way toward explaining Lapolla's own aesthetic approach. While his fictions are rich with the realistic specifics of place and people — East Harlem and the Italians who once lived there — the pastness of these very specifics lends them, even from the perspective of the 1930s, the luster of historical romance. Furthermore, Lapolla frequently imbues his settings with firelight, moonlight, shadowplay, and religious iconography, elements more typical of Nathaniel Hawthorne or Edgar Allan Poe than William Dean Howells or Henry James. The traditional Southern Italian folk beliefs fictionalized by Lapolla — with their fascinating interplay of Christian providence, saint worship, Marianism, and occult mysticism — further add to the otherworldly romanticism of the novels. Finally, Lapolla's novels feature characters who attempt to rise above their sordid urban surroundings toward a transcendental plane of spiritual and — given the recurrence of the artist figure in all three of his works — artistic fulfillment.[24]

The Fire in the Flesh and The Grand Gennaro

The Fire in the Flesh, Lapolla's first published novel, certainly fits this description. Set in turn-of-the-century Italian Harlem, the novel puts into motion both a business plot and an occasionally intersecting love plot that ensnare its principal characters as they make their uneasy adjustments to the ways of urban America. In the love plot, which begins in Villetto, Italy, protagonist Agnese Filoppina bears the child of priest Gelsomino Merlino and, while bearing the brunt of the village's scorn, marries simpleton Michele Dantone and leaves with son Giovanni for Italian Harlem. Never truly loving her husband, Agnese saves her affection for her business rival Antonio Farinella and Padre Gelsomino, who flees Villetto for America soon after Agnese leaves. Meanwhile, in the business plot, Agnese builds, from humble beginnings and through often-dubious means, a real-estate empire that dazzles her fellow Italian immigrants and shames her do-nothing husband. While these characters endlessly pursue love and money — "the fire in the flesh" that motivates them — one character, the young painter Giovanni Dantone, seeks transcendence from his prosaic surroundings through art.

Its first chapters set during the late-nineteenth-century flood of Italian immigration to the United States, Lapolla's third and final published novel,

---

[23]*Ibid.*

[24]As Lawrence J. Oliver writes, "Lapolla's novels display the ethical idealism — the belief that the people can rise above corrupting and degrading influences to a higher moral plane — that marks [. . .] romantic literature in general. Indeed, if a label must be applied to Lapolla's novels, the most appropriate would be that coined by Frank Norris, 'romances of the commonplace'" ("Beyond Ethnicity" 18–19).

The Grand Gennaro, tells the story of Gennaro Accuci, a Calabrian immigrant to Italian Harlem who rises from a small-time laborer to owner of a junk business, and then "minor dictator" of the local Italian-American community.[25] By pluck, luck, and unscrupulous business practices, Gennaro is able to "make America" and become "The Grand Gennaro," in effect an Italian-American "Great Gatsby." Modeling himself after the worst of the actual robber barons, Gennaro, who at the beginning of the narrative is a penniless laborer, violently wrests control of his friend Rocco Pagliamini's junk business. Gennaro's assimilative program of hyper-masculine greed and brute force is ironically underscored by the series of women he beds (consensually or not), molests, or otherwise abuses — before and after he finally sends for his wife Rosaria and his children Domenico, Emilio, and Elena.

Toward the end of the narrative, however, Gennaro grows increasingly uneasy with his aggressive Americanism. He humanizes his business practices and, remorseful for having robbed Rocco Pagliamini of a livelihood, makes his old friend the manager of his rag business. Gennaro also sees the fruition of a long-term project: the construction of Saint Elena the Blessed, a Catholic church for local Italian Americans. Initially a monument of self-serving hubris, the church, in Gennaro's state of moral reformation, becomes a kind of penance. Rocco, however, has never forgiven Gennaro and even stirs up discontent among Gennaro's workers, who threaten to strike for better wages. When Gennaro manages to settle the labor dispute peacefully and beneficially for the workers, Rocco, enraged by another defeat by his former friend, murders Gennaro. Like so many other European immigrant protagonists — Abraham Cahan's Yekl and David Levinsky, Guido d'Agostino's Emilio Gardella, and Samuel Ornitz's Meyer Hirsch, to name just a few — Gennaro is made to pay for his hyper-assimilative indiscretion.

MISS ROLLINS IN LOVE

In a mostly negative assessment of the novel, a *New York Times* reviewer describes Garibaldi M. Lapolla's second effort as "a ponderous, heavily subjective account of the impulses and heart-action of an inhibited school teacher."[26] Olga Peragallo, writing in the 1940s, was more generous. She considered the novel "more subtly and finely drawn, less carnal and melodramatic" than *The Fire in the Flesh* and "written with a richness and a fine mastery of the English language."[27] Published in 1932, the novel takes education as its central focus and privileges a student-centered, culturally pluralistic progressive pedagogy theorized by John Dewey in the late nineteenth and early twentieth centuries and practiced by Italian-Amer-

---

[25]Rose Basile Green, *The Italian-American Novel: A Document of the Interaction of Two Cultures* 74.
[26]"A Schoolmarm in Love" 21.
[27]Peragallo 140.

ican Harlem educators and writers. *Miss Rollins in Love* interweaves two plot threads, one in part documenting the challenges confronting the exceptional Italian-American student Donato Contini, and the other in part documenting the challenges confronting the idealistic, Deweyan educator Amy Rollins. Although the story Lapolla tells is by no means conclusive, the novel suggests that while Donato Contini finds success as a puppeteer and sculptor, many, if not most exceptional students like him do not achieve such greatness. Instead, they are neglected by a traditional public school system that is ignorant of immigrant students' cultural situations and unconcerned with their specific needs. Furthermore, such a school system is shown to be in many ways hostile to the efforts of well-meaning teachers like Amy Rollins, who notice and wish to nurture the potential of Donato Contini and students like him. While *Miss Rollins in Love* suggests that success is rare given the long odds, it also suggests that the only hope for success lies in the progressive, culturally pluralistic pedagogy theorized by John Dewey and practiced by Angelo Patri (1876–1965), Leonard Covello (1887–1982), and Garibaldi M. Lapolla. The two plot threads join together in a romantic relationship between Donato and Amy that has symbolic implications for the relationship between teachers and students.

In the novel, Donato Contini — the son of Sicilian immigrants, his father a master puppeteer named Emanuele — is earnest and serious in his studies as a young boy, but lives in what we would now call an "at-risk" family environment. His parents are poor, and his brother Giulio is said to have been a gangster who had been sent to the electric chair for his participation in a botched robbery that had led to a fatality. The reader also learns that Donato's mother had died of a broken heart shortly after hearing the bad news. Both Donato and Giulio are said to have had little guidance from their father, who, for example, would often strike both boys no matter who had misbehaved. The lure of the street had been strong for both brothers. However, Donato had managed to escape Giulio's fate by immersing himself in schoolwork and in the marionette theater. Lapolla makes certain the reader understands the many challenges facing Donato and real-world students of his ilk. After a powerful description of Giulio's crime, trial, imprisonment, and execution, the narrator states, "It was in this atmosphere that Donato grew up."[28] Indeed, Donato encounters many pressures faced by Italian-American students in the early years of heavy Italian immigration to the United States. For example, he wonders if he shouldn't leave high school early in order to help his father earn money. At one point in the novel, he is placed in a reformatory for a violent altercation in a speakeasy. Even though he is studious and successful at school, he faces outright bigotry from educators such as Mr. Sidon and Mr. Crabbing who don't believe Donato and immigrant students like him are worth the effort Amy Rollins puts into their education.

Described by Rose Basile Green as "the incarnation of the missionary

---

[28]Lapolla, *Miss Rollins in Love* 123. Hereafter referred to in the text as "*MRIL*."

zeal and sincerity of altruists who have helped immigrants to realize their own success," Amy Rollins sees the potential in even the most coarse and untutored students of her Latin classes and views teaching as a kind of "work that satisfied and blessed" (*MRIL* 41).[29] Like John Dewey, and almost as if she were following the advice of Angelo Patri and Leonard Covello, Amy Rollins believes her "main objective as a teacher" is to "enter into the life of the promising students in her classes, know about their families and their surroundings, become friends with them and eventually a force in their days" (*MRIL* 44). As Lawrence J. Oliver and Martino Marazzi have argued, Lapolla demonstrates that this idealism inevitably competes with the reality of "large classes, burdensome clerical duties, a sense of complete division between teachers and pupils, and a general air of pessimism and cynicism about teaching and its results" (*MRIL* 191).[30] One day as she walks toward Donato's home, one of many acts of teacherly outreach she performs in the novel, she ponders her teaching of language and literature and the edifying effect is has upon poor immigrant children, who might otherwise fall victim to the circumstances of their daily lives but instead are allowed to "utter the music of their hearts above the confusion of the streets." "Such was Donato," Amy reflects, "and such might have been his brother, Giulio, could he have been saved" (*MRIL* 192).

While some of her colleagues are sympathetic — like, for example, Principal Polter, who is loathe to administer heavy-handed discipline, has a friendly relationship with teaching faculty, advocates "heart-to-heart pedagogy," and views ethnic students favorably — most are not (*MRIL* 100). For example, there is the authoritarian Mr. Aborn, who in trying to establish control of Amy's classroom, refers to Donato as "pretty bad stuff" (*MRIL* 55). Then there is Mr. Sidon, a teacher called on for "disciplinary cases too serious in character to be considered sporadic or negligible," who berates Donato and accuses him of being involved in "organized crime" (*MRIL* 58). When Donato inquires about establishing a sculpting club, Amy consults with an art teacher, who responds cynically: "It's an idea [. . .] but who'll give you one? Where's the money and where's the program committee to put it in? Talk to the principal? What's he care? Who cares about art?" (*MRIL* 106). Eventually, Amy comes to see her colleagues as "leering effigies around her," "frustrated in part by the limited pay of their profession, in part by the narrow circle of contacts it allowed, in part by the poverty of their own vitality" (*MRIL* 197). Amy herself on occasion struggles with her own despair over the state of her profession and the cynicism this could foster.

The reader is led to understand that Amy's Deweyan pedagogical approach genuinely benefits Donato. As Lawrence J. Oliver argues, "Amy [. . .] instills in her pupil-paramour a love of classical poetry that refines

---

[29]Green 74.
[30]Oliver, "Great Equalizer" 117–18; Marazzi, "King of Harlem" 200.

his sensibilities and that leaves its mark on his mature art."[31] While Donato is Amy's student, she is supportive of his desire to form a sculpting club, much as Angelo Patri and Leonard Covello were supportive of their students' extracurricular interests. Throughout Donato's academic career, Amy frequently encourages him to stay in school. After Donato is forced out because of trouble with the law, Amy encourages him to return to his studies. When Donato takes a college summer art class, Amy is supportive of his idea to put on a marionette show there with his father. When Donato is released from the reformatory, she makes room in her rented household for him to live and provides him with materials and with the support needed for him to put on a successful art exhibit. After the exhibit, Donato tells Amy, "It's yours, Amy — it's all the poetry you taught me out of Virgil and Horace and Juvenal . . . it's all the poetry you gave me out of your own life" (*MRIL* 346). A further implication is that Amy's teaching of Latin literature, in keeping with Angelo Patri's and Leonard Covello's recommendations, has instilled some measure of pride in Donato for his distant ancestral past. As Lawrence J. Oliver has argued, Donato becomes a well-adjusted, assimilated, yet still ethnic, artist, and the titles of his successful works support this claim: "*The Pioneer Grandmother, The Immigrants at Ellis Island, The Marionette Director*" (*MRIL* 368).[32] Donato is not unlike the memoirists studied in articles by Maria Parrino (Rosa Cavalleri, Bruna Pieracci, Grace Spinelli, and Clara Grillo) and Caroline Pari-Pfisterer (M. Bella Mirabella, Louise de Salvo, and Marianna de Marco Torgovnick) in that his education does not quash his sense of himself as Italian American but rather affords him a more confident understanding of what Italian American means.[33]

Lapolla places Amy's professional life on equal footing with her romantic life; indeed, as the plot evolves the latter becomes symbolic of the former. Lapolla has Amy reject a series of suitors, each of whom embodies qualities undesirable for a devoted Deweyan teacher such as Amy. Stephen Bennett, for example, wants Amy to quit work altogether and live a carefree life as his wife. Mr. Crabbing is miserly, petty, even bigoted, and lacks the generosity of spirit required of the progressive pedagogue. Mortimer, a man Amy meets while vacationing in Italy, is a New York schoolteacher himself, and he shares the cynicism of many of Amy's colleagues. Much as he intertwines, even conflates, the desire for money and the desire for love in *The Fire in the Flesh,* Lapolla merges Amy's desire to teach well with her desire for love. As the novel progresses, Amy develops romantic feelings for Donato. At one point, when Donato is no longer Amy's student, she reflects upon what she considers to be her failure as a teacher: "Somehow it had something to do with Stephen, with Crabbing, with Donato. If it could but bloom and be, it would do more than merely display

---

[31]Oliver, "Beyond Ethnicity" 12.
[32]*Ibid.* 16–19.
[33]Parrino 72; Pari-Pfisterer 19.

its flower, like one of the plants she was so carefully tending at home. It would radiate color, it would burst into flame, and the flame would be warmth and fulfillment. In its radiance, teaching would acquire a new meaning" (*MRIL* 249). On more than one occasion, Amy compares Donato to the Greek god Hermes. Compared to the great messenger of the gods, "Stephen and Crabbing and Mortimer now lacked bulk and form, were nothings in a distant world that had suddenly become shadow" (*MRIL* 283). The reader cannot help but reflect on the rejected suitors' failures as love interests and as Deweyan intellects.

Taken literally, the reader would disapprove of the love relationship between Donato and Amy, which is first signaled while Donato is still Amy's student but is fully realized while Donato lives with Amy after his stay in the reformatory. Taken symbolically, however, the relationship serves as a hyperbolic statement of the need for a more productive, symbiotic relationship between teacher and student and the need for the traditional boundary between the two to become more elastic. The fact that Donato does *not* return to school after his stay in the reformatory, in fact finds success without school, and the fact that Donato and Amy's relationship is not allowed to continue suggests that at the time of the novel's writing, the ideal, Deweyan relationship between teacher and student had not been achieved. However, at the novel's end and in a chapter entitled "The Cactus Blooms," the reader discovers that Amy Rollins has relocated to New Mexico, where she lives with her brother Philip, who has recovered from shellshock after his service in World War I, and Donato, Jr., a young son she vows never to tell Donato about. So while Lawrence J. Oliver is correct to suggest that Lapolla was highly skeptical of the ability of the public school system he knew to assist most immigrant children, and that the bright Italian-American schoolchildren of his fiction — Giovanni Dantone of *The Fire in the Flesh* and Donato Contini of *Miss Rollins in Love* — find success almost in spite of their studies — the presence of a Donato, Jr., at the end of *Miss Rollins in Love* indicates an optimism for the future, when a better realized relationship between teachers and students will work for the benefit of generations of schoolchildren to come.[34] But why does Lapolla insist upon bringing Amy Rollins to New Mexico? It is likely because these desert environs allow Lapolla the use of the cactus metaphor he announces in the title of the final chapter. In New Mexico, Amy becomes a successful cactus gardener, and the implication of this is that the best of teachers, like Amy, are able to nurture the social and intellectual capacities of their students even in the harshest of environments, like those faced by urban ethnic students such as Donato. They are able to get the cactus to bloom even with the laws of nature seemingly arrayed against them. Lapolla may have gotten the metaphor from Angelo Patri's educational memoir *A Schoolmaster in the Great City* (1917), in which the author tells the following story after the first act of a play given by the

---

[34]Oliver, "Great Equalizer" 120–21.

students of P.S. 4:

> 'My friends,' I said, 'I have brought you here to enlist your collective help in the work of the school. Acting together as a moral force in the neighborhood you are more vital to the education of the children than is the school. You remember the story of the cactus plant, how once upon a time, the cactus was a fine flourishing plant with luscious fruit. Then there came a change over that part of the earth where the cactus grew. The mountains heaved and the wind shifted. The valley that was once rich became barren and the plants died. They all died but the cactus plant, which, in answer to the new needs that the changing earth brought, toughened its skin and grew needles all over its body. The winds came with their sandy blasts and the cactus plant withstood their attacks. It had become ugly, repellent, and the beasts of the field could not touch it. Thousands of years after, a man came by who took the cactus plant and put it in his garden. Here there were no hot sandy winds. There was moisture and soft breezes and wonderful soil to grow in. The cactus plant changed and became once more the thing it had been in the beginning, a fine plant with luscious fruit. So it is with your children. You are the soil and the wind and the light in which the child, your plant, grows. You are the environment, the compelling force which by its influence, can make the children fine children, or can make of them warped and twisted natures unfit to live with, unworthy to carry on the ideals of your souls. Even if we could take upon our shoulders all the responsibilities of the home and relieve you entirely it would not be good for you and for the children. The children need you. You cannot afford to have the teachers take over your responsibility. You must share the common burden. You must all work together to make the conditions of life under which the children are living such that they will grow up healthy, intelligent, sympathetic, of fine American citizenship.[35]

From the idea that schoolchildren need to be nurtured, to the idea that schools require full community involvement, to the idea that education prepares children not only for work but also for American citizenship, this passage conjoins many of the recurring themes and stated ideals of progressive pedagogical literature.

---

[35]Patri 65–66.

BIBLIOGRAPHY

Note: GMLP= MSS 64, Garibaldi M. Lapolla Papers, Historical Society of Pennsylvania, Philadelphia

Adler, Mortimer J. *Philosopher at Large: An Intellectual Autobiography.* New York: Macmillan Publishing Co., 1977.

Blackburn, Marc K. "Register of the Garibaldi Mario Lapolla Papers, 1930– 1976, MSS. Group 64." GMLP.

"Editor's Notebook." *Sunday Herald* 21 June 1953.

Ferraro, Thomas. "Ethnicity and the Marketplace." *The Columbia History of the American Novel.* Ed. Emory Elliott. New York: Columbia UP, 1991. 380–406.

Green, Rose Basile. *The Italian-American Novel: A Document of the Interaction of Two Cultures.* Rutherford, NJ: Fairleigh Dickinson UP, 1974.

Hornsby, Robert. E-mail to the author. 2 Oct. 2007.

Lapolla, Garibaldi M. "The American Novel." Box 2, folder 3, GMLP.

___. *European Trip Diary.* 1953. GMLP, Box 1, folder 9.

___. *The Fire in the Flesh.* 1931. New York: Arno Press, 1975.

___. *The Grand Gennaro.* 1935. New York: Arno Press, 1975.

___. *Italian Food for the American Kitchen.* New York: Wilfred Funk, 1953.

___. "Letter in Answer to Dr. Lefkowitz about So-Called Communist Teachers." GMLP, Box 1, Folder 2, 3–5.

___. *Miss Rollins in Love.* New York: The Vanguard Press, 1932.

___. Returned letter. New York, to Mark O. Lapolla, 25 Dec. 1944. GMLP, box 1, folder 3.

___. Returned letter. New York, to Mark O. Lapolla, 7 Jan. 1945. GMLP, box 1, folder 3.

___. Returned letter. New York, to Mark O. Lapolla, 15 Jan. 1945. GMLP, box 1, folder 3.

___. Returned letter. New York, to Mark O. Lapolla, 31 Jan. 1945. GMLP, box 1, folder 3.

___. Returned letter. New York, to Mark O. Lapolla, 6 Feb. 1945. GMLP, box 1, folder 3.

Lapolla, Paul. Telephone interview. 25 June 2007.

___. Telephone interview. 11 Nov. 2007.

Lear, Paul. E-mail to the author. 1 Oct. 2007.

Luisa, Maria. "Le Conversazioni del Giovedì." *Il Progresso Italo-Americano* 2 Apr. 1953: 1.

Marazzi, Martino. "King of Harlem: Garibaldi Lapolla and Gennaro Accuci 'Il Grande'" *'Merica: A Conference on the Culture and Literature of Italians in North America.* Ed. Aldo Bove and Giuseppe Massara. Jan. 2003. Rome and Cassino, Italy. Stony Brook, NY: Forum Italicum, 2005. 190–210.

Meckel, Richard A. "A Reconsideration: The Not So Fundamental Sociology of

Garibaldi Marto Lapolla." *MELUS* 3:4 (1987): 127–39.

"Missing Flight Officer Now Is Reported Killed." *New York Times* 6 Jan. 1946: 30.
    New York Times Jan. 1954: 29.

Oliver, Lawrence J. "'Beyond Ethnicity': Portraits of the Italian-American Art-
    ist in Garibaldi Lapolla's Novels." *American Studies* 28.2 (1987): 5–21.

___. "'Great Equalizer' or 'Cruel Stepmother'?: Image of the School in Italian-
    American Literature." *The Journal of Ethnic Studies* 15.2 (1987): 113–30.

Ontario Post. 2 Sept. 1917.

___. 29 Sept. 1917.

___. 8 Dec. 1917.

___. 20 Apr. 1918.

___. 25 May 1918.

___. 1 June 1918.

Orsi, Robert Anthony. *The Madonna of 115th Street: Faith and Community in Ital-
    ian Harlem, 1880–1950.* New Haven, CT: Yale UP, 1985.

Pari-Pfisterer, Caroline. "Divided Worlds: Autobiographical Literacy Narra-
    tives and Italian-American Women Writers." *VIA* 22.1 (Spring 2011): 3–20.

Parrino, Maria. "Education in the Autobiographies of Four Italian Women Im-
    migrants." *American Woman, Italian Style: Italian Americana's Best Writings
    on Women.* Ed. Carol Bonomo Albright and Christine Palamidessi Moore.
    New York: Fordham UP, 2011. 55–77.

Patri, Angelo. *A Schoolmaster of the Great City: A Progressive Educator's Pioneer-
    ing Vision for Urban Schools.* 1917. New York: The New Press, 2007.

Peragallo, Olga. *Italian-American Authors and Their Contribution to American Lit-
    erature.* Ed. Anita Peragallo. New York: S. F. Vanni, 1949.

"Principals Lose Pay Case." *New York Times* 2 June 1950: 12.

"A Schoolmarm in Love." Rev. of *Miss Rollins in Love,* by Garibaldi M. Lapolla.
    New York Times 28 Feb. 1932: 21.

Sinclair, Upton. *The Goslings: A Study of the American Schools.* Pasadena, CA:
    Upton Sinclair, 1924.

"Teachers Oppose Loss of Royalties." *New York Times* 17 Sept. 1946: 7.

"Teachers Secretly Quizzed on Loyalty." *New York Times* 17 May 1922: 18.

Thomas, Norman, et al. Letter to the editor. *The New Republic* 26 May 1917: 109–11.

Www.ancestry.com. Accessed 28 March 2015. http://search.ancestry.com/
    cgi-bin/sse.dll?rank=1&new=1&MSAV=0&msT=1&gss=angs-g&gsfn=g
    aribalde&gsln=lapolla&mswpn=1652382&mswpn_PInfo=6-%7c0%7c165
    2393%7c0%7c2%7c3244%7c35%7c1652382%7c0%7c0%7c0%7c&uidh=ejd
    &pcat=ROOT_CATEGORY&h=2210235&recoff=8+10&db=NYCmarriag
    eindexes&indiv=1&ml_rpos=2

MISS ROLLINS IN LOVE

by

GARIBALDI M. LAPOLLA

Author of THE FIRE IN THE FLESH

THE VANGUARD PRESS
NEW YORK

to

Priscilla

as gracious in her doubts
as in her appreciations

CONTENTS

CHAPTER   PAGE

    I.   Freedom   35

   II.   Stephen   39

  III.   Decision   43

  IV.   Experiment   48

   V.   Rejection   57

  VI.   Donato   62

 VII.   Loneliness   73

VIII.   Crabbing   86

  IX.   Hermes   97

   X.   The Marionettes 105

  XI.   Summer Session 116

 XII.   Donato's Summer 125

XIII.   Another Decision 133

XIV.   The Marionette Show 141

 XV.   School 147

XVI.   Selma's Party 165

XVII.   The Fall Session 172

XVIII. Sabbatical Leave 185

XVIX. Mortimer 196

  XX.   The Reformatory 211

 XXI.   Transfiguration 218

XXII.   Fulfillment 228

XXIII. Change 237

XXIV. Angel 246

XXV.   The Cactus Blooms 259

I. FREEDOM

-1-

IT WAS the morning after Miss Rollins had returned from burying her invalid mother, who had dominated her life for the past eight years. Sleep had smoothed out all signs of grief. In fact, as she lay huddled under her covers, with the blown spray of straw-yellow hair about it, her face seemed haunted with shifting lights of childhood not altogether suppressed by adult controls.

A slight breeze had raised the corners of the shades, and held them up like the leaves of a book one tries to separate with one's breath. Sunlight — the bright sunlight of an April Sunday — was a spatter of magnolia petals on the dull-green shabby Axminster between Miss Rollins's slightly more shabby mahogany four-poster and the dust-shredded curtains on her windows. The Chippendale mirror with its dog-eared corners was too far removed to catch much of it. In consequence, it reflected only dimly the chintz-covered boudoir chair, the old chest of drawers with several handles missing, and the low cedar chest with its pathetic jumble of black dresses and black hat. The patent leather shoes fared better, for they glinted with spots of sheen that effectively reduced the impression of the run-down heels, the zigzag cracks in the uppers.

There was a kind of mischief in the play of wind and light, a mischief that purposed to lift the corners of a sad mouth into flickers of smiles. Occasionally Miss Rollins made childlike gestures with her hand to brush off the light that fluttered from mouth to eyes, from eyes to temple, fingered the loose strands of her hair, or welled quietly in the accidental hollows of her throat.

The sun at last succeeded in awakening her. She jumped up with a start and, like a child, rubbed her eyes with her fists, looked around half-frightened and seemed uncertain of her whereabouts. The next minute she had leaped out of bed, tugged at the shades and allowed the deluge of sunlight to pour in. She risked a thrust of her head and shoulders out into the open — shoulders bared by slipping night-dress, hair winnowed by the wind — and with audible intake of breath saw the wonder of the spring in the backyards of the dilapidated brownstones: clumps of neglected forsythia bravely alive with yellow, an apricot waving whitened tufts, a bed of stunted tulips.

She had no memory of the intermittent copses with their new leaves, bright splashes of the Sound, the unbroken rows of suburban dwellings with their display of gardens as she might have seen them on the funeral

35

trip to Maston or on her hasty return. She had refused to spend even the night with friends or relatives, and had left them all amazed and their tongues loosened. Spring was touching her only now, and there was more than delight in the sight of its few glories. There was the buoyancy of a child let out to play.

"It's my day — a whole day before I go back to school."

She stood her full length to say it and to draw in breath after breath as if only by so doing could she strengthen resolutions that had begun to recall themselves to her.

"It can't be wicked. I do feel free. She's dead, and I am — alive, alive!"

-2-

Several minutes later she stood on her bathroom mat with a towel in her hands pulled straight across her back. The early morning light pearled in the drops of water not yet dried on her smooth skin — pale usually but flushed now like a seashell. The mirror in front of her had taken up her image and filled the tiny globes of water with iridescent life as they coursed in unpredictable directions down the sides of her firm breasts and shapely torso. She could not resist the impulse to halt the operation of drying her back and, as she glanced rapidly at the blithe reflection of herself, shiver slightly with delight. For though she might be past twenty-eight, no lines marked the years in her face, and her body was youthful and gay. Yes, gay, gay was the correct word.

"Catullus might have used it," she reflected, and her thoughts shot ahead to the next morning when she would be back in the classroom.

"But this whole day is mine — mine — the first in years. . . ."

She let the words slip slowly off her tongue, tasting each one like a sip of a delicious beverage.

She rummaged through her suitcase and slipped on the black and red kimono with an air of enjoying the silk on her body and then sat down on the bed with the final vigor of resolution.

"The first thing, collect all mother's clothes and let Mrs. Nilins have them. And, Amy, no sentiment about it. Why disguise your feelings? As long as she lived . . . but she's dead. . . . Then tidy up the rooms. And move — soon — these board floors with their cracks and their paint! . . . Two rooms in one of the new apartment houses . . . better than four here. Philip will have to look out for himself — it will be the best cure for him — your life's ahead of you at last. . . ."

She got up again as though her determination required the confirmation of physical movement. Whether the light, pooled in the looking glass, had awakened the impulse, or whether it was still the same impulse that had caused her to survey her body in the bathroom mirror, she went quickly up to the glass and looked in with a gesture of complete abandon.

"It may be shameless — but I do feel like Narcissus. . . . I have had no ears, no eyes for years, years. I do find myself beautiful . . . everything in me's alive. . . ."

Again she shivered with delight, and laughter escaped her brittly like thin glass falling. She scrutinized herself with frank approval, her uplifted arms revealing the soft flaxen curls under her armpits, the gentle curves of her muscles as they ran like quiet billows into the globes of her breasts.

And again her movements were sudden and the result seemingly of notions formed in previous silences and now becoming vocal in fact. She almost skipped, again like a child, her eyes quick and eager, as she made for the telephone in the next room.

"Yes, yes," she kept repeating, "Stephen Bennett. . . . Mr. Stephen Bennett . . . Miss Rollins . . . tell him . . . Amy . . . Amy Rollins."

She waited restlessly, the kimono drawn about her smiling.

"Yes, Stephen, Amy. . . . Yes, I got it . . . a very kind note . . . I know . . . no one came . . . no one knew much . . . Philip? Stayed in Maston. . . . Yes, I left immediately . . . couldn't stand it another minute . . . oh, they'll talk, I know . . . think it shameless . . . oh, but if they had the nightmare I went through — eight years, Stephen . . . night and day . . . then the morphine habit she developed. . . . I don't see why I didn't go mad . . . they left it all to me . . . Stephen." Her voice lowered, and her cheeks reddened, "Stephen, I want to see you, today. I can't stay in this place all alone — not all day . . . you remember . . . you said once to call you if I were ready. . . . I am . . . don't think me shameless . . . I am . . . I am . . . today . . . no, not here . . . on the Drive . . . at eleven? You will? Oh." (Her pleasure was unmistakable) "Stephen . . . you don't . . . you don't think me shameless?"

–3–

There came the climax of laughter and little bursts of song. She had pulled a sheet off her bed and with nimble unhesitating gestures thrown into it dresses of her mother, several pairs of shoes, a number of hats, underclothing. She drew the opposite corners of the sheet together, knotted them, and then, seizing the overlapping knots in her hand, was about to deposit the bundle on the floor. Something stirred in her. It surged into a thought that carried all her impulses toward freedom and assertion, all her desires to plunge into a life that was not the dull routine of perpetual sacrifice, upward and forward to a peak of action that should be a symbol in itself. She threw the bundle over her back and, her kimono loose, her hair cascading down her back and sides, with firm eager march she paraded up and down the rooms, through the intervening hall, into the kitchen, unaware of open windows, pulled-up shades, the warm clear sunlight, shouting.

"Old clothes . . . who'll buy old clothes? Old clothes!"

She stared into the mirror, aghast at the blue of her pupils white-washed with horror, had a chance to note how needlessly full her eyebrows were, and then, features aglow, the energy of desperation expressed in her craning neck, she cried into the glass as if it held a whole mob of purchasers who must be shouted at.

"Will you buy . . . old clothes . . . will you buy? She's gone . . . they're for sale . . . old clothes?"

What happened exactly at this point she never could quite recall. As she told the story to Stephen later on she said that her face, multiplying into the semblances of shoppers crowding into windows, took to pinwheeling with immeasurable rapidity. The pinwheeling continued for a time that seemed incalculable to her. It ceased with utter suddenness, and the whirling mass of faces sharpened into one. But it was not her own. It was her mother's, looking steadily at her. The muscles were let down into the perpetual whimpering and querulousness that had become part of her. Her eyes had gathered their light into points of the saddest and most dictatorial remonstrance. Amy watched it with horror, stared at it like a baby being scolded, just as she had been time and time again. The remonstrance changed into pain, pain visibly cruel in spasmodic eyelids, twitching lips, contorting jaws — her mother's face when the desire for morphine had become acute agony. But Amy did not recoil. She craned her neck still further, placed her face close to the pleading agony and cried:

"You can't . . . you won't rule me from your grave. I was dutiful to you for years . . . for years. . . . I slaved for you . . . stood for all your abuse. Slaved for you and Philip. Where was Anna? Married and gone . . . never a cent from her . . . never came on to stay a day. . . . You can't have me now, too. I am myself at last. Philip will have to go. I am going to live, mother, do you hear, live. . . ."

And she repeated her hawker's cry, "Old clothes . . . old clothes . . . who'll buy?"

Laughter moved out of her in a series of trills, slight, assertive, even gay. She could hear it between the sound of her steps and her cry of old clothes. But it seemed not to be her own, rather to proceed from the interior of walls that had no outlet, from the throat of one imprisoned within them and incapable of rebellion except in laughter. She had got back to her bed, still crying but in a half-frightened whisper, "Who'll buy? Old clothes . . . who'll buy?" She stopped abruptly. On the bed lay the lace shawl with its thin fringe of blacker silk — the shawl that her mother had worn over her slight, drawn-in shoulders, shoulders like a plucked bird's. Tears blurred her sight. Her body trembled, reeled.

"Mother," she wept, "mother. . . ."

She fell on the bed sobbing, her whole body moving in one piece.

II. STEPHEN

STEPHEN BENNETT was waiting on the Drive. "Never believed it — never — not now at any rate," he repeated to himself. He sat facing the Hudson, noting leisurely the hurrying whitecaps breaking noiselessly, and just as leisurely following the drift of a cloud toward the Bay, and musing just as leisurely that the Bay was filled with immeasurable bustle, but a quiet bustle rendered even more muted and muffled by the occasional shriek of a ferryboat.

Life presented itself to Stephen as most alluring when it wore this genial aspect of activity without much fuss and noise. All the events of his life had slipped out of each other as one portion of cloud detaches itself from another and moves on to join with still another gliding as unperturbed as the first. So had he drifted into college, into law, and then the inside work of writing briefs. He had drifted from one set of friends to another, from one man-friend to another, from one affair to another untouched, unhurried, unexcited.

The Palisades struck him as an appropriate symbol of the ideal existence. They had remained unconcerned despite the variety of excitement that had worked itself upon their face, presenting a constant demeanor of goodwill and serenity even where smokestacks had leaped across their view or a ferry burrowed itself into their foundations.

It was not so bad waiting here with a view of western skies blue enough to pick out the pinks and greens and creamy yellows in the groups of houses on the cliffs. It was warm enough, too, for him to remove his gray stitched-cloth hat and lay it beside him on the bench. The sun would be soft and demulcent. He felt the spring warmth on his head like the restorative lotion he was in the habit of rubbing into his scalp with its pink corridor of baldness between full swards of silk-brown hair, and he listened, as it were, almost impersonally for the subtle recordings in the nerve meshes of the medicinal softness he so loved. "This is what you call basking," he said to himself and averred there was nothing he loved more. Suppose Amy were late. She would come eventually.

He was past forty now and had at last decided to marry. Would he tell Amy? It presented itself to him as a problem without much real point. After all, what would it matter? There certainly had been no discussion of marriage with Amy.

He recalled vividly his first meeting with her — how worried she looked, her eyes taking in without registering a thousand things at once. She had been living at that time at some remove from the school and used the subway. Later he learned how close a margin of time she always allowed herself. She was constantly late and getting herself in trouble with the heads of the school. Stupid, he thought, no matter what the reason. Suppose her mother did have one of her weeping fits and clung to her daughter's hands with her bony little ones like a pigeon's claws, begging, "Stay home today, Amy. Stay home today!" Amy simply had made her worse by giving in.

"Oh, yes," his thoughts returned to the original meeting with her. A strike had made using the subway dangerous. He had decided on a taxi. Amy was standing on a corner, a huddle of books under one arm, bag dangling from her hand, making despairing gestures to the filled taxis that whizzed by with noisy unconcern. He saw her stamp her foot and ordered his driver to stop and back up to her.

"Come in," he said, sympathetically, holding the door open. "Oh, it's all right. We've all got to get downtown some way. . . ."

The whole conversation floated languidly through his memory, as languidly as the canoe he beheld through half-closed eyes, not quite real, not too remote.

"School teacher?"

"Yes, Latin. . . ."

"Always liked Latin. *Et haec olim meminisse* – "

Amy shrank into a silence.

"Only thing I remember from college is Latin. Always liked my Latin teachers too. Seemed always so engrossed they could sit in one place without minding. . . ."

Amy had looked at him with an incredulous smile and he realized that his languid, unperturbed manner interested her and frightened her too.

But she laughed, "That's a queer reason."

"Isn't a better one," he answered. "You like people for the things they do and you like things for the people that do them. . . ."

How directly she turned her head to him, losing sight of the cinematographic tape of the scene without, into which she had been restlessly peering for a sign as to their whereabouts!

"Won't be long now," he assured her. "You said Seventy-third Street?" He caught sight of the tawny hair escaping under her blue felt hat, pressed close over her head as if from the fine shape of it to take comfort for its own shabbiness. He added, "Teachers – women teachers I mean – are funny people. They suggest unusual wisdom to their pupils, and I always wonder if they possess it. Take yourself. You seem to be worrying about getting to school on time. They can't chop your head off, certainly not during a strike. . . ."

"Oh, but I've been late so often. . . ."

Her face, slightly flushed with a feeling of having said too much, was nevertheless turned appealingly toward his. Stephen enjoyed languor and ease not so much on principle as from the fact that all his body moved slowly. But his perceptions were rapid and his sympathies alert and sure.

"You're a very troubled person," he informed her slowly, as he placed upon her shoulder a hand that yearned to be remedial. "Can't imagine why a school teacher should be troubled. Leads a quiet life — monastic life, one might say. . . ."

She laughed, but her laugh mingled a note of bitterness with a suggestion of embarrassment — embarrassment, Stephen imagined, because to her mind talking so frankly with a stranger in a taxi must be reprehensible.

"Of course, you're troubled . . . you show it . . . I don't know why, Miss. . . ."

"Miss Rollins," she filled in the blank.

"Well, now, Miss Rollins," he repeated jovially, but suspended the genial note long enough to open the door of the taxi and throw out the cigar butt he had been holding in his fingers.

"My name is Bennett," he told her, "Stephen Bennett. . . ."

"I must go . . . just a few blocks. . . ."

"Be at the same corner tomorrow," he said "Oh, put that money away . . . I have to pay anyhow. . . ."

"But I couldn't if you didn't let me pay."

"Tomorrow maybe," he promised, with ever the slightest pressure of her arm as he helped her out.

She confessed the next morning that it had been with much misgiving that she had ultimately decided to wait for his taxi. Her greatest fear was the shame that she would feel were he not to come, and so she had contrived to leave the house a few minutes earlier than usual.

"But there you were waiting. . . ."

How often she had repeated the story, and how often she exclaimed the same thing with her air of ingenuous delight.

"You were waiting. You had not forgotten."

The canoe had been headed for the Jersey shore, and he had pursued its progress as he kept thinking of Amy. It had reached the shore and was turning back. If Amy had not put in an appearance by the time the canoe had come halfway back, he would walk to the corner and back again, wait a few seconds longer, and then. . . .

Brown on blue, changing shape like a water sprite, ruffling the waters but itself unruffled, the canoe lazied toward Bennett. All other images left his mind, and as he sat with his head exposed, one arm over the back of the bench, the other in his trousers' pocket, he was conscious of pleasure bathing his face in smiles as one is conscious of sleep billowing over one with its softness. The pleasure was for the tiny craft that cleft the waters without fretting about its exact position or emitting the slightest sound of approval or disapproval. The unheard rhythm of the paddle alone had a kind of vocal quality, and it kept saying to Bennett, "You've caught the notion, caught the notion, caught the notion . . . why the fret . . . why the bother . . . everybody restless and unhappy . . . watch me . . . here I toss and here I dip . . . here I catch the spray and here I hiss into a trough . . . and I keep going and you hear no murmur of complaint. . . . That's the path for Amy. . . ."

A touch on his shoulder awaked him.

"Mr. Bennett," it was the shrill whisper of Mrs. Nilins, "Oh, dear me, Mr. Bennett . . . you must come . . . Miss Rollins, she says, you must come. . . ."

"Why bless my heart," he said, without more than rising politely. "Bless my heart, Mrs. Nilins, you look frightened. . . . Nothing wrong?"

Mrs. Nilins always spoke in a whisper, possibly because she was afraid of spilling her little gray topknot, or because everything that happened always seemed to her a mysterious event without cause or purpose. And her whisper always conveyed a vague persistent excitement. When she was emphatically disturbed, she placed two fingers under her upper lip and snapped them nervously forward as if she might be twanging on a jew's harp.

"No, Mr. Bennett . . . it's crossing the street . . . I don't do it often . . . no, nothing . . . Miss Rollins would like you to come. . . ."

III. DECISION

STEPHEN FOUND Amy in a state of nervous indecision. It had all been so dreadful, coming back to these stuffy rooms with their reminders of the horrible years of suffering, of being shut in, confined in a pen with sick souls — her mother, Philip. Surely she had meant every word of her statement. She was ready. She would go at once. She laid an apologetic, an uneasy hand on his knee, looked up at him like a child.

"Oh, this is wicked, Stephen . . . wicked to draw you into my troubles. What am I to you?"

He blinked, too overwhelmed by her outburst to say anything. But he was not unaware of the pallor of her skin, the sunken cheeks, the drawn lines, the fright in her eyes. He would have smiled incredulously had she told him of her exultation at the sight of her body in the bathroom mirror. Nevertheless, as she sat next to him in loose kimono, loose hair, despite the restlessness that swept her features like wind over water, he had a definite sensation of pleasure — pleasure evoked by her supple athletic body not yet awakened but lying like a machine waiting to be set purring with activity and meaning. And yet, this feeling was not altogether the trivial smugness accompanying the assurance of another conquest. The brave smile that cast sprays of gayety into her eyes and quivering mouth touched him, and a gentleness and a sympathy stole into his mood. He drew her quietly to him.

"Look, Amy," he said. "See that tree in the backyard. Well, that's only one. See that bush full of yellow flowers. That's only one — see. Do you know what you need? Thousands of them, and water, and sky overhead and stars and. . . ."

"You, I suppose. . . ."

The hint of archness in the question did not escape him, and he replied smiling, "Maybe that too. But I wasn't thinking of that. You've got to have a chance to be like a bulb in the ground, or a turtle in mud, you know what I mean, sitting around doing nothing, letting all the things around you warm you. . . ."

Her whole body quivered as it pressed against his, as if an internal commotion of nerves and tissue rendered it incapable of quietness. He thought, "What's this, an hysterical woman?" Love to him was always something characteristically quiet and even, like water in a deep well. The slightest jar to its placid surface transmuted its qualities into those of a cracked mirror; all of its functions remained but none of its beauty.

"I don't see how I can get away. . . ."

"You've got to . . . with me or alone. . . ."

"I couldn't stand myself. . . ."

"We ought to make a break tomorrow. . . ."

She clung to him with both hands.

"There's school, Stephen. I've been absent so long. . . ."

"But you've got to get out of here . . . out of the city. . . ."

His gestures, palm perpendicular to wrist, fingers outspread, conveyed more of his feeling than words.

"Oh, I know . . . it's a stuffy old place . . . musty . . . that's why I kept looking out at the yards. . . ."

"It'll make you fit. . . ."

She was persuaded to write to her department head. Her mother's death had not been altogether unexpected, but it was sudden and for years it had all been a trial. She was exhausted. She needed to recuperate, get back some of her energy . . . the letter was humble, self-effacing.

Stephen was moved to exclaim, "What do they think in a school anyhow, that they are the high gods of what?"

He was already familiar with Amy's constant fear of her superiors and so thought the letter another proof of it. He failed to detect in her apology a desire to withdraw from the adventure upon which she had invited him. It never occurred to him — man of many successes — that an accident of mood might cause her to change her mind. He sensed implications not altogether satisfying. He was not accustomed to fervent pleading, to high-strung situations. Love and serenity were synonyms in his lexicon. Something undesirable had crept into the episode even before it began. And yet, she did need the rest, the change of scene. The sonata could be played even with a broken string. . . .

-2-

Early the next morning, somewhat before the main stream of trucks had filled the highways, without more than a soughing of the wind that accompanied its movements, his car rolled in front of the flaking brownstone steps of Mrs. Nilins's place. Stephen patted placidly the rubber bulb of his expensive horn and listened with an air of simple delight to the gentle moo that issued and spread softly throughout that street exactly as if it were in a spacious landscape of fields and hills. Amy had hurried down so rapidly that he had no opportunity to assist her with her brown imitation-leather bag. One look at her, and he concluded in his own mind that the place he had chosen for them to go seemed the right one.

"She never will be a dresser," he said to himself as he noted the shabby patent leather shoes and blue serge coat trimmed with black braid. "God, she could get another hat. I've seen that baby blue felt for a generation now."

"Not even a cigarette puff of a cloud," he remarked gaily as he made sure the door.

But Amy had not looked up and said good morning in a whisper without a smile.

"Want to give it up?" he asked in tones so low that they were lost in the oily meshing of the gears.

The tear in her eye, gay with the forced smile of protest, compelled him to busy himself with this and the other devices on his dashboard. They were soon on the Drive and speeding with a smoothness that seemed a happy omen. But the unbroken silence of Amy, no matter how he turned the subject of his talk, gradually had the effect of wearing down the uninterrupted calmness of his behavior.

"Perk up, Amy, for God's sake," he pleaded. "What's the good of a two-hundred-mile drive in the country?"

She sat back, looking straight ahead, missing what he thought to be subtle therapeutic qualities in the changing glories of the landscape. Castle-like dwellings pillowed in verdure, cherry blooms haunting gay arms like dancing girls to the music of the winds, the infinite murmur of the privet hedges as the car stirred the flanking air, little sounds like bells dropped from unseen belfries and imperceptibly mingled with the echoes of footsteps.

"Can't you imagine Horace in a car like this?"

"Yes," she answered, and kept looking straight ahead.

"*Quid sit futurum cras fuge quaerere.* Can't you hear him as he took in all these hills without snow but hiding many a *fons Bandusiae*? I'm telling you . . ."

A surprise flash of sunlight forming a silver lake in the unrippled blue of the river made him turn his head rapidly.

"Look at that, Amy. God, I can still be a kid and get a thrill out of a thing like that. Oh, this is going to do you a lot of good. Nothing like nature. . . ."

Stephen kept wishing — for Amy's sake he insisted to himself as people always do who desire things for themselves — that a fine effluence might come out of the sight of these beauties of sky and land that would travel through her being like a transmuting fluid, work the sorrow into intenser strains of feeling and give to her attitude and movements depth and vigor and the graciousness that accepts fully.

–3–

Stephen's wish was more than just a shadow of the truth. Amy was delighting in his talk, in the unfolding landscape, the quick roll into copses — their new verdure shining with an air of festivity — the sharp ascents to catch breathtaking glimpses of the river, wooded hills, farms trimmed and furrowed with such precision that it seemed that they had been first wrought by quiet-limbed lapidaries at their benches and then set out in the sun. Most of all it was the sun that played with her thoughts and memories, loosened them from each other and gave them back their individual beings so that the grief that had accumulated like a glutinous substance around them no longer deprived them of vitality. She watched the sun with particular delight, noted its wayward play on leaves, diminutive silver feet galloping to keep abreast of the car, fan-like sheaves radiating from hanging lamps now unlighted, intensified shimmering pools in windows. Everywhere it struck was vigor visible and incessant, unmanifest life made to perform in the open as by a conjuror's wand.

Rock plants gleamed in a dozen shades of crimson, the mock-orange bushes winked masses of yellow eyes in a sea of white, tulips lifted their open mouths to drink in the radiance, from the roadside dogwoods extended their palms in adoration like choristers at a high mass. Amy let her head remain sunk back, made no movement, though now and then she was troubled with impulses to cry out into the great tranquility. What gentleness, what calm — like the quiet after the organ has pealed into a diapason and then rolled into stillness! After the months of pain this was a new sensing of energy, particularly because it required no exertion. Life folded itself around her and the silence seemed like so many series of softest tissue wrapping up her mind, her heart, her body. She was thankfully aware of Stephen with his hands loosely resting on the wheel; she heard his voice raised just a shade above the purring of the motor and the whole intermingled with the serenity to affirm it and make it definite. She could utter neither word nor sound; instead scraps of Latin verse sang themselves in her head, echoing like waters at the foot of a hill from which one had just climbed to the top. *Fulsere quondam candidi tibi soles.* It was a soft sensation of sinking into pillows with music and warmth and darkened lights.

Oh, she was grateful to Stephen! What though she did, metaphorically, put her fingers over her eyes when she was conscious for a second of the meaning of the trip? She kept reiterating to herself, "You can't go back on it now. After all, he thinks he is doing you a wonderful good. Stop being frightened at yourself. *Nec dulcis amores sperne.* Don't you remember, Amy, how these words and many others ran through your veins like a wine? Only ten years ago at college, how literally you took them. Let the dead bury their dead, Amy, Amy . . . *nunc pede libero. . . .*"

Stephen saw the glitter of a smile leave her eyes to be lost in a pink fulfillment of color in her cheeks. He stroked her hand, as he had done several times already, as if it were a kitten lying in her lap. How pleasant it was, she thought, that and the sun like another hand rapidly brushing her knees, or reposing on them for a second until the warmth passed through. Would her lover be to her always as the sun in her first days of living? — for these would be days of living, not of dragging a weary weight of body through a narrow passage filled with the cries of loved ones in pain.

The question wove in and out of the snatches of Latin, in and out of the memories that the sun loosened in her mind, in and out of the sensation of beauty in wood and water, in and out of the echo-like talk of Stephen. What was it she was seeking and why did it frighten her? Was there not too deliberate an air about it? Would Stephen expect her to go on with it? But how could she know that this was the solution rather than plunging with renewed vigor into her work and studies, recapturing the zest of her graduation days and applying it anew in the service of youth? What was the quality of this experience she had been denying herself, which others sought only in marriage, which she now snatched at to ease the infinite frustration in her heart?

Stephen was talking.

"Look, Amy. See that tall mountain — in the last of the ridges there beyond the shore? Notice how heavily wooded it is. Now look carefully. See a kind of string running through the woods. It glistens here and there? Well, that's a funicular railway. Martin Van Tuyl Maarten built it some years ago. At the top of the mountain he had erected an imposing kind of castle — all solid rock like a castle on the Rhine. You can see the tower among the trees. It's abandoned now and I suppose nobody would live in it if he knew the story. They thought he was crazy when he built it. Anyhow, he had a big housewarming. God, they say he spent thousands on the affair. It lasted weeks. Then it was all over. He dismissed all the servants, didn't keep one around. Then guess what? He must have got into the railway and in some fashion snapped the cables. Seems crazy to believe he had gone to such elaborate preparations just to commit suicide. The fact is they found him crushed like a spider under the splinters of the coach. . . ."

Amy looked at the mountain that still held the vacant mansion. Its woods lifted hazy green billows into the immense quietness. Stainless, serene and vast its forested summits beckoned. She could hear the wind in the remote treetops sighing languorously, "Why not come here where it is high and lonely and quiet?" The next second she saw a taut ashen face, eyes glittering, headed with incredible velocity to the base. Did it seek even intenser quietudes? Was the solution there in the broken limbs under splinters?

The car glided past continuous box gardens, toy-like new houses, slumberous fields with grass so newly green it caught the sun like water and white-capped in the breezes. What fragrance, what stillness! How good to lay one's head back and feel oneself propelled through an infinitude of whispering emptiness, beyond clustered houses, and on to a room shadowed in trees alone on a mountain side!

IV. EXPERIMENT

THREE DAYS had already passed at the mountain lodge, but between Amy and Stephen there had been no closer relationship than the friendship with which they had begun. Stephen laid it to the nature of the place. He lacked the shrewdness to perceive how unimportant time and place are to a person like Amy. Her coldness lay not in her emotions so much as in her habits of thought.

The huge four-square house, sprawled like a bulldog under the shadow of a locust clump, had managed in its long career to make fantastic acquisitions of gloom in the most unlikely sections. The dining room collected the gloom from the porch; the fireplace with its spacious hearth and the room that housed it, gathered the gloom of the porte-cochère; the sitting room, screened from the sun not only by thick-growing locusts but by the precipitous slope of wooded hill, drove out the early morning brightness, and hugged to itself premature afternoon darkness.

Stephen had been stirred to pity of Amy's condition when he had first seen her. He planned the excursion even at the expense of delaying important work in the office. He sincerely wished to bring some freshness and relaxation into her life. Alone with her, however, he felt the promptings of desires meshed closely in the reactions which a changed Amy awakened in him. She was looking now budded and quiet like a faded flower that has drunk the healing freshness of water. Sleep and freedom from the small routine of her life, the sight of green and the growing blooms had remade her. The stately beauty that was hers had emerged triumphant from the drooping and hysterical sufferer. The drawn lines had softened and light had danced into her blue eyes.

"What a figure she has," thought Stephen again and again, and allowed himself to slip into anticipations.

They were alone save for the old Negro cook. They had been alone from the first day — a fact which had disquieted Amy more than the place, the remnant of an old estate that had been permitted to fall into disrepair. They had pulled up on the first day over a cobbled road overgrown with mosses and weeds. Sunken flags, slightly tipped, led to the pretentious sweep of steps running up to the porch. Between the cracks, cinquefoil and wild mustard spiked upwards with their yellow heads and invited the eye to follow through to the unpainted pillars of the porte-cochère, the broken lattice around the porch, and upwards to the mansard roof with its rusty railing. The stillness whispered around the corners of the house, welled in the tree shadows, and made small sounds in the grass where insects had already been building themselves in for the summer. It was not the stillness of activity subdued: it was the quiet of disuse — a quiet touched with sadness.

"Not too tired?" inquired Stephen.

He patted her on the knee and looked up into her eyes. Something in them disturbed him, and he whistled thoughtfully as he proceeded up the porch and pulled the knob intended for the bell. He heard neither bell nor steps in answer. He tried again. He looked into the window and saw no one. He walked around the porch, his steps hollow and distant in the silent heat. He returned to find Amy still reclined in her seat, her eyes fixed on nothing save the totality of the immense blue overhead.

"Not a soul around," Stephen ventured.

"There are birds. . . ."

Amy smiled.

"Not very romantic, hey?"

Amy smiled again.

"Place is ramshackle — ought to keep it up. I hope they have something to eat."

"They've stopped living here, Stephen."

"No, I got them on the wire last night — said to come right up. I'll try again. . . ."

Amy laughed softly. "Why, Stephen. I thought you didn't take things so seriously?"

"Yes, but this is spoiling the party."

"But the country's heavenly. Look at those spires, and the hills. They're like purple velvet. . . ."

They decided to stroll to the brook. He helped her out of the car, saying to himself, "Funny. I haven't kissed her even."

Nothing quite so deliberate and glacial had characterized any of his other episodes. There had been laughter and banter, none of the solemnity preceding a mystic rite, full of constraint and embarrassment, such as this affair had assumed.

"Better chuck it," he thought. "Be the good Samaritan. Then leave her. She's as cold as a hydrant."

"What'll we do," he said aloud, "go on to some other place?"

"If you wish."

Amy had placed her palms on a bed of Kennilworth ivy and ran them over the petals as if smoothing out a wrinkled material delicately precious.

"Amy, do you want to go on with this?"

"Don't you?"

"It all seems so cold-blooded."

"Shouldn't it be? Didn't I call you up that way?"

"Well, not quite."

"Why, Stephen, I am here."

She realized, however, that something more than her mere presence was expected — a continuous display of affection in gesture and modulated voice such as she had observed on bus tops and boat decks. She shuddered inwardly, but nevertheless placed her hand on Stephen's with a pressure meant to be sweet.

"You're already beginning to show the change, Amy . . ." he said, acknowledging the pressure by a pleased twinkle.

"It's going to be lovely out here. . . ."

They were interrupted by the sound of the automobile horn. Stephen hurried back and returned soon.

"Well, they're alive after all. Thompson, the old Negro . . . says for us to go to our room. . . ."

Stephen noted that the singular had caused Amy to blanch slightly. Once more he wondered about the wisdom of it all. They had to find the room alone, Stephen carrying both bags.

"Is there going to be no one here besides us? Haven't they somebody to help you?"

"The season's early . . . and they haven't been expecting anyone. . . ."

The room was huge, with a fireplace topped by an old colonial mantelpiece, redwood shutters to the windows, cherry-stained doors of individual paneling, an immense four-poster mahogany bed with provision for a canopy, all the other furniture in keeping.

"This is almost regal," Stephen smiled.

"I thought we should have two rooms."

He tried to take her elbows into the cups of his palms, but withdrew at once as he sensed her whole body withdraw.

"There's a door to another room. We have a suite."

He was amazed to find that the door actually led into another room of similar design. The wallpaper a rich blue, like velvet, intertwined into shadows and brighter tinges to effect final clusters of leaves and grapes. In the first room the walls were rose scenes of pastoral occupations.

"Well, we have two rooms. . . ."

A bell above the door, swung from a bracket, dangled.

"Old-fashioned place," Stephen was moved to comment. "Means lunch is ready."

Amy took her bag into the next room without a word.

Stephen realized for the first time how cliff-like is silence — a fortress that guards approaches to souls and the meaning of things. He opened his bag with his usual slow gestures.

"Got to give her a chance to thaw," he said, and whistled.

-3-

They had taken walks into the woods, had climbed to the top of the mountain through woodcutters' roads already beginning to be heavily bordered with ferns. They found leafy places where they could sit and talk.

"Stephen," she said one morning. "You're too good to me. I am worse than a little girl. I have all her fears and, what's worse, a lot of doubts. You've been so good. So patient . . . I love you for it . . . I lie awake and I keep thinking, 'How important is this thing?' There are the psychologists. They say dire things happen — if you do, and if you don't . . . tell me, Stephen, what is there to it?"

"You're a type, Amy," he answered. "What you need most is rest and sleep — the sight of all these marvels . . . You look a marvel yourself. Your color, your eyes, your walk . . . why, Amy, you're a fulfillment. You are lovely — altogether lovely — not made to spurn life. Why grow sour?

"Maybe it's your training — it's almost damned you. . . . Why follow somebody else's pattern? . . . I have my own — I want all the things other people want, but I don't want to fret, worry over consequences . . . I make no bones about it, Amy . . ." he cried, forestalling her interruption. "I got interested in you right away — wanted you — completely — I thought you would break through, be a little wild, even.

"I wanted to pass my hand over your breasts, your thighs . . . without these things — say, life's harsh enough . . . You see I need this sort of thing . . . maybe you don't . . . I am beginning to think so. . . . You perceive its importance — logically. You admit there are the emotions and the impulses, the muscles and the energy, in your body, your nerves. . . . All the thing needs is a beginning." He smiled and lost himself in thought, as if following the smoke of his pipe into the great distance. "Amy, a satyr must have been a marvelous being. I think we should cultivate the type. His heart must have been an imprisoned melody, storing up memories of mad moments and promises of wilder ones, beating all the time with the normal rhythms of life . . . God, to accept every impulse as action and have no puling about it! What a difference between the ancients and us. The ancients were afraid of forces outside themselves; we're afraid of things in ourselves. Sex — for instance; we want to keep it subdued. If we can't, we've got to spin pretty yarns about it and dress it up in sentiment and poetry and junk. . . ."

There was a pause. Stephen sat up and scrutinized the rock where he had been lying — its bits of mica glistening in the sun — almost as if he might make it a trifle softer for reclining.

"Amy, I think I know why we choose rocks to sit on. It's instinctive. . . ."

"Castigation of the flesh, you think, Stephen?" Amy inquired in a whisper, not without a note of archness.

Stephen merely took out a cigarette and threw away the extinguished match with an uncommonly vigorous gesture.

"Forgive me, Stephen."

Amy sat up and came close.

"It's funny," Stephen suddenly cried. "People simply won't take sex like food and sleep and walks in the country . . . at least, not us. God, I've known people would read tales of the most horrible crimes, revel in descriptions of mashed-in heads, ripped-up bowels, and yet they won't listen to a risqué story. . . . Here we are together . . . you came with a definite intention . . . I never believed you would. But here you are, and you fight shy of it. You shudder if I touch you . . . withdraw your whole body . . . look hurt . . . maybe it's what you've gone through. . . ."

Experience is not a guarantee of wisdom; otherwise Stephen would have understood Amy's silence. He interpreted it to mean that she had been impressed with his arguments, rendered passionately, almost as if he had put poetry into one of his briefs. She had been impressed, but with the logic only, not the feelings. For his abstract notions she had little sympathy and not altogether the understanding which might have been termed acceptance. She realized all too keenly that the sensual in Stephen had felt itself balked and forestalled, and that it was making him unhappy. And she was conscious of a partial revulsion to him despite the gentleness and patience he showed. On the other hand she was intelligent enough to perceive that lacking the experience of intimacy and the delight that it must mean, she would be unjust in visiting upon Stephen any anger at his demands.

In fact, she went beyond. She condemned herself for failing to carry out her part of the compact. Her silence was a telescoping of her thoughts and sensations, of her revulsions and her sense of justice into a climaxing exercise of will. In reality, the more she was removing the purdah of her constraints, the farther she was withdrawing her whole body from the gaze of the multitude, although the multitude in this case was only Stephen.

"Stephen," she said, "forgive me. I have been terribly selfish. You are right. I came here . . . with a definite purpose. . . . You understand my hesitations . . . I am not excusing myself. . . . But my mother's image . . . my own habits . . . you understand . . . and maybe some false delicacy . . . what shall we call it? It must be false, Stephen . . . that's the word, isn't it . . . ?"

"Let's go back to the house," is all he answered.

She walked alongside him, talking as if to one of her pupils, anxious to soothe him, to bring them together again. Occasionally she stopped to point out a wild flower.

"Look, Stephen, there's a meadow lily, and did you hear the sapsucker a minute ago?"

"Got enough already," Stephen was saying to himself. "I'm going to make a beeline home. You would think she was the arc of the sacrament. . . ."

And despite the things she uttered, Amy in turn was saying to herself, "What a poor sport you are, Amy . . . suppose you have no real feeling . . . you've come here . . . go through with it. . . ."

-4-

The house was always unoccupied. To the darkness in the hallways was added the silence of dust that never lifts. They passed the dining room, its multitude of tables gray in the premature dusk, only one set.

At the door of their rooms, Stephen and Amy stopped and looked at each other. She held out her hands. He took them and said:

"I don't want you to hate me, Amy. I think I had better leave you here and go. . . ."

"Stephen," she cried, and for the first time since their arrival put her head on his shoulder. He took her into his arms.

There she stood, pressing against him with a kind of fear recording itself in slight tremors throughout her body. And yet Stephen noted that here was no surrender but hesitation and doubt. She might just as well have been a mannikin. To Stephen the love that breaks through the encasements of a steel-like will should have the energy of flood tide. Short of that, the ensuing ecstasy is abortive spluttering of flame without glow and without warmth.

"It's just fear," she said through tears. "It seems so unnecessary. You really do not need me. It's I who need something — somebody — how should I know? I thought it might be this, but when I got here something happened . . . it made me shudder — it seems so unnecessary — for you — and for me. . . ."

Stephen patted her on the back. What more could he do, what could he say? He was conscious of a vague embarrassment and uneasiness; the desire to end it all became acute. But Amy lifted her head and said, her lips twitching and smiling:

"Let's go to the cliff this evening and watch the moon come up. It'll be our night. . . ."

-5-

The evening came on slowly. They sat on the edge of the cliff overlooking a valley completely filled with foliage. The side of the cliff was sheer with a short drop from the edge to a natural terrace below it — a ledge-like terrace that itself was precipitous and looked into the leaf-filled hollow. A violet gauze-work of shadows moved over it like mist lifting and forming again.

Stephen, stretched full length, his hands behind his head, gazed upward into the quiet skies. Amy sat close to him, her skirt tucked in under her. The blonde of her hair caught the frail radiance of the lights fading out of the air. The three days already had begun to show in the clear tinge of pink suffusing her light skin as if a petal denied the sun for days had repossessed its original tints.

Stephen turned to look at her. The satyr in him gave his eyes a dancing quality that both agitated and disturbed her while the Puritan in her, detecting the cloven hoof despite her reason and sense of fair play, reduced the energy of the impulses gradually rousing within her.

The sky encased them and the hills as if they were equally unimportant in the vastness in which all things achieve a similitude. This was the thought which fell upon Amy with the soft pressure of a hand that intends directing one to one side or another, and she communicated it to Stephen. In fact, Stephen said:

"It's something like what I was thinking. I was watching the drift of the smoke from the village. As I watched it I seemed to lose control of my body and felt drifting with the smoke too. . . . Everything seems drifting with it . . . the leaves are moving in that direction and the clouds. . . ."

"And we too. . . ."

"I never get sentimental, Amy. You know it, and that's one reason for your hesitation. But something in the spaces around here has got itself worked into my system and in yours too, and I want just to lie by you indolently, quietly, without effort. . . ."

". . . and drift into another a affair. . . ."

Amy completed his sentence with a bit of laughter as a climax, and he who was unsentimental felt jarred out of his composure. The word "affair" was like a stone thrown into the still pools of his contemplation.

"What's the use of effort, Amy?" he questioned without showing his irritation.

"Oh, Stephen, you're a big boy. You're hurt, aren't you? You want your pie and you want to eat it too. You hate to have this — affair — called just that, and you say you aren't sentimental. You're a big boy. I wish you were more of a big boy though and needed me lots . . . needed me for comfort and for sympathy and to look after you because you were sick at heart or something. . . . But you're so well and your soul is at peace with itself and what am I to you?"

She went closer to him and ran her hands over his face as if actually he were sick and she were attempting to soothe him by the gesture. Then she bent over him and kissed him. He put his arms about her and drew her closer to him. The sprays of her hair fell about him and the weight of her body lay on him without restlessness, without urgency — just the sort of evenness that he loved. He allowed the full measure of the sweetness to enter into his being before he returned the hesitant kisses, the vague touch of her cheeks, the accidental pressure of her breasts.

The wind that had been barely blowing the smoke and the leaves toward the west, had lifted with slightly more strength, and now it seemed as if the drift were not a visible effort of forces but a voice out of depths. For their eyes were shut in the dusking of their embrace and what was once visual was now audible. The leaves made a scattered melody on reed pipes that knew no shrill notes and a whisper sang it in every corner of the sky. It was as if the smoke and the clouds were like fingers tapping loosely a thousand tenuous strings and then passing on a tap a thousand more.

"Stephen," she murmured. "Be a little boy and say you need me. . . . You're sweet to me, but do I deserve it?"

"But you know I need you. . . ."

"To fill in a gap . . . because I am a different type. . . ."

"Because you're beautiful and not dumb. . . ."

She laughed quietly in her chest, and he knew she had been pleased by the sally.

"You're the golden girl for whom Horace had so many names. . . ."

"Yes? But are you the *gracilis puer*?"

"Just a boy. . . ."

The wind stirred in the trees. The far-flung whispering melodies merged into a crescendo, dwindled, and died into a hum.

"Amy, if it rained here and you lay beside me, I should not move. I should still keep my arms about you. I should still be kissing you, pressing close. . . ."

"Silly boy," laughed Amy.

He held her with increasing pressure, placed his lips close to her ears, talked gently and without interruption. Amy lay unmoving in his arms, letting outbursts of soft laughter fill in the brief pauses. . . .

"But I should not, Amy. And do you know why? It's because you were in reality made for loving. In classic times, your place would have been among the bacchantes and the maenads. You would have tossed your arms like the branches of saplings and your fingers, like twigs twinkling with blossoms, would have fluttered to the twanging of lyres. . . ."

"What a lovely translation. . . ."

"Out of a pony, Amy. . . ."

"Did you always have to use a can book?"

"It's surer to love by rote. . . ."

"Then all of this — you don't mean. . . ."

"Why, of course I do. . . ."

"How much of it?"

"Every word. . . . Listen. The wind is galloping with little feet over the treetops. . . . Isn't the whole place like an ancient temple to the Venus of Paphos and the sound of the wind the sound of the satyrs bitten by the ecstasy and dashing after escaping nymphs? . . . Amy, loving is sipping out of huge vats of nectar. One never can get enough, and it matters only that the heart is ready and the lips are eager. Poetry springs up like the wind among trees one knows not from where or why. . . ."

–6–

She lay under him with the inertness of one listening to thoughts singing themselves in the mind and allowed the flow of Stephen's words to pass over her as one bows in silence while the organ sighs a benediction.

The sound of the pines on the hilltops, soft and sibilant like many whispers, the thudding of branches in the nearby copse, the infrequent lifting of a bird's note in the dusking — how blessed they all seemed to Amy. For, think as Stephen might, that at last the frustrated impulses in her being were breaking through the habits of her will, Amy lay quiescent not only with ecstasy but also with fear. Fortunately for him and for her, however, the place was as a holy vault, dim and silent, in which one might feel exalted, and for the breathless minutes of their ardor abstracted them from realities that pain.

Practiced lover as Stephen thought he was, anxious to sense the essential difference from all other women which was Amy, he had not entirely lost himself in the mood. It was otherwise with Amy, for both her rapture and her fear had sharpened her senses, and as she listened to her lover's voice and the sounds of leaf and wind, she also was acutely aware of the sheer physical delight he was taking in the touching of their bodies. She shuddered slightly but let herself be held with firmer and firmer hold, and the pressure of it was sweet and the warmth like an incense that quiets and exalts.

"No more than this," she kept repeating to herself, "no more than this now and forever . . . do not let this blessed moment change. Is this forgetting pain, or remembering something sweet? Stephen," she called, "Stephen."

And then it was that Stephen, sensualist as he was, felt his moment had come, and with a swift gesture he had drawn her bosom to his, pressing it hard, and with the other hand stroked her thighs slowly, with fingers that closed on the flesh. The fears that had mingled with her ecstasy rose like a storm in her.

She struggled to free herself of his embrace, struck him with her fists on face and shoulder, seized the loose end of his coat and desperately pulled on it. Struggle was not in the code that Stephen had developed, and to him what was not freely given and as freely accepted was simply not worth the effort. The principle was on a plane no higher than that. But the impulses that had channeled into energy were too strong to arrest in full tide, and he continued, despite the blows and the resistance, to cover her neck and her cheeks with kisses and desperately seek to bring back to her the repose and composure of a few minutes ago.

"Amy, just let yourself go," he whispered into her ear. "Throw back your head and do nothing, say nothing. . . ."

With a violent movement, however, she pushed him away from her and sat up.

"Stephen . . . Stephen," she cried, her eyes filling with tears.

Her body shook as in a fever, and her gaze rested appealingly upon him as a sick person gazes into the eyes of an attendant.

Stephen looked at her without saying a word. He stroked his head slowly and stood for a moment in thought.

"Amy," he said finally, "I'm not your man. We won't quarrel about it. I'll leave tonight. . . ."

V. REJECTION

AMY HAD sat on the edge of the cliff until the night had fallen. She rose and walked back slowly to the lodge. The path lay through scrub pine and a rock-filled slope once the bed of a stream, and she was forced to pick her way carefully.

Let Stephen think what he might of her. She had been schooled too long in the tradition of sentiment and poetry. She could not now accept love, illicit and furtive, no matter how blinding, meant only for a day.

She recalled the girls at college during the days of the war — the gay insouciance of their actions, the breakdown of all customary reserves, the drinking parties and the late dances, the rides into the night with their soldier friends. How she had envied them, and how she had longed to join them! She remembered Lucy Dauz, red-haired and with a turned-up nose that seemed symbolic insolence. And there was Marjorie Lexall, and Kate Devlin. They had disguised nothing, feared nothing, demanded everything. Pretty, all of them, not particularly good in their lessons, but they were laughter itself shaking both its sides and tripping with the gayety of assured delight in themselves, in their youth, in their desires.

Could she not have been as they? Was her beauty of so classic a mold that it deserved an alabaster niche? Amy smiled at her own sally, deserved satire against her inveterate dignity. The men she had met, first awed by the quality of it, had been frightened away by her incapacity for the light-o'-love banter, the unmeaning kiss, and the forms of affection not meant to be sincere. Why could she not, like Lucy Dauz, jump on a man's lap at one of their parties, only because he was good-looking and made you understand he would stop at nothing? Why was she repelled by the slangy badinage of her classmates and, later, by that of her younger colleagues at the school?

"Amy, you're a born old maid with all your fine mind and with all your classic beauty."

With that as a final shaft at herself, she made her way back to the house. She had put Stephen out of her mind entirely.

She went down to breakfast and noted the absence of Stephen. She had expected it and yet it was with a shock that she saw his empty chair. As she ate, she decided to return to the city. She was anxious to resume her work. There was only a little more than a month before her classes in Cicero would be up for their final examinations, and they needed her.

But especially did she think of her small group in Virgil, dreamy boys, many of them, pathetically sincere in their ambition to master the quiet surge of the great poet's lines. Like her, they too had been led, by chance or some trick of their own personalities, into these retired walks of learning, far from the noise and fret of every day, in the search of a wisdom that would eliminate the heartache and the thousand natural shocks of living. She would return to them and enter into their spirit no matter how aware she was of the essential emptiness and falsity of it. The day would come when they too would discover that in the capsuled golden dust of poetry was not contained the opiate of understanding or the stimulant of experience.

For she had devoted hours and days to it, and while she heard the noise of dancing feet and the laughter of gay hearts, often had she said, "But here is the wisdom of the race, here in these lines, and they will bring me later to the heights." It had all been well, so long as she had shouldered the responsibilities of her sick mother and her shellshocked brother, and had not yet been overborne with the fatigue and the weariness of flesh and heart that it had entailed.

And now, here she was, the ruins of an attempt at life before her, and stretching far behind years devoted to study, to the pursuit of those things which the pages of books averred to contain the wisdom that would bring serenity and calm and the satisfaction that makes one neither smug not self-assured.

Stephen had found it in living; Philip thought to find it in battle and had returned incapable of ever again achieving it; she had sought it in books and discovered that books reduced her to impotence when confronted with reality. And there was Mrs. Nilins — she had found it after her fashion in the slow accumulation of money which she never spent; there was Amy's department head, white-haired, laughter always on his lips, satire dancing in every word that he uttered, real master of the Latin which he taught so enthusiastically — he had found it, but where? In detective stories which he read by the dozens, in the athletic games which he never missed, in the statistics he was forever compiling.

Had her other colleagues found it? Those young girls just out of college, giddy with their positions and especially with the attention of the young boys in their classes? Every morning they gathered in the teachers' rest rooms, cigarette smoke forever trailing from them, decked out in the newest styles, laughing as they told of theater parties and the dances afterwards, of cocktails and highballs, late hours and the struggle to get out of bed and get to school on time. Had the forlorn-looking young men who had come into teaching after graduation found it? Most of them timid boys — like herself — not willing to chance the risks of the competitive world, pulling quickly into a windless berth. Or did those middle-aged but not querulous women find it — women who listened to the talk of the young girls with eagerness and never questioned? Or those old ladies who still puttered around — little shawls on their backs in the winter days, and their dresses of all vintages, always running to the office with complaints against the students and their boisterous ways and their failure to study, always raising the banner of good taste and decorum and morality, talking in whisperings in their own corner — faded, drawn, grey? Or has life a way of tormenting people like these, like herself?

But there were her boys in the Cicero class, in the Virgil class. They needed her, and she needed them. Only now she realized the quality in work that satisfied and blessed. But Amy was too honest not to sense a quality in her boys which added to her work something fulfilling. Even now she recalled how thrilling it was to have the boys crowd around her, talk excitedly about their work or ask her questions just for the fun of asking them. She welcomed even the impudent snickers of the cynical when she burst into perfervid translations or read with sonorous energy to demonstrate the strength of the ancient language.

She recalled how a group of them had stayed one afternoon for a few minutes after the bell, evidently in a concerted plan. The leader among them had been pushed forward. One of the boys had catcalled, "You don't dare?" The leader had finally settled into a kind of mock-seriousness that made the other boys hold their mouths to keep from laughing.

Leaning over the desk, head thrust out, his face glowing, taking no notice of the boy pulling mischievously at his leg, the leader asked insinuatingly, trying not to appear overworldly or impudent, "Miss Rollins, do you ever go out? If so, I should like to ask you out sometime." What a straight face she had kept, how natural she had made the whole episode appear, just as if to be asked out in this fashion was the most customary thing in the world! Not even the slightest glow of the flattery the incident was to her shone in her eyes or smile.

"Why, yes, I do go out," she had answered. "But really, Donato, I am not in the habit of being asked out this way."

She noted that the rebuke made an impression upon him. He ran his hand quickly through his heavy mass of chestnut hair, and with wide-open eyes gazed at her, as if transfixed in that position.

"I don't want you to go, boys," she had finally added. "Of course you have been rude. . . ."

Nervous laughter, hurried shuffle of feet, and then a great silence was all the answer she had.

"But since you have all come, why not stay? Why can't we just talk? Here's Donato. You know I have always wanted to know what was in that head of his. And in yours too, Stewart, and in yours, Grabinsky." The latter she addressed by their last names, but Donato Contini she had called by his first.

The episode was vivid to her now. Her memory filled with the details. Donato had wanted to leave at once, but the other boys had finally said, "Yes, let's all stay. Maybe Miss Rollins will read some more Latin to us."

Although she knew that the boy had not meant, except in mockery, what he had said, she replied at once, "That's an idea. Let me see. I bet you boys don't know what horses' hoofs sound like pounding on the dirt in races. Virgil did it beautifully. You don't have to know the meaning of the lines. Listen, I have found it. . . ."

She had remained at school for an hour, and the most exciting thing about it had been how most of the boys had stayed too, and listened to her read, and how they had got into a wrangle over the usefulness of the language as a study, and from that branched on to the utility of the whole high school course. Boy after boy had poured out his doubts to her.

She remembered Stewart, fastidious dresser, high up in the athletics of the school, a good mind in his clean-cut, shapely head.

"I get it, Miss Rollins, when you read it. Seems great then. You hear Cicero making a speech-like. Gee, but when you've got to plug it out for yourself. . . ."

"What's the use of it, anyhow, if Miss Rollins does read it?"

"Only it's good to listen to . . . that's all I know."

-3-

The joy it had been! She must get back to them. Or was it Donato she was most thinking of — the slender Italian boy with a figure like the Hermes of Praxiteles surmounted with clusters of curls? His eyes, grey and almond shaped, pooled into thought at the slightest question she addressed to him. And then, as if from his mind there proceeded an energy like a sudden wind, his eyes danced like the surface of water, a light shone in them, and he rose to answer rapidly, with uncommon seriousness, following each thought with vigorous persistence, incapable of stopping until he had made his reply as complete as possible. Particularly, she liked about him a trait which at times annoyed his classmates. Interrupted by another question or unceremoniously told by an impatient youngster to sit down, he would turn either to the class or the teacher quite earnestly and continue, "But you see I mean. . . ."

And then, with a horrifying perception that he had talked too long, he would sit down, and not say another word. She looked at him at such times without his noticing it and saw that he had been hurt, that the force of his thought had held him like an inspiration and left him quivering. How few were the boys these days so stirred by ideas as he was, so much in earnest about his studies that he seemed to have found in them an escape from something he dreaded. She had meant often to talk to him, to do what she had resolved was going to be her main objective as a teacher, enter into the life of the promising students in her classes, know about their families and their surroundings, become friends with them and eventually a force in their days.

But the increasing demands of her mother, the added worry about her brother, so oppressed by the disillusionment of the war that it had become a mental derangement, the lack of calm and freedom that all these entailed, had made impossible carrying out these cherished hopes. This was in spite, too, of the evident regard her pupils showed for her, a regard at times assuming the characteristics of an alarming attention. Many had been the occasions when she had heard a boy remark about the loveliness of her person, the fine quality of her reading, her voice. She had seen once in a while — the effect of her person in the eyes of a student, and she had not recoiled from it, rather had it put a spring in her gait and a touch of light in her cheeks. Donato she had surprised gazing at her with his head down as if her effect on him had been to make him sullen and irritable or possibly ashamed of himself.

She would return to school. There were six weeks left and during those weeks much ground to be covered, difficult examinations to prepare the students for, clerical duties which she should not force upon a substitute. It would be her first chance to devote all of her energy and attention to the profession which she had chosen. She realized now that her selection of it had been a measure of her personality.

She had done brilliantly at college, not only in her major subjects but also in mathematics, and had in fact distinguished herself in a survey that had shown her to possess distinct abilities as a statistician. In consequence, she had been offered a position with an established firm of accountants. There would have been opportunities for hurried visits to the larger cities of the country, even the possibility of making a residence, for periods of varying length, in several of the more interesting ones. But ever since her childhood in Maston-on-the-Sound she had visioned herself as a teacher. Curiously enough she had a striking memory now of one of her reasons. She recalled the difficulties some of the teachers had with the larger unruly boys, fresh and impudent specimens, who seemed to delight in the anger of their teachers. She would show others of their kind some day! Take that big boy in the corner, who thinks he is so good-looking and smart. She would. . . .

A wistfulness crept into her mood. She looked out on the locusts and above them the pines on the hillslopes. Hints of rain hung about them as they drooped. The sky seemed to have neared and to be on the point of encircling house and hill and woods so closely as to require a gesture of remonstrance on her part. She rose and went to the window! What a sharp desire to push at the sky with her palms and by the force of her movement to drive it back! For the wistfulness that crept into her mood was a dream of a freedom that she feared now would never become fact. This sky that was closing her in, making her as it were the depth of a vortex that whirled about while she remained stationary, this sky was a travesty of freedom. Freedom for her lay in the work she had undertaken to do, work which had become habitual and comforting in its routine, a groove to slide back and forth in, assured of motion without the uncertainty of its direction. Enough for experiment. She was not of this generation. There had alighted no mystic touch upon her. The old moralities still held good. . . .

VI. DONATO

AMY LEFT home earlier than usual. She wanted to arrive at the school before most of the other teachers and the great hordes of boys that would stampede through the corridors and catapult into the rooms with the irrepressible energy of their kind. She wanted to get away from her stuffy rooms — they still were filled with the painful memories of the last eight years and held no charm either of equipment or newness. Besides, she had received a letter from Philip, a letter that had so filled her with anxiety and awakened so much of her spirit of self-accusation that she had not slept. Phrases of it kept thundering in her mind.

"Too bad I spoiled your chances. Mother spoiled your chances too. Let me salute the modern martyr and the saint. A thousand battles, Amy, to one of your tears — it were blessedness. As long as my mustard-gas mind, my shell-shocked nerves hold out, I'll stay on my own. I'll hit the road. The stars shall sing to me and who knows but that the gibbet will beckon as they sing. Mine be the freedom of the open skies — yours the drinking-bowl and the satyr's dance. Don't forget, the rake is father to the saint. You will wear a halo yet but it shall be lighted by the alcohol of a thousand cocktails. . . ." It had gone on, irresponsible in its accusations, bitter in its complaints, disturbing in its uncertainties, the forlorn Philip become flippant, sourly gay-hearted. There had been no address, she would not know how to reach him, would have no word of what he was doing or what was happening to him. The night had been a long debate. Would it not have been better to go on taking care of Philip as she had for her mother? Was she not made to take care of people?

And spinning in and out of her thoughts had been another letter. Why was it she had been so pleased to get it? Was there something in it which caused her to rise earlier than necessary? Why had Donato Contini's name made the letter seem sweeter?

"As president of Class 6G1 I am writing to let you know that we all sympathize with you, and the flowers we are sending are just to show you our appreciation for your work with us and our friendship for you. We are all very sorry.
DONATO CONTINI
President, 6G1

P. S. I want to say for myself alone that I am really very sorry."

The funeral had taken place too soon after the death of her mother for either the flowers or the letter to have come before she left. The flowers were now all faded. In some ways, however, their color and their perfume, the sentiments that clustered about them, had been preserved in their entirety in the letter. It was all the more gracious a gesture as she observed how loth are boys of their age to express their emotions. It must have been the suggestion of someone more inclined to show feeling than the others. It might have been Donato himself. The thought was warming. She could not tell why.

And so she was glad to have come to school before the "whole gang," as everybody put it, the hundreds of teachers and the thousands of boys. A cathedral calm pervaded the building. In most of the rooms the shades were still drawn. The corridors were long and dark like the aisles of a church, and the half-light coming from an open room here and there suggested niches ensconced in unexpected places. She had walked through the crowded push-cart markets already alive and noisy, had smelt the accumulated fetidity of packed human masses, caught glimpses of sleeveless men at the windows of factories, had images of the river craft smoking past the clefted streets. And from the very first the building had had all the effect of a retreat from life that is too blatant, too scabrous, too full. The mosaic in the lobby, the flicker of the stained glass windows, the quiet, had all contributed to the totality of an impression which her heart had yearned for — of being alone in a holy place where the impulses are stilled, the blood is quiet, and the call of the whirling mobs is softened into a music that enters the spirit.

The elevator man had greeted her with perfect casualness, as if she had not been absent for some time. No words had passed between them and so she could retain the fullness of her feelings. Then as she stood at the door of her room, she heard the faint sound of an organ. Someone in the music department had come early too. He could not just be practicing. The peaceful strains rising throughout the building were too much like the gentle, persistent fervor of a spirit yearning in pain. It was soft and melancholy, like the voice of one who longed for things that could not be. There were no other sounds in the building. There was no sign of activity anywhere. She would be alone.

-2-

She entered her room. In the semi-darkness, with the green shades pulled down, the rows and rows of seats seemed eternal parallels reaching out into vast distances. The air was heavy and still. Silver films of dust glinted on windowsill and desk tops. She entered quickly and went to the windows to open them. She stopped suddenly. Someone was in the room.

"Good morning," she heard.

"Why, good morning, Donato." She spoke as if she had been startled, and as if she had need to be grateful that it was he and not someone else.

"Can I speak to you alone?"

"We are alone. . . ."

"I thought maybe you would come early. . . ."

"Open the windows, Donato," she said, this time in the matter of fact tone she knew she should have used at the beginning.

Donato had thrown up the shades and windows both, and stood with them behind him. Outlined against them, he looked a young god stepped out of a classic temple, a figure admired throughout the school and much in the comment of both teachers and students. Especially clear in the light were the well-defined lines of his features. Nowhere was there bulge or depression. The forehead molded itself out of the massed curls of his light chestnut hair, the nose carried the line surely to a point where the eye of the spectator must seek for the lips and the chin, both well-proportioned to the rest and demanding no extra attention. The mouth alone, because it was never entirely shut tight nor open sufficiently to reveal the teeth, seemed always to quiver with expression and so drew ever the slightest extra attention to itself. The eyes were large and almond shaped with long lashes so much darker than his hair that when his lids were closed they shone against the olive of his complexion. A gentleness, a dreaminess, but not altogether of quiet things, gave distinction to his grey pupils, so grey indeed that they blended imperceptibly with the other section of his eyes. He stood erect, without nervous movements of any kind. Unlike the Italian he was, he was given to few gestures except when he was stirred to more than ordinary feeling. This time he had raised both his hands, palms upward, as if in prayer, and said,

"Could you help me out, Miss Rollins?"

The distress in his voice was real. Amy looked quickly at him.

"Why, what's the matter? Come here."

Donato took a seat at the foot of her desk which was on an elevation a few inches above the floor.

"They suspended me, and they won't take me back."

"Why, what happened?"

It was the boy's turn to be affected. There was distress in her voice, and it startled him enough for him, too, to raise his eyes quickly.

"Maybe you can't help me. If it's going to get you into trouble. . . ."

"Why, I don't see how, Donato. But this must be dreadful. What have you done?"

She tried to laugh and to smile both, and leaned toward him in a friendliness that would reassure him.

"I struck a boy — hit him in the face and knocked him out. . . ."

"You did!"

"Yes."

An embarrassed smile hovered about the corners of his mouth and sought refuge in uneasy eyes. Something in the tone of Miss Rollins' "You did!" suggested a real interest, an interest akin to that of a person who might belong to her own set. It was completely natural and he felt he could pour out his troubles to her and be understood and condoned.

"This is dreadful," she said. "No wonder they suspended you. Just what did you do it for?"

"They'd been losing things out of their rooms, the teachers, you know, and some of the boys, too. They found a gang that were taking fountain pens out of the boys' pockets in the locker rooms and other places and going through the teachers' desks. The gang sold the pens and other stuff and were making money out of it. . . ."

"Were you in it?"

His mother might have asked him the question, hurt and horrified but not lacking in sympathy. Donato looked up at her once more, amazed and touched.

"No, really, I wasn't. But I bought one of the pens and I wouldn't tell who sold it to me — you know that. Mr. Sidon knows that. Why should I tell? When I said that, the teacher, you know, Mr. Sidon, the man in charge of the squads, he turned to one of the boys in the room, and he asked, 'Didn't this boy buy a lot of your stuff?' the boy stood up and said, 'Yes.' That was a lie, Miss Rollins I swear It was a lie. So I up and asked him myself, 'What, do you mean that?' Mr. Sidon told me to shut up, but I asked him again and he saw there was fire in my eyes and he said nothing and just looked at the teacher and I said, 'Say it again, did I?' and he said 'Yes,' or I thought he did, and so I punched him. Gee, but I punched him. He fell back and they had to get an ambulance, and Mr. Sidon wanted to get the cops and have me sent to jail for assault, but the principal said he wouldn't have it; if the boy's father wanted to make a complaint all right, but they suspended me and said I am too old anyhow to remain in school, and they could discharge me if I didn't tell the truth. . . ."

"And did you?"

Donato looked up frankly, and she returned his look as frankly. For a second they gazed at each other's eyes, aware of nothing but them. They did not hear the gongs clang through the hallways as a sign that the boys might enter, nor the sound of running feet, the yelling of the students one to another, the banging of doors. Or rather they did hear, but a quality in their expression had put them momentarily beyond the limits of the present. In some fashion they had communicated to each other a mutual need. Amy could not have said just what it might be, nor Donato himself. The look, however, had been intense enough to have rendered them both a trifle uneasy and for a second they said nothing, aware that the bells had rung and that boys were coming in.

–3–

Most of the boys ran past unconscious of anyone else's presence as if Miss Rollins had not been away for more than two weeks. Several stopped at the desk.

"Glad to see you back," one diminutive chap piped, taking off his cap hurriedly, and smiling all over his tiny, inquisitive face.

"Hope you're well, Miss Rollins," another boy said, leaning over the desk most confidentially. He was an oversized lad already aware of his nearness to adulthood.

"I see you're growing a mustache," is all Miss Rollins, answered, smiling.

"Trying to. But they're all kidding me about it, so maybe I'll take it off. . . ."

"It looks nice," Amy vouchsafed, not without a suggestion of the "kidding" that he seemed to resent.

"Oh, don't tell him that," several boys spoke up at once, crowding around her.

"Gee, he's conceited enough already."

"Thinks he's the cat's whiskers," another added amid the laughter of the group.

"He sure ain't no Romeo with or without," another cried.

The boy was unable to answer back. They had pushed so close to the desk that he could not move nor straighten himself up. Miss Rollins was all smiles and looked so happy, despite Donato's story, that could Stephen have seen her he would have avowed that the country had worked wonders with her.

The other boys in the room had in the meantime found other occupations. Several were engaged in a veritable struggle to wrest a cap out of a boy's hand so as to throw it out of the window. One was shouting at the top of his head, "Cut it out, will you, and let me read this stuff."

The door opened to admit a heavy set man with enormous shoulders and a head that was leonine in proportions.

"What does this mean, Miss Rollins? Can't you keep your class in order?"

"Why, Mr. Aborn," she gasped, standing up, while all the boys made a beeline for their seats. But the boys in the back of the room continued their wrestling for the ill-destined cap.

Several cried, "Shut up, there."

"Quiet," yelled the man in the doorway. The command began in a roar but ended in a voice that broke and thinned off into a shriek. The wrestling boys ducked for the nearest vacant seats.

"You go downstairs to the office," he cried again. "All of you back there." Several of the real offenders rose to go downstairs.

"You too," Mr. Aborn cried. "And you . . ." pointing to one boy and then another.

"But I didn't. . . ."

"You too, I say," screamed Mr. Aborn.

The boy went out sheepishly, if rebelliously, while all the others kept steady faces, but any observer, save Mr. Aborn, might have noticed that they were all on the point of laughter. Mr. Aborn turned about and was proceeding to go out when he retreated a few steps and said,

"I'm glad to see you back, Miss Rollins. We've been having a lot of trouble with the noise in the morning and there's a campaign on against it. . . ."

"Thank you," she said quietly, as he turned to leave. No sooner had he left, however, than the class to a boy raised a roar of laughter. The cap had sailed through the air and was making its way out of the window.

"Why, boys," is all Amy said, looking injured, and rapping the desk.

Fortunately the laughter had subsided when Mr. Aborn poked his head into the doorway again and beckoned to Miss Rollins.

"That boy, Contini," he said to her in a whisper. "He's pretty bad stuff. He has got into a nasty mess. Don't listen to his story. . . . It's too bad; we all thought him so nice. I'm sorry I had to speak about your class this morning. . . . You generally keep good order. . . ."

Amy gazed at him without expression or manifest reaction. Unable to understand it, Mr. Aborn continued talking.

"Sorry about your mother." His voice broke again. "We all hope you're going to get right back into things . . . you're looking well. . . ."

He would have talked endlessly had not Amy put her hand on the knob of the door and said, "There's plenty ahead for me to do. . . ."

-4-

The day proved to be more trying than she had expected. The classes had been in the hands of numerous substitutes, who not only had been unable to maintain discipline but had failed to keep the students up to the standards of achievement required for her grades. She realized from the start that only the brighter among the pupils were going to be able to pass the examinations and that the others were so discouraged that they would sooner or later lay down their arms and refuse to go on. Several born rowdies had discovered their innate propensities for creating mischief in the soft reign of the substitutes and were prepared to attempt conclusions with Miss Rollins. The mere physical task of suppressing these troublemakers rapidly depleted her stores of energy. By the time she had gone to the teachers' restroom for lunch she had begun to show her tiredness.

Besides, she had been unable to throw off the problem of Donato Contini. She was aware that her interest in him was as much personal as it was that of the teacher attending to a routine case of discipline. She would have interested herself immediately in any boy with a similar story. There was a trait in Donato, however, which arrested her attention, had done so from the very beginning. Even several terms back, before he had dropped out of school for a year, there had been evident in his manner of speech and address — it was noticeable even in his posture — a furtive quality of fear as if he were standing off to one side and watching both himself and his interlocutor. Yet once free of this tendency, he became open and frank, almost confessional in his talk and ways. His voice was deep and full and had a singing quality which immediately suggested the artist or at least one who is sensitive to beauty, to subtle combinations of ordinary things. It was this that had attracted Amy, this and a real interest and ability in his work. His translations at times were couched in an English not as idiomatic as she would have liked, but there was always present the unusual word which lifted an obscure Latin phrase into distinction, threw light on the rest of the sentence and occasionally caused considerable comment and questioning among the other members of the class.

Once, she recalled, he translated, "' — and the rest of the men and women, they had to bend their necks to the yoke. . . .'"

"But, teacher," another lad had protested, "it doesn't say that. It says, 'had to pass under the yoke. . . .'"

"I know," Donato replied, "but I just used my imagination. . . ."

The answer was that of a boy, and Miss Rollins smiled. "It's really an inaccurate translation, word for word. But it does catch the spirit. . . ."

There were times when he seemed lonely and aloof, as if he made a practice of keeping to himself. With thousands of boys to choose from, he had few companions. She observed, however, that he was on friendly terms with all of them and that he was universally liked despite the fact that he rarely entered into their sports, their parties, or even their school clubs. Once there was a group of boys who had wished him to run for president of the school organization, sensing in some fashion that his handsomeness, the slightly imperious manner, withal so gracious and so pleasant, that characterized him, would make a wide appeal. But he had refused the honor. As a matter of fact, he had absented himself from school for several days, saying to Miss Rollins on his return,

"I couldn't come. I can't tell you why. My father didn't write a note. But really, Miss Rollins, if you knew, you would understand. . . ."

"I am not supposed to excuse you without a note. . . ."

"I know. . . ."

And then he had turned to her his grey eyes with their troubled brilliance, and she had signed his slip, "Note recorded," and heard his low, "Thank you," and watched him leave, wondering why she had done it.

As she walked to the teachers' room, these incidents came back to her. Here he was now, throwing himself upon her completely. She would forego lunch and run to the principal's office. No, she would see him first and find out more. Donato had been ordered to remain in the office of Mr. Sidon, a teacher in charge of disciplinary cases too serious in character to be considered sporadic or negligible.

As Mr. Sidon bent over his desk, the noticeable droop of his shoulders brought his head closer to the desk top than necessary and caused him to look over the rim of his huge horn glasses. Amy was taken aback. He had so much the look of an inquisitor, especially in this dark room, sunk, as it was, below the level of the street, with its high windows heavily screened and barred. She had heard numerous teachers complain of his high-handed police-like methods with the boys, but before this, she had never seen him in his room. He was talking to Donato, looking at him over his lenses, his elbows spread out on the table. His raspy voice was sarcastically superior, high-pitched, and attempted quick drops into low registers and stage whispers.

"This is the last time, young man. You'll make an open statement, tell me everything, or you'll go up the river. This is not a school offense, this is no kid's prank. This is organized crime — do you hear me?" (His voice mounted sharply and dramatically.) "Organized crime. Fellows like you ought to be behind bars. . . ."

Donato kept his head lowered. His posture was one of infinite patience, but color had flooded his cheeks, and so he gave the impression of being able no longer to stand the repeated attacks upon him. When he saw Miss Rollins, a smile came to his lips, and he looked up brightly as if he thought deliverance were at hand.

"Mr. Sidon," Amy said, "I beg your pardon. I am interested in Donato. I heard what you said just now. . . ."

"You haven't heard the half of it," replied Mr. Sidon, sliding on his swivel chair, and dropping his voice into a tone of confidence. "We've unearthed a nest of incipient thieves and gangsters, and this slick article seems to be the leader. . . ."

"Why should he seem so pleased with it?" thought Amy, and then she said aloud, "Could I see him for a few minutes? I have something to ask him. . . ."

"He's remaining here in this room. Everything he says, he says in my presence. . . ."

"But it's between him and me. . . ."

"Nothing is between him and anybody else. He'll be in the hands of the police . . . he is in the hands of the police. . . ."

Donato jumped up, his face flushed, his whole body trembling.

"You can't do that, Mr. Sidon," he cried, "You can't do that. . . ."

"You keep your seat, and don't say another word," Mr. Sidon yelled at him.

"Is there any reason for this anger?" thought Amy. "What a way to handle a youngster — he's no gangster. . . ."

"Mr. Sidon," Amy spoke quietly and earnestly, "if you will let me talk with him alone, I think I can help you. . . ."

"Only in my presence!" Mr. Sidon slammed his open palm on the table.

"You're a brute, you're worse than the cops, you're. . . ."

"Worse than the cops, hey, worse than the cops!" Mr. Sidon had jumped to his feet and dashed toward the boy shaking a long knotted finger at him, and raising his voice in sing-song glee. "Worse than the cops . . . well, well. There you cooked your hash, young man. There you spilled the beans. What do you know about cops, hey? Tell me that. What do you know about cops and their ways that you can make the comparison, hey?"

The teacher's voice hinted at dark and mysterious knowledge. His eyes he fixed on Donato with the look of one closely scrutinizing a puzzling object.

"So . . . so . . . ." Mr. Sidon took up his sarcastic chant. "You get pale, and shaky a bit, hey . . . pale and shaky . . . you know something about the cops. . . ."

Amy was so intent upon observing the course of the incident that she had approached closer to Mr. Sidon, not only horrified by partly fascinated by the intensity of the man. She was at a loss to account for this manifestation of what to her seemed sheer brutality, although in her own mind she was willing to admit the enormity of the offense and possibly Donato's complicity. She had just turned to look at Donato. Again Mr. Sidon raised his voice.

"Maybe you know a thing or two about the cops. Maybe it is not the first time you have been a fence. . . ."

What followed occurred with great rapidity. She saw the color rise in the boy's face, his eyes became bloodshot with anger, the muscles of his face quiver. Then as Mr. Sidon renewed the accusation, Donato threw himself forward, striking wildly with his fists. Without the slightest hesitation Amy interposed her body. The blows that had been intended for Sidon fell upon her. Later, as she thought of the incident, she wondered why they had not hurt, why they had not floored her. She watched Donato's fists, like one bewitched, exulting in their falling on her and not on Mr. Sidon. What might have resulted from the assault she dreaded to think. Added to the original accusation of larceny and injuring a boy, would be violence, violence against constituted authority.

"Stop, Donato," she cried. "Are you going crazy?"

"I'm sorry, Miss Rollins," he blurted, his face pale, his body shaking.

Mr. Sidon, too, was pale and standing without motion or word, too bewildered for either.

–5–

Amy alone seemed to have retained her composure. But she, too, had colorless cheeks and scared eyes.

"Shame on you, Mr. Sidon," she said in deliberate whispers. "Shame to provoke a boy in this way. Suppose he is a thief. It isn't for you to do what you are doing. After all, he is a student here and just a boy."

"I'll not be criticized by you, Miss Rollins, nor by anyone else. He's not the kind of boy we want here, if I know anything about him. This will be the last thing he does in this school. . . ."

"I came here, Mr. Sidon, to see Donato and have a heart-to-heart talk with him. I ask you again to let him come with me. . . ."

"He's in the hands of the police, I tell you. . . ."

"Then let me talk to him here alone. . . ."

"Very well . . ." and quivering with emotion he left the room, slamming the door.

Donato and Amy looked at each other.

"Well?" she asked, as if they had known each other for years.

"It's all a lie, Miss Rollins," the boy wept, lifting an agonized face to hers. "It's all a lie. All I did was buy the fountain pen. I needed one and the boy said it was his and he wanted to sell it cheap. Maybe it was his, maybe it wasn't, but why should I have to tell? I'll tell you, Miss Rollins, it's because that man Sidon, he knows something . . . I didn't think anybody knew . . . I stayed out of school a year . . . I came back for my father's sake . . . he's an old man, Miss Rollins, and he's all broken . . . and I'm all that's left to him . . . it killed my mother . . . and this man Sidon he knows but. . . ."

Donato had burst into tears. He fell into his seat, and buried his head in his hands.

"You poor boy, you poor boy," was all she could say as she watched his body shake with his sobs. She had an intense desire to place her arm about him and to wipe away his tears. Genuine tears they were, tears that came from the depths of great sorrow. She began to understand that some cruel secret had made him the morose and distant lad he appeared to be. She began to understand, too, that this must have been the source of the real wisdom he displayed, of the sensitiveness and appreciation that he evinced when, with other boys of similar intelligence, it was only a case of rote comprehension.

Donato stopped crying as quickly as he had begun.

"I'll tell you all," he said. "I wanted to forget, and my father too. My brother . . . you didn't know my brother . . . he came here for a while . . . he was a fine boy . . . I know he was . . . a fine boy, Miss Rollins, but he got mixed up with a gang and they wanted to pull off something big, and they roped my brother in . . . anyhow they held up this man with all the money . . . they say it was pay money for workmen . . . I don't know . . . that's what they say, see . . . but instead they killed him and another man with him . . . my brother he didn't shoot at all . . . they never proved he had a gun, see . . . they never proved it . . . they didn't, Miss Rollins . . . but he was with the gang . . . laying for the police like . . . you know . . . well, they gave him the chair too . . . they gave him the chair too. . . ." He stopped, his lips tremulous, unable to go on. His eyes had misted and a great sadness seemed to filter through them like a light behind a fog. "He was only nineteen, Miss Rollins," he added, making a rare gesture, an impotent fist held for a minute suspended and then brought down slowly to his side.

Again, "You poor boy," was all Miss Rollins could utter.

"They think I'm in with the gangs. Mr. Sidon, I mean, because he knows about Giulio, see, he knows . . . it killed my mother . . . if they tell my father about this . . . but it isn't true . . . I had nothing to do with it . . . I didn't know about it . . . honest, Miss Rollins, you believe me. . . ."

"Of course, I do. . . ."

She wanted to stretch her hands out to him. But the door opened. The principal of the school and Mr. Sidon entered in great hurry and agitation.

"What is this, Miss Rollins?"

The principal asked the question politely and calmly, but she realized that Mr. Sidon had either misinformed him of her intentions or that he himself had drawn erroneous conclusions from the situation. Mr. Polter was a man of considerable girth but insignificant stature. Despite these disqualifications, he had developed a ponderous moustache which became bushier and bushier the farther it extended from the upper lip. Nevertheless the impression he made was neither ludicrous nor incongruous, for his quick blue eyes, penetrating and genial, gave his mobile face an alertness which stamped him as a leader at once. Students and teachers alike esteemed him, and though several nicknames, not altogether flattering, were constantly associated with him, he managed to leave upon them the marks of a personality interested in their welfare, understanding of their needs, devoted to the ideals of an education which, unfortunately, only too rarely is achieved.

Both Miss Rollins and Donato, despite the tone of severity which Mr. Polter suggested, felt relieved at his entrance. She explained at once in answer to a direct question that she had no purpose of interfering with Mr. Sidon. She had foregone her lunch because she had been deeply moved with what the boy had confessed to her in the morning and had been so disturbed by his manner and his attitude that she wanted to help him. She caused Donato to repeat his story. Mr. Sidon grew red. He had not told this portion of the incident to Mr. Polter and showed in his manner and expression an immediate desire to make an explanation that would clear himself in the eyes of the principal.

"Let him talk," commanded Mr. Polter. "A boy isn't a criminal because a brother was one. . . ."

"He wasn't, Mr. Polter, he wasn't. You didn't know him. He was a wonderful boy . . . he went around with bad companions . . . my father thought he'd be something some day . . . then they gave him the chair. . . ."

Donato broke down again.

"Miss Rollins," said the principal. "I'm going to leave Contini with you. We're pressing no charges, Mr. Sidon. What's a school for? We're not policemen and we're not judges. We're not catching criminals in this school nor helping to make them. There's a lot to this boy. . . ."

VII. LONELINESS

AMY THREW herself on the couch as soon as she got home. The fatigue of the day was as nothing, however, to the sense of complete loneliness. No object she looked at but reminded her of her mother, and with it came the impulse to perform some little act, to answer a question, to ask, "A little better today?" But the impulses lost themselves in the silence like waves that roll upon the beach and dissipate into nothingness. And as they did so they left a pain behind, the sharp consciousness of the futility of being apart and alone, of having to care for oneself just because one is.

"Don't let the madness come on me again," she cried in her own heart. "Don't let the feeling of utter loneliness seize me. . . ."

She lay on her back, with her hands across her eyes. She resolved she would lie there relaxed, drop the cares of the day, forget the fatigue and the worry. Donato, after all, was a boy, a vigorous, intelligent young man bound to make an adjustment. Philip would throw off the obsessions that rendered him useless and dependent. All he needed was to be given the chance of depending on himself. It would be his cure and his salvation. As for her, like a child she had placed a foot into the ocean, fearful of its power, its beauty, its joyousness but filled with the desire to feel its buffets, its soft caressings, its cleansing, vivifying strength. But like the child, she had withdrawn her foot, had run back to the shelter of her assurances — her work and the routine it involved. It had been satisfying, had engaged her full attention, had sapped enough of her energy to render her now inert, desirous only of stretching out in thorough and definite languidness. The fatigue of the day ran through her veins like an opiate, and gradually she fell into the softness of sleep, discarding her thoughts, tasting the sweetness of resting.

She woke up with a start. The room was in darkness. Night had come upon her unaware, and with her perception of its presence, she shuddered. For it had blotted out the images of furniture and walls, of frames and windows. The room expanded about her like space without confines. She peered into the places where she knew corners must be. Distant lights cast uncertain reflections in the oddest spots. She recognized the small rocker near her radio. Again she shuddered. It was so irretrievably empty.

How often her mother had sat in it and rocked and rocked, listening to the miraculous voices, the magical music box. She rose and ran to the radio. A solemn voice was announcing: "*For your body, Bell's Pure Soap.* . . ." She shut it off, stood stock still.

"But I must talk to somebody, must. . . ."

She had let her hair fall on her shoulders. She placed her hands on it and stroked it as if it were some living creature in need of love. And as she stood thus, she said to herself, "I've got to find something to do . . . take a course at the university . . . complete my doctorate . . . it would be easy now . . . so much time on my hands . . . I'll join a swimming club too . . . . What shall I do all summer . . . school closed . . . everybody off to Europe. . . . ?"

Gradually her own mind added to the pressure of the empty chairs, the silent room, the uncrowded darkness, just enough weight to render almost unbearable the burden of her loneliness. She became like one in a fever before getting home and to bed, incapable of finding comfort or ease, assailed as if by physical violence by every object within sight and hearing. She made little gestures with her hand like a kitten trying to keep a huge dog at bay. She placed the balls of her palms into the hollows of her eyes and pressed and pressed, trying to flood the interior of her thoughts with the sporadic borealis of the irritated iris. Then, as if she had found a way of driving out the sense of being alone with no purpose, no joy, no hope, she ran to the electric switch and threw on the light. The chairs the small table with its red glass jar, Whistler's *Carlyle* on the wall, the ivory replica of the Parthenon on the mantelpiece, the old spindled Windsor chair near the window, and the room itself, as if it too were an article one could pick up and deposit in another place — all jumped into the vision, and as they did so assumed an individuality with contours and a voice appropriate to it.

"Only *you* here for me. . . ."

"Can you gaze on me and not want to share me. . . .?"

"From couch to me, from me to the couch, like your mother. . . ."

"Just a door — a door into the kitchen where you will cook — cook? — for whom? — you alone, you always alone. . . ."

"For you I keep the time, that you may be at school early, come back to note how many hours before you must go to sleep . . . day in and day out . . . think how you will watch my hands move throughout the summer months. . . ."

"Yes, for flowers . . . cut flowers . . . bought flowers . . . what time you will have now to change their water, cut their stems, wash their petals . . . yes, you could have pots . . . grow rare blooms . . . that will fill your time. . . ."

"Books are the essence of a master spirit embalmed . . . dead? — yes, dead . . . but with exquisite exhalations as of mummies washed in myrrh and frankincense that never lose their scent . . . not living souls . . . dead but filled with agony that does not pain, with joy that does not dry the tongue, with fear that does not chill the blood . . . I am Caesar and I tell my little story as if I were a god . . . and I am Tacitus and know that the grains of wheat may spell destiny or defeat . . . Ovid I, who knew delectable nights and the ways of the amorous . . . and come with me, fifty parasangs away, a hundred parasangs, a thousand parasangs, and there the sea bursts into view the sea, the sea. . . ."

Amy had walked to her bookshelves. They were several mahogany racks without windows or doors, tiny cherubs carved along the edges with dust collected in the folds of their bodies. She stooped to look at the titles, to finger this book and now the other, trying to decide to read one. Each one, however, seemed to be shouting at her and the shouting seemed mockery and the mockery seemed to come out of the depths of disillusion, and the disillusion seemed permanently fixed in the titles as in a scroll fantastic, distorted. . . .

She put her fingers to her ears. How strange, but the books were actually vocal, advertising themselves in loud voices, making desperate cries to disprove her lack of faith, swelling now to positive disbelief. Would they ever cease it? And the shelves are joining in. . . .

"Out of the forests of quiet depths we came, to hold these silent utterings of the great dead that you may have the means of filling in your days. . . ."

These *were* voices. Why did she not succeed in shutting them out?

She ran, like a little animal, scared by unaccustomed noises in the grass . . . ran quickly into the kitchen, and closed the door after her. But the sounds continued . . . "We will wait . . . when you are alone . . . you will be often alone . . . and you will prepare lonely meals . . . meals for you . . . for you alone . . . you have few friends . . . you had so little time to cultivate them . . . they dropped away. . . ."

But the sight of the gas-range, egg-blue enamel now covered with the dust of weeks, and of the pans hanging from hooks under the dish-closets, shining dully and bulging from the wall like overfat insects clinging to boughs, they also seemed to shout at her . . . "Eat, eat, eat . . . alone . . . ." A feeling of nausea came upon her. She reeled. She wanted to rush back into the other room and run to her bed, but she was afraid, afraid. . . .

-3-

Just then the kitchen door opened with such suddenness that she started and gave a little cry.

"It's me, Amy, me . . . Mrs. Nilins, dear, Mrs. Nilins. . . ."

Mrs. Nilins' small figure teetered in the doorway, overcome with the sight of the pale frightened Amy, eyes wide open, her fists pressed to her cheeks.

"You aren't frightened of me?" Mrs. Nilins' head shook, and the top-knot along with it.

"You poor child," she said, going up to Amy who was crying as if in an hysteria of delight at seeing only Mrs. Nilins and no phantasm. "You're frightened so, and shaking, and sick-like. . . . Miss Batten is outside . . . came to see you. . . ."

Mrs. Nilins had put her arm about Amy's waist and was holding her as if she were in reality sick. But Amy smiled and patted the hand on her hip. "You're awfully kind, Mrs. Nilins . . . I don't know what happened to me . . . maybe the heat and having nothing to eat all day. . . ."

"Oh, Amy, how dreadful! You look dreadful! Oh, here sit down, by the window . . . do get her some tea. . . ."

Miss Batten's voice, approximately a baritone, boomed her distress and sympathy all through the rooms.

"Why, child, you should not have come back to school. It was too much for you. I heard all about it. . . ."

"She hasn't had a thing to eat, Miss Batten," interposed Mrs. Nilins, "and it's so hot. . . ."

"How dreadful," explained Miss Batten, taking off her hat, and throwing it, as a man would, on the couch. "We'll repair this at once. That's your kitchen . . .?"

The energy exuding from the enormous proportions of Miss Batten was overwhelming. Amy looked on with amazement, wondering how Miss Batten always managed to keep so cool and controlled when she possessed so many immense contours. The contours bayed themselves into space, however, with unmistakable assurances redundant but satisfied.

"Now I am huge, Amy, but I eat no more than a sparrow. . . ."

"There isn't even enough for a sparrow in the kitchen . . . I forgot I'd be alone . . . Philip would have done the shopping. . . ."

"Well, then, you'll get yourself together and we'll make a beeline for Tony's around the corner. . . ."

-4-

Mrs. Nilins' brownstone house had lost whatever distinction it once boasted. She had moved into the place on the day of her wedding over forty years back and had remained. It was all she had in the world.

She was the last of a family if not of a generation. Her husband had died exactly twelve months after her wedding, and several months later she buried her infant girl. A sister had come to live with her and she too had died. From that time on, Mrs. Nilins had decided to live alone, at least to have no relatives near or distant, few as they were, risk their lives. The house appeared to have deadly properties. She alone seemed to have the proper immunity.

For a period she had remained, solitary, retired, unhappy. After several years, she found that the money left her by her husband would not be sufficient to maintain both her and the house. She took in a family, at first on the top floor, and as she did so she prayed fervently that no harm might come to them. It was an old man and his spinster daughter. In less than a year the old man had died and the girl had moved out.

So it had continued. Every family had buried one or another member and then moved out and as they moved had left Mrs. Nilins the clothing of the deceased. This Mrs. Nilins had carefully sorted, reserved for her own use the more likely apparel, and sold the rest to the old clothes man who invariably rang her bell instead of merely calling out his presence. She had needed very little for her wants, had bought next to nothing for herself, and was reputed now to have a considerable sum of money safely invested or possibly stowed away in the manner of an older day. At the present time, she was in mortal fear lest Amy move away too and had resolved to exert her utmost to retain her. This was not altogether because Amy was a desirable tenant, but Amy had stirred her imagination and awaked memories that had begun to achieve new outlines as she grew older.

"You have the hair of my daughter. She would now be a mother many times over if she had lived." This she had told Amy time and again. "She had your skin, too, and your blue eyes . . . it's as if God had made her and didn't want to lose the pattern, so he made you. . . ." Mrs. Nilins' fingers snapped between her open lips as she spoke these words: sure signs that she was deeply moved.

Now she stood on the stoop, watching Amy and Miss Batten going down the stairs.

"She's just as alone as I used to be," Mrs. Nilins thought, moving her fingers slowly over her mouth. "She's just a lonesome thing. . . . What would she be doing moving away? I am lonesome too and the days with her away were not so nice . . . I'm getting too old to be alone and she's too young. . . ."

She shook her head sadly but with the mechanical effect she invariably produced, as if alarmed that her topknot would topple off her head. She shook her head as she watched the cars roll out of the garages across the street, from doors through which had pranced high-spirited horses and shining carriages. She looked at the lights proclaiming the cleaning and dyeing shop of S. Levinsky. Again she shook her head.

"Mrs. Baird lived there once. What a lady she was!"

Further down was a house, similar to her own, with all the windows of the second story lighted. Back and forth and kicking up their toes, whirling and mincing and tossing their bodies from side to side, were the figures of numerous girls in tights and slight body coverings, learning to dance. The window panes blazoned forth the fact. A fat man in shirt-sleeves, belt holding in the ponderousness of his abdomen, plain in the bright glare, kept clapping his hands, or waving them up and up as if the toes of the dancing girls could rise until they touched the ceiling.

"That was the Stuart house . . . the Stuarts!" Mrs. Nilins shook her head,

"Old Mr. Donald would turn in his grave . . . deacon of the church . . . never missed but four Sundays. . . ."

A car sped past, sounding its horn in blatant hilarity, packed with boys and girls piled upon each other, laughing at the top of their voices. Mrs. Nilins watched them pass one car and then another, weave in and out, make a frantic turn to the right all in a desperate endeavor to catch up with something, or just keep going, going, going.

"What youngsters!" thought Mrs. Nilins, smiling.

Only two memories she spoke about, and these only rarely. Talking was an effort and her whispering voice annoyed people. There was the little girl who had died before learning to sit up . . . she would have loved to talk of its blue eyes, its yellow hair, its tiny fingernails. And there was her husband. She loved to talk of him too, but not to reveal his kindliness, his affection, his thoughts. Rather did she want to tell people that he invariably, invariably wore a Prince Albert, even to his business, mind you. And he had vests — ah yes, waistcoats that were the envy of the other men. They still hung in his closet, each on its own hanger, purple velvets, green silks, white piques, striped ones with mother-of-pearl buttons. And on the shelf immediately above, were his hats: high hats and derbies, and several beavers.

"He always cut a figure, Amy," she would say. "He was a gentleman and you knew it at a glance. . . ."

-5-

Amy shrank from contemplating the image of her own father who had only been a foreman-plumber and had never been able to establish himself as a boss or storekeeper, try as he would. The picture of him was of one who never was out of overalls, overalls never free of smudges, smudges with incorrigible propensities for spreading out and out until they burred into his shirt and deposited concrete symbols of themselves under his fingernails. Prince Alberts and high hats, spats and waistcoats — Amy could see the grand gentleman proceeding down the street to the park, and on his walk through the park to catch the coach and four on Fifth Avenue.

Her own father glimmered into view, hurrying out with a tin dinner-pail in his hand, the overalls that would come back smeared, and a face whose straight regular features seemed to be peering with painful assiduity into a future that he could never fathom. His face remained perpetually clean, as if to suggest that an immense gulf stretched between the work that he was doing and the thoughts that filled his mind. Never the slightest taint of his work found lodgment in the fair skin, soft and pink like a baby's, nor in the hollow places where the chin curved from the jaw or where the nose sloped from the cheeks. And the blue eyes that Amy had inherited glowed, glowed perpetually, as if they were lighted by fires within that had nothing to do with the routine of his life.

Mrs. Nilins took a seat on the upper step of her stoop and looked around, her head shaking with mechanical precision, her topknot barely holding its place of pinnacle on the surface of it. Young couples and old filmed past like shadows, sauntering groups, voluble, wordless, excited repressed. They all passed her by. She had been too long accustomed to loneliness to feel it keenly now. Something there must have been, however, in the still heavy air of the June night, the oppressive warmth that oozed its way into every nook and crevice of the pyramidal apartments on the avenue and crowded out the inhabitants, something there must have been in the diffused jollity of the moving throngs, the lighted stores, the whirling vehicles, that touched the gregarious centers of the brain, filtered into the hollows of the heart.

For Mrs. Nilins looked on the scene with more than her accustomed cursoriness. There was curiosity and interest, a desire to understand. And she peered into the darkness, peered as if hoping to recognize someone, someone to whom she could call; or was she puzzling out an explanation for the satisfaction everybody was taking in being with someone else, in being propelled along in a crowd, jostled and pushed, stared at? She, she was perched there, alone a frail figure unknown to anyone, like a child left at the window to watch her parents going out into the big mysterious world beyond her little ken. For the first time in years, a sadness pervaded her few obvious thoughts. She had a sudden desire, a desire that she was afraid would become too overwhelming to resist. She wanted to cry out into the night, call some chance name. "You there, Mr. Robinson, why do you pass me by? Why won't you stop and talk with me?" Her fingers snapped back and forth, back and forth between her open lips, now in complete awe of this confused and swirling world in front of her.

"It was seeing Amy like that tonight," she said. "I never feel this way . . . not anymore . . . it must have been Amy . . . she must not be allowed to go on this way alone . . . alone like me. . . ."

And then the pompous gentleman who used to fill the gorgeous Prince Alberts came into her thoughts and with him the short period of their wedded life. Visions of the room on the second floor with its canopied four-poster, its stuffed chair, the ornate pier glass between the windows, sailed before her eyes like a cloud that suggests details of a definite scene but never is complete. And she saw the gentleman that had occupied the immense spaces within the Prince Alberts, saw him quietly asleep, the soft smile of delighted exhaustion on his features, and she remembered the few sweet moments, the occasional delirious rise into joy. Like Amy, she too seemed to feel a slight touch of fever.

"It must be the heat," she thought, snapping her fingers, "the heat and seeing Amy that way . . . oh, she must never, never be allowed. . . ."

"And here we are back," almost bellowed Miss Batten at the base of the stoop. "Look at the little girl now. She needed a good meal and some talking-to. . . ."

"Oh, she needs more than a good meal," whispered Mrs. Nilins, "much more than a good meal."

It was surprising how the whisper carried above the noise of the street.

"You're a wicked woman, Mrs. Nilins," roared Miss Batten. "I know just what you want to say. . . ."

"But she needs a companion . . ." whispered Mrs. Nilins, more vigorously than ever, shaking her head with more energy than she generally expended. The topknot appeared ready to topple over.

A chill went through Amy. The words she heard seemed coarse and vulgar. It was as if her friends had pried into her intimacies and invented ribald stories about them.

"Miss Batten," continued Mrs. Nilins, "I have been a widow and I know what it is to be alone. . . ."

"Come, come, old girl," shouted Miss Batten from the lower capacities of her chest. "You must not make an old maid like me feel sorry for myself. . . ."

And with that she turned to Amy and said,

"Good night, Amy. I'll see you in the morning . . . I wouldn't worry about that old fool. . . . Everybody hates him. . . ."

–6–

Miss Batten had taken Amy to Tony's and, as if instructing a child, made her take a seat under one of the fans. Despite the fans, however, the air hung grey over the counters, their showcases filled with pies, and slices of curled tomatoes, withered lettuce, mayonnaise disintegrating into its component liquids. The tables were covered with tablecloths upon which previous dinners had left traces of coffee. Crowds poured in and out, ran up to the food counters with trays, deposited the trays on the tables, ate as if they had not eaten before, and left.

"This is as nice a place as any," said Miss Batten. "You sit here and I'll get you something. . . ."

Amy sat quiet, not daring to manifest the revulsion she felt at the sight of food exposed in such quantities and at the sight of so many men and women eating, eating, eating. Laughter now and then made the thick air seem thicker and the crowded tables all the coarser. She had rarely eaten out, and when she did eat away from home, she chose unpretentious little tearooms with clover leaves for emblems, or a dainty name: "The Mossy Rest," or "The Wayside Niche."

Miss Batten set down both trays with violent confidence that the salads and the coffee would retain their positions forever. Her own bulk she lowered with more care, again took off her hat in the manner of a man, and reached over to a nearby hat tree to hang it up.

"Never go to tearooms," she explained in loud tones. "Give me a man-sized cafeteria where you can get something for your money. I don't eat more than two thimblesful a day but I want them full. Forget the things you don't like, Amy," she commanded, "and you'll be surprised. That salad will be just the best thing. . . . That's it, nibble at it. . . then go to it . . . and for God's sake," she continued, breaking a roll in two with angry vigor, "forget about that Sidon wretch and his filthy little nose. He's always poking into the dirtiest corners. . . . Mr. Polter got taken in by him. . . . Oh, they won't do a thing to that Contini boy. . . . He's got too good a record. . . . Too bad you had to come back to school after what happened to you and face a thing like this. Why, I wouldn't leave a stone unturned to get that boy out of any mess even if he were guilty. . . . He's got some manners . . . innate manners . . . ever hear him talk to the other boys? . . . He's always quiet . . . and to the teachers? . . . Of course, I'd worry about him . . . but don't. Say, life's too short, old girl. . . . I got my own worries and so have you . . . we've ourselves to worry about. . . . Say, you are not married and you won't be if you don't hurry and get a man. As for me, I am hopeless . . . nobody wants to take care of my immense developments. . . . Men have been scared of me ever since I started making eyes at them. . . . But you, Amy . . . you ought to get yourself a man. . . ."

Miss Batten talked and talked fast, but she seemed capable at the same time of administering generous helpings to her mouth in an endeavor, presumably, to maintain its energy at par. She looked up and saw that Amy had not eaten much. . . .

"Young lady," she said, "I brought you here to eat. Don't be a ninny about eating in places like this. . . . You haven't too much money, and you must be saving. . . . Why, I wouldn't spend more than a dollar ninety-eight for a hat and in these days to find a hat at that price you've got to currycomb the five boroughs of New York. That's just what I did today. . . . Why, I even went to Brooklyn and finally had to land in Williamsburg. Ever try finding your way around in those parts? I lost at least ten pounds, but I got the hat. And I am not going to spend two dollars for a meal when I can get one for seventy-five cents. I got things to do with my money. I live in style but not in this God-forsaken hole. I work here and don't mix pleasure and work. As soon as school's over, I'm off for Europe . . . there's the place . . . there you can't trust the cheap hotels . . . they'd soak you anyhow . . . so there I live in style . . . that's what you ought to do, Amy. . . . I don't teach mathematics for nothing . . . I calculate everything . . . say, where would one be if one didn't? That's why I came around to see you . . . I knew you were going to be alone and I knew how badly fixed you were and I want to give you a piece of advice . . . get married as soon as you can if the man can support you; otherwise save your money . . . you'll be old sooner than you know it . . . there are plenty of men will marry you if you stick to your job and keep the larder full . . .

but I wasn't brought up that way, Amy . . . a man's got to support me . . . of course there's a lot of me and maybe too much . . . but that's my slogan . . . there was a man once, but I saw right through him and I haven't had the offer repeated . . . that's why I went to Europe . . . they tell me my size specimen has a chance there . . . enjoys a kind of preference . . . that's the tale I heard, but I think it's a legend . . . say, maybe I didn't try to land me a man! Almost hauled one in Palermo one summer . . . talked English with perfect downtown New York accent . . . woik and toid and all that — had made money and gone off to spend it in his hometown . . . wife dead and children all married . . . and handsome, Amy . . . had a face like King Humbert, mustache, hair and all . . . ever see one . . . ? Have one in the wax work in London but . . . the family put their heads together and said I was too much for them to handle or words to that effect. . . ."

What there was of frankness and vigor and wholehearted self-understanding in Miss Batten's speech and manner must have communicated itself to Amy. She had eaten what she had placed before herself in perfect synchronization, as she talked, with the movements of her jaws. The effect had been so amusing and her carefree speech so infectious that Amy began to disregard the confusion and the cheapness of the restaurant and to peck at one thing and another on her plate and finally to eat it all. She stared in utter amazement at the huge manlike woman in front of her, and could not make up her mind whether to admire her or to pity her. It was perfectly obvious to Amy, sensitive and understanding at all points, that this breeziness of manner, this braggadocio insouciance were like huge coverings she was spreading over a soul not altogether so pleased with the world and what it had offered as Miss Batten wanted Amy to believe.

"A lonely soul, too," thought Amy, "but she it not letting it get the better of her."

As she listened, she went over in her mind first one and then another of the numerous suggestions her companion threw out.

"Oh, why should I bother myself with the case after all? Donato will be able to take care of himself. Of course, I could be of some help to him. I should go and call on his father, see where he lives, what he does with himself. There's ability in the lad . . . don't be silly, Amy, you are not just pleased with his good looks. . . ."

-7-

The food began to have it effects. Some of the color came back to her cheeks. Although she was fatigued, she knew it was not abnormal and that she would sleep and sleep soundly. She wanted to get back to her apartment and get back soon. There were so many things to straighten out. Why not change the couch and the table around and have a shelf put up right under the east windows where she could try to cultivate several rare species of house plants? She might even get some better curtains. There was Mr. Whiting at the school. Some of his paintings were highly imaginative and colorful. The seascapes in particular seemed refreshing in their simplicity and their direct communication of the power and charm of infinite waters rolling under sunshine. He had offered her one some time back. She would hang that in the living room and get a lamp too. . . . The place was *lonely* looking. It needed brightening up. . . . Miss Batten would know where to get things reasonably . . . It needed something to give it life. . . . Possibly if Donato were terribly unhappy at home, she might . . . what a thought! What sane woman would think of such a thing?

"Yes," she heard herself saying in answer to a direct question from Miss Batten. "I have always wanted to go to Europe. I majored in Latin and Greek you know, and have longed for a sight of the classic ruins. . . ."

"That's just the ticket, old girl," bellowed her friend. "Come, let's pay the check. Your share's thirty-seven cents . . . I'll pay the extra penny and there's no tip . . . when you're saving, Dutch treat's the word, Amy, keep that in mind. . . . Why, Europe would remake you. There's more health in a fast gallop through Europe than in all the gyms in the city. . . ."

"I ought to go," Amy kept thinking. . . . "I can't make it this summer," she said aloud.

"Not going myself this summer . . . getting a sabbatical in February and spending the spring there. Intend taking a camel route too . . . maybe go into Africa a bit . . . haven't seen the place and would like a little hob-nobbing with some of the natives . . . say, that's the ticket for you . . . the very thing . . . you'll be out of the dumps in no time. . . . Well, how do you do, Mr. Crabbing? Well, now, how do you do!"

Miss Batten had taken the hand of the stranger and was shaking it with such vigor that poor Mr. Crabbing's scraggly goatee bobbed up and down in a protest the rest of his body was not in a position to express. Amy looked up at him and laughed to see his long bony face contorted with real pain which he was too much of a gentleman not to want to conceal.

"Don't make believe it hurts, Crabbing," cried Miss Batten as a small group of people about to enter the restaurant stopped to see what was happening. "And don't you say 'ouch'. . . . I never forgot the day we met at Wendell out in Ohio, and you shook my hand the same way and I vowed you'd never be the first again. . . . Amy, you know Crabbing . . . in the Spanish department. . . ."

There was a quality in the way in which Crabbing bent his elongated body as he lowered his hand to hers that caused Amy to withdraw slightly within her skin and just barely hold out her entire hand to his. The slight puffs under his exophthalmic eyes, the quick flickering of his eyelids as if they were upper lips smacking from a sweet taste, the points of his teeth revealed despite the full mustache and the goatee that began at the lips and knobbed out before making its final sharp descent — these unmistak-able elements of eccentricity in conjunction with his strung-out limbs and thin proportions, both repelled and fascinated.

"Glad to meet you out of school," he announced in a resonant basso. "And before you say you are, too, let me make a confession, may I?"

He turned to both quickly, holding his eyelids raised so as to reveal the smile diffused in his bulging eyeballs and bringing his lips together hastily for fear of exposing too much of his angled teeth.

"Of course," said Amy, hoping to induce him to talk at once and change the expression of his face. Again she had a feeling of revulsion, and at the same time a definite running of little thoughts throughout her mind, like ants scurrying away from an intruding animal. She felt them, too, as if many ants with little feet were crawling all over her. She heard them, what is more, actually heard them, and was afraid, and as she looked up at the man wondered what he would have to do with her life. Was this a premonition of something disastrous, of the convergence of many lines of fears and desires and forecastings into an event that would determine and shape her years? And what she heard was, "Maybe it is this man, Amy. Why not he as well as any other? This man is looking at you the way Stephen did, and others too, only he is licking his chops doing it. . . ."

Above and around the crowds and the noise, movements which had begun to force themselves upon Amy the longer she was conscious of the feelings of repulsion, his voice sounded . . . a deep bass that was not unpleasant, rather modulated so precisely as to give it the quality of cultivation.

"I got to the school only this term, Miss Rollins, and I have seen you around in the lunch room and thought it would be more than nice to know you. . . ."

"Well, well, Crabbing, but you are the sprightly gallant," boomed Miss Batten.

"That's nice," said Amy.

With that, she took Miss Batten's hand, as a child does its mother's, impatient to be gone.

"You are the gallant, sir," cried Miss Batten, as they began moving off.

Crabbing put his right hand over his left shoulder in the manner of a Frenchman and bowed very low, as he said, "Good evening, ladies," smiling again but only through the area of his eyeballs.

"That's one of the men I told you about, Amy," said Miss Batten. "Desperate for a woman, or why ask me? Widower or divorced or something like that. . . . Sometimes I say it's a good thing we have the boys in our classes. They help preserve the illusion that men are human beings too."

They walked the block to Amy's resident for the most part in silence. Miss Batten occasionally blurted out a word about Crabbing. "Got money sewed up somewhere, and never changes his suit. Pours the coffee in the lunch room so it spills into his saucer and then pours it back into his cup and that way has two helpings . . ."

"Maybe he is saving too. . . ."

"Of course, but for what? He just saves, the starved little soul. . . ."

"You make me shudder to think of the sort of people around us. . . ."

"The school crowd's a decent crowd . . . God, those girls and a lot of the men too, you can't get a harder working herd of cattle anywhere . . . the harder they're driven the more they like it . . . and they like it, really . . . . Why, Amy, even I get sentimental about those kids . . . they're a rough species, and uncouth a hundred ways . . . but aren't some of them good looking, and haven't they minds? And when they take your work seriously you could hug them. . . ."

Amy agreed with a little laugh, and said, amazed at the unconscious manner of her speech, "There's that Donato boy. . . ."

But Miss Batten did not allow her to go far. "Yes . . . and yet when you think of Sidon . . . bah . . . what a piece of offal that man is. . . ."

VIII. CRABBING

-1-

AMY WAS destined to see more of Crabbing, and to hear the hundred and one bits of gossip, some malicious, some just tittle-tattle, all emanating from him and much of it involving her.

The school organization was extensive. Composed of upwards of two hundred persons, it was a physical impossibility for one teacher to know all the others even by sight. The entire group met on four or five occasions throughout a term of six months. Some sort of entertainment for the whole staff was arranged by a set of the more social-minded and party-loving. Nevertheless, entire sections of the faculty were strangers to each other. Newcomers were months in getting themselves known and young men fresh from the colleges were all too frequently mistaken for the pupils.

It was at a time when prevailing economic conditions favored the bold and adventurous among the college graduates. In consequence, only a limited number of the new teachers were recruited from the male colleges. Most of the incoming ones were young women, or men who had taught in small towns outside of New York, like Crabbing, because they were unable before this time to meet the difficult standards and to pass the exacting examinations. Dozens of young girls, hardly older than the seniors, pretty, vivacious, just barely possessed of the dignity that coming into one's majority inevitably brings, were in charge of huge classes of boys. Their presence in the faculty was a source of uneasiness, among the men for obvious reasons, and among the older women for reasons not so patent — reasons imbedded in the jealous impulses of those left behind by time and circumstance.

But these feelings were not all confined to the older women. Men, too, withered men, whose retirement from competitive living had sapped the juices of their youth and diminished the exuberance of their energy, no longer capable of attracting attention despite the substantiality of their learning and the massive dignity of their pedagogical success — these men, too, felt the stirring of jealousy. Grooved in their routines, penned in the narrow family life necessitated by small incomes and lack of opportunities for numerous contacts, they stewed in bitterness, their complaints at a world that had been only kind and had withheld any excessive generosity, distilled into a poison that warped and dried them.

Crabbing was the extreme example of this type. Prone to indulge himself in careless and pointed comments about other people, he was reticent about himself and his doings but not about the desires that fitted leers into the corners of his lips and eyes and made him avid to hear the many ribald and coarse stories retailed by the men in the privacies of their rest rooms. On several occasions he had attempted to strike up an intimacy with women he met by chance in the subways or in stores, but something in his manner and his physical composition caused them to laugh at him outright or to fail to meet him a second time.

Miss Batten had talked to Amy about his habit of having only coffee in the teachers' lunch room and then of helping himself to more than his allowance by overfilling his cup. She had not heard of other habits similar to this which, more than his manner and his ungainly appearance, set him entirely apart from the rest of the group. He never failed to see a pencil stub, or a castaway cap, or pieces of writing paper that might still be used without picking them up, stealthily indeed as if they were held precious by someone else and would be denied him were he to ask for them. It was a form of penuriousness which had settled into distinct miserliness, but a miserliness that had overflowed from the bounds of the material and what was exterior to him as a person, and had inundated the interiors of his soul, forcing out sweet and generous thoughts and feelings. Crabbing was the first to rise in protest at the smallness of the teachers' salaries and the first, too, to dodge the collector of funds to make possible a campaign for increasing them. Having found it impossible because of this niggardliness, both of purse and spirit, to attract a woman as a companion or wife from the mass of those outside, he had conceived the notion that there must be several of the definite old maids in the school — that's what he himself called them in his own mind — who would welcome the attention of any man.

Two considerations were strongest. First of all, he did feel the need of a wife and a home. He was getting on in years — approaching fifty. Secondly, both his years and the years of the woman who would accept him might preclude the necessity of children, and that would mean that she could continue at work and the two of them might "pool their resources," as he always put it, and over these resources he would eventually be certain to exercise such control that he might to all intents and purposes consider himself their sole owner. The prospect warmed him. It put new energy into him. It made him rush to the door at the end of the school day and stand by the clock as the teachers filed out to punch their time cards. He smiled at one and then another and would finally make up his mind to leave, casually as it were, with one of them, walk alongside as she made her way to the railway station, and proffer some remark about the weather or the work of the school in the hope of starting a conversation. So he had struck up anew what he thought was now a promising friendship with Miss Batten.

"Things are humming already, aren't they?"

"They're roaring, Mr. Crabbing," she bellowed back.

"Oh, yes, but I mean the program committee is certainly efficient.

Imagine programming six thousand boys individually. It is as big a task as a railway manager's. . . ." Mr. Crabbing's basso was always deliberate.

"Who cares?" growled Miss Batten.

-2-

The beginning of this renewed acquaintance had been unpropitious, but the next morning a chance discovery of her saving ways whetted his interests and gave him the urge to persist. He heard some one remark at the lunch table, "If I had the system that woman has for saving her nickels and her dimes, I'd kiss this job goodbye and give the Rothschilds a run for their money."

Although he weighed the cost of a telephone call, he did try to telephone but, finding the wire busy, gave a whoop in his own mind and decided to walk to her apartment. This he had done for several days until he discovered at what time she prepared her evening meal. He tried from then on to synchronize his appearance with it.

One night he had happened in exactly at the minute when Miss Batten was thinking of peeling potatoes. She turned them over to him, and went into the other room. He heard a great sloshing of water and heavy breathing as if a seal were in the bathtub disporting itself in the small amount of water allowable in so narrow a circumference. Hungry and uncommonly pleased with the simple but ample meals that Miss Batten prepared, he hurried with the peeling. As he did so, he kept glancing about the room.

"She's the economical genius," he kept saying to himself. "I bet she paid less than I did for those deal chairs and table, and painted them up herself too . . . they're prettier than mine."

"Put them in another saucepan and change the water," yelled Miss Batten to a continued accompaniment of sloshing water.

"Miss Batten," he called out in his turn, "shall I strike a match under them. . . ?"

"No, indeed," came back the cry, "don't you dare, sir . . . those are for my stew tomorrow. . . ."

Miss Batten had appeared in the door frame, completely blotting out the entrance, all dressed and ready to go out.

"I thought I'd put you to some use, sir," she added. "And now, Mr. Crabbing, you're taking me out to dinner. I have given you a meal six evenings in the last three weeks. Your turn. . . ."

The glow in Miss Batten's face only helped to deepen the pallor in Crabbing's. His goatee made impotent movements up and down, while his upper lids had withdrawn like rolltop covers behind the protuberant balls.

"I'd love to," he managed to stammer. "But I wonder if I have brought sufficient funds. . . ."

"You've got them all right, and besides I'll take you to a cheap place."

The vigor and decisiveness of her movements and the neat trick she had played upon him, a trick in his own manner but not tinged with the slightest stealthiness or meanness, served to enhance his admiration for her. Although he anticipated with horror the expenditure from which he could no longer withdraw, he kept saying to himself, "She'd certainly make a perfect wife, a perfect wife. . . ."

"In my circumstances, Mr. Crabbing, every penny has its purpose, and I have none to spend on entertainment unless, sir, it is returned tit for tat and in kind. . . ."

It was through her that he had discovered Tony's and for that much he was more than grateful. As she sat opposite him, her bulk displacing as much of the heavy gray air as two others might, he gazed upon her with admiration. His lids moved as if they were lips smacking over a rich morsel. His goatee jerked spasmodically as his neck muscles quivered with the unformed words in his thorax. Miss Batten looked at him in dismay.

"For God's sake," she said, "Can't you sit there without bobbing that beard of yours up and down?"

"Why, Miss Batten!"

"Sorry to offend you," she answered. "Awfully good stew, isn't it? Get the most here for your money. I advise it, sir. . . ."

Admiration once more overcame his anger, and with it, the decision that was forming in his mind, came to a head. . . .

"Miss Batten," he exclaimed, running his napkin across his beard. "Miss Batten, Miss Batten. . . ."

"Mr. Crabbing, Mr. Crabbing. . . ." She looked at him and saw queer soft emotions struggling in the depths of his bulging eyes.

"You'd better say it, sir. . . ."

"You know, we're much alike. . . ."

"You wouldn't say that twice, sir. . . ."

But Crabbing ignored her and plunged into the remains of his speech. "I think we could pool our forces . . . resources, lives, Miss Batten. . . ."

"Eat your stew, there, and be yourself, sir," she roared at him. "I'm too old for that sort of foolery, and you too much the miser. . . ."

But Mr. Crabbing did not altogether cease his attentions. He once went to the extent of purchasing a dozen roses — roses which he had seen in a department store at a great reduction. They had already bloomed and the petals not only were stained with the signs of decay but were falling off. When Miss Batten opened the package in his presence, more amazed at the unexpected gift than she would have been had she suddenly contracted into the slenderness of Amy, she looked him up and down, and it was the remark she made then that put at end all his hopes.

"There are ninnies, Crabbing, in this world, but I never thought you'd stoop so low as to buy an old crone like me a bunch of roses, and roses that stink, besides, sir. . . ."

-3-

But Crabbing was not the sort of man who is altogether defeated by life. Whatever aids the one objective he sets for himself, to a man like Crabbing, possesses the mysterious essence that is elixir to the ego and emulsion to the wounded heart. As he counted the sum total of his investments, drew up the account of the savings he effected yearly by the regimen of persistent self-denial, his horizon expanded with the light of rising suns. But the future appeared not entirely so roseate. A wife, and a wife who would not waste his substance, would not even cost him too much, nay, who could contribute to the amounts he had already amassed — such a wife would mean real achievement.

Miss Batten being unattainable, he cast about for another teacher who might be more amenable and possibly lacking the substantial demerits that attached themselves to her person. Amy became a vivid thought. He discovered where she lived and how she lived and decided that she could be taught to understand the mode of life which he had developed. Besides, she was lonely and she was lovely. He could not choose worse and for that matter few could choose better. In consequence he felt himself transported by the chance meeting at Tony's and the next afternoon hung over the counter in front of the clock. He hurried after her. He understood at once that she was aware of him. She hastened her steps and took another direction. But he caught up with her as she stopped to allow a truck to pass. She felt his hand grasp her arm and heard his voice, and shuddered.

"Let me help you across, Miss Rollins."

She said nothing until they had got to the sidewalk.

"Oh, how do you do, Mr. Crabbing?"

"Nasty street. No business having a huge school on this kind of a street. Throwing good Norman architecture away — pearls before swine, I say. . . . You're in a hurry?"

"Yes," and she hurried up the Elevated steps, hurried as if she had to free herself from the man or die of nausea. Her direction was north but she bounded a south-bound train. Several boys in her classes doffed their caps. One sat down next to her.

"Gee, we're glad you came back," he said. "I was sure going to fail, but you came back and now I'm not. You can make us work. I like a teacher who can make us work. Some teachers just say go ahead and do this and we don't. . . . You can't tell why, and you can't go up to them if you got something on your mind that's worrying you. I wanted the history teacher he should tell me what books I should read this summer because I don't go to camp or anything and I got time and he said 'don't bother me. . . .'"

Miss Rollins smiled and looked so gracious that the boy turned to her quite eagerly.

"Maybe you can tell me. I got into an argument about God and if he exists and I want to meet this chap again and have some pointers for him, see, that would stick him. . . . We had a club but Mr. Sidon busted it up where we discussed these things. . . I suppose it's bad to but what isn't bad I'd like to know the way he goes for everybody. . . . Gee, we all heard the way you got Contini out of a scrape . . . he was innocent I think, but all the other boys say maybe not but they're glad you put one over on Sidon. . . ."

Amy left at the next station and crossed to get her proper train home. The words of her pupil had disturbed her. Donato's image flashed across her vision but instead of the dreaming face with its regular features and the grey eyes that melted into soft lights, there was a smirking countenance like Crabbing's. Crabbing's goatish mien with its knobby eyes and bobbing beard flashed before her mind too, but it had lost some of the meanness and the animal-quality it possessed and borrowed the gentle lines of Donato's. It was all so confusing. Why did she have to let these things remain in her thoughts for a minute? Hitherto she had hastened home, knowing that her mother would be there, anxious for her attentions, insane with the desire for morphine. Philip was there too, stretched out in his chair, hands in his pockets, ready to burst into an unending stream of complaint. She could hear him now.

"College did you some good, Amy, but how about me? They trained my mind to appreciate the subtleties and then drove me into battle where there were no subtleties. They pumped me full of gas and they let shells crash around me, and my digestion got shot to pieces and my nerves got jangled . . . and here I am, a useless contraption of slats and knobs and springs tied up in fibers with a box on top of it all filled with the world's disillusions. . . . Day in, day out, Amy, I hear those goddam shells and I smell that goddam gas, and Calvary splinters around me and the Parthenon goes up in smoke and Christ and Moses and Zoroaster get into a hell of a fist fight right before my eyes. . . ."

It never ended, this outpouring of the most bizarre images. And it mattered not at all that no one listened to him; he kept on, as if by emitting his jargon of half-poetry and half-profanity he fed himself a medicine that soothed and exhilarated him. Mrs. Rollins occasionally raised a thin voice of protest.

"Amy, Amy, can't you make him stop?"

"Nobody can be sick around here except her. Ever since father died she's been at it. . . . There's nothing wrong with her; just got to have attention. That's what's wrong with me . . . give her some morphine, Amy, if you're not too broke to buy a fresh supply. . . ."

–4–

As the train rattled on, she heard all this again, and she knew now that as long as she had been compelled to administer to her mother and to Philip nothing else in the world had mattered. She had definitely put aside all thoughts of marriage, all hopes of continuing with her studies, all friendships. Stephen had been an accident and a blessing. He had forced her by dint of constant urging to go out with him for a walk or a drive in the country, and once or twice to the theater. It had all been so casual, as if it meant nothing either to him or to her. She had soon learned about him and knew that there was nothing to look forward to except this companionship and something more intimate, but furtive and sporadic. When freedom had come, how impossible she had found the very thing she had spent hours dreaming about. And now that all the afternoon was hers and all the evening, now that she had no one to engage all her attention and all her energy, every incident became enlarged, fraught with drama, an event of moment.

She realized that the change in habit had brought a change in proportion. But why should this boy Donato have come to bulk so large on her horizon, and the larger he bulked the smaller he grew, as if all her life was definitely and irretrievably to be concentrated in him, that his personality and his doings were to become the measure of the space she occupied?

And this man, Crabbing, what of him? What was there about him that frightened, that said unmistakably, "Lady, we are component parts of a scheme, and together we are fulfilling a destiny." She made little movements with her hands like a child trying to push away something too big for her to manage. As she did so, she saw that she had been surprised making the gestures. She felt embarrassed and once more changed her position. This time, however, she moved into the next coach. But, instead of finding the place a safe retreat, she found herself facing Mr. Crabbing.

He rose at once. "How did you get here? Delighted. You get off the next stop?"

They walked together to her apartment, talked of school, of the difficulty of language teaching, the necessity of going to Europe to keep up with one's subject.

"I have been several times. But I always go with a group . . . no, not teachers. They're always charged too much. A carpenters' international convention I went with last time. They charter so much room on a boat and can't get enough of their men and throw open the privileges to others. Never amounts to as much as half what teachers pay. . . ."

In the morning he contrived to intercept her on the way to school. To dodge him she took the circuitous route through the park. The ruse was successful for only one day.

"You're not trying to avoid me?" he laughed a low basso. "No, Amy," (this use of Amy was a self-allowed privilege) "I'm getting to like you too much. . . . You do like me a trifle, do you not? I am such a lonely person, Amy. I have been a lonely man all my life. . . ."

"Certainly I have not been the only woman in it?"

"No, of course not, of course not . . . but so many things have prevented, Amy, any of the things a man craves, companionship, a home. . . . I thought Amy, now that you are alone . . . you understand what it is to be alone and hungering for the sight of some one . . . a friendly word . . . we could pool our resources, our lives, don't you know . . . ever since I saw you . . . you understand . . . I am not too old . . . we can go away this summer. . . ."

Crabbing had interpreted Amy's mood surely and had decided to play upon it. The extreme necessity of winning someone who would be able to "pool her resources" along with his had aroused his cunning. His earnestness sounded so real that Amy for a moment was lost in thought. The possibility of marriage with the man at her side seemed the wildest and remotest dream. Her impulses were to laugh outright into his face, and then leave him to nurse his bewilderment in the traffic-ridden street. But his mention of his loneliness slowed up the full stream of her contempt for him, and the momentary hesitation she manifested encouraged him to continue.

"I have not known you long, of course . . . but I have seen how lonely you are, too . . . they avoid you at school. . . . You seem so dignified, so aloof. And you have reason — what a pack of sniveling fellows they mostly are . . . what one could tell about the men, and some of the women! What can we expect of our boys? That man Sidon, for instance, a sneaky little worm . . . who is he to be the guardian of boys' conduct? You have a right to avoid them all . . . they're not worth a second notice. But it has made you lonely and I saw it at a glance . . . we're both lonely. . . ."

Amy was too dumbfounded to say a word. The desire to laugh at him had turned to pity, but by a natural gradation pity had changed to contempt. There was a corner store directly in the line of their path, a store that had several exits.

"Pardon me," she said, "I have something to get here."

She walked in rapidly, ran out, hailed a taxi, and made her way to school, once more the feeling of nausea having seized her in all reality. She wondered at herself as she rode to school, at these sensations of disgust, of insects crawling over her, the feverish restlessness when she was alone in her apartment, the desire to welcome people into her life and the inability to accept them. Was she getting to be like Philip? Had she inherited her mother's incapacity to cope with life?

–5–

The sight of the large building with its numerous turrets and its Norman-Gothic squareness, a quiet pile in the confusion of traffic and business all about her, calmed her nerves. She dismissed Crabbing from her mind. Hundreds of boys were crowding into the building. Their carefree manner, their shouts, their hair, for the most part exposed to the air but all slicked down, shining with oils, and parted in frank and unabashed vanity, their pell-melling into the doorways — what a relief they were! She welcomed the day of work. . . .

Crabbing was not to be put off so easily. He had arrived late but nevertheless rushed into Miss Rollins's room. Despite the boys, he blurted,

"Did you shake me on purpose, or were we separated?"

His goatee quivered with his emotions, and the lids of his eyes retreated behind the whites. There was consternation and indignation expressed in the way he stood, the way he looked, the way he talked.

"I shook you, Mr. Crabbing," Amy answered turning a frank gaze to his.

"Shook me, shook me?" he asked again and again incredulously. "Shook me, Miss Rollins? Very well," and he made a right about face in military precision and slammed the door after him as he left.

That afternoon Amy had remained after school with several of the boys. They needed special coaching to fit them for the coming examinations. Donato had asked to stay, as he felt he was in as great need of assistance as the others despite her assurance that his work was satisfactory. While he read to her at sight from the text, the other boys were at the blackboards that lined the three windowless walls of the room, busily writing out various Latin forms. Donato was leaning over the desk, his soft voice translating in whispers the resounding periods of Cicero. His head was bent over his book so that the massed curls of his hair was the only portion of his head Amy could see. As she heard his voice, grown already into its full adult range, she shut her eyes, and a smile came to her lips. One of the boys at the back of the room had turned around to ask a question and had as quickly resumed his writing. Something in the expression of her face deterred him. It was at this point that Crabbing opened the door and looked in. He, too, saw the same expression.

"I beg your pardon," he cried. "I did not know you were so busy."

He stayed long enough to afford her an opportunity to see the expression on his face, one of apparent indignation at being slighted for a mere stripling but one, too, conveying a menace, a menace of being discovered by one like Crabbing. She realized its full import at once, but said and did nothing.

Several days later she was called to the office of the principal so unexpectedly that she felt like one of the boys reporting for discipline. She had had few contacts with Mr. Polter personally and had been satisfied that they were not more. Not only she but the large bulk of the faculty dreaded the extreme bluntness of his manner, a bluntness that seemed boorish lack of tact but in reality covered a sincerity that amounted to sentiment. In consequence when teachers' were asked to pay a visit to the office, despite assurance to the contrary, they felt shaken with fear. On this occasion, Amy hurried to the teachers' room to straighten her blouse, catch the straying straws of her hair, and otherwise to calm the agitation within her.

"Got it straight from Crabbing," she heard one young woman drawl as if not to move in any way faster than the smoke of the cigarette dangling between her lips. "He's a sponge for scandal. . . ."

"That man's an old woman," another one offered facing Amy as the door opened, and hurrying out immediately. The silence that ensued fell on Amy like a material load. Her lips quivered as she tried to shake off its weight. She dared not look around.

The three other women had exchanged rapid glances and then dropped into a tense silence. While she made hasty adjustments to her hair in front of the mirror, Amy saw their reflections. Unaware that she could be seen, the young lady with the cigarette, making a pretence at drawing a puff upon it, had been trying to form words with her lips. "Do you think she heard?"

To Amy, the expression, although unuttered, thundered throughout the place. The noise of it was terrific. Amy knew she was trembling, but why did the geranium box in the window tremble too, and the snake plant on the table, and why did one of the other girls take a pebble out of the pot and throw it at the smoker? The door opened suddenly. Miss Batten sailed in, an armful of papers clutched tightly to her bosom.

"Well, by heaven's mighty deeds," she exclaimed, "the place is quiet. The scandal mongers are silent for once, and a body can do some work. It's buzz, buzz everywhere you go . . . buzz against this one and buzz against the other, and it's not the women folk only . . . the place isn't decent. . . . Now, if any body so much as lifts her voice in this room I give notice," she whispered dramatically, slamming down her papers on the long table running through the center of the room, "I give notice right now. I don't report it but I'll eject that very person from this room myself personally. . . ."

Amy took advantage of the confusion Miss Batten had added to run out. But the words she had overheard had drawn the color from her cheeks and she felt in no mood to face the principal. However, her free period was fast coming to a close and she hurried.

"Miss Rollins," Mr. Polter exclaimed, as soon as he saw her enter, "this is the first opportunity I have had to thank you personally. Take a seat, and I'll tell you. You know our greatest trouble here is not so much teaching a lot of dead heads. It's remaking some of their characters and it's a big job. The last few days I have observed the effect you have had on your class and especially on that Donato Contini boy. It's fine work. A bit more heart-to-heart pedagogy and our task becomes a simple one. Get the boys with love. . . ."

For a quarter of an hour he carried on like an orator. "Get the boys with love," formed the text of his discussion. Too much impersonality was rendering teaching a mechanical process like a factory routine. The staff was interested only in the paycheck at the end of the month. Of course, there were exceptions — Miss Rollins and some of the serious young men from the colleges, their ideals still unwarped, their enthusiasms still fiery and unspent, their knowledge still a vivid acquisition that meant something to their souls.

"Give me pedantry all the time, Miss Rollins . . . yes, pedantry. It's a thousand times better than cynicism, lack of sympathy, lack of love. Love is what we need and the pedagog's task is accomplished, wars are abolished, degradation in business, graft in politics. That's why I say your influence is the finest. The Contini boy has been weaned from the gangs he grew up with, gangs that sent his brother to the chair . . . a pupil of ours, too, he was. You've done wonders with his brother, wonders. . . ."

Amy left more shaken than she had been when entering. All the while Mr. Polter had fired his volley of sentences at her, she kept smiling, but it was a conscious effort to stem the tears that were rising to her eyes. She was aware of an immense tiredness in all her muscles as if she had not been away to the country at all, as if she had not really thrown off the years of toil amounting almost to immolation. She gazed at his mobile face, a face of such soft musculature that, as he moved his jaws, lines formed and unformed rapidly over its surface. She was amazed at its softness, a softness that ill consorted with the reputation of hardness that he had gained among the faculty. And as she gazed at it and was at the same time aware again and again of the fatigue that oppressed her, she caught herself saying in her mind something which caused her to jump with terror, but only in the quietness of her own thought. "He would understand." "Understand?" she asked herself. "Understand what?"

She glanced away from him and was grateful to the Alma Tadema opposite her, the young Virgil reading from his scroll while his companions lay about in many poses, overcome with interest, keen, alert and dreamy, too. She carried the picture away with her in her mind, and attempted to see only that and nothing else.

"But what can he know?" she asked herself as she hastened to the elevator to make her next class on time. "What can he know? Love . . . love . . . is it? Is it?"

–6–

That afternoon, Donato had remained in the room after the other boys had been dismissed.

"Miss Rollins," he was saying, "I've never studied so much in my life. I'll make the grade in everything. I'm taking up modeling too. My father . . . you know he used to make marionettes and had shows for the people here and in the old country . . . I used to help him. . . ."

"Really?" she exclaimed, and the sound of her voice filled with a joy that startled him. He raised querying eyes to hers, and as she returned his look, what had been only the sound of joy and admiration in her voice, became a light and revelation in her eyes. She saw a flush spread over the boy's features, a flush that deepened the grey of his eyes and made them also fill with a light that was revelation. And so they glanced at each other, and the glance became the magnetism that holds two hearts that understand, and understanding, pulse with delight and fear combined. How many seconds they stood thus, their eyes fixed upon each other she did not know. In a flash, she was conscious of other eyes gazing upon her. Her color fled, fled so instantly that Donato turned his head quickly. There in the rear of the room stood Mr. Crabbing, a malicious gleam in his bulging eyes, stroking his goatee with his bony hands.

"Sorry, Amy," he bassoed with even greater deliberateness than he affected as a rule. "Sorry if I interrupted anything. . . ." And he shook his head in a kind of grotesque fatherly admonition, smiling his bizarre grin. . . .

IX. HERMES

DONATO AND Amy walked home together. It was surprising to her how many things he had to tell her. She could not help but compare him to a small boy. She recalled the one time she had visited Anna, her sister, in Boston, whose oldest child, no more than six, had learned to read, to manipulate a scooter, insisted upon bathing alone and even drying himself, and who perpetually boasted of his prowess. She and Ned had walked for blocks in the same way as she and Donato were doing. Ned had talked incessantly.

"Want to see me jump two flags at once Aunt Amy?"

"I can run faster than Peter!"

"Why have policemen got belts across their chests?"

"I beat Peter throwing a ball. . . ."

Irrepressible, eager, alive, like a puppy, nosing into everything, looking up for approval, glad to get it and forgetting about it if he did not, sure of himself, full of the present and hurdling the future by the simple process of amalgamating it with the passing moment! She recalled his blue eyes — the Rollins eyes — the pug nose, the small ears close to the head, the curling yellow hair, his long thin legs, his long thin torso, his long thin neck. The more Donato talked the more she thought of her nephew, grown up now, sixteen and at high school, just like Donato. Was he interested in the same things? Did he attach eternal values to the simplest theme? Did he argue heatedly about wood as a medium for sculpture to replace clay and stone? Did he get excited about marionettes and the way they should be worked — with strings, with wires, by the interlocutor or by a supernumerary?

"My father, Miss Rollins, ran a big place in Messina. I was born here, so I don't know. He says dukes and nobles came to see them. There were ones that became favorites. Britomart and Paladin, Orlando and Carlomagno . . . he doesn't get tired talking about them, and there was Pulcinello too, and Columbina, and Scaramuccio . . . . He's got them all in the backyard shed. He tried to have a place here but it didn't pay. . . ."

They dodged the trucks, they waited for each other when one did not make the crossing. They both laughed if one of them was compelled to perform one of the numerous acrobatic stunts necessary to avoid traffic in New York. They sat down on a bench overlooking the Hudson.

"I don't come here often. When we were boys we used to walk across town. A whole gang of us . . . we were funny. Some of the boys just had enough clothes on to get by. We hitched on everything . . . taxis and trucks, turned over garbage pails, shoved the kids into pushcarts. . . . We got to

Columbia College one day and the boys dared me to go in and apply and I did. There was a man with a bald head, and a little red beard and glasses, and he always smiled. I made up my mind I would get there some day, the place was so quiet and cool, and the ceiling so high. . . . My brother was along . . . you ought to have known him, always full of life, up to any stunt. . . . That day they dared him to stand on the top of the statue out in front . . . what do they call it? He did, all right, and then they dared him to take the scepter out of her hand. . . . He got into a fight with the boy who dared him. . . . 'I'll punch you in the jaw for that,' he said. . . . 'You know I'll do it if you dare me twice.' 'I'll dare you twice and three times and four times, and I'll bet you a half a dollar you can't . . . .' 'Think I want to break it?' 'Scared cat, scared cat. . . .' the other kid yelled at him, and my brother swung at him and threw him down and made his nose bleed. 'You're afraid anyhow,' the kid answered crying and wiping his nose. . . . 'I ain't . . . and I'll show it to you tomorrow morning. . . .' He yelled for the crowd out of the window the next day. The crowd came upstairs and then we all went to the shed in the backyard where all the marionettes were and he shut the door after us and he dug into an old box and he pulled out the scepter. They wouldn't believe it. He swore black and blue . . . he had to convince them, so he took them up to the place again and there the scepter was gone, but the kid wouldn't pay the fifty cents and my brother punched him again and then that night he went and hid the thing in a restaurant near the college. . . ."

-2-

She let him have full rein. It was amazing how he poured himself out to her. There was no mistaking the fact that he had starved for the affection of someone older than he to whom he could unbosom himself as he was doing now.

It became his custom to wait for her to come downstairs after school. It was too near the end of the term for it to have become noticed by the other boys or by the teachers. It was a common practice for intimacies to spring up between the pupils and their instructors, especially between the youngsters and the men. In addition to the athletic events and the constant practice they required under the supervision of the faculty, the students had developed interests in hundreds of directions, and had there been men or women sufficiently equipped or deeply enough interested there would have been nothing that is done by the adult world that the boys would not have done in school. Donato wanted a club of sculptors.

"Why can't you, Miss Rollins?"

"But I'm no artist . . . get one of the drawing teachers. . . ."

"There's no one can model . . . may be I'll do it myself, and you can just sit with us. It's required. Yes, let's do that. I'll work hard all summer.

I've got a pile of wood my father used to use. . . . He just goes to work now by the day and I stay home and look after him, clean up and cook and so I'll have a lot of time. You ought to see the knives my father has, knives to carve with. They're curved and long and some thin as a needle almost. . . . Yes, that's what we'll do . . . and you'll be the faculty adviser. . . ."

The project appealed to her enough to consult one of the art men, a cherub-faced, florid little man, always nervous about one thing or another, with a shock of crinkly black curls, and eyes that blazed as he talked, never capable of making up his mind, constantly in fear that his nerves would be affected, perennially complaining that he had no time to do the big things for which nature designed him.

"It's an idea, Miss Rollins, an idea. The boys and everybody for that matter, think art's only painting. We ought to have sculptors . . . sure, we ought to have sculptors too and a class . . . a modeling class — but who'll give you one? Where's the money and where's the program committee to put it in? Talk to the principal? What's he care? Who cares about art? Did you ever see my painting — *Barren Island in the Twilight* . . . matches Whistler. . . . I never had the luck. . . . Have you been to my studio? . . ."

"Well, what do you say, Mr. Gonle? Do you think Donato could swing it, if I stayed afternoons?"

"It's an idea, it's an idea . . . I'd be afraid though . . . they always find fault with you, you know . . . why should you stay — a Latin teacher? They'll say the art department's not on the job . . . it's an idea. . . ."

Donato and Amy lived with the idea for weeks. For the last days of the term such a mass of clerical routine was necessitated by the winding up of one organization and the formulation of another program that the teachers, on several occasions, were compelled to remain after school hours until late in the afternoon. Donato stayed to assist Miss Rollins, dictating to her long strings of marks, running after records, totaling figures, arranging interminable packs of cards alphabetically or numerically, by colors or by sizes — the thousand and one details which teaching in a huge system entails.

They were in a room together on one of these afternoons. The room overlooked the Hudson once the eye could leap the jumble of paint factories, tinsmiths' lofts, and gas tank. The hot June day shone on the river with unremitting glare. The water seemed to come from depths of molten glass, swing upward for an escape, and then, realizing the impossibility, plunge awkwardly back into the original mass. Huge smokestacks threw parallel shadows on the sun-beaten surface, the piers and buildings between huddled at the base of the cliffs, effectively hiding the fresh green that clung to their sides.

The school was practically empty. From various corners came the sounds of teachers' voices. Occasionally a boy ran headlong down the corridors, his footsteps echoing and re-echoing in the still building. An elevator door slammed metallically. Donato had climbed up on the table and then upon a chair on top of that.

"Better not leave this painting here for the summer. We'll take it down with the rest of the things. . . ."

Amy spared no expense to make her room reflect some of the spirit of her subject. On the windowsills paraded statuettes of classic deities; postcards of scenes in Athens and Rome daubed the bulletin boards; prints of the Greek theaters, pictures of temples, hung on the walls. Between them glittered mottoes in red and black. *Non scholae sed vitae discimus.* A bronze Hermes lifted his caduceus on high as he tiptoed on one foot ready for flight. It was a small thing but the admiration of the pupils. In front of the reproduction of the Pantheon was a miniature Jove with clustered locks and bulging muscles. The picture that Donato wanted to remove hung above the desk. Atalanta, her kirtle held close to her body with her right hand, was stooping to catch up with the left the golden apple at her foot. To either side were signs: DON'T FORGET. VERBS IN INDIRECT DISCOURSE TAKE THE INFINITIVE. There was little classification or order, but there was the sense of other things besides the immediate. There was the suggestion of something hidden somewhere for the heart and the mind to follow, something upon which the imagination might erect its frail structure of dreams.

"We'd better take it down," Donato repeated, rising on one foot, and reaching up with his hand.

She looked at him, and something like a shadow from a world beyond passed over her. The marvelous slim body of the boy, the chestnut curls almost amber in color, the grey eyes turned upward intently — why, he was, he was the Hermes on the stand, grown to human size, become human. Messenger of the gods he was, and he had come to her, here on this hot day, in the midst of factories, in a quiet spot dedicated to what was not worldly, had come to her personally to reveal to her that she had found what she was seeking.

"Donato," she called to him, with a sweet urgency that surprised her. She folded her hands as if in prayer, "Donato," she called again.

"Oh, I won't fall," he answered. "Never catch me falling."

"But, Donato," she called again.

He gazed down upon her and saw her upturned head. The blue of her eyes was brilliant with an emotion that communicated itself to him too. Her folded hands, held close to her full high bosom, seemed to be imploring, to be thanking at the same time, to be holding the tense body still, subdued, a barrier against the floods from its soul.

He stepped down from the chair, and then from the table, and went up to her.

"Miss Rollins," he said simply.

"Donato," she answered.

The stillness of the empty building took on the steadiness of a hum. Neither the shrieks of tugs, nor the occasional upflare of stacks in the gas yards, nor the screeching and clattering of trucks disturbed the sweet monotone of the silence. They looked at each other, and for a second time a quality in one winged its way to the other, and they stood still like neophytes in the presence of the deity they never had seen before.

"Oh," said Donato, "I'd better get that picture down."

It was the work of a few seconds. Then they both set to work with great energy to remove the other objects and stow them away. They worked without talking. When they had finished, Amy put her hat on without saying a word. At the foot of the stairs, she turned to Donato.

He presented her a surprised face.

"You had better go home."

She left him brusquely. He stood watching her cross the street and when he had lost complete sight of her in the crowds, whistled low to himself and started for home.

–3–

The thoughts that disquieted Amy persisted until long after she had got home. She threw herself on her bed, lay on her back, and allowed her mind to wander freely. Stephen came back to her and the expression in his eyes. Especially conscious of that, she strove to keep it in front of her mind's vision. "Possible?" she asked herself. "Could it have been the same, what Donato saw in my eyes?" A slight tremor went through her whole frame.

There was no denying the nature of the feeling she had developed for Donato. Ever since her girlhood she had been certain that she would know when love came to her. Housekeeping as few girls of her set were, devoted to her studies both at high school and college, possessed of a stature and a carriage which suggested a dignity amounting almost to aloofness, she was aware that she attracted young men and young men attracted her. But a barrier always intervened, a barrier which was an amalgam of this exact physical component of her own personality and a quality of the spirit, a distillation of her reading, a belief in the legends and the romances of love which assured her that she would know it when it came. She would know it by the sadness it would inspire, by the sense of her being helpless in its presence, divorced of will, as if in sight of a holy shrine become animate because the spirit in her was intense and vibrant.

"As it was, as it was," said she over and over again.

But the more she suspected the true nature of her attitude toward Donato, the more she measured its danger and its futility. The years of lonely sacrifice had rendered her sufficiently solitary to confer upon her a sort of immunity against the fear of people and of their talking. It was not that she feared her own position in the school, in society, among her few friends. She feared the effect upon the boy. "He is just a child, Amy. . ." she shuddered thinking about it, shuddered, and then placed her hands over her eyes, and shut out the world.

In the world of darkness into which she plunged by the simple act of shutting out the light, she could allow the fibers of her body to feel immersed in a great coolness. There in this world under the world of immediate sensation she would dwell forever. There she could take Donato into the silent paths of her living and walk hand in hand with him. There she would listen to the voice of the young god, musical and serene, unconscious of the world's soilure as she would become unconscious of it, too. In that world, removed from the living, she would live. The hidden life of her soul would be the fullness of experience. Away with the Stephens and the Crabbings. . . . The bell jangled, she jumped back into time and space.

–4–

"A telegram," Mrs. Nilins was whispering in her ear.

She sat up suddenly as if she had been roused from a deep sleep.

"I thought it might be important. I never have got over feeling frightened at a telegram, Amy," continued Mrs. Nilins, snapping her fingers between her lips. "And you look frightened, too. I hope it's nothing. . . ."

"It really is nothing, Mrs. Nilins . . . nothing at all, but that's why it's terribly disturbing. What did you tell Philip when he came back?"

"Oh, not much . . . nothing, Amy . . . really nothing. . . ."

Her head shook with a kind of emotion that Amy could not understand. Had Mrs. Nilins taken upon herself to tell Philip how much of a burden he was?

"You gave him my letter, and that's all?"

"Well, no, Amy. You see I thought somebody ought to tell him. He's a grown man . . . carrying on the way he did . . . doing nothing . . . sponging on you . . . ordering you around. . . ."

Amy said nothing. She reread the telegram. How similar to his letter it was, sent as it were out of the depths of his bitterness, a bitterness that was the sum total of his rebellion against a generation that had been aroused to enthusiasm over a war in which he had no interest, which was fought for an ideal that was an empty boast to him, with weapons that were too subtle, too treacherous, too unmanning for a man of his temperament. Philip was trying to be strong, making a desperate effort to get out of her life and give her a free path. Poor Philip! Little did he realize how like him she was too — educated only in her mind, her perceptions entirely intellectual, her knowledge without reality, her aims based on notions not actually operative in the world at large. Like him too she had emotions that derived their intensity from forsaken gods. She knew but could not sense; she sensed and could not do. She belonged completely neither to the new nor to the old generation, and so she was alone and would be perennially alone. And so would Philip . . . poor Philip, the brilliant student who fell like a vivid bomb in battle, sputtered and died without so much as splintering a twig, frightening a man, scattering dust.

"Westward with false lights in my breast and the quittance money from Uncle Sam in my belt."

What did it all mean? Where could he be reached? She would recall him and they would merge their lives in each other. What else could she do? She would have ample funds, and he with his monthly remittance from the government would not feel a burden. He needed her . . . needed her as her mother had needed her. . . . She saw him now: his long legs outstretched, hand in his pocket, head thrown on the back of the chair, exposing the stringy muscles of the neck. How his face lighted and dimmed with quizzical smiles giving way to amusement, tolerance, superiority, the lids closing slowly over his eyes, and then suddenly opening like a shutter loosened by a wind. "It will be the chance you need, Philip . . . to be alone . . . on your own . . . . You'll come back remade." He had replied nothing, just kept his head back, while the smile shadowed and brightened on his thin face.

And Amy thought, "Yes, I must find him."

But no sooner had she framed the statement than the old sense of having been shut in, of having been denied the light in which to flower, became a pain and a desire. She must, she must discover interests that would give meaning to her life. She had tried and failed with Stephen. It had all been so coldblooded, so designed, like a remedy. School . . . school . . . it must be in that; in that she would find the solution. Men became absorbed in their work; their work was more to them than family, than love, than dreams — it was family, it was love, it was dreams. She was too much aware how secondary to her colleagues was their profession, and she could not believe that it would release all her potentials and give moment to her life. And yet, it was a pleasant way, and you could hug the boys, as Miss Batten said, when their eyes gleamed with understanding and their responses were keen and bright. Even when they were problems, of discipline, of retarded intelligence, of maladjustment — how interesting they were, challenging, fulfilling. Take the case of Donato — Donato with his grey eyes and the sadness that lingered in his smile — Donato — dear Donato. . . .

Again she shuddered with the reality of her feeling for him. She walked up and down in her room. Tomorrow she would not see him. Today she would bid him goodbye in a few words, shake hands with him, and forget.

–5–

The last day of school came, and with it a sadness which fell upon Amy like a mist that blurs the sight and enters chillingly into all the senses. Everybody was bidding gay goodbyes, bound for a thousand places. There was the agitated group that was going to Europe, jumping out of their skins, as Miss Batten said, with their feeling of importance. There were the ones who had planned to go automobiling through the states and were full of camping talk and the size of tires. There were those going to the universities — a bit ashamed of their simple projects. Then there were those whose faces glowed with the tremendous excitement of their marriage days ahead, brides to be, or grooms to be, who passed you in the hall, nodded benignly but not without a suggestion of pity that you too had not announced your engagement. . . . The halls emptied quickly. Save the clerks tapping away at their typewriters, the department heads stewing over belated reports, everybody had brought his work to a close and left. The students had just stayed away, their reports already in their hands, nothing for them to do. Only a few had come, some to beg, with tears in their eyes, for a change of rating, others to wish goodbye to a favorite teacher or to assist her.

Donato had come early, but Amy had told him simply that all her work was done. He glanced up at her and saw none of the sweet light that had passed over her face in the days previous. A chill fell upon him, and, as if transformed into a bronze image of himself, he stood facing her. Through his mind there ran a fire that quickened the sadness in his eyes. But save in the glittering of his pupils, it left its mark nowhere else. He smiled, said "Goodbye, Miss Rollins," and left.

No sooner had he gone than the bright light that poured into her room vanished as the sun does with the coming of a storm. She looked around on the bare walls, the unswept room, the papers scattered all over the floors. What a barren prison cell! Where, where was the beauty of the school? Fled . . . fled with the sad boy who had run out . . . run where? But he too needed her; he, too, like Philip, needed her. Oh, was she never, never to love someone for his own sake only, for the beauty of his sweet mouth, his passionate body?

X. THE MARIONETTES

DONATO CONTINI, despite what he had told Amy about his closeness to his father, in reality had achieved maturity without much personal guidance from either of his parents. The same had been true of his brother, Giulio, whose execution at the age of eighteen years and six months had been a front-page story for weeks. But whether his tragic end might be ascribed to the incapacity of his family to offer direction and point to his character and ability will never be known. The school authorities attempted to learn from him to what he attributed his leanings toward gang life. For statistical purposes alone they wanted to discover what the attractions were which overpowered the controls set up by the school in particular and society in general. They had sent to interview him one of the teachers in the school who had shown particular interest in him before and in whom he himself had reposed considerable confidence. But he refused to talk except to beg to be let alone.

Sometime before the tragedy, he had related in detail his ambitions to amass a fortune before he was twenty-five. Giulio, despite his reticence about his devices and plans, spoke freely about his objectives. Unless one had money, what was one? Doctors, devoted to a supposedly social service, what were they but money grabbers of the worst sort? They even refuse to perform critical operations unless paid beforehand. His own mother for example. . . . "What do they think they are, gods, kings, tyrants, what?" They had seen her suffering. They said she needed an operation. Did they do anything for her? Only when his father had pawned everything! And lawyers, what were they? He knew about the shady business deals, too, of contractors, and he saw money shelled out to the cops for protection. Say, what did they think he was? He had seen his father go down and down.

His father had a café once, and he had a reputation for the best *pizze con ricotta, taralli, sfogliate* . . . all the fancy things that only Italians can make. On the corner of the avenue, the store made money. In the back there was an old backyard tenement — a small brick house. He had fitted it up for a marionette theater. His heart was in that. He had devoted more time to it than to the café, but it was the café that made the money to run the marionettes. He was constantly adding to them. They were his whole life. The café, though, did not continue making money. Why not? The other cafés did, and they were not as good. . . .

"I'll tell you why, I'll tell you why. . . . The others sold rum for the coffee, see. . . . An Italian likes rum and brandy in his coffee, see. And the others sold it, and spirits, too, for cordials, and the cordials . . . and they got away with it, see. They got away with it because they paid off the cops, see. And my father didn't have enough money for everything. He wanted to start a big marionette theater and have big shows, and he needed the money, see, and he didn't pay the cops. . . . You've got to have money. I'll make it before I'm twenty-five and my old man is going to have his theater and we're going to be on easy street . . . my brother, for instance, Donato, you know . . . he's an artist. Ever see the heads he makes for the marionettes? Beat my father's . . . they're great. Gee, they laugh at you, and they're angry, and when it's the head of the Turk, Solimano . . . you ought to see it. It makes you want to fight him . . . well, can we send him to school? No . . . you got to have the dough, see?"

Mr. Barr had been attracted to Giulio in his first term, a wide-eyed lad who got into controversies with everyone, resented comments on his behavior or work, found cause for quarreling just in being jostled, spoken to, anything. He was not morose, but he kept his own counsel except when there was an opportunity in the class discussion for him to take the opposite side and be at the same time in a conspicuous minority. He had done unusual work in Mr. Barr's English class, was the exception in understanding the classics, in composing imaginative incidents. But, chief and outstanding trait, was his air of cynicism and his refusal to believe anything, whether it was teacher or pupil who announced it.

Unlike his brother, his hair was straight and unruly hung over his eyes and ears, was rarely combed. In his boyhood he had become involved in a fist fight and had suffered a severe injury to his nose. His face had fallen into sinister lines because of it, the nose having been bent to one side and flattened unnaturally over one nostril. His eyes were even a lighter grey than Donato's and whether or not because of the deflected nasal lines only one possessed any brilliance, but it was a sharp metallic luster that directed a straight shaft and fascinated one. Possibly because of this strange disharmony between the eyes, a general sense of sadness shone in his face and lingered particularly in the lips, lips that seemed always ready to quiver almost as if he had been hurt by an utterance of a mysterious force with which only he could have communication.

Both he and Donato had grown up practically without the guidance of their parents. They were both Sicilians from the city of Messina where they had maintained a marionette theater, the legacy of his family. They had had two daughters who had married and left Sicily to make their homes in the Argentine. Ever since their departure a wistful sense of failure had seized upon the father, the failure that life appears to an older person who has never ventured beyond the small confines of one business and who sees the younger generation experimenting, adventuring, gay. America became a land of wonders to his imagination.

He had heard that the marionette theater had become popular in New York, and soon after his daughters' departure for South America he had made up his mind to crash into the life of the magic metropolis beyond the sea and to dazzle the entire city with his marvelous puppets. They represented the work of generations of marionette makers and were a complete assemblage of all the social classes and of all the legendary figures of Italian literature and of Italian life. The transportation charges he discovered would be excessive. He would have little or nothing to start with, and where could he borrow money? He hit upon the scheme of writing to the Italian papers in New York. Some comments appeared in their columns, but no impresario had rushed to offer to back him. He came, nevertheless, Giulio about to be born, a silent unseen member of the family.

The friends he already had did everything in their power to assist. They were enthusiastic but for the most part lacked funds and technical knowledge. He was compelled to start his shows in a small store. Rough wooden benches, a rude platform for a stage, candle lights of the kind he employed in Messina — stuck in little tin boxes and affixed to the wall — a canvas curtain painted with pell-mell castles, fields in the distances, roads without perspective, horses with unnatural buttocks and preposterous necks highly bedizened knights, bleeding forms sprawling in all manner of anatomical grotesqueries — this constituted the entire equipment. The entire equipment, the total assemblage of properties, the mere material side of *Il Grande Teatro Unico Marionettista dell'America* all these were — but what a poor thing indeed in comparison to the remarkable voice of Signor Contini.

–2–

Don Contini had a voice as large as his nose and his nose had gained him the appellation of *Pepperone* — huge pepper. But, although his voice was large, it was the voice of twenty people at one time. It covered the whole range of emotions. It was plaintive with distressed maidens and stentorious with overbearing knights, champion or defender. It whispered and it bellowed; it spoke words of love and it rose to tumultuous pitches of anger. It imitated the clown's mock cooing and yodeled peasant songs. And as the marionettes stepped out in front of their long spit-like handles manipulated by Don Contini from invisible spaces in the rear, they dispelled the present world and conjured back the Middle Ages and the back streets of Old World towns where macaronics and fanfaronades were the order of the day. His audience burst into laughter and into tears too. Gradually they began to recognize the various personages and to hiss and applaud before they performed their deeds of foolery or of villainy. The children of the neighborhood flocked in, and in the beginning the older persons too.

But somehow the feeling spread that all this was puerile, belonging to an older time, to another society. It was too laughable. Were there not the movies and the peep-show arcades? It was all a thing of the past. Better be back in Messina, they told Don Contini and broke his heart. But they did not persuade him to give up the enterprise. He carried on the business of the café, he and his quiet devoted wife, who washed the dishes and superintended the baking, gave out the cards for the games, served at table, sprinkled sawdust on the floors, and always kept a serene smile on her pale, almost yellow face, with its early wrinkles playing like stirred water about her eyes, her hair always smoothly pompadoured as if she never hurried or became ruffled, her apron doubled over and tucked into her waist in the manner of a gleaner during the harvest.

She never complained, and she never showed that she worried. But her heart was filled with a bitterness that only her smiles recorded, for her smiles were invariably soft and gentle, as if it were painful to shape them, and yet no one ever divined the truth of it. The bitterness was there, however, and it was the bitterness of a mother who had in reality lost two daughters — married off as they were and living thousands of miles away in another country, with no prospect of seeing them again. It was a bitterness augmented by the sad realization that she could do nothing for the two boys, the last of her children and the only two who had survived of the six born after her daughters.

The boys roamed the streets, were involved in all the gang fights in the neighborhood, were perpetually in mischief and in trouble with the police and the teachers, stayed out at nights until all hours. What could be done? There was a living to be made and someone had to be in the café.

Don Emanuele Contini appreciated the conditions too, but he could do less than his wife. The only corrective he ever applied was to burst into extreme rage whenever a report on their bad conduct came from the school or one of the boys came back with his pockets stuffed with pilfered goods — fruit at times, but just as often cards of buttons, safety pins, small toys stolen from the pushcarts or a poor stationer's shop. The rage ended in his beating the two of them mercilessly no matter whether one or both were guilty. In fact, so furious was his anger that the blows he administered resulted in physical injuries — blackened eyes, strained wrists, contusions. For days the boys were kept indoors, Don Emanuele confining himself along with them and nursing his wrath the entire time. But worse than nursing his wrath he allowed himself to fall into a devastating despondency in which he cursed himself in true Italian fashion for coming to New York and, even more, for being unable to assist his wife as much as he wanted, and for his stupid devotion to his marionettes. And then he would come out of his fit. He would call Donato to him and ask him what he thought might be done to improve the leg movements of Arlecchino, or how could they brighten up the smile on Don Stefano, the monkey grinder? Then he and the boys betook themselves to the old brick house in the backyard and busied themselves with the marionettes, redressing them, reshaping their faces, changing the hair dress, making a new suit of armor, painting, varnishing. Donna Angela kept busy in the café and never interfered with either the beatings or the reconciliations. And so it continued year in and year out.

But both Giulio and Donato could not entirely shake off the influence of the street life in which they participated. A gang reported immense possibilities in a raid on a new building where it would be a simple thing to yank out the lead pipes and resell the metal to the local junk dealers. Giulio and Donato both were approached and one or the other, but generally Giulio, jumped into the adventure. Or there was a chance of making money by holding up one of the "cash-clothes" men that were constantly crying out in the neighborhood. Particularly worthwhile was it if the peddler had a long beard and wore a long coat — sure signs of his Jewish origin. Then they tormented the man, and that was exquisite sport — pulling his beard, snapping like little dogs at his coat, his trousers, yelling foul names. Donato had begun to draw away from these wild pranks and find more and more interest in the marionettes and in his schoolwork in which he was becoming proficient. Giulio made brave attempts too, and for months on end set himself the ambition of never leaving the house, assisting his father and mother, studying his lessons. However, the call of the rough-and-tumble life of the streets was too great. One night he would not be home, and the next day he was ready to offer his mother a handful of bills.

"Well, don't papa need the money? What do you mean where did I get it? I did something for somebody. . . . God all mighty, won't you believe me? Why will you always call me a thief?"

–3–

His last year in the elementary school was his best year. He studied hard, stayed home, graduated and finally decided upon going to high school. During the summer his father had managed to obtain work for him in a bank. He learned about huge payrolls being put in bags and carried out by messengers. Again he was approached by his old cronies, and he heard the old call. Donato had told the truth. Giulio had had no part in the shooting: he carried no gun, but he had given the gang the details of the messengers' movements and had been posted as a lookout while the others were to carry out the robbery. They had promised him that they would not shoot and that they would have no weapons. Days after the capture of the group, he kept repeating the phrase, "They promised . . . they promised. . . ." No one knew that he meant they had promised not to kill.

He refused to talk to his lawyers, to his father, or to his mother. The day before his execution his father had gone to see him. They stared at each other in the dim light of the meeting room. Giulio maintained his silence throughout. The father had broken down and begun to weep. He complained of his decision to come to America, blasphemed the saints, called for God's wrath on the judge, the jury, the attorneys. The guards were escorting him out. Only then did Giulio turn to his father. He smiled feebly and said in a firm voice, "I thought you would tell me about the marionettes. I hope you can do something with them. They say the colleges are giving lectures on them. . . ."

It was in this atmosphere that Donato grew up. Several months after Giulio's execution, the patient Donna Angela took to her bed. She died, like her son, without a word. The café had drifted out of her consciousness during the agonies of the trial. After the final brutal day, it had vanished as a place definite in outline and in purpose. She tried to wait on the guests. For a while they had become more numerous, attracted to the place out of curiosity. Many were genuinely sympathetic and had no way of showing their feelings except by coming to the café for a cup of coffee and a *dolce*. But she could not face them. What heart could she have for this thing? She did not even smile. She looked up with her great grey eyes and stared as if she might find some word written in the distant air that would explain what had happened to her. She finally took to her bed, really not sick, just exhausted, and died without uttering a word. She saw Donato close to her bedside one day and stroked his hair. That was the extent of her farewell greeting. The next day she lay in her coffin.

Don Emanuele found it equally impossible to carry on the café. The business was given up and he went to work in a piano factory, polishing the wood. At night he came back to his son Donato. They had moved into an old white brick house, with a stoop and long iron balconies bracketing a series of similar dwellings from the first to the last story. The basement apartment was occupied by a rag picker and his family. In the backyard he had constructed crude sheds of castaway boxes and rusty tin to keep the rain out of the accumulations of rags and junk. One of these sheds he rented to Don Emanuele, and in it Don Emanuele stored his marionettes.

-4-

They hung on wires, their feet barely off the earth floor, grotesque in the musty darkness, smiling perpetually, or with their mouths open in unending surprise, or with their features contorted into violent anger time without end. The first months after the death of Donna Angela, Donato and his father were drawn closely to each other. The old man sat at the window of the rear room — the paint flaked off the walls, the bare boards gaping with crevices, the coal stove rusty with age — and looked out on the backyards with their innumerable sheds, their clothes poles towering gaunt and thin into the air.

He looked out upon it all, and nothing was revealed to him. His mind had become blank with the grief of the past year and so nothing but memories floated through it — squares of bright light, for the Duke of Santo Maggio had come with a complete retinue to view the new Arlecchino and his minions; a panorama of Stromboli and the blue sea, for the girls and their aunts and he had hired a donkey cart and were spending the day in the country. Letters came from his daughters. He read them without comment or surprise or joy. He folded them up and laid them somewhere — on the old bureau they had salvaged from the wreck of the home above the café, or on a backless chair, on the bare wooden mantelpiece. And then he forgot them.

Donato with his fifteen years was troubled about his father but had not the wisdom nor the experience to help him. The boy would sit in the same room and watch the old fellow, his tall frame still straight, his curled hair without a trace of white, the long fingers that had communicated life to so many puppets just as steady as ever. But the luster had left the fine face with its distinctive nose, its laughing blue pupils, its sensitive large lips, and the mustache with its drooping ends that were always alive and vigorous had become merely hair that grew and had no reason for being.

On his own initiative Donato had begun getting the meals for both of them, tidying up the rooms, even scrubbing the floors. One night he had just put away the two white plates with their innumerable nicks, which served for all their courses. A frying pan with the grease of sausages and the red peppers still uneaten, was sizzling quietly on the stove. Dusk had filtered into the bare rooms. An accordion player had gone out on the fire escape and was singing dolefully about the sad love of a bandit boy, an Old World song that has not yet died out. Don Emanuele sat at the windowsill, tired from his work in the piano factory, looking out on the sheds. Donato followed the old man's gaze.

"Let's see what they are doing," he whispered to his father.

"Who?" Don Emanuele almost shouted. His thoughts had been on Giulio and Donna Angela, and the suggestion had come at a point in his reverie that made it horrifyingly appropriate.

"The marionettes. . . ."

Don Emanuele looked at his son. The sadness had become miraculously transformed. Smiles played about his lips and the corners of his eyes.

"I've been thinking, too. . . ."

"They've been alone ever so long. . . ."

"Britomart needs more color on her cheeks. . . ."

"Orlando's sword is broken. . . ."

"It must be damp father, in that kennel. . . ."

They went at once, using a candle to light their way.

A miracle of love happened at this point. Father and son busied themselves with this puppet and the other, adjusting a dress or fixing a buckler. Some were laid aside to be brought upstairs where there would be more light to apply a coat of paint or carve another line under the eye or near the nose to give the face a bit more meaning.

"Giulio made this head," Don Emanuele said, displaying the features of a common soldier in bare armor and plumeless helmet. "It's good — it's a frightened soldier but you know he will fight."

"Giulio was clever. . . ."

"Your mother made these dresses for the dancing girls. They're good, aren't they?"

"She loved them all too. . . ."

"But you, Donato, you always were the ablest. Your heads. . . . Look at them! What skillful noses, what speaking mouths! Who taught you such things? Ever since the tiniest tot. . . ."

"From you, papa," said Donato happily. They had rarely talked together this way. "I watched your fingers, the way you used your knife, the way you held the wood in one hand and worked with the other. . . . That was all. . . ."

He saw tears in his father's eyes, tears for the first time since the terrible tragedy. He went up close.

"Papa we'll have to have shows . . . shows just for you and me, and maybe later try another store. . . ."

So they decided and went up to their rooms with their hearts flooded with a feeling of peace, as if purpose had once more entered their lives. But more than peace was understanding and more than understanding was resolve — resolve that from then on their days were dedicated to each other, that they would live so that Giulio and Donna Angela would know that no more sadness was to come into their hearts.

"Donato," whispered the old man as they went to bed.

"Yes?" inquired the boy.

"I shall sleep tonight. . . ."

"And I too. . . ."

–5–

Three years had elapsed. Donato had gone to high school and had thrown himself vigorously into his work. Teachers and pupils knew that in some way he was a sad boy. Only occasionally was there anyone who had learned about Giulio, and no one about the marionettes, the marionettes which were his father's whole life, the marionettes which performed for both of them after the day's work was over. Both secrets Donato guarded carefully. When he had been implicated in the organized stealing of fountain pens, his pain had gone like a knife into his heart. His father was not to hear of it. It would kill the old man as the other tragedy had killed his mother. He had no one to whom to appeal.

For too long a time he had been solitary and reticent. There was no teacher with whom he was friends. There was Miss Rollins alone . . . ever since the incident when he had asked her out with him as a joke in the presence of all the boys. He had stayed afternoons studying in her room, he had found it sweet to listen to her as she talked, and for the first time since his mother's death had realized the difference between the love that springs up among men and the affection that develops between man and woman. His sensitiveness, rendered even keener by the sorrow at his heart, brought into focus feelings and understandings hidden from the vision of most people.

His instinct to trust in Miss Rollins was a sure one. The months following the episode that had brought them together in the kind of intimacy which he had never experienced before, had been sweet months. And what was more than their sweetness, they had been months in which he had grown and was aware of his growth. He scanned the life he was leading, and he knew that it was as good as most boys led despite the two mean rooms in which he and his father lived, despite the ugly disgusting street with its immense crowds, its dirty stores, the countless pushcarts that lined it night and day and, like a herd of animals, left their refuse behind to pollute the air.

But the hours of joy together with his father! How alive the wooden images became at those times! What poetry came to his father's lips! What glowing lands beyond all life and all dreaming swam into his imagination and slowly vanished, cloud within cloud, sun behind, and then the innumerable stars! And now these hours with Miss Rollins . . . hours in which he could pour out what had gathered into his heart of hope and ambition! School became as much a country of the mind as the places in which his father laid the stories enacted by the marionettes.

And so it was that the first weeks after the closing of school, Donato was unhappy and could not conceal his unhappiness from his father. The vacation to him stretched out as a time of infinite boredom. Not that it was not going to be filled with work. There was the home he kept for his father, there were the marionettes on which he constantly had something to do, and there was the project he had imposed upon himself — to learn about modeling in clay and stone and wood. Already he was skillful with the knife, and out of much of his father's old hickory, out of broom handles, out of kindling wood, out of pits of peach and apricots, had been fashioned by his own fingers a grotesque arab, a replica of a gargoyle, his recollections of queer heads among the boys, storekeepers in the neighborhood. There was a soap box filled with them; some only heads and necks; others, grinning faces at the ends of long sticks; others, countenances sunk into wood, their muscles flowing naturally out of the complicated mesh of the grain. Don Emanuele amused himself taking them out of their storehouse and talking to them.

"Well, well, you old idiot of a groceryman. Now I can tell you what high prices you charge. And you, Commare Rosa bella . . . you think you are good looking. But my boy knows better. He has seen what a shrew you are and how you yell at your husband and your daughter and your old mother too. That's why your eyes are almost popping out of your head and your neck is swollen with veins . . . . And you, little fellow. I bet you think you are smart at school. You make good marks, but you are not a good boy at home. You disobey. Why do your eyes shift that way then, hey, you bad boy? But you are at heart a good lad . . . you look bright. . . ."

There was all this for Donato to do, but there was no one to whom he could go, no one in whose presence was erased the shadow of a boy who died before his time, and of a mother who did not even smile at him as she lay waiting for her eyes to close. The lonely life with his father was becoming more and more a dream, and the noisy life around it receding out of space. Occasionally memories of the old ways with the boys came back to him, especially at night when he could not sleep. But he heard his father's breathing and the faces that beckoned disappeared, the call of the adventure was lost in the silence.

–6–

Those who have matured to their full capacities and have developed habits in conformity with them are as much the resultant as the prime movers in the process. They have fallen into molds which they have not made but which have shaped themselves out of the aspirations and the trials of their living. Donato was still too much in the gristle for the habits of solitariness to have become the mantle under which his whole life moved. He had grown to love his father too intensely ever to desire to upset the older man's routine to the extent of rendering him in the least degree unhappy. He made his father happy by studying, and he studied; he made his father happy by carving, and he carved; he made his father happy by being the audience at the puppet shows and he sat through them. Only on infrequent occasions were there visitors — old customers of the café; some of the neighbors, peasants who had not changed their simplicities and gazed in stupefaction upon the inanimate mimes that battled and sang and performed deeds of valor; the children of the small but congested tenement in which the Continis lived. Donato was as happy as his father and found more joy in the hours he spent carving a tiny apricot pit into the miniature head of a giant than in all the other things he did or dreamed he might do.

Nevertheless, as he grew into adolescence, as he observed the boys at the school at their numerous activities, as he listened to the stories of their adventures with the girls of their acquaintance and saw them called to the platform for being heroes in the games, there began to flow through his thoughts an undercurrent of uneasiness, a restlessness born of new and tantalizing desires. Several boys of the school, Stewart the athlete, and Lobishinsky the debater, had struck up friendships with Donato, walked out of school with him, met him in the crowded lunch room and discussed everything under the sun, roughhoused with him during the gymnasium periods, and, in the manner of boys growing into manhood, had exchanged views as to their aims in life, or just sat looking at each other and guffawing for no reason whatever. At school they were inseparable, but outside of school the story was different. Asked to their homes, Donato had found excuses never to go, and he never once invited them.

Now the summer loomed ahead as a dismal stretch of time. Filled with the ferment of youth and visited by dreams that were touched with a light that shifted as he attempted to focus it, he was a reservoir of unused energy, of intensities that did not let up, of wants that deepened his reticence but sharpened his desires to reveal himself. The light in the eyes of Miss Rollins had been like lightning in a dark storm. He had seen the high towers of magic cities and the broad plains of the country beyond them. The flashes had been disturbing. They had filmed themselves in the agitated spaces of his thoughts and in doing so had quickened his pulse and whetted his sensitivities. What had been simple before became complex; what was ugly had a touch of the beautiful; what was merely desirable became a craving. His craving therefore assumed significance; his interest in Latin broadened into a devotion; his life with his father must be made to yield greatness and beauty.

These had been the thoughts that kept up a constant movement in his mind. Ever since his encounter with Mr. Sidon, life had become a different thing. Miss Rollins had in some manner, like a creature in the magic stories that the marionettes told, laid a charm upon the days and the nights. The dreams became truth, and the experiences of the day the dreams. He had worked harder than ever at his modeling and hoped to have shown her the head on which he was working. The skulking head of Catiline was drawing away from the denunciations of the great orator. But in the wide-open eyes, the fallen lines of the mouth, the dilated nostrils, were revealed the high-spirited youth, unable to talk and defend himself against the accusations, as if he had been in the grip of uncontrollable forces which urged him to a task no one but he could understand.

But she had left him on the last day of school with a curt, "Goodbye. Have a good time." That was all. The summer would be again the sad and stupid one it always had been. For his father denied him the privilege of working; dreaded having Donato become involved in another such episode as his brother had; would have kept him locked up with the marionettes if he could. There was only the possibility of chance walks in the district where she lived, of meeting her accidentally, or of boldly writing to her and calling on her.

XI. SUMMER SESSION

AMY HAD decided to attend the university for the six weeks' summer course and actually found exhilaration in the hurrying crowds on the campus. She knew it was the exhilaration of feeling oneself once more like an undergraduate. How important it had felt to hasten to the library for the rare book reserved for the exclusive few of the world to understand. What joy to be bound for the lecture room where the visiting professor was to expound the profundities of the Vedas in the light of Spencerian evolution. The same thrill came flooding back. She let it pass through her with an epicurean's delight in the effect of an old vintage now newly tasted. And yet, as she was aware of the spreading warmth, she was aware too of the slowness of its movement. Involuntarily words rushed to her lips: "Is there going to be nothing to rouse and stir me?"

The summer weather had stripped the students of heavy garments. It was as if gardens had burst into sudden bloom to watch the young women with their light dresses of a hundred colors in great excitement crisscrossing over the brick walks. What a constant chattering and how many strange accents! What fresh faces filled with the delight of being in the metropolis miles from home! Teachers mostly they were, finding in the combined routine of the class work, and the freedom of the hours after, an amalgam that was a fire in the spirit — a fire that swept away age and flamed with magic for the youthful. Gayety had touched the brow of solemn thought, and purpose had placed a gentle restraint upon freedom. All moved about in groups held together by friendships already established or formed only in the first days of the session. Amy was one of the few who walked by themselves.

She sat down on one of the benches and watched the rows of poplars swaying in the soft breeze from the river. Over them clouds, puffed and shirred in endless series, floated with summer laziness. The red and white buildings etched themselves in clear-cut outlines, lost occasionally behind a curtain of leaves or softened in the grey-blue shadows cast by the slow clouds. Voices all about her rang with the happiness of new activity, and the feet of passersby seemed echoes of a joyous spirit. Amy gazed upon it all and again the sense of being alone became an intolerable pressure.

Why had she not followed Miss Batten's advice and taken a student roomer with her? Why had she not arranged to see her colleagues who were staying in town, taken their addresses, their telephone numbers, planned excursions and parties, trips up the Hudson, swims at the beaches?

She opened her volume of Paterculus. One of her courses was the reading in Latin of sources for the reign of Tiberius. The professor had assigned her as a topic the defense of that sinister emperor against the contemporary accusations of dissoluteness and degeneracy. She fingered the yellow pages of the old volume. The wind played with the others. She began to read. But the words seemed to go off with the wind and mingle their sounds with the stir of the willows nearby in an inarticulateness that attempted to be the utterance of all the sentient things about. No matter how she tried, she could not read. It was the place. She would go into the library.

"Well, well, well," she heard a familiar baritone.

Mr. Crabbing had sat down on the bench with her.

"What a busy person, what ambition!"

Mr. Crabbing, in an old Palm Beach suit, wrinkled and spotted, with his thin uneven face still unshaven, and his goatee slightly undefined, therefore, in the general scrawniness that lifted itself out of his collar, smiled and smiled after delivering himself of his surprise and admiration. Amy smiled back too, partly glad at having seen someone she knew.

"Summer session makes one solemn," Crabbing attempted a witticism.

"No." Amy was amused at the earnestness of her reply.

"Seems to me you'd go away."

"Oh, where would I go? One place is as good as another."

"And it's not such a drain either," replied Crabbing eagerly, as if finally the conversation had taken its proper turn. "One can do so much more in New York too. Of course, I am too old for a course of any kind. I should like to have tried the examinations for departmental head, don't you know? It's a cool thousand more, but they tell me you have to have pull. . . ."

"Oh, really?"

"Well, not to pass the examinations, to get a place after. . . ."

Amy looked at him without saying a word. He looked at her and stopped talking. She wondered what had made him sit down next to her, and he, whether she would consent to walk with him.

"Oh, yes," he resumed. "Pull's the thing . . . everywhere . . . nepotism of the worst sort . . . talk of the church and the popes . . . why there's no institution today, public or private, without the old taint of nepotism . . . good men have no chance take myself. . . . I have worked hard in the schools . . . always good results in my classes . . . know my subject . . . written an article or two . . . nothing to boast of . . . little letters of protest, don't you know, against crazy new methods . . . where have I got? I should like the higher position . . . at my age, Amy the sense of having failed — stuck in the classroom . . . it's a miserable sensation. . . ."

–2–

Amy, however, was not listening. Her eyes were elsewhere. She had seen a familiar figure cross the campus and enter the small brick building where the new applicants enrolled. She wondered. Was it Donato? What would he be doing here? She kept her eyes on the door. He must soon come out.

"You're bored with me?" asked Crabbing, placing an arm on the bench behind her back, and bending toward her at the same time.

"Oh, no," she exclaimed in a kind of fright. But why fright? she kept asking herself.

"I forgive you for the other day. . . . I really understand you could have no feeling for me on the short acquaintance we have had, and for me to have asked your hand in marriage . . . pool our resources. . . ."

But she was not looking at him. He followed the movements of her eyes, silent, offended, as if he had been invited to sit down by her and then been summarily dismissed.

"You are not listening to me at all, young woman," he exclaimed, his goatee having become agitated and his lids drawing behind his eyeballs as they did often in the classroom when he reprimanded a youngster.

"No, Mr. Crabbing, I am sorry," she turned appealingly to him.

"You have been rude. . . ." He talked as if he were scolding one of his pupils.

"I am sorry. . . ."

"Good morning. . . ." He rose stiffly. "I had intended asking whether you would walk with me. . . ."

Amy had risen too. She had seen Donato coming out of the registrar's building. It was Donato. Why should her breath come and go so, and her face flush? It was so stupid, so stupid, and Mr. Crabbing near.

"I'd be glad to," she said, without really understanding that she had seized his offer in self-defense. "I was thinking I'd like it too. . . ."

They started off, Crabbing taking her arm to help her down the narrow stairs leading from the campus to the street level.

"The river is a glorious sight these days. . . . I never understand why people should want to spend so much money to see the miserable little Arno creep along. What is there more wonderful than this?" he asked finally, sweeping in with a gesture of his gaunt arm the whole length of the river with green cliffs rising like a perpendicular reflection of the water itself. Amy stopped as Crabbing stopped, and pretended to be admiring the view. But already her original revulsion for the man at her side had become intense again.

"We ought to sail up the river, Amy," he said. "We could take lunches . . . you'd provide something and I would bring along something else . . . we should be back in time for our dinners. . . ."

His words ran over her like thick warm liquid. She wanted to escape and kept thinking of some way of doing it. But there was another fear that held her where she was. She had decided once and for all she must not. She must not meet the boy. If he had enrolled in the summer session, she would have to leave, go to the country, out of the city, at a distance, somewhere. . . .

"What do you say for Saturday . . . no, Friday would be better. . . ."

"Yes," she heard herself say, "yes, Friday, after classes. It would be nice."

-3-

They had stopped to allow the traffic to go by, before crossing the park and taking the walk along the wall. Despite the constant movement of automobiles and people, the uncoordinated noises of the river craft, the flash of smoke rising and falling like a curtain over a light, there was a sense of serenity in the scene, a serenity derived from the long shadows cast by the tall apartments flanking the Drive. The shadows drifted out like a liquid, engulfed the lighter and more restless shadows of the trees and shrubbery, and then spread quietly out and out until they became part of the river and sky. It was but an extension of the campus, a small square of grass plots and brick walks with copses of poplars and willows at stated intervals, but nevertheless a place that suggested retirement, a stopping place on a long flight. Its spirit sent out its quietness and the steady flow of cars became a hum, a hum that merged into itself the activity of the city, subdued it, cast it into the cadences of music.

She was grateful to Crabbing for having invited her on the walk. She was too unused to such simple pastimes to have discovered the joy of them for herself.

"Isn't this lovely?" she exclaimed. "Look at the long rows of trees, and the water, how still, and the apartment houses! Why they're beautiful really. . . ."

She turned to look at them and scan their surfaces until her eyes rose to the blue above. As she did so, she had a feeling of being watched by curious glances, and the thought came to her that she might cause a crowd to collect in the fashion of casual gazers among the hordes in the lower sections of the city. She made a quick movement to see who or what it was that gave her the strange feeling. There on the corner at the top of the steep street stood Donato, hatless, shirt open at the neck, his chestnut curls glistening in the morning air. She looked. The same sensation of being in the presence of a Hermes come to life once more passed through her like an echo of a poem she had committed to memory and forgotten.

"That apartment with the convex wall skirting the bend of the avenue . . . it's a bold piece of architecture," Crabbing was saying. "We don't give our architects sufficient credit. . . ." How hateful the voice was, baritoning so complacently while within her flitted the ghosts of a hundred desires. Would he not stop it? And why could she not take her eyes away from the figure on the summit of the street, perched like a god, but like a god puzzled by a new landscape, the landscape of a world not of his making? Why did he sum up for her in a living person all the ecstasy she had had in the swing and imagery of the Latin poets? Why did he stand there? Why did he not run down to her and like the god he was seize her and carry her upward?

"Yes, Amy," Crabbing continued. "We are in the presence of beauty and we don't acknowledge it. We spend money on the theater, go to expensive cabarets, buy high-powered cars, go in for elaborate entertainment, and what do we get out of it? A simple walk like this. . . ."

Amy put her arm suddenly under his.

"Let's walk up the river," she suggested quietly.

All the while she kept saying to herself, "He waved his hand, waved his hand as if I were but a school girl. Impudent fellow . . . he must not . . . I must not see him. . . ."

Much to the surprise of Crabbing she quickened her step. In fact, the rapidity of her pace communicated itself to him. Was it an awakening of tender feeling? Did she not take his arm of her own free will? Did she not press close to him as they hurried?

He looked impressively down upon her, reelingly conscious of her beauty.

"But this is great, Amy. That's how I like a walk, brisk, continuous. . . . Oh, it's good to be in sight of heavens and water and beauty — like yours," he added, making his voice low and syrupy.

Amy shrank within her skin and hurried the faster without daring a word or looking up. The young god was pursuing . . . he must not catch up.

-4-

At luncheon with Mrs. Nilins, she learned that a young man had called on her that morning.

"That's a nice salad, Amy. You must eat it . . . you haven't eaten well for a month or more. . . . Just a young boy seemed like a foreign boy, curly hair, open shirt. . . ."

That Donato knew her address disquieted her. Of course, had he not sent the flowers? He could not have made a special effort to obtain it! Moreover, was there not the telephone book? She must instruct Mrs. Nilins never to allow Donato to wait for her. She must tell him, "Miss Rollins is out, and will not be back."

She plunged into her work with a vigor that astounded her. Following the direction of Prof. Filtray, she scrutinized each statement about Tiberius, attempted to discover the validity of each separate item. It was a revelation to her that no statement, even one lacking entirely in the scurrility and malice characteristic of the writings about that unfortunate Emperor, should mean the same thing on a second or a third reading. Gossip had a way of giving itself its own lie, thought Amy, unless one is disposed to accept any remark only because it has its bit of barb or its smell of scandal. She was dissecting a paragraph for evidence of evil intentions, a desire to foment discontent, a bitterness caused by withdrawn privilege or withheld rewards. She suddenly sat up and gazed straight ahead at the wall.

"If I were seen too often with Donato, would not they all talk? And if they all talked, would they not believe, and be believed? And is not belief proof of a fact?

"Amy, Amy," she cried aloud to herself. "Be on your guard . . . your nerves have just got jumpy. . . . Crabbing is better than the horrible mess. . . . It isn't true that you wish to help the boy . . . because you, you need him. . . . Forget about him. . . ."

That afternoon another disturbing telegram arrived from Philip.

"Prison is like Milton's Hell. To escape it, one must jump out of one's skin."

This telegram, like the others, was without date or place. What was going on his mind, where was he, what was he doing? Anna, her sister, in answer to a letter of inquiry professed complete ignorance. Amy could see his long frame stretched out in utter relaxation, a loose, sour smile on his lips, his eyes observing everything with an air of infinite disdain. And yet he exacted sympathy, almost dictated an attitude of pity, for all his face had sunken, cheeks and mouth and eyebrows, sunken into lines of pain. He, he, it was, should have taken the morphine! What was he doing now when his chest muscles began to contract, and his lungs like empty bellows seemed to have collapsed, and he stared with agonized pupils upon a world he felt distrusted him? Amy put her fingers over her eyes, shut out the light, and in doing so tried again to drive the world from her mind entirely, slowly lowering herself into the darknesses under our beings where the pain and the anguish are blotted out for good.

The lack of knowledge as to Philip's whereabouts was keener pain than the realization that he must be suffering. And he was suffering not only the effects of the gas poisoning that would not leave his system, but the sensation of having been advised to get himself together, try to depend upon himself for his ultimate rehabilitation. She had meant it for his good. He must know it — for his good.

If only she could locate him now and bring him back, not only his problems might partially be solved but her own also would be nearer an end. What she most required of life was to sacrifice herself without return. Habits that spanned so many years could not be broken overnight. . . .

–5–

To fill in the hours when her studies palled and her mind failed to work with the clarity her task demanded, Amy had begun to rearrange the furniture, shop for new things, try her hand at raising plants. She had got herself catalogues from a well-known horticulturist, had gone to the public libraries for books on pot plants, indoor blooms of an exotic kind.

Buying a canary had been a moment's impulse. She came home with one that had just achieved the power of its wings. Many hours of her day she spent training it.

Before the summer vacation was over she had taught it to skip a rope across the entire room, jump on to another rope leading into her bedroom, and from there hop to each of the four knobs of the poster, and then return.

It ate from her fingers, hopped at command upon the table, flew in and out of the cage at her bidding, and at the ringing of the alarm clock burst into long-sustained trills. Her first thought on entering her apartment was to call, "Bezo" and then wait for the flutter of wings and the answering whistle.

Bezo performed his tricks for everyone. Mrs. Nilins was amazed at his proficiency. She never tired of seeing the bird go through his whole repertoire. Later Miss Batten amused herself with him as much as Amy did and taught him the added trick of climbing up her outstretched arm until he reached her fingertips, leaping to her other fingers, and then running down the other arm to the other shoulder. Miss Batten kept doing it over and over again.

The only visitor who caused Bezo annoyance was Crabbing. No sooner had Crabbing entered than Bezo would insist upon flying back to his cage. There, behind the protection of the wires, he would chirp angrily, make shrill sounds, flutter his whole body against the enclosure. Crabbing attempted to ingratiate himself into Bezo's favor by putting a finger into the cage. Bezo only pecked at it viciously with his bill.

If either her plants or her bird were ailing, Amy would be as disconsolate as over a human being. She studied the books in detail, learned the best type of food for both plant and bird, kept them out of drafts or placed them where the sunshine would flood them to the full.

One day she came home and called out archly, "Bezo!" There was no answer. She called again and still there was no answer. Real fright seized her. She summoned Mrs. Nilins. Had she failed to shut the windows? Had a stray cat found its way into the room? She ran quickly into the apartment. Mrs. Nilins followed, her topknot teetering on her head, whispering in her bated manner, "Poor little fellow, poor little fellow."

"No feathers, Mrs. Nilins, no sign of any kind. . . . It couldn't have been a cat. . . . The windows are all shut. . . . It's not in its cage either. . . ."

"In the bed room, Amy. . . .?"

They searched the bedroom but there was no sign of Bezo. Amy sat down on the bed and tears came to her eyes.

"But, Amy, I know . . . I know how you feel." Mrs. Nilins stroked her hand, held her shoulders, sat down beside her.

"Oh, it's so foolish, Mrs. Nilins, don't I know? . . . It is . . . but it seems so horrible . . . hear it sing in the morning and find it gone before nightfall . . . and really without exaggeration. . . . Oh, I know you will laugh at me . . . I'm laughing at myself . . . after all I have some little sense . . . really without exaggeration. . . . I love it, love it . . . love it like a person . . . but more . . . Mrs. Nilins, you maybe think I am losing control of myself. . . . But the illusion is complete. . . . I almost think it is one of the Greek gods of old in a new transformation . . . an epiphany they called it. . . ."

Mrs. Nilins looked up at her with wide-open eyes and lips quivering with desire to say, "You poor child, you poor child . . . you should never have stayed in the city . . . you should have taken the summer and gone off into the country."

Amy, however, was unconscious of the effect she had produced upon her friend. She had got up from the bed and stood as if on tiptoe with ecstasy, gazing upward in a wonder that was like that of music heard far off and to which one listens intently, putting the stray cadences into bars and the bars into melodies that echo one's own feelings.

Like a young god, Mrs. Nilins . . . it might be Apollo . . . Orpheus . . . no, Hermes, the messenger, fleet of foot . . . . It is Hermes the messenger . . . it is. . . ."

And with that she fell upon the bed and wept in an agony that communicated itself to Mrs. Nilins.

"The poor dear, she's all nerves. . . ."

Just then there was flutter of wings and the call of a bird.

They both ran into the sitting room. Bezo's call was unmistakable. The spasmodic movement of his wings and the quality of the call left no doubt that he was in pain. But where was he?

"Bezo . . . . Be . . . zo. . . ." Amy called.

There was the reply. It came from the region of the mantelpiece. She hurried to it, and there within the interior of the replica of the Parthenon was Bezo, imprisoned. How it had worked itself in was a marvel. It was caught as in a trap and could not easily be removed. It was not until Crabbing came that they succeeded in extricating it. But no sooner had Crabbing managed to take the bird out of the temple and return to its cage than Bezo snapped with his beak at the deliverer and raised his angry chatter.

"You would think he'd be grateful. . . ."

"I am," Amy assured him.

"Oh, grateful, yes . . . I have restored you your bird. . . ."

"But I am, Crabbing, but I am. . . ."

"Of course." His goat-like face tightened into an expression meant to be partly affectionate and partly reprimanding. "But, Amy, how about your real feelings, hey . . . how about them?"

He tiptoed over to her and placed his hands together finger to finger. To Amy he appeared in that position possessed more strikingly of the traits that made him repulsive. The bulging eyes, the agitated goatee, the sparse hair over his forehead achieved a singular distinctness.

"Let us go to Tony's," he added benignantly, unaware of her feelings. "We'll talk it over again over our dinner. . . ."

Despite her repeated negatives, and the obvious ruses she employed to escape him, Crabbing persisted in telephoning to her and obtaining invitations to come for the evening, for supper, for tea. When she was not in, or refused him admission to her rooms, he called anyhow and spent the evening with Mrs. Nilins. Throughout her widowhood, Mrs. Nilins had not had the attentions of any man. So, she could not now fathom what pleasure Crabbing derived from her company. She laughed to herself. "Is the old crow making love to me?"

What he most persisted in discussing rendered her suspicious of him altogether, but she discovered no way of refusing to receive him. In fact, the evenings when he came seemed pleasant enough. For so long a while now she had been solitary. And these strange attentions . . . they were at least amusing.

"My father knew how to buy a house and sell one too, Mrs. Nilins. . . . Just a rural minister, five hundred dollars a year, and eight children. Well, you may judge for yourself. We simply had to practice economy from the beginning. We preserved everything . . . the wrapping on parcels, the strings, old newspapers . . . they made excellent linings for our boots. We all went to school but there weren't enough pencils to go around . . . we were allowed each a half one, some times only a third . . . and it had to last us all the year . . . now I have so many little stubs . . . see . . . pockets full. When I call on my sister . . . married a wealthy old fellow in the lumber business . . . he has a balance I wager you, Mrs. Nilins . . . owns half the county . . . . Well, if I show my sister a handful of stubs . . . pick them up in school you know and in the street, too, at times . . . can't resist picking them up . . . seems so wasteful letting them lie around . . . if I show her a handful, she cries with joy, 'Richard, Richard!' and when I give her some, she weeps, she weeps, Mrs. Nilins. . . . But my father could buy a house and sell one at a pretty price . . . how could we ever live? I suppose, though, you found it more profitable just holding on to this . . . they tell me real estate in this section has taken a tremendous jump since the war . . . you ought to realize fifty thousand . . . cash too . . . Mrs. Nilins . . . fifty thousand . . . imagine. . . . One thinks about it in awe, Mrs. Nilins . . . of course, one may save and save . . . like me. . . . I work nights, too . . . Mrs. Nilins . . . but I wonder . . . if I ever could have fifty thousand all at once . . . all at once. . . ."

The bulb-like eyes of the man flashed with mysterious lights, and all his face worked with the emotion of contemplating such a figure. The expression was persistent, almost fantastic. Mrs. Nilins, frightened, rose from her seat and moved away.

XII. DONATO'S SUMMER

–1–

DONATO AND his father had sat up one night discussing his future, "I am getting old and worn out, Donato, and you are still young. . . ."

"Maybe we should go to the Argentine. You would be happier. . . . Rosina has children. . . ."

"No, Donato. My place is here with you . . . your place is here . . . you know the language . . . you are getting an education . . . you will go to college. . . ."

His large frame had grown thin and in his shoulders, slightly drooping, were visible the ravages of his sorrows. His hair, thick once like his son's, was greying in long streaks as in a woman's. For the most part, he sat at the window, pipe in hand, gazing over the backyards with their jumble of sheds and junk carts, his eyes half-closed as though by holding them so he could see under the surface of the meaningless scenes. It was only occasionally that the old spirit came back.

"This, Donato, your mother made completely, even the head . . . not a very good head, but she has expression . . . she's the Chinese lady that received Marco Polo. Watch her walk with tiny steps, watch her make her little bow, watch her turn to see what her father, old sour looking Mandarin, is thinking. . . . And see her advance to the throne, so appealingly, so humbly . . . she loves this stranger. Bow, One Hundred Petals, . . . bow to the great emperor . . . and say what's in your heart. . . . 'Do you wish to sow rice seeds of sorrow? They will fill all the marshes of my life with sweet blooms . . . but they will choke my spirit . . . .' Oh, I don't suppose she spoke that way . . . but my audiences would weep, Donato, weep. . . ."

On this particular night, the day before Donato had registered for the modeling class at the university, Don Emanuele had felt in no mood to show his dolls. They sat together talking of the future.

"Your place is here. . . ."

"But you are unhappy. . . ."

"No. Donato, you will make me happy . . . you will be the girls and your mother and Giulio too . . . all of them. . . . Yes, be an artist . . . you are a born sculptor. . . . I suppose you will make little money. . . . Who cares for art in this country? Maybe there are the rich who do. . . ."

"I could go to the modeling class this summer. . . ."

"As long as my work holds out . . . we shall have money. . . ."

Father and son looked at each other. In the pale light of the early evening their eyes seemed the only brilliant stars. The dreams of youth and the hopes of the old burned with equal fire. They looked at each other in silence, and though in the background of their thoughts was the great sorrow that had come upon them, there was joy in their communion.

"I shall register tomorrow. You'll see what I can do. . . ."

-2-

At the university Donato applied himself with the zeal of a novice. In a short time, however, he had realized that the class was no place for him, and the instructor had realized it too. The professor was a huge man with a head like Rodin's, heavy with hair, ponderous, even ungainly, so out of proportion was it to his thin straight legs and small chest. But something slept in the deep eyes, cavernous under his full black brows, that was all poetry and exquisite delight, delight in himself for his delight in things, delight in the sun, delight in the modeling of trees, and the shape of hills, delight in the curves of the rails before a speeding train, delight in the work done by his pupils no matter how crude, how lacking in intelligence or skill.

"Ladies and gentlemen," he cried at the beginning of session, "did you see, did you see the sun over the Hudson last night? The purple bands, the gold lakes, the filigree lavender lace . . . and the boats, the boats! We must catch that in the eyes of some of the heads we shall shape. Ah, to put such joy in the eyes of an inanimate bust . . . that is the art of sculpture . . . but not only in the eyes . . . in the muscles that flow from the mouth, that curl about the points of the eyebrows, in the quiver of a nostril. . . . This is the dream of the ages that stone shall be spirit, that clay shall cry with music. . . ."

Donato felt his body tremble. He gazed with unabashed wonder at the man. He felt his breath come and go, and in his eyes was the reflection of the light in Mr. Borriner's.

"You marvel of youth," exclaimed Borriner at the first head shown him by Donato. "You're an artist . . . you're not a teacher like me . . . like these. . . . I can teach you nothing . . . nothing . . . Ladies and gentlemen," he cried . . . "Ladies and gentlemen . . . will you form a circle? . . . This young man has actually performed the miracle. . . . Do you recall at the beginning of the session what I said about making the face talk? Look at this. . . . Notice . . . elongated grotesquely, ending in a beard like a goat's . . . eyes bulging . . . lids withdrawn behind the eyes . . . hair combed to suggest the devil himself . . . a bizarre head but human . . . you will see how human when I pass it around . . . a marionette's head it would seem . . . heads such as I have seen in marionette theaters in Italy . . . but note the eyes and the cheeks and the lips . . . the ears too . . . they all converge to a point with the eyes . . . to a point far beyond . . . as if he were looking at something. . . ."

The nondescript class gathered round: women in their forties bent upon bringing back something new to their classes, young women who, disillusioned with the classroom work, yearned to shake off the routine in a blaze of enthusiasm for what they called art, men and women taking this course in desperation, having already taken so many and having been bored with them all. They were impressed. They laughed their appreciation, exclaimed, "Wonderful," "Simply great," "Grand."

One of them, a Jewess, approached him after class.

"But, Mr. Contini, you are not going to teach?"

Donato looked at her in amazement. He had never had anyone before come to him as if he were an unusual person, possessed of traits that rendered him worthy of homage.

"But you are an artist, Mr. Contini, an artist!"

Miss Selma Kreymdorf let her wide eyes, her full lips, her mobile cheeks singly and in combination reveal the great impression he had made upon her. The fine fuzzy hair, neither black nor brown nor dark nor light, but just a mist that clung to her head, blew about her temples.

Donato smiled, and as he smiled the full beauty of his face acquired the peculiar charm of which Amy was always so conscious. Not yet eighteen, he looked older than his years. His close life with his father, the memory of his brother, dark and bitter, the gang experiences at an early age — all these and a natural reticence, a thinking quality, and sensitive perceptions had given a turn to his thoughts. They had placed a touch on his features which added to the sense of his having matured to understanding. Like Amy, Selma saw the unusual in Donato and rapturously responded to it with the volatility characteristic of her race, strengthened by the determined ambition to be considered one of the intelligentsia among the circles in which she moved.

"But you are an artist," she exclaimed again, with slightly in-drawn breath, and eyes that darted her admiration.

Donato was too unused to this sort of effervescence to reply. He continued to smile and as he smiled his olive features became suffused with color.

"I hope you are not going to stay in this place. You need freedom, a chance to live. . . ."

"Oh, I'm just beginning. . . ."

"But what a place to begin in, Mr. Contini! You should be among artists, downtown, in Paris, at Cape Cod, somewhere else, but not here, my Lord, not here! This is the graveyard of genius and the arena of the mediocre . . . get out of it. . . ."

Up to this time Miss Rollins had been the only woman with whom Donato had talked on intimate terms. Girls he had not known, not even the girls of his neighborhood, shop girls, or if home-staying girls, for the most part of peasant origin, interested in getting married as soon as possible, with no thoughts in their heads of the type Selma geysered so effusively. Very early in his life, like many of the wilder boys of the district, in a riot of guffawing and snickerings, he had been initiated into the so-called mysteries of sex, had been in a house of prostitution, had heard of vile obscenities, had known of practices which had heated his blood to the point of disgust and horror. Quite without being aware of it he had been making a distinction between women. One set he placed on an elevation, considered them entirely without thought of sex; the rest were easy women, without feeling, without sweetness, of a low sort, with heavy voices, coarse manners, foul desires. They were desirable too, infinitely desirable, but to be abandoned, shunned as soon as possible, not made into companions. Before the summer was over he was to add to his knowledge, but the knowledge upset him, changed the color of his world, soiled the beauty he had been finding in it.

This strange creature walking at his side, with her swinging gait, her full hips, her high bosom, suggesting the languor of dim boudoirs and soft music, talking in terms of notions which set his heart afire with dreams and hopes of self-discovery and, therefore, pedestaled her too — what was he to say to her? How address her? He could neither look at her nor straight ahead. He kept his eyes on the ground, feeling himself reddening, aflame.

"I suppose you're no more than twenty. . . ."

"No," he answered, without meaning to lie but too overwhelmed to offer a clear statement, a statement which would lead to more explanations and those to still others. He was anxious to be gone, to get to his own bare room overlooking the motley fetid backyards of the rag pickers and shovelers, and there in the quietness at the center of all the noise and activity he could think over what the professor had said, what this young woman was saying, what his own heart was throbbing.

"Imagine . . ." cried Selma, making no pretense at hiding her admiration. "You must have had a teacher. . . ."

"No, just my father. . . ."

"Is he an artist too?"

"No . . . he used to make marionettes. . . ."

"How thrilling! Imagine. . . ." she had stopped to look at him, and for the first time since their meeting he had raised his eyes flush with hers. Her open neck, the frank expression of her eyes, the voluptuous fullness of her arms and bosom, an essence, which she emanated, of something natural without coyness and without restraint, her low-toned rich voice — all these laid a disquieting hand on the boy. Desires long since suppressed by the quiet life he had been leading with his father, leaped and tore through his frame. They danced in his eyes, quivered in his lips, trembled in the muscles of his neck.

Selma laughed deep in her chest an inarticulate low laugh which only served to gather the varied impressions of her personality and cohere them into one more personal and yet general, too, and remote — a definite inescapable sense of her being a woman stirred by man, and by the type of man for whom she had always been reaching out in her waking moments, in her vision, in all she had been doing. And as she laughed, she said,

"I only came to visit Mr. Borriner . . . we're sort of friends . . . a very interesting man . . . but a failure . . . perceives with his feelings, feels with his mind . . . no real ability . . . doesn't get lost in work, only in words . . . he uses them beautifully — just the kind of man to teach . . . but not you . . . you're beyond him already. . . ."

She talked on and on, aware that he was disturbed and why he was disturbed, but unable to break the tension. They had stopped under a group of poplars, slim and tall, the color of their leaves like the fresh green of lettuce. Every movement of the air in the branches was music and the murmur of the twigs fell into the conversation and drifted out with the words. As Selma stopped, they were both rendered acutely conscious of the sweet stirring overhead, and they looked up, Selma laughing once more in her chest, Donato turning uneasy eyes to her.

"Loveliest of trees . . . like dancing girls . . . I often think they skip over the grass long before people are stirring in the dusk. . . ."

"I shall make a head to show them as they skip," Donato said in one forced breath.

"That will be glorious. . . . Will you bring it to me . . . in my rooms?"

"Yes," he said. "Tomorrow. I shall work on it all night. . . ."

"What a silly boy. . . ."

"I do it many times. . . ."

"For whom?"

The question rippled out on the tones of laughter, and Donato reddened more violently. Yet he knew it was meant to be bantering, and he smiled too, showing the even row of white teeth flashing in unison with the sparkle of his eyes.

"For myself, and my father. . . . I have heads of all kinds. . . ."

"Will you bring them too?"

"Yes . . . if you want to see them. . . ."

"All you have. . . ."

They walked toward the subway station, unconscious of the talkative crowds of students, the trolley bell, the roaring of automobiles. At the entrance, they stopped.

"You know," said Selma, "you never asked where you are to come. You won't make any kind of lady's man even if you are an artist. . . ."

More than anything else she had said or done, more than the undulant body she possessed, than the deep luster of her eyes, these words coursed through his veins with the vigor of flame. He looked up at her, and he wondered at this creature, so wise, so frank, so upsetting.

When she had disappeared into the subway, he turned at once and ran, ran for a while and then walked, quickened his step and then increased it to a run once more, stopped dead and thought, and once again ran, ran. His daily walk home took him down the steps of Morningside Park, still a quiet place of many trees and shrubs covering the cliffs, making sallies into ravines, leaping on to terraces. As he hurried down the steps, he thrust a hand upward to touch an overhanging branch or he pulled at the bushes that lined the walks. What a riot the thoughts made in his mind, a crisscross of impressions that burned like candles or floated into drifts like clouds lighted with the sun.

"I'm an artist . . . an artist . . ." he laughed with the thought, and he wondered what his father would say. "And she likes me. . . ." And as he said this there came to his memory the scenes of a world he had left far behind, scenes that were flashes of heat in his heart.

"And Miss Rollins — she will like it too."

-3-

That night he wrote Amy a letter. He told her he had tried to see her, hoping that she might advise him as to what to do for the summer. But she had not been in and he had gone of his own accord to the university and had asked about courses in sculpture. She remembered how he had spoken of starting a club at the school and that she had consented to stay with the boys as faculty adviser. The course he was taking was an advanced one and he was allowed to enroll but without credit. Mr. Borriner was a remarkable man and called him an artist. . . . He was going to work hard. He would let her know. He had met a woman who had called him an artist too. He wondered whether he ought to come back to school. Should he not just study sculpture?

But it was not until long after his meeting Selma in her rooms, as she called her apartment, that he once again saw Miss Rollins. She had replied at once to his letter, expressing great joy at the work he was doing and advising him by all means to devote his time to sculpture.

"My dear Donato," she had said, "you must not leave school. It is always an anchor to windward, especially for one in your circumstances. You cannot get far without an education even if it is the poor sort one gets in the schools. I should not be a friend to you were I to tell you anything else.

"There is one more thing, Donato, which you said which disquieted me not a bit. You are still a young boy but you seem ever so much older, so much so in fact that you are easily mistaken for a grown man. This is not said to flatter you. You have talent, you have ideas, you make an impression. You must be careful of the acquaintances you make. I should hate for you any experience that is not sweet and lovely. I do hope your new friend will prove a real inspiration. You see I feel I can talk this way because you did place a good deal of confidence in me. . . ."

Amy had wanted to destroy the letter no sooner had she written it. Had not Mrs. Nilins come upstairs at the moment to say that Crabbing was waiting for her, she would have destroyed it. But she did want to answer Donato at once, and so she sealed the envelope and wrote out the address just at the moment Crabbing entered the room. He glanced over her shoulder and made a wry face. Bezo, as usual, whether by hearing or by sight had divined the presence of his disliked visitor, and set up a vigorous twitter of annoyance.

"Is that Contini boy still bothering you?" he asked.

Amy looked up amazed and bewildered. She recalled the incident in the classroom when Crabbing had surprised Donato and her in an exchange of glances, and with this recollection there flashed through her mind all the other moments with Donato, his standing tiptoe like a Hermes, the first meeting with him after her return from Eston, the walks and the long afternoons.

She did not know how to answer Crabbing. She realized that in his own way he was being sweet to her, that he had not proved altogether as repulsive as his manner at first indicated, in fact that he could be interesting, that his mind was quick and well-trained, too well-trained possibly, that his information was broad and detailed and ranged over many subjects.

Imperceptibly he had grown to believe that she was accepting his attentions in the spirit of the proposal she had so definitely, crudely, rejected. That she knew, too, and she was grateful to him for not having renewed the proposal in words. And she was grateful, too, for their days together, days sailing up the Hudson, or at the beach, when he had been attentive in gentle kind ways. She sensed the difficulty, the struggle he was having in laying out money for their excursions and did nothing to increase the expense of them, filled with pity for the man at such times. A dollar expended by him was the pouring of lifeblood in sacrifice, and the sacrifice he seemed to be making out of a feeling that was developing into affection. His hard hairy hand on hers had at first been like the passing of many beetles over her, but gradually it had rested ever so gently upon her fingers, unpressing, without boldness, and she had begun to find it bearable. And yet she sensed that in subtle forms the possessiveness at the bottom of his character, like a sour brew, was permeating his attitude toward her, and that in continuing to see him she was permitting him to assume the attitude with justification. How answer his question?

"I never liked that youngster," Crabbing added, walking toward the window with his hands locked behind his back, unmindful of the canary that clasped the wire of his cage, and again twittered its violent distress.

To reply would be to accept the implied accusation; not to reply would be tantamount to a discourtesy he would resent and never cease bringing up. But why should she be disturbed at all? She had refused Stephen; was she to fall into the mess that a life with Crabbing might become?

"You would not carry a stamp?" is all she said.

"No," he answered, lengthening the vowel to suggest annoyance.

"We'll stop for one on the way out. Will you take the letter?"

"I don't mean to interfere in your affairs, Amy," he said, looking straight at her as if entitled to assume the air of the offended lover. "It's not my business, but we are friends . . . I have seen you two together a good deal. . . . And it hasn't seemed to me like the sort of thing one expects. . . ."

"Mr. Crabbing. . . ." Amy, unaccustomed to displays of anger, had merely turned pale, and whispered this in a kind of fright.

"He's a no-good sort . . . worst type of foreigner . . . lives in the most miserable place associated with the rowdies of Harlem all his life. . . ."

"What are you making such a fuss about?" she finally said. "What's the fuss about? First of all, what do you really know of the boy? And what right have you to talk in this manner, Mr. Crabbing? Please take this letter and see that we mail it. . . . You're too far gone in years to play the adolescent. . . ."

"Yes, I have been a fool, a fool," Crabbing replied, putting the letter in his pocket. Amy, however, had turned about to put on her hat, and did not observe the mean radiance that filled his eyes, and the deliberate stroking of his goatee.

"A man at my age! You are right, Amy . . . but you understand. . . ." he lowered his voice tenderly . . . "I have grown fond of you. . . ." He once more went to the window as if the view of the scrubby yard and the rear of garages would assist him. Bezo retreated to the top of the cage and thrust out its head and bill as if ready for an encounter. Actually as he talked, Crabbing was once more taking an inventory of Amy's four rooms and finding them suitable. There would be no need to buy another piece of furniture. The armchair was comfortable, there was a good daybed and a good four-poster, the rugs were a bit shabby but they could be used . . . the rent very reasonable. . . . Mrs. Nilins was not the one to raise it. . . .

"I have grown fond of you, Amy . . . it can't be flattery to you but you are the only woman I have been fond of. . . . I ask if it is love? . . . . I have been a lonely man . . . my boyhood was a confined one — my manhood hard toil . . . I had no time for the amenities, Amy. . . ."

Amy had acted as if she had not heard. This was the first time since their outings in the summer that he had spoken so frankly of his feelings. He contented himself hitherto with stroking her hand, gazing dreamily at her through his knobby eyes, calling her "Amy" in tender tones. She had dreaded moments of this sort. But now she could listen to him talking, his back toward her, trying to be dramatically affectionate, playing the shy lover, and smile in a sort of flattered contempt of him. And yet she kept saying to herself, "Your days are going fast and your chances too . . . forget about Donato . . . that's an insane passion . . . passion . . . yes . . . but insane . . . forget about him . . . take this man . . . it will be a fence around you. . . ."

"Crabbing," she said aloud (she could not bring herself to say Richard), "Crabbing, listen to me . . . you are being a big boy . . . and so I am laying down a number of caveats for you . . . no more talking on this subject of your overwhelming passion for me. We're neither of us spring chickens, and so we can do without syrupy sentiment . . . take what you have and be content. . . . Are we going on this walk or are we not?"

"But Amy. . . ."

"But Crabbing," Amy retorted in lugubrious imitation of his cry. "Don't try to look distressed . . . let's go . . . and I'll make you happy later. . . ."

"Really. . . ?" He could barely frame his surprise.

"Yes . . . I'm paying for lunch — it's my turn you know."

XIII. ANOTHER DECISION

BEZO LIVED a self-sufficient existence — proud of his tricks, and proud of his mistress. When alone he maintained unbroken silence, contenting himself with pecking on seeds, on cuttlefish bone, on the wires of his cage, or swinging himself with adroit mimicry of languor, and making, as he did so, a gentle gurgle at the bottom of his throat. If the sun shone brightly through the window, he grasped the wires of the cage and gazed out into the spaces beyond with a persistence that might be called wistfulness. He found an equal cause for attention, however, in the debris of lunches and breakfasts at the base of his hanging world of steel and chintz. He made a great to-do with his claws and his beak, moving the grains and the chaff about from here to there and back again, and then taking an immovable pose, he cocked his head to one side and gazed in sage fixation upon some indeterminate point on the horizon. Amy, alone, and Mrs. Nilins who looked after his daily wants, electrified him into an energy of song, discontinuous for the most part, and an unending fluttering of wings.

Amy had returned from the university. She had made no friends, at least none whom she might have asked home with her or whom she might have taken on excursions and trips about the city. Thanks to the interruptions planned for her by Crabbing — the better for her that they were simple and quiet — she had contrived to throw off the sense of desolate isolation which had entered into her life ever since the return from Eston. Tiberius, ill-starred and lonely, became an absorbing figure, emerging gradually from the foul wrappings of scandal and scurrility, a man who found in reticence and withdrawal the perfect answer to his critics and therefore led his own life of embittered contemplation beyond the eyes of a curious world. His punishment was just that — that the more he withdrew the more he aroused envious tongues to babble and spread evil-report of himself, his doings, his policies. It had set her mind thinking about herself, and the more she saw the true disillusioned leader turned sour philosopher, the more she wondered about herself and her incapacity to mingle with her fellows. What she desired most, she dared least, and what she obtained came unsought and unwanted. Most distressing was this habit of self-insulation and with it the lingering energy of the old faiths: to live in the light of standards, to distrust the emotions that channeled deep streams through her imagination.

Bezo had seen her come in, and had chirped his welcome.

"Hello, hello, Bezo," she exclaimed, putting a finger in the cage and stroking the bird's head lowered in contented anticipation. "What would I do without you, you big beast, you?"

She opened the cage and Bezo rushed out, a murmurous flutter of yellow, and flew in energetic delight throughout the room.

"On my shoulder, ugly one!" she commanded, and Bezo descended from his perch on top of the window jamb.

"Make the circuit," she cried, and Bezo jumped on to her head, hopped to the other shoulder, and back again.

Just then the bell jangled violently.

"Who can this be?" Amy asked, taking the bird on her finger and putting his bill into her mouth.

–2–

At the door stood Crabbing, his goat-like face lighted with unfeigned delight at finding Amy in.

Bezo had jumped immediately to the safe vantage of Amy's yellow hair, seeking protective assurance in its elevation and had begun almost at once a violent twitter of indignation. Why had this man forced himself upon the quiet of his play with Amy? Why had he entered at all into the sequestered confines that he and Amy occupied? So the bird seemed to be questioning, and for once Crabbing felt moved to retort in anger.

"Quit it, you little pest," he cried, snapping his finger close to the bird.

Bezo betook himself to the top of his cage and, like one who has been pursued and finds himself safe from seizure, had turned around and retorted in turn with an even more violent twittering than before.

Crabbing, as well as Amy, was forced into laughter.

"He certainly doesn't like you, Crabbing."

"Dogs don't," he confessed, taking a seat. "But why a diminutive nothing like that. . . ."

"This is unexpected, sir," said Amy, changing the subject. "I meant to complete Suetonius. . . ."

"I had a piece of news for you. . . . When did you leave the university?"

"Just a short while ago. . . ."

"Did you see any placards. . . ."

"There are always dozens. . . ."

"About the Contini marionettes. . . . ?"

"What?" exclaimed Amy, reddening.

"Famous Italian marionettes in a performance of Ariosto. . . ."

"Of course, it must be Donato's father. . . ."

"The boy himself was tacking up the announcements. . . ."

"Well, I am glad he has found something for his father. . . ."

"And a young woman with him . . . older of course, but handsome; in fact, I should say a provocative sort. . . ."

There was no mistaking the malice with which Crabbing expressed himself at this point, a childish gesture that alarmed as well as amused Amy. In her own mind, she said, "What a fool to tolerate the man," but was acutely aware, as she spoke the words, that the hurt he knew would come was there.

"That's why he has not replied to my letter," she ventured. "He must be tremendously taken up with all this. . . ."

"I suppose," suggested Crabbing, looking out of the window, "they'll make a pretty little penny out of their show. Fools and their money, you know, and especially in summer schools."

"Oh, I suppose," answered Amy, and then asked quickly, "What's out there that's so interesting?"

"A sneaky looking cat. I wouldn't be surprised but he has smelled the presence of your little feathered friend. . . ."

He faced Amy with these words, and at the same time approached close to her.

"Amy," he cried suddenly, knobby eyes, bearded chin, and the pouchy wrinkles on his cheek bones in a frantic motion to exhibit no feelings whatsoever, "Amy, you like that boy a lot . . . like him the way you would a man . . . don't you, don't you?" And as he questioned her he put his face closer and closer to hers, so that she saw the fine mesh of lines in his protruding eyeballs. "You really don't give a rap for me, do you, do you? And yet you permit me to come here day after day and go out with you and you arouse my hopes. . . . Amy, I am not a spring rooster . . . I am getting on in years. . . . You must not play with me. . . ."

"Crabbing!" cried Amy, as much in censure as in amazement.

Her voice had a quality in it at this moment that evidently suggested none of the Amy Bezo knew, and just as if he were a third party to the conversation, the canary flew about the room in great distress. Finally he found a perch on the window top and from that elevation twittered in undisguised anger at the intruder who had irritated his mistress.

"Crabbing," cried Amy, "I ought to tell you to leave at once. . . ."

"Isn't it too late now? Why did you not do it before you made me want you . . . want you, Amy, with the affection of a youth. . . ."

"Why too late, Crabbing?"

And as she asked the question, there flashed across her vision lines out of her Latin texts, lines of gossip which assumed the dignity of truth once they had been sufficiently repeated.

"You know I love you now. . . ."

Hateful thoughts crowded into Amy's mind: her stupidity in dealing with this rammish monster in front of her, anger at herself for cutting herself free of the feelings she had been having for Donato, greater anger even for not accepting Stephen, anyone, and not letting herself drift into a foul mess with Richard Crabbing.

"Amy, Amy!" she heard his words slip through his teeth, and the last syllable linger with a note of appeal. "I love you now . . . you must know it. Men have told you how superb your figure is . . . how charming your smile and your blue eyes . . . they have told you about that to win you . . . to have you a moment, a day . . . but I, Amy, I love you. . . ."

The afternoon was a hot one. The heat filtered into the rooms like an unseen mist that one could brush aside with one's hand and keep off like a curtain. Amy felt it press on her body, a clammy cloth that clung and clung to her. She tried to pull it away and thrust it aside. With each word that he uttered the sense of being smothered in the damp thick cloth of the heat increased, and with its increase she felt her whole body quiver with the chill of incipient nausea — a sensation that she invariably perceived in Crabbing's presence without experiencing it. She knew that he could have no suspicion of her feelings and dreaded that he would come nearer and, as he spoke, endeavor to put his arms about her. He would put his arms about her. . . .

"I am getting on in years, Amy," he continued, "and I do not disguise my thought . . . I do need a wife . . . you . . . we could be happy. . . ."

He did approach her as he spoke and he did hold out his hands. She could see each separate hair between his knotty knuckles, the fringe of long bristle-like hair under his cuff, every wrinkle in his coat sleeve, the creases made in his face by the strain of his unusual pronouncement.

"Oh, Amy," he cried, while all his face lighted up with a grotesque smile. "Amy, tell me you will marry me. . . ."

He was holding her in his arms, without strength, without impulsiveness, timidly, as if feeling his way to the end of the episode, fearful of consequences. The breath of the man mingled with the heat moving in the air, and encircled her neck, crawled up to her cheeks and ear.

Why could she be gentle with him? Why could she not drive him away as she had done Stephen, with her fists, her whole energy? Was it because he was so mean, so pathetic, so remonstrant? The questions were vivid streaks in her mind like matches one strikes in the dark. But they helped her not at all to do the very thing she most desired: push him off so that he would fall and tumble in some odd and antic position. Then she could laugh at him without hurting him, without malice or superiority, but with sufficient contempt to make him get up, walk away and never again cross her path. Instead however she felt his lanky arms fold her in, courage coming to him the more she failed to assert her unwillingness.

"You are making me happy, Amy," she heard in a whisper, a grateful whisper as an old man might employ to whom one has given a coin for alms. "I know you would like me . . . we shall be happy in this little nest . . . too big for you, too big for me, but snug and comfortable for two of us. . . ."

All this while she had said nothing, done nothing. Was she to allow him to put his bearded lips to hers, see his eyes shut with emotion? She shuddered, withdrawing into herself, but he was lowering his lips to her forehead . . . it was too horrible, as if all the clamminess of the heat were concentrated in them . . . she must get away. . . .

–3–

The bell at the top of the kitchen door jangled. Crabbing released her at once, looking at her like an embarrassed boy caught in mischief. Bezo made his shrill sounds of anger, flying about the room. Mrs. Nilins entered, and ran up quietly to Amy.

"That Italian boy, Amy . . . he's outside, says he wants to see you. . . ."

"Yes, let him in. . . ."

Only upon speaking the words did Amy realize what she had done. With them there surged into her mind like a full billow a complete summary of her many sweet moments in the companionship of Donato, and the memory of it was strange and refreshing like a wind that blows from nowhere and goes at once. She knew Crabbing was looking at her, and she knew too that Donato stood in the entrance between the rooms, framed in the light, his bronze features more than ever like the young god Hermes.

"There's your satyr, Stephen," she heard her mind saying, "that lean goat with his bulging eyes . . . and there, there is beauty, in that young boy . . . come from the gods . . . innocent . . . even as I. . . ."

"How do you do?" she said aloud. "This is a surprise, Donato. . . ."

Crabbing seemed to be looking at both of them at once as the boy advanced with outstretched hand, his face glowing with pleasure.

"I wanted to tell you something . . ." he said simply in a clear voice. "I shouldn't have come without letting you know . . . but the time is so short. . . ."

He saw Crabbing and stopped. A chill seemed to descend on them all.

"How do you do, sir?" he asked, bowing slightly.

"Oh, how do you do, young man?" answered Crabbing, condescendingly.

It was the first thing he had said in some minutes. He must have aroused the ire of Bezo thereby, for Bezo had flown back to his cage, grasped the wires, and chattered furiously. They all looked at the bird, everyone smiling except Crabbing.

"Oh, hush there," commanded Amy with a smile, and at the same time invited Donato to sit down. "Mrs. Nilins will bring a cold drink. . . ."

"No," answered Donato, "I can't, Miss Rollins. There's some one downstairs waiting for me. We were passing by. . . ."

"Bring him upstairs. . . ."

"I can't," he replied, smiling in an embarrassed way, but all his features aglow as if he were making a frank confession of something not altogether wicked but in some way reprehensible, sentimental, emotional. "It's a lady, Miss Rollins, in my art class. She helped me get up a marionette show. My father is showing his marionettes. Haven't you heard? She has a car, and we're carrying them to the college. . . ."

"Isn't that perfectly marvelous?" exclaimed Amy with genuine enthusiasm. "Perfectly marvelous. Why, I think it's a grand idea. . . ."

"Yes," continued Donato. "Miss Kreymdorf thought of it . . . I showed her all the heads I made. . . . I spoke about them to you . . . she said they were fine. And then she wanted me to show them in an exhibition but I said that my father's marionettes were better and she thought we ought to have a show and spoke to Mr. Borriner . . . so that's why we're having it . . . next Friday night . . . you'll come, won't you. . . .?"

"Of course, Donato," exclaimed Amy. "It's just too grand an idea. . . . I hope it will be a success."

"My father's gone crazy over it. . . ."

"You're charging admission of course. . . ."

"Too much, I think," interjected Crabbing.

"Do you really think so?" asked Donato innocently.

"One dollar's too much. . . ."

"I told Selma that . . . Miss Kreymdorf. . . ."

Donato for all his youth could not fail to note the slight change of color in Amy's countenance. It puzzled him, and he contented himself with merely looking at her with his grey eyes frankly open in query.

"Of course, I'll come," was all she said, however, and turned to Crabbing. "You'll take me, won't you, Mr. Crabbing?"

Crabbing complained openly about the price, thought it excessive for a fool thing like a marionette show.

"I meant you to come on a pass, Miss Rollins . . . and you too, Mr. Crabbing," Donato assured them. "I hope you come . . . it'll be fun . . . really . . ." and, smiling, he left.

–4–

"It ought to be amusing," Amy laughed, excited.

Crabbing kept looking at her through half-shut eyes, silent, motionless. Amy was acutely conscious of his feelings and the thoughts in his mind. She knew she had not been able to hide her pleasure at the sight of Donato. She knew too that like a little girl she had revealed how it had cut her to hear Donato speak of Miss Kreymdorf as Selma.

"It will be the remaking of his old father. . . ."

Crabbing reopened the subject of his proposal. There was no hesitation now in Amy's reactions.

"As I told you before, Crabbing, we had better not discuss it . . . if you love me," she said, her eyes appealing to him with a touch of laughter in them, "please do not talk about it. . . . I suppose you can see no reason, can you, for my asking you not to . . . ? There really is none. . . ."

"Then you do not care to see me . . . ?"

Crabbing had risen with great suddenness, as if he had been insulted by the remark he himself had made and stood facing her grimly, sourly.

"You look too funny for words, Crabbing. Sit down. . . ."

"It's that boy. . . ."

"Mr. Crabbing, please. . . ."

"You have played the fool with me. . . ."

Amy laughed, but Mr. Crabbing in his anger could not realize that it was hysterical laughter, an escape from a dilemma she could not solve. She remained in her chair, one knee over the other, her arms dangling at her side, staring at him in utter amazement, an amazement that was a compound of surprise and fear, surprise that he should have read her feelings correctly, fear that he meant to employ the knowledge in a sinister way. And yet what had she done? she kept questioning herself. What fear should there be? All the time that Crabbing maintained a steady stream of complaint and abuse, she kept revolving in her mind every aspect of her friendship with Donato, almost as if there had occurred between them reprehensible episodes, as if the feelings that rushed over her like waves had in reality carried her beyond into the regions of danger. She could hear Crabbing's voice and she could watch his expression, alternately alarming and then subdued, and yet not answer.

"You have strung me along, played the fool with me. . . ."

"There's been enough of this," finally Amy answered. "Will you please leave? I have heard enough. . . ."

"You will hear more."

This episode — an episode which Amy could not help but laugh at when she held it out as something detached from herself — and the events surrounding the performance of the marionettes on the grove of the campus, brought matters to a head for Amy. Added to them was the long letter from Philip, which for the first time since his departure gave some information about his doings.

The letter narrated in detail another attack of the combined asthma and nervous disorder which shook him to the marrow, depleted him of all energy, and made him capable of nothing except sitting up in his bed, like a sawdust bag folded in two, his neck craned to the perpendicular, his eyes bloodshot and staring helplessly into space. His vivid account of the several days and nights in the hospital, with his description of the frightened nurses — "they stood in the doorway of my room eyeing me cautiously as if they were on the threshold of hell" — recreated for her the last years of agonizing routine with both him and her mother. The whole evening after Crabbing's stupid outburst she went about her rooms like one afraid to go back to bed for fear of a nightmare returning with redoubled horror. She could not read, she forgot to water the flowers, and Bezo kept chirping away with a dogged gayety that evoked no response.

Snatches of Philip's letter dinned in her ears like the sound of coal running down a chute. *"On my own, Amy, with no imp shrieking in my insides 'don't pluck the strings out of your sister's life!' . . . it's a consummation, I tell you, sweet fratricide. . . . Whether the grave at the end of this new trek westward or a boxcar speeding through the madcap night, my heart's pumping*

*away regardless . . . what a meaningless tune it pumps to . . . inheritor of the ages'
culture, refined into a useless lilied dandy of learning, broken on the pinwheel of
a war, plaything of the giant idiots of the race. . . . Laugh at your cocktail parties.
. . . I saw how you longed for mother's death that you might be alone . . . life's a
flagon that's either too heavy or too light. . . . I have found it too heavy. . . . Hoboes
shall be my companions, roughnecks jumping the freights, rats sneaking in dives
along the wharves. . . . I want to feel hunted. . . ."*

And then she sat down deliberately, pencil in hand, and decided to
jot down what was the matter with her. Why could she not have taken
Stephen, or Crymble at college, or been bold enough to have left the city
with Donato as her companion? Why did she not attract other men — not
men like the impossible Crabbing? What rendered her incapable of making friends with the women at the school, or those in her classes at the
university? "It's not that you lack beauty" . . . she wrote out definitely in
long hand . . . "but you are endowed in your own mind with classic qualities that stamp *forbidding* all over you. It's not that you lack a mind, but
that you have believed that mentality is important. It's not that you lack
a sense of humor, but that you let it interfere in crucial moments — in the
case of Stephen, for instance. . . . It's not that you have no feelings, but that
your feelings are too intense and you keep them down. . . . It's not that
you cannot plan your life, but that you let yourself drift. . . . Amy, you're
a fool." She underscored fool several times and then laughed outright,
laughed so loud and so long that Bezo mistook it for a form of singing and
burst into his own gay arias. Then something strange occurred to her; she
heard her own laughter as if it were another person's and it frightened
her. She rose from her chair, and ran to the mirror, her hands in her hair,
and gazed fixedly at her image. Her fine regular features seemed to have
sagged, and the slightly overfull eyebrows to have jutted out as if attempting to shade the excessive brilliance that had flamed up in the eyes. The
corners of her lips had drooped and she could see them quiver, them and
the immediate cheek muscles above.

"But I am lovely," she cried to herself, and once more the narcissism
at the core of her being asserted itself — the narcissism which in some
fashion made her feel that she was meant to be of importance in the life
of others, that it was venial to employ her beauty in self-gratification, that
her body was too sweet to waste. She seized her blouse with both hands,
tore it open and gazed unabashed at her white bosom.

XIV. THE MARIONETTE SHOW

THAT AFTERNOON was the last Amy saw Mr. Crabbing for the summer. The night of the marionette show he did not come. She finally went alone and occupied a seat far in the rear. By the time she arrived, everybody had moved as far forward as possible, seizing even those seats distinctly marked "Reserved." The performance had been hastily arranged. Many difficulties delayed the showing of the marionettes and caused considerable confusion in the fairly large audience. Seats meant to sell at higher prices were taken by those who had paid less; there was much excited talk. The irritation of the audience was unmistakable. Mr. Borriner's big head bobbed up and down among the rows of the seated heads while there emanated from his mouth an unending series of apologies. Selma Kreymdorf seemed to be pursuing him and adding her own excuses. Her large frank face glowed with uninterrupted smiles. As she maintained her chase of Borriner she stopped to talk to this one and the other one.

Amy was aware of an undercurrent of dissatisfaction, and in her heart, despite the annoyance at Crabbing's failure to appear and despite a restlessness of mood as if a sharp and peculiar catastrophe was ahead of her, prayed that the thing might come off successfully, that Donato might achieve the distinction she thought would accrue to him. She looked around anxiously for a glimpse of him and managed only to see Borriner followed by Selma, and she knew at once that this was the woman of whom Donato and Crabbing had spoken.

At once she saw that there was something in the manner of Selma entirely lacking from hers, something which won to immediate happiness without brooding, without questioning, without doubts. She admired her vigor, her ready words, her quick repartee. She admired the laughter in her voice, rich and deep, like an accompaniment so deftly played that one fails to distinguish it from the entire melody. And Amy realized, as if her aloofness, her diffidence and the timidities that they inspired had rendered her intuitions doubly keen, almost clairvoyant, that in the solicitousness of Selma for the success of the enterprise was more than the interest in an art form of another day and another country.

All about her, they talked of nothing else. Commedia dell'Arte, Punch and Judy, famous Pierrots and Columbines, old mummer customs and the comic mimes of the Greeks, the new art of the pantomime in the movies, the feeble attempts at pantomime on Broadway . . . the air buzzed with learned gossip, a babble of pretentious interest. Two hatless ladies sat next to Amy, fanning themselves with the programs, gazing at everyone, rising occasionally from their seats.

"Irma look that's Professor Thornbit. . . ."

"He doesn't look much, does he?"

"Well, what did you expect he'd be — like a senator?"

"When will they start?"

"Oh, don't be impatient so soon, Irma . . . you've been impatient ever since you've got to New York. . . ."

"Oh, I suppose this'll be just another fool thing. . . . I haven't seen anything yet. . . ."

"You ought to have stayed home. . . ."

"I ought to have and there's no doubt. . . ."

"You would have to go to Europe to see a thing like this. . . ."

"I could have died happy without seeing it. . . ."

"You're positively tiring, Irma. . . ."

"If I didn't need to pass that course and if the professor had not insisted we see this . . . what's it got to do with Shakespeare, I'd like to know. . . ."

They were grey-haired and gently withered, their thin hands wafer-like in the uneven lights of the Japanese lanterns that swung from the trees and clung like glowworms to bush and fence. The weariness that comes from an occupation without variety and without excitement had settled on their features. Curiosity had left their eyes. Amy looked at them and shivered slightly.

She turned her head and craned forward. What was happening behind the heavy blue canvas stretched across the corner made by the meeting of the two iron fences? There were lights behind the canvas that outlined it vividly and cast into prominence the painted horseman in armor against a background of hills daubed with the carelessness of improvisation. And the same light brought into focus the marionette warriors at each end of the curtain, erect and superb in gilt armor and sword, vizors down, guarding the entrances. But the interest she was taking in everything, the happiness she felt at Donato's getting the opportunity to do a thing of this sort faded away before the persistent sense of being alone, marooned in a sea of people, desolate with hunger for love and companionship. She had fallen into a reverie out of which she was startled by the clapping of hands. Selma Kreymdorf appeared in front of the tiny stage to explain. How Amy envied the young woman's aplomb, the assertiveness of her gestures, and especially the open face playing with smiles that never showed a symptom of nervousness or constraint.

Her explanation was simple.

"Just a boy in the clay modeling class . . . we'll have to have an exhibition of his heads, and we want you all to come to it. This is just improvised, you understand, a little hasty, we are afraid, but it represents the marionette theater as you would see it in the crowded streets of Messina or Naples before the movies. . . . You have no idea of the variety of their figures . . . literally hundreds . . . after the show we want you to remain and come up front and they'll be lined up for you. . . . Now I know you

are impatient, but I must tell you about this marvelous boy's father . . .
a marvelous old man himself . . . full of the romance of old Italy — and
how many of us have not felt it? — steeped in Ariosto and Tasso and the
legends of chivalry . . . why, it's just too marvelous to think we can have it
all transferred here on the banks of the Hudson in this commercial town
. . . he tried to start a theater in Little Italy, but like other artists in this in-
dustrial age, especially here in this huge and bustling metropolis, he was
neglected and now we hope that possibly this will be a beginning of a big
movement to restore the simple art of illusion — real illusion it is — this
marionette theater. . . ."

"She's going around in a circle and ought to sit down," piped Irma.

"Irma!" pleaded her sister.

"She ought to at that," insisted Irma.

Amy shared her sentiments but from different motives. Amy's simplicity consisted largely of the belief that everybody else plunged directly into the
thing over which she hesitated. Selma's aplomb and decisiveness not only
aroused everybody but were proof that the delight manifest in her words,
the praise that they hinted at, was not without strong personal feelings for
Donato. Amy wondered. Donato was handsome; this young woman — so
different from her. But . . . the boy was so young. Selma would not dare. . . .

"And here is Mr. Donato Contini," smiled Selma, dragging the boy by
the hand and playfully thrusting him forward. Against the bright square
of light, his head was sharply defined with its classic regularity of feature,
the compact curls of the hair, the straight even neck. Once again the sense
of being in the presence of Hermes become human and returned to live
among mortals, possessed Amy. She could not mistake the impression he
made on the audience, and she knew it was not because he was presenting
a marionette show. The applause was general and real. She knew it was
his splendid chiseled figure, the head like a young god's, the eyes that
were wells of brightness if quiet and dim and sad. And she rejoiced, and
she knew that her rejoicing was not completely for the boy's success.

"It's my father's show," is all he could say . . . "I'm helping him. . . ."

He was about to go when Selma came forward again, put her arm
through his and turned him once more toward the audience.

"What's it all going to be about?" she asked.

"The fight before the walls of Jerusalem between Tancred and Clorinda and the death of Odoardo and Gildippe . . . and if we have time how
Orlando slew Gradasso and how Flordelis joined her lover Brandimarte
in his grave. . . ."

As he spoke he smiled and the smiles revealed the unusual ancient
Greek quality of his countenance much as if in him had been preserved
and then recast the lingering influences of Athens in that island whence
his people came — the melting pot and filter of the races that have lived
and fought on the shores of the Mediterranean. Once more Amy knew
that it was this and not the performance that won the crowd to him.

Selma had been right. Despite the alien tongue in which the dialogue was spoken, despite the angularity of the puppet's movements, despite the queerly painted drop of the tower of David, the illusion was complete. Smiles and even laughter greeted the procession of the knights, male and female, that purported to come out of Tasso's pages and fight in the flesh before an audience that could not know the anguish and the chivalry of the Crusades. Amusement rippled through the spectators as Clorinda, clad in yellow-painted armor, a tiger at the top of her helmet, on a stuffed horse with mane and tail flowing with ribbons, galloped to the center of the stage, raised her diminutive spear, and shouted in the powerful voice of a man tuned to the inflections and lightness of a woman's:

"*Indarno, indarno chiedi tu mio nome . . . codardo . . . perche, perche . . . combattere ci dobbiamo e alla morte. . . .*"

They laughed when Tancred, huger, on a horse more grotesque, daubed with blood, a gigantic mustache drooping from under his vizor, rushed after her, and bellowed:

"*Barbaro discortese, alla vendetta.*"

The audience would have smiled even more superiorly could it have known how distorted and badly quoted were the words of Tasso. As it was, they found the combat between the lovers thrillingly conducted, and after their first outburst of laughter, settled into real enjoyment of the dexterity with which horse and rider were managed, the skill with which the swords and then the battle axes were manipulated, the range of the voice that spoke for both the combatants. And when the lovers lay dying, both wounded to the death and for the first time recognizing each other and the short hour they had to live, the audience fell into a silence. The voice of Don Emanuele, despite its tremolo, its occasional break, was filled with the accents of poetry in the grand manner, and the vigorous lines of Tasso, truncated, amended, and filled in though they were, fell with force and melody into the air.

"*Amico, hai vinto; io ti perdon . . . perdona*
Tu a me. . . ."

Genuine excitement seized the audience when whole squadrons of paynim horsemen clashed with dozens of the crusading knights, plumes waving, spears brandishing, gyves and cuirass clanking, horses falling, and above it all the voices of the unrelenting killer, the defiant vanquished, the whinnying of wounded chargers. Oaths and the battle cries of Christian and of pagan filled the air. . . . This was no mere replica of a battle . . . this was battle idealized and eternalized, its distinguishing elements brought into quick and poignant focus. . . .

"Don't you think it grand, Irma?"

"Well, well . . . it's stupid but I wouldn't say I'm not moved. . . ."

Amy woke to the reality of the moment when they spoke. Could this be possible, she thought, and do they know at school of this remarkable boy? They call him thief, and they say his brother. . . . Her heart surged with feeling. Something must be done. Had they seen the home in which he lived? Did they know his poverty? . . .

Several other scenes followed. There was a humorous one where Orlando resisted having his senses restored to him. The divine buffoonery of Ariosto leaped into vivid life. The strutting, loud-voiced Rodomantad, the gallant Rinaldo, the love-consumed Flordelis, and a half-dozen other famous heroes and heroines of the old romances quickened into activity, once more alive, alive in an imagination that had forgotten towering apartment houses, clanging trolleys, the screeching of the boats on the river. . . .

Once more Selma was pushing Donato in front of the audience. His head seemed preternaturally enlarged, and yet the features once more wore their guise of an ancient god's. The people crowded around him.

"You must do it again. . . ."

"Just too marvelous for words. . . ."

"You must exhibit your carvings. . . ."

Amy stood indecisively on the edge of the group that had surrounded the miniature stage. Don Emanuele, glowing with excitement, had drawn the inner curtain and showed a network of rods from which were hanging dozens of puppets, each one dressed in the full regalia of its personality. He took one down and passed it around. Exclamations of surprise and admiration punctuated the hubbub.

"My son, he made that one, that one with the anger on her face. . . ."

Professors of English expounded on the remarkable fidelity to the text that had been displayed in the performance.

"Closer to the story than the movies get," Dr. Thornbit was saying, holding up the timid form of Erminia, seated on a bedizened palfrey. "This one for instance . . . remarkable . . . such devotion in the features, unrequited affection, sadness on the lips perennially quivering to speak out the secret of her love. . . ."

The lecture room manner boomed in his voice. The younger people left him. Donato attracted them where he stood at Selma's side. They plied him with questions.

"My father's father too . . . we all helped. . . . I made many of the heads . . . oh, when I was a boy . . . my mother and sisters made most of the dresses . . . no . . . we don't show them . . . never went on the stage. . . ."

As they left him, Amy heard remarks and comments that made her happy.

"He ought to make money. . . ."

"Nothing like it in this country. . . ."

"Stunning, isn't he?"

"Simply stunning. . . ."

Amy, however, had no opportunity to offer Donato her congratulations. She would not push through the circle surrounding him, and evidently he had forgotten all about her and would make no attempt to seek her out. She waited until the attendants came to remove the lanterns and pile up the seats. She saw Selma put her arm through Donato's and go behind stage. There she saw them taking down the puppets and putting them in boxes. She saw them looking at each other, laughing over this or that, smiling if their eyes exchanged glances.

The illusion created by the diminutive figures was still strong in Amy's consciousness. The figures of Don Emanuele, and of Donato and Selma appeared larger than the natural size. Something grotesque at first attached itself to their movements. But as she stood watching, she lost the feeling of this distorted reality, the enlarged figures seemed to have fallen into a pattern of hugeness as in a dream, and somehow, when she caught sight of Selma and Donato facing each other silently, nervously, their eyes glowing with feeling, Amy could not believe it. Nor could she believe that the next second Selma had raised her hands and, pinching Donato's cheeks, had drawn his face close to hers and kissed him, laughing gaily in the night.

XV. SCHOOL

SUMMER SESSION came to a close, leaving Amy four weeks with no definite routine. Since the marionette performance she had studiously avoided places where she might encounter Donato. At the university she had maintained the aloofness which rendered her incapable of making friends. Professor Filtray had been impressed with the skill of her translations, the soundness of her judgments, the organization of her material. He spent a whole period analyzing her paper on Tiberius, reading selections from it, and getting her to elaborate orally various of her comments. Several of the students remained after class to express their admiration.

A fussy little fellow offered her a nervous hand. He wore glasses that cut into his nose and temples, had sparse hair that streaked in all directions on his head, a small ball-like chin, ball-like cheeks, and short ball-like nose.

"Just grand, Miss Rollins, just grand. How did you do it?" His voice was sharp, thin, apologetically nasal. "Would you show me your notes sometime? Mrs. Barritson is working here with me this summer, and she would ever so much like your coming over to tea. Could you possibly?"

Amy excused herself with thanks, and the thin voice shrilled his grief.

"We're just the two of us, don't you know. We have seen so little of people here. Professor Filtray thought he could come too. Well, well, I am sorry. . . . Couldn't induce you. . . ?" He cocked his little head roguishly and his eyes twinkled far behind his enormous spectacles.

"Poor little man," she thought, as she walked out in the company of the professor and several students. And as she said it, she felt angry with herself, and she thought, "Poor little you . . . with your airs!"

Professor Filtray never moved ten steps without an inordinate collection of books under his arms, and he always walked as if he took two steps with one foot before daring to move the other. One was always surprised that he made any progress. It was the same with his voice and all his gestures. He did come to the end of sentences, and those who heard him invariably blinked their eyes in a sort of consternation at the advent of the period. If he raised his long excitable fingers to punctuate a remark, one got interested in their uninterrupted movements and the persistent poise of the hand in midair, and one heaved ever the slightest sigh when the hand did finally find a lower level. But he never was too busy to stop and talk, no matter how many books weighted down his lanky arms. He always had a good-morning or a good-afternoon, but he never talked of anything not connected with Roman history, and if it were not connected with Roman history he was certain to find a parallel in Roman history.

"Miss Rollins," he drawled as he stumbled alongside of her, "that was an excellent thought that the truth of a personality is never revealed to even the shrewdest observer, like the rose deep in the center of a bud . . . excellent . . . excellent! How could mere collectors of gossip like Suetonius know so much about the motives of Tiberius? Excellent, Miss Rollins!" He turned to her most eagerly: "Would you call on Mrs. Filtray and me? We could expand on the subject."

Amy confidently said she would call. But when she had got home, she sat down on the couch, her books on her lap, stared into spaces far beyond the walls of her room, and though she was unconscious of space and time and of the mental processes that cohere us into ourselves, she shook her head and she knew she was not going to the Filtrays'. Instead she phoned and though she was compelled to wait for fully a minute to hear the end of the professor's sentence of entreaty and regret, she found it impossible to change her mind.

She spent that evening trimming her flowers, making a list of ferns to complete the arrangement for the northern windows. Bezo hopped about, perched on her shoulders and chirped, allowed himself to be carried on the tips of her outstretched fingers, and then suddenly dropped. At such times he flew, as if in a temper, to the top of his cage and chattered ferociously. Mrs. Nilins had taken to coming upstairs in the evening, sitting in the small armchair Mrs. Rollins used to occupy, folding her hands in her lap, and rocking gently and interminably. Only occasionally would she find it sufficiently worthwhile to interrupt her motion and silence with a remark to Bezo, or a comment that had no relation to any immediate concern of either hers or Amy's, and always in her bated breath.

Crabbing had apparently disappeared, Donato had neither written nor called, and for weeks there had been no letter or telegram from Philip. Miss Batten alone had written scoldingly.

"For shame to stay in the city these hot months. Pack up your bag, young girl, and hoof it up here to the mountains. No men, attached or otherwise, to ruffle your placidity! We simply sit in chairs and let nature do the rest. No men, I say! A few untrousered specimens who find it herculean to knot sweaters around their necks, there are, but three young unskirted females and the most abbreviated pants have appropriated them. What they do away from the porch all day is a secret that only solicits winks from the rest of us. . . ."

Amy was not persuaded. The four weeks passed wearily but not unprofitably. She had become acquainted with all manner of house plants and the best methods of caring for them. She had studied the history of bird training and the available birds which might be trained. She had set her mind on purchasing a myna and later a finch and hoped to cultivate among the three of them interesting tricks of association. In her own mind she had definitely concluded that for the rest of her life there was to be school, at some future date a trip to Europe, possibly a trip very soon to Italy. For years she had longed to go, extend the trip to Greece, visit the scenes more familiar to her from her reading than places she had been to in this country. One thing was certain, that unless there occurred an accident over which she had no control, this routine would have to suffice. She had thought of tracing Philip and recalling him. She could look after him. The two would be sufficient unto each other.

–2–

Only one interruption intervened during the four weeks, an interruption which was to mean more in her life than she could possibly have suspected. Selma Kreymdorf sent her a little note on thin, blue, three-by-four paper. It was written with a stub pen in a handwriting that allowed her only ten words to a sheet.

"A matter of importance dictates this note. Please do make it possible to see me this Wednesday morning." The finished product looked like a batik pattern.

She dashed in without apology of any sort and, unabashed, stared at everything. She admired the bird, the rows of flowerpots; she admired the replica of the Parthenon, the fine print of Whistler's *Carlyle*.

"Imagine the tricks of the bird! Well . . . imagine . . . ivory is it? And this print! They do wonders nowadays. Imagine having something almost like an original. . . ."

Her close blue felt could not entirely enclose the brown mist of her hair, while the pink boucle suit brought greater color to her cheeks. As she leaned forward, her full luscious figure, the glowing skin, the well-tended nails, the slight scent of perfume, made Amy understand that here was a person meant to love and to accept love when it came and as it came.

"It's about Donato, Miss Rollins. You must help me to orient him properly. He's a genius. A marvelous boy, really. Imagine what he has done in his environment!"

Besides greeting her visitor, Amy had said nothing, except to make short answers regarding Bezo, the Parthenon, and her flowers. In no case had she added more than Selma wanted to know. She had glanced at her guest's rich clothes with the hasty thoroughness women know, and then, as if she had not seen or admired, looked up and waited for Selma to speak.

"He's told me a lot about you . . . ever since I met him this summer. But he tells me he is tired of school, wants to go in for sculpturing. He has genius. Oh, he has genius, and I admire his ambition. Don't you? But it would be silly leaving school, wouldn't it? He ought to remain until he graduates . . . shouldn't he? . . ."

Amy made no attempt to interrupt her.

"He has become restless. . . . His father can get him to stay at school . . .

but the boy doesn't want to . . . shouldn't he, though?"

"I haven't seen much of him recently. I don't know what's prompted him to this. . . ."

"Seeing a bit of the world, I suppose . . . his success with the marionettes . . . his exhibition. . . . He's been asked out a good deal by a lot of giddy girls. . . . He had seen so little of big restaurants, sumptuous homes . . . then all of a sudden. . . . You see what has happened? You'll help him. . . ."

"Can't you, Miss Kreymdorf?"

Amy did not change either the tone of her voice or the direction of her steady gaze, undisturbed, unpenetrating, but fixed and interested. Despite her poise, Selma displayed ever the slightest flutter of eyelids, a flutter which did not escape Amy and which seemed to acknowledge that something more was intended in Amy's simple question than met the ear.

"I have tried, Miss Rollins. . . ."

Selma suggested the greatest despair in the emphatic drawling of the "tried."

"You have done so much for him. . . ." Amy said, still feeling her way to affirm the suspicions that had gathered in her mind since seeing Selma kiss Donato.

"We've been very good friends this summer. . . . He's really a marvelous boy, but Latin, don't you know . . . so Latin . . . so much feeling and so many enthusiasms . . . and such abrupt depressions!"

Amy had understood enough. Selma's words revealed nothing, but the quality of her inflections, the earnestness of her statements, the pleading in her tone. . . . Amy was sure that between Selma and Donato had occurred more than the simple friendship of which she had been told. She would see Donato. But why, why? What was it to her? She leaned close to Selma.

"If you see him soon, will you tell him to call me up?"

As soon as she had spoken the words, both she and Selma knew that they should not have been uttered.

"But I couldn't do that . . . he doesn't know a thing about my coming here . . . and I don't see him very often. . . ."

"Should I write to him? You see," explained Amy, "that would be impossible. I would have to mention something about your visit . . . not that you were here, but the purpose of it. How would he take my knowing about his plans? How would he know that I knew?"

Selma smiled, sat back in her chair, and employed the occasion for so much movement to place her white leather bag with its facing of sea-blue design on the couch to her side. But before doing so, she had taken out a scented handkerchief and held it lightly to her lips and nose.

"I have just the slightest touch of hay fever," she tried to explain, holding in her breath for the imminent explosion. There was no explosion, and so she replaced the handkerchief and the bag.

"Very grand lady," thought Amy. "Very grand indeed . . . but not the type for Donato . . . he'd be just a little pin in her corsage. . . ."

"In a way it's a good thing I have it, Miss Rollins. Always gives me an excuse to get away. . . . I should cultivate it if I didn't have it. . . ."

Amy smiled most dutifully, and hastened to say,

"Possibly I should shut the windows . . . or is it the flowers?"

"Oh, no, oh, no," replied Selma, with both palms raised. "No . . . I must be going . . . there are all kinds of reasons for my getting away besides the hay fever . . . maybe you understand. . . . Donato is so young. . . . We have got to like him a lot. . . . Mr. Borriner and I and some of our friends . . . but he's so young. . . . We trust to you . . . he ought to be at school . . . after all an artist must be given a background. . . ."

"I shall try," answered Amy in a whisper.

The whisper, designed to hide a thought, exposed it completely. Selma smiled. And her smile intended to hide her knowledge of a thought, revealed it fully.

"But, Bezo, Bezo," cried Amy, a minute later, addressing the bird as it clung to the cage, head cocked to one side and eyes fixed with great intentness upon his mistress. "Bezo, such a thing can't be, can it, can it?"

–3–

Miss Kreymdorf had left in a cloud of perfume with a profusion of apologies and thanks that still echoed throughout the room. There was no doubt in Amy's mind as to the relations between Selma and Donato. The thought left her numb, overpowered, as if she had been struck by a weight that had fallen slowly and crushed only her feelings. Selma had suddenly dramatized Amy's struggle, for she was the kind of person that arouses not only envy but the anger that is inverted wistfulness in women like Amy — women born too late to accept the attitude of denial with utter resignation and born too soon to have accepted the newer philosophy of experiment.

"Can this thing be?" she asked Bezo, stopping slightly after each word. "But he is so young . . . so young . . . he must be (she paused for so long that Bezo pecked at a bar, annoyed to have no voice addressed to him) saved, (Amy smiled at the word, and yet she used it again) saved. . . . But from what, Bezo, from what? You tell me that, you imprisoned brute, you ugly little monster with the ugly little voice . . . tell me that. What have you done with yourself in your tiny cage? You never had a chance to try your wings and fly the length and breadth of the woods and seek the unending blue spaces beyond them, and stop at hilltop pools to bathe, and garner the grain out of the fields, and peck at cherries? What do you know about it?"

How Bezo enjoyed the sound of the voice! He turned his head to one side and another, stood perfectly still, flew a few inches up the bars, chirped once or twice and manifested every symptom of attention and delight.

"What would you say if you could talk, Bezo, hey? I know. Let Donato alone . . . let him seek his own ways . . . school is bad enough. Why crush him in the traps of other uniformities and conventions and routines? Let him alone. But he must go to school, and he must be a good boy while there and do his work and stay away from me. . . . He will want to start his club . . . . Shall we let him, Bezo? But he is a dear boy . . . what does he want with me? . . . look at how I dress, Bezo dear . . . aren't you ashamed of your Amy? Just a plain little print at the bargain counter, and, oh, I am afraid they'll all think my shoes don't match and, look, not a bit of jewelry around my neck . . . but it is a firm neck, Bezo, and well-proportioned and tall. . . ."

–4–

Instead of writing, Amy decided to call. She had hoped that Donato would be home with his father, and she would give her interest in their dolls as a pretext for her visit. On her way she recollected how she had looked forward to making friends with her pupils, to knowing about their home life and their parents. She smiled as she reflected that it had taken two months of teaching to show her how such idealism had become submerged in the weariness of large classes, burdensome clerical duties, a sense of complete division between teachers and pupils, and a general air of pessimism and cynicism about teaching and its results which was but a reflection of the war and had settled upon the school like a blight.

This was actually her first sally into the dim regions that were the pupils' homes. They might just as well have lived on desert isles or among the ice floes of the poles. They could just as well have been the sons of blackguards and drunkards as of respectable hardworking laborers and store keepers. She did not know them, nor did many of the teachers. Occasionally one of the parents did come to school, harassed, or irritated, not knowing what it was all about. The time to discuss with them the children and their welfare was always so limited.

But as she walked now through crowded sections in which the noise of trolleys and cars was a persistent dull accompaniment to the quick jangled medley of voices, she wondered more and more that the children should learn anything at all. What could Latin be to them, Virgil, Caesar? Or for that matter the Euclidian mysteries or the fall and the rise of empires? What the delicate cadences of Keats or the sinewy lines of Browning? Or could these boys and girls find these subjects, so remote from their living, escapes and retreats? Some of them did, and many of them emerged remade. Witness her colleagues . . . sons and daughters of immigrants, transformed by the process. But they would have been by any process. Vitality and genius break through the fetid shells of these dirty buildings, come to flower in the malodorous piles of garbage in the gutters, utter the music of their hearts far above the confusion of the streets.

Such was Donato and such might have been his brother, Giulio, could he have been saved. Saved? Yes . . . as she was trying to save Donato.

But saved from what and for what? Like Philip, for instance? . . . Philip, counterpart of Donato, with a mind attuned to the thought of the ages, a poet in every fiber of his being, educated in the time-honored curriculum, and thereby incapacitated for living in the world of machinery and business. She would turn back. Let Donato take a fling at what he wanted to do. Why interfere? Who could be sure that any pressure, any guidance would be the right one? It would be all hit and miss in the long run, and the finished assemblage of ideas and skills and information would bear no particular relation to the efforts put into it. And who was she to offer assistance? What could she do except repeat the platitudes and say amen to the traditional? What had she done with herself?

As she climbed the foul-smelling steps to Donato's apartment these thoughts became hissing metal in her consciousness as if the formed mind had melted into its component metals and was now seeking to return to the original earth whence it came. Unpainted walls, steps that had been worn into troughs, accumulated dust of weeks, warm puffs of cooking odors from the open doors, the shrieking and crying of children, laughter above it all, and the sound of mothers scolding, radios in full blast, damp darkness. . . . Amy shrank with the sense of hopeless unrelieved limitations . . . like life under moist stones, crawling, compact, tumbling. . . .

–5–

Don Emanuele opened the door in great surprise. All the other doors were opened too, and out of each one several heads craned out, and out of each head issued a question in a whisper, or a shout, "Who is she, what does she want?" The word went round that she was a teacher, and the word teacher was repeated over and over again like an echo.

"Come in, come in," said Don Emanuele, bowing profoundly.

He offered her the only chair with a back. He stooped to brush the dust off, using a bandanna from his neck. His long mustaches with their vigorous ends, upstanding and twisted both, belied the sagging muscles under the eyes, the sallow hollows of the cheeks and the colorless lips. Only the eyes brightened with similar energy. The stoop of his shoulders had become more accentuated and the head unsteady so that the light of his pupils was never fixed and quiet but fluttering like a flame on a candle stump and as disturbed by the slightest movement.

"You excuse me," he said, spreading out his palms and nodding to the sleeveless undershirt that covered his body and to the blue denim overalls held up by a cord-like belt. "You excuse me . . . it is the hot day, and I am just this way . . . it is the great honor. . . ."

The smiles that flowed up and down his features relieved the tired face of a portion of its sallowness.

"I am not working today . . . no work for many, many days now . . .

we have hard time. . . ."

Amy's inexpensive print dress and little straw hat gave her an extraordinary distinction in the poor room: coal stove under a dirty white mantelpiece, uneven and uncovered boards for flooring, blue oilcloth table cover zigzagged with dust-filled cracks, a gas jet hanging from the middle of the ceiling with a broken mantle and finger-stained globe. Amy shuddered, and as she shuddered resolution coursed in every vein. Donato must be saved; he must be led out of all this. At a glance she saw the story of his father's present condition, and it must not be recapitulated in Donato's career. The same grey eyes and the same brilliance, but the same sadness and the same too hurt sensitivities, the same dreaming and the same quick lapses into despondency. That Giulio's death had not meant the death of the father seemed to her miraculous, but that they lived in this fashion, that he could not make his cafés and his marionettes paying enterprises was not at all difficult to explain.

These walls meant nothing to Don Emanuele. Any other sort of walls would have meant the same with all their grime and their flaked paint and the gaps that revealed the slats beneath. Walls close one in. Stoves heat and enable one to cook. Backless chairs provide seats. What more does one want? The light from the windows, hot and glaring, was the only reality of the world outside the barren rooms that made its way inside. And as she took the scene in, surveying it almost without shame at her frank scrutiny, she recalled the voice that had leaped all reality into the realms of romance and endowed the angular puppets with an animation that was the breath of life itself. It had been a subtler and more fluid protoplasm than that which makes bones and the muscles of the heart.

"It is the great honor," Don Emanuele repeated, "the great honor, Miss Rollins. . . ."

"Where's Donato, Mr. Contini? . . ."

"Oh, Donato!" Don Emanuele raised his palms to the level of his cheeks and shrugged his shoulders. The smile vanished and the light in the eyes became sadder.

"I came to see him, and you too. He is a fine boy . . . a fine boy."

Amy shouted the word *fine* as if she might convey by that means that it was not quite the word she wanted to employ. She did say finally and in a shout too, "He's a marvelous boy . . . a genius . . . a genius. . . ." And as she said so she was conscious of having repeated Selma's language and wondering whether she might have made a similar impression — a thought which amused her when she thought of it later.

"Donato?" asked Don Emanuele. "Who knows where Donato is? He is not here much now. He have money in his pockets, and he goes. Where? Bought fine suits. . . . I do not work now . . . but he has money from the marionettes. . . . You saw the marionettes, no? You like them? It is the great art, the art of marionettes . . . but the art is not great in this country . . . they will not come . . . they like the cinematografo . . . no . . . the marionettes, they are the old world. . . . 'Donato,' I said. 'Donato, you will try to make the success with marionettes, no? a teatro . . . it will make money . . . ' 'No,' he say, 'I will be the scultore. . . .'" Don Emanuele shrugged his shoulders and again a great sadness came into his eyes. "He is the great artist . . . you see the heads he make. . . ."

He ran into the windowless room just beyond the kitchen and came out immediately with an old soap box which he placed at Amy's feet. He himself kneeled on the floor in front of her and continued talking, offering her one head after another.

"This head, you see, it will be Alessandro il grande . . . and this one Clitimnestra . . . you know Clitimnestra . . . she was in Donato's book and he make . . . he make all these gods and he will make the play . . . but this . . . oh, Miss Rollins" (she loved the way he accented the second syllable and caressed the whole word)" this show how great, the genius. . . . It is Ercole . . . you see the beard . . . all the fine curls so close together . . . and the nostrils? You see the nostrils? You see he breathes . . . he works too hard . . . the muscles pull and the nostrils must breathe in air, more air, more air . . . you see. . . ."

Again that strange voice of many rises and blends transported him beyond the dreary precincts of the wretched tenement, crashed through the poverty-stricken confines, and carried her away too. She looked in amazement upon the transformed face, filled now with color, the eyes brilliant, the lips open in animated query. She saw too how he loved the boy and saw again how utterly without knowledge of the immediate values that bring comforts and security he was. And as she understood it, again the determination became strong that, come what may, she must bend every effort to save Donato — saving having become by this time so general a figure that it symbolized all that was fine and beautiful without suggesting anything concrete enough for her to have defined it. As she scanned the various carved countenances, she marveled not so much at the dexterous fingers that wrought so tenderly and so surely but at the resemblance between father and son. Here he was now, out, spending money doing what? Had he fallen in love with Selma or with one of the other girls she had mentioned, and was he now giving all his time and all the few pennies he had made to live as those girls lived, to go into waters beyond his depth?

"But he is still making these things, is he not?" she asked.

"The school close, and he stop. No . . . he is away now . . . all day . . . and at night too . . . he is where all the time? I don't know. . . ."

"He will go back to school?"

Don Emanuele rose to his feet, several of the diminutive heads in his hand.

"He will not go back, he say. He will get work, and he will study in art school too. I think it not so good. You think so too?"

"Why, yes," Amy cried out, so eagerly that she was afraid he might attribute her agreement to feelings other than those of a teacher's interest.

"Why, yes. He is a good student. He has one year more. He must get his diploma. We all must have as good an education as we can. . . ."

But as she spoke the words, her cynical young colleagues at the school ranged themselves in leering effigies around her. She recognized that the infinite contempt that they expressed was the reverse of their longings, frustrated in part by the limited pay of their profession, in part by the narrow circle of contacts it allowed, in part by the poverty of their own vitality. But she dreaded the sharpness of their language, clever, sparkling, epigrammatic. "Education produces the arrow collar boys and strangles the artist in his infancy." She heard the statement repeated in a hundred ways. "Those who have ability don't need an education; those who haven't are not spoiled by it." Could she defend her conduct before them at the luncheon table? And yet, she sensed in some dim way that in the formal schooling ahead of him for the next year with the imposed necessity of application and fixed hours and steady tasks was to be found the salvation of this boy, whirled at too tender an age into the false gayeties of parties and lovemaking and. . . . The words seared her thoughts even as she said them, and only the resolution that she must bring him back to his studies remained throbbing, alive. . . .

–6–

On her way home, Amy had an almost irresistible desire to laugh. And it was not so much a series of mental perceptions that revealed the grotesque and the incongruous in the spectacle of her having made this sally of a moral missionary. It was rather a physical movement of muscle and nerve, something over which she had no control. It continued for several of the long blocks she had chosen to walk to reach a subway station and rendered her incapable of other sensation almost as if it had become the point of concentration for all the nerve processes of her being. The shrieks that filled her ears suddenly with flashes of imminent horror alone forced her out of her mood. People were shouting at her from all sides as a huge truck seemed to be bearing directly upon her. The dexterity of the driver in steering it abruptly to the wrong side of a trolley car saved her from being crushed. She hurried across the street to avoid the glances of the crowd and to be out of earshot of the foul oaths of the truck driver. The incident had so frightened her that it had paralyzed her thinking and her feeling, and she rode the entire distance to her destination as one who has been rendered numb and inert.

The air and the walk through the park revived her. At the corner of the street upon which she lived was a dress shop that was displaying unusual values in the garments just about to go out of style and give way to the fall creations. Amy did something she was not in the habit of doing. At the best the store windows elicited a passing glance from her. When she needed a new dress or a new hat she went to the nearest store available and asked for what she wanted. She spent little time in going over the numerous items placed in front of her. She made up her mind at once and left immediately. On this occasion, however, she stopped in front of the windows and made a careful examination. She ruled out at once the white and cream ensemble with its tan polka dot yoke, lingered over the light blue organdie with its series of frills around the skirt, and finally decided that she must go in and investigate further. She surprised Mrs. Nilins when she arrived with several boxes, a new hat, and a face glowing with unwonted pleasure.

"Bless you, child," whispered Mrs. Nilins, snapping her two fingers. "You look happier than I have seen you in years. . . ."

–7–

The next day, as if she knew that Donato would come, she had dressed herself in her new clothes and stood in front of the cage.

"What do you think, Bezo? A great psychologist once said that you can have all the emotions you want if you just make the gestures. That's what I am doing today, and I am going out, Bezo bird, and I shall not see you the whole day."

She turned her begonias about. She snipped a leaf or two off her blue African lily, changed the position of the lady's eardrops with their red petals, ran her hand over the ferns and finally decided upon washing them. Over the yellow satin she had placed a white apron and was about to begin her task of washing the sword fern when her bell jangled and she knew Donato had come.

She ran downstairs to open the door herself, and there she found him standing in the doorway in grey striped flannels of the newest cut, his matted chestnut curls uncovered, his shoes reflecting the thin edge of his trousers. She was startled by the transformation. He was no longer a boy. Even the awkward smile did not altogether erase the impression of a quick maturity of poise and grace. His tall slim form, straight as a young warrior's, seemed to have come not out of those foul-smelling streets, out of the dingy fallen-down tenements, but rather out of the clean atria pictured in the *Alma Tadema* she so much loved. And it was in only a second that the same illusion that he always produced upon her rose before her vision. He was, he was the young Hermes come to earth in human form, and the dreams that filled her mind as she read the classics as a girl were fulfilled, and she knew she was like one of the wood creatures of old, or those that sprang out of the bushes that grew by the wayside as Apollo passed, or the golden-haired Dionysus, or Hermes the fleet-footed, the light of heart.

"You're just on time," she said. "I was just going out and you may come with me. . . ."

"You look grand. . . ."

"Well!" There was no mistaking her pleasure, and she thought imme-diately that she could not blame Selma for having kissed him.

"Nice of you to say it," she added, laughing. "You look grand too, young man."

Donato laughed in his turn and adjusted his step to hers as he swung his cane with adroit grace.

"What have you been doing all summer, Donato?" asked Amy, look-ing somewhat reprovingly and maybe too much the teacher. She had prac-tically to pilot him across the street, so fixedly was his gaze turned on her in an evident effort to discover what was the intent of the question. They came to a trolley stop and she let go his arm.

"You must tell me everything, Donato."

It was in the nature of a command but the laughter that accompanied it was infectious enough for Donato to laugh too but also to look away as if embarrassed.

"Of course . . . if you make it an assignment," he said, flinging his cane out and then resting on it debonairly.

"What poise!" thought Amy, as she felt herself helped up the steps. "What an air!" something studied in his modulation arrested her too, and in his eyes there was an added dreaminess, intenser, more fulfilled. His laughter was richer, his gait more manly, his gestures more assured.

"Of course, Donato. I do make it an assignment. But I suppose I don't really dare. You have grown so much, sir, in six weeks . . . you frighten me."

Again the rich embarrassed laughter. There was not much opportu-nity for conversation in the crowded lurching car until Donato found a seat for both of them.

"Yes, Donato," she resumed, scrutinizing the young man from head to foot. "You have got an air. You must tell me the secret. So many of our boys could profit from a little instruction in manners."

Donato smiled with all his teeth and chuckled, continuing to spin his cane between his legs as if he had been accustomed to canes all his life. But she could see, nevertheless, that he was disturbed, that a note in her remarks went deeper than merely impersonal query would suggest.

"Our boys don't meet enough people out of their set, do they? They don't get around. Isn't that it, Donato?" She was trying to put the dis-cussion on the level of a classroom debate on the proprieties of conduct. However, she was aware that the longer she looked at him and the more persistent became her questioning, the greater effort he made to conceal something in his thoughts behind a mask of smiles. And in doing so, she knew that the more she must have been revealing how undiminished was the feeling for him which she had openly displayed in the closing days of school. She was glad, finally, that he frankly peered out of the window to determine their exact location.

"We're going to a small art shop on Madison Avenue, Donato. I want some pictures for my rooms. Needn't be so impatient. We'll have lunch in the neighborhood and then proceed to the museum."

"Oh, no, Miss Rollins, oh no . . . not the museum. . . ."

He accented the first syllable with tremendous emphasis. He threw a great deal of contempt into his pronunciation of it. A suggestion of bored nonchalance became accentuated with sharp decisiveness in his manner, in his speech, in the lift of his eyebrows as his teeth smiled.

"Oh, I got dragged there, and dragged there all summer. We did the sculptures up brown. And what's there to it? The American pieces are childish imitations of the Greek. I told Mr. Borriner that they were afraid to make the faces laugh out, spit, swear . . . you know what I mean. Rodin's the only thing they've got. . . . No, Miss Rollins, you must excuse me. I'll come to the art shop, but to the museum . . . really!"

They had to get off to change cars. Donato it was, this time, who took the, lead. "What have they done to the lad?" she kept thinking, especially as with dramatic elaborateness he extended his hand for her elbow when she was about to jump off the car. She smiled at the picture of this boy made over into a replica of a Greenwich Village dilettante with a touch of Park Avenue. "Young man," she said turning to him without any effort to conceal her amusement and bewilderment. "You certainly have got too grand for me. Why, you as much as tell all these big fellows that they're nobodies. . . ."

"And they are! Leave out St. Gaudens . . . and even his Diana is stupidly Greek. Have we no symbols of our own? Haven't we ideas, people around us?"

Intensity was stamped on all his face, in the sharp concentration of his eyes, in the pulled muscles of his jaw. He was no dilettante really. He was talking with the fervor of one who has just discovered a new faith. The dream in him had become reality, and the reality was a thing apart from the street noises, the traffic, the glare of the late August sun and yet a higher transmuted version of them all. She stood looking at him somewhat overwhelmed, brought to a silence that penetrated her like a light, a light that must have given her eyes the sudden and strange beauty which they acquired. For Donato stopped talking. His eyes had met hers, and the light in his quivered and then broke like sheen on water ruffled by the accidents of wind.

"Let's take this car," he said simply.

She smiled sweetly as if she had had no stronger emotion than one feels at a casual tea. But she knew that a shadow had been passed between them and that in the shadow they saw with unabashed distinctness that they were closer in spirit and in feeling than they had ever before divined. However, as they entered the car, their momentary bewilderment had disappeared. Again the street cries, the banging wheels became audible. "No, really, Miss Rollins," Donato said. "I can't come to the museum. Besides, I must meet someone later."

Donato could not have known the effect of these simple words. She spun with them out of the present to the night of the marionettes and she saw once more the kiss that Selma had given him and then. . . . She shut her eyes. She dared not allow her imagination to follow Donato and Selma.

"You shall keep your engagement," is all she said.

The art shop had been a pretext and Amy was happy to find it closed. "I have been to several of these places too. Mr. Borriner thinks it important to go around if I'm to do anything as a sculptor. They've lovely things in them. But they remind me of school. They do things that seem to have no life."

They entered a drug store and sat at a small table. Amy ordered iced drinks.

"You have got around a lot this summer, then, Donato?"

"A little bit." His face broke into a smile that was not altogether frank.

"I saw your show of course. It was great, Donato. You ought to do something with the idea . . . play the universities . . . hire a small theater . . . work up a fad. It will take time, surely. And you will need money and a backer . . . and then you must get through with your high school. It's complicated. . . ."

They exchanged smiles. They looked at each other without speaking. Their eyes danced with unfamiliar lights. In Donato's manner was concentrated the sense of his being in the presence of a force far above him, the image of all that he had hoped and longed for in the classroom: knowledge of things beyond the immediate, the distinction conferred upon the spirit and the personality by association with what has been of the highest in thought and deed throughout the ages enshrined in the school unto a life everlasting. Amy gathered into her person all these things and more. She was even a sweeter symbol: she was human understanding and love. She was the imponderable warmth in affection and sympathy, the love that he had not had throughout his boyhood. And despite this, he could not hide the effect that her loveliness of body and face, the charm of her interest in him, had upon him, sensitive passionate Latin that he was. The physical touched his reverence with a light that was flame and Amy saw it in the intense gleaming of his eyes.

"I wanted to see you about that, Miss Rollins. I hate going back to school. It seems stupid to me now. I want to give all my time to sculpture. I'll have to work in the daytime to earn some money. You see how we live. My father doesn't make much. At night, I'll go to art classes . . . I'll carve and model in all my spare time. . . . Selma thought I ought to talk it over with you. And she made me promise that if you said I was to go back I would go back and get my diploma. But I hate it. I'd rather drive a truck. Imagine all those kids, Miss Rollins. They don't care for a thing . . . what's anything to them? What's school to them or to anyone . . . ? It all seems so stupid now. . . ."

The "now" seemed a conclusive word. Amy inferred at once that it was the verbal demarcation between childhood and adolescence, that the "now" presented his having crossed over into the vivid lands of knowledge. The way in which he spoke of Selma, the appropriative intonation he gave her name, confirmed her deductions and for a minute a sadness settled on her which estopped all utterance. She was conscious only of his interested face, animated with his statement, for the first time lacking the hints of disingenuousness and embarrassment which it had worn ever since their meeting.

People passed back and forth. She could hear them ordering the most incongruous things: nail files and writing paper, absorbent cotton, linseed oil. She was conscious of the differences in their steps, their voices, the size of their bodies, vaguely informed by shadow and movement as to whether they were young or old, in a hurry or without thought of the next minute. And Donato's voice acted merely as a kind of frame to hold them all in as if by so doing he could emphasize the trivialities of their occupations in contrast with the vision of his sculpture.

She heard him continue. He had stretched his cane out to a distant point and was slowly manipulating it as if seeking some obscure solution of his problem in the zigzagging lines of the floor designs. With his head lowered, his dark lashes resting on his olive skin, the curls of his hair compacted into the semblance of those on ancient Greek heads, he looked to her with redoubled vividness the reincarnation of the Praxiteles Hermes. The reality of it was so sure an item in her consciousness that she could understand that several of the customers stopped to look at him.

She heard one girl whisper to another. . . . "Stunning, isn't he . . . perfectly." And she was in some unaccountable manner happy because of it. She listened as he talked as if she were the younger one and he endowed with all the qualities that he ascribed to her: understanding of the world, sage advice, sympathy based on wisdom.

"I don't want to go back to school. It means nothing now, nothing. I want to get into a studio, help around, be a model maybe. Selma says I'd make a good one. I could watch the sculptor work. It would give me a chance to get hold of tools too. They cost money. Selma and Borriner showed me lots of things, and school became nothing to me. Selma's afraid she's put it out of my head and has a conscience about it. It seems so unnecessary. What's a little more Latin? Imagine spending ten weeks reading one or two books in English. I can read them in one night and a dozen more before the week's up. I couldn't stand it. Don't say I've got to go back. I promised Selma I would if you said so. . . ."

"Do you care a lot for Selma?"

She leaned over the small black marble table so that her shadow filled it and somehow caught Donato's eye, for it was in that and not at her that he stared.

"And she cares a lot for you?"

She asked the question in a solemn sort of whisper and as she asked it she felt both like shrieking with laughter and weeping at the same time. She possessed too sharply the power of regarding her actions with detachment not to appraise at its full value this touch of utterly adolescent seriousness which had been injected into the conversation. But she could even look with detachment at this very detachment and put it down to morbid self-consciousness, to fear at acknowledging the effect that Donato had upon her. But she repeated the question without either laughing or weeping.

"Because, you know, if you do like her and she does like you, there would be nothing so nice as to follow her advice. She's right, really. You do have to finish your course. It isn't what you learn in so much detail. It isn't even the introduction it gives you to the past and the culture of the race, Donato. The practical value of it, too, counts. People have faith in education. They think it's important to have a diploma. At least while you're young. It makes little difference after you've proven yourself. I know all that too, Donato. You could prove yourself right away. But get your diploma first. It will be something to fall back on. . . . Selma will like you the more for it. . . . She's the girl that helped you with the marionettes?"

"Yes. She put it over really. . . ."

"You've seen a lot of her, haven't you?"

No sooner had she uttered the words than she knew she should not have asked the question. The steady gaze he tried to maintain was too painful and the color that suffused the pale olive of his skin had mounted too rapidly for her to fail to understand. She trembled with excitement. She felt a rush of cold and warm feelings alternately possess and vacate her body almost as if they were peculiar sorts of phantoms, for she could not make them out. Was she envious of this Selma . . . jealous could not be the word? And what did she envy Selma? The surer impression of beauty which she made, or that more inestimable, unmeasurable impression that she had erected no barriers between herself and life? If she, Amy, could lean over now, now as she longed to, as the wild fluttering heart in her sang to her to do, if she leaned over now and like Selma placed her palms on his cheeks and then drew his face toward her and kissed him, would he sense the same quality in her too, and show in his eyes, in his manner, his having been touched by something that was poetry and vision? Would it be too terrible to satisfy this longing? She leaned over closer and asked again:

"You have seen lots of her, haven't you? She's done a great deal for you. You've grown up since the beginning of the summer. You are no longer a boy. You understand. Life has called to you. That's why you're so ambitious. It's really astounding how surely you understand yourself and know what you want and what you ought to do. Selma has done all that for you. Do something for her now. Go back to school. Postpone your program for a while. It's only for another year. You'll then be ready for your own work. You needn't go to college. . . . And so I say Selma is right. I'm so glad you met her, Donato. Remember what I said in my letter. . . ."

Donato interrupted at once. There had been two girls standing in front of them, not directly looking at him and Amy, but attempting to accomplish that very thing by deft electric flashes of the eyes over their backs.

He had noticed them and had looked up and just stared vacantly at them. But when he heard Amy mention a letter he had suddenly withdrawn his gaze and said abruptly.

"I never got a letter from you."

The girls giggled and he looked up again and they giggled some more because, although he had seen them and must have known that they were making desperate efforts to catch his eye, he presented such a blank un-seeing face. His tone was one of having being hurt. Amy knew by the way that he had said the words that he had laid great store upon receiving a reply from her, and as she realized that she wondered why the letter had not reached him.

"But I answered at once, wrote you the very same day. Mr. Crabbing mailed the letter. . . ."

"I never got it. You know you were so short with me the last day of school. You said goodbye so matter-of-fact like. I hesitated about writing and then I did and I got no answer. I thought I had been too bold and I said I wouldn't try to see you again. And then I saw you on the campus with Crabbing — Nanny, that's what the boys call him — and I thought you saw me but you walked away with him and wouldn't let me see you. I thought I had been too bold. . . ."

The words came fast like an apology. She felt that he was offering an explanation and she knew that he meant to offer it by way of accounting for his companionship with Selma. It was all very adolescent. She won-dered at herself and a wild desire came upon her to seize the boy by the shoulder and shake him and say, "Why are you talking this way? Do you think I am a Selma? Do you think I am like these silly little girls that are staring at you and giggling?"

Instead she smiled and said, "It must have gone astray, Donato. I did answer and I want you to forgive me if I hurt you. . . . But it's getting late, and you have an appointment. . . . Shall we go? Only promise me you're going back to school."

He had laid the stick over his arm and he bowed as she left him. But Amy did not go to the museum. She walked very slowly at first until she had turned the corner and then an irresistible feeling to run and run wild-ly took hold of her, and run she did for a short distance. She seemed to be running from the scene of a personal shame. Several people turned to look at her and she saw an old lady smiling. She stopped and walked qui-etly. A taxi whirled up to her and came to a dead halt at her side. Without knowing what she was doing she had entered it and had given orders to be taken to her home.

"I'm in a great hurry," she told the driver, and as the cab careened around corners, dashed past cars, she gazed out and felt herself inundated with excitement. There was something immensely satisfying in the speed they were making, in the sensation of passing millions of cars each vowing not to be passed and threatening to give chase. Deafening noises assailed

her ears, the city crowds seemed even huger crowds than usual, the buildings more numerous and taller, the advertisements larger and more glaring.

Everything had begun whirling about her, so much so indeed that her
own body seemed to be whirling too. The stairs whirled as she ran to her
rooms. And the rooms whirled as she entered them. Bezo's twitter turned
into shrills, and the shrills into flaming needles piercing her ears.

As she fell on her bed she heard it no more. But she spun around diz-
zily as if seeking a lost line of direction, and then finding it, moved out
into space beyond the roofs where there was silence and light like a silver
dusk gleamed perpetual and soothing.

XVI. SELMA'S PARTY

WHEN SELMA told Amy that they were both so much older than Donato she had not misstated the facts, but she had exaggerated. To all intents and purposes she might have been forty instead of the twenty-three she was; she had already been married, and had been divorced, and was now living not only on her alimony but on the added bounty of a rich lawyer connected with a personal loan association. Her marriage to Samuel Kreymdorf she always claimed to have taken place at the request of her father. Kreymdorf and Saltenberg were both in the ribbon business, but Saltenberg's affairs had not prospered. He had sent Selma to college, from which she had graduated at the age of nineteen. In great desperation he had shown her his accounts the night of the elaborate party he had arranged in her honor.

Kreymdorf had been at the party, stout for his twenty-five years, sleek-faced, with eyes that sparkled in cups of cheery fatty wrinkles, hair pomaded close to his head for fear that the incipient baldness might be too hastily exposed. His laughter was the laughter of a stout person pleased with himself and the world. He was headed for immediate prosperity on a large scale. He had already taken a prominent place in the trade association and was slated to become an officer of the bank the trade was organizing. These things were like a fine wine drunk with a fine dinner. The stout, middle-sized man showed it in all his actions. He spoke with authority, and whether or not what he said was funny, they all laughed at what he said; he laughed too and laughed the most heartily. Even after his listeners had stopped laughing, his chuckle could still be heard, and he was not averse even to renewing the remark.

"So I said to Selma, maybe you could marry Isaacson's money but accept my hand . . . ha . . . ha . . . ha, ha. . . ."

He liked to carry everything before him and made no bones about it. The night of the graduation party he had been its mainstay. He had risen to propose the toasts, he had held forth at great length on the value of an education, he had praised Selma to the skies, he had slapped Mr. Saltenberg on the back, he had put his arms around Mrs. Saltenberg and kissed her with a loud resounding smack squarely on the lips.

"Say," he cried turning to the fifteen guests at the table, who had all been finding the proceedings amusing, "say, Papa Saltenberg knew a good thing."

Selma squirmed. Her bright fluffy hair, fine as a mist, clung precariously about her broad rosy face. Her hazel eyes glowed with the excite-

ment of the party, the heavy tokay she had drunk, the praises she had
heard of her beauty, her learning, her youth. But she squirmed. She had
a horror of bad manners, of the thoughtless vulgarity of her group, their
frank ways, their appetites, their broad laughter. She had insisted upon
going to an old American college where she could get away from them all.
In her heart she had a great deal of love for her father and mother but she
was also ashamed of them, ashamed of them and their friends. And now
that she knew she was expected to marry Kreymdorf she wondered what
it had all meant to have gone to the last boundaries of New York State, to a
college where the great majority of the students were native stock.

At college, she had put up with a good deal of snobbery, but she had
been willing to put up with it. She knew she was obtaining something
she never could have had in New York. She even accepted an invitation
to a dance from one of the Gentile men when she knew that he had tried
to induce other girls to go with him and had finally turned to her as a last
resort. On the skating rink, her glowing cheeks, her bright hazel eyes, the
misty brown of her hair escaping coquettishly from under her pink tight-
fitting cap called attention to herself, and many the young man who had
turned around to smile, and later to skate with her, and then to take her
to a small ice cream and coffee shop for a talk together, and hopes had become high and like a heat within her. But the young man had not invited
her to the Saturday dance. He had not invited her for reasons which she
understood too well and despite the ardor of his first words, the spontane-
ous compliments, the pressure of his arm about hers as they had walked
back to the campus. She had gone through all this, gone through it all
because she had wanted something she could not get at home, something
indefinable in intonation, manner, gait.

Her own set told her she had acquired it, told her without words in
open admiration, with eyes, and a courteous diffidence in her presence.
They were all impressed with her and especially Kreymdorf. He had met
her at the station in his new car, shining with nickel, luxurious, noiseless.

"You're like the belle at the inaugural ball . . ." he had told her, laughing. "You look great. Imagine the little kid that left New York last summer,
and the summer before. You're a real queen, Selma. God, you'd knock out
Zeigfeld's eye. Hey, folks, what say, wouldn't she now?"

–2–

She had lived with Sam for five months, but after the first weeks had
refused to give herself to him. There had been family conferences, plead-
ings from her mother, frantic attacks from her father. He was a little man,
with ever the smallest chinks for eyes, skin preternaturally wrinkled, tiny
bony hands.

"Will you shame your old father?"

Sam stayed away from home. She sued Kreymdorf for a divorce.

"On any grounds," he told her. "Just get out of my sight. Sure, you can have money. Think I'm the same kind of piker?"

She lived alone in a one-room apartment overlooking uptown Broadway. She indulged her tastes in modern prints, modern furniture, modern rugs. She sought out a radical set in the Village and spent her time with them although she would not live where they lived and as they lived. She made a point of picking up young geniuses and escorting them around from place to place. But she had resisted all importunities for closer relationships until she met Shelley Londin, a prosperous lawyer.

He had a head formed on the framework of an isosceles triangle: narrow forehead with scalp and the hair attempting to seek an apex, big jowls that bayed out at the cheeks and hurried in fatty contours under the chin and down into a thick neck. He had a tremendous torso in keeping with his face and head, but his legs were small, his feet diminutive, his hands thin, tapering, almost colorless. The skin of his face was as pink as a child's and without the trace of a hair, and he had no eyebrows and no eyelashes. But his eyes were filled with a keen, quiet intelligence, an intelligence that was further manifested in his soft voice, never hurried, never excited, never troubled. His reading had been universal and his knowledge was vast and accurate. He could discourse with equal lucidity on the latest researches in physics and give a capable explanation of the various orders and mysteries which composed the mythological religions of the ancients. He was married, had seven children, two of them brilliant young men both engaged in newspaper work. He had been married at an early age to a woman who had grown immensely fat after a few years, who had had no education, never acquired any, and seemed as the years advanced to have reverted further and further to the coarse peasant habits of her nondescript Galician ancestry.

He was attached to his family, however, spent most of his evenings with them, alone in his own room, reading, except when one or another of his children bounded into the room, jumped on his knees, pulled him off the chair, compelled him to tell them his endless stories. He made up the stories as he went along and never could repeat them, much to the disgust of the children.

One night a week he spent away from home with Selma in her small apartment with its exquisite prints, colorful carpets, modernistic divan, indirect lighting that teased one's imagination with suggestions of spaces beyond spaces, rooms beyond rooms. On such nights he brought her a first edition of Emma Lazarus, a reprint of Thomas Browne in new type and binding, with illustrations by the newest Mexican artist to make a sensation in New York. Occasionally he obtained an obscure eroticon done in bizarre lettering, with pictures the lewdness of which was relieved only by the undoubted artistry of the execution. They glanced over it together, making no comments, save on the technical dexterity of the bookbinder, the family of type employed, the decorative quality of the pictures. Only when he read to her from the text would there be any laughter, and then it was the soft rich laughter of lovers in passion. The evenings thus wore on to a silent midnight with a drink taken slowly and held up often for the lights from the brackets on the walls to shine through, and then an hour together on the large many-pillowed divan with its oriental softness and color.

He never questioned what she did or where she went the nights and the days when he did not see her. Occasionally he called up on the telephone and enjoyed talking with her, especially if he had discovered a volume of particular interest. Or at rare times they would both attend a concert or the opera. If she told him about a young boy out of the slums who was writing the best verses she had seen in years, or the equally young violinist who added greater dreaminess, greater intensity to a Brahms waltz, he listened appreciatively, said "He ought to go far," and waited for the next story. In such fashion he had heard of Donato and had seen several of the heads he had carved. But the manner in which Selma spoke of this new find must have been sufficiently different for Londin to have looked up at her and taken her by the chin. "You like this youngster?" he asked. But that was all.

-3-

Selma had had a party on the night when Shelley was coming. It was with his consent, in fact, practically at his request. He had wanted to meet Donato. There were very few persons in town to invite, but Selma could always depend on Borriner, and Borriner was always in touch with a number of young men and women who had come to New York with their ambitions and their hopes and their poverty. Among them this time was one not quite so poor, a Kansas girl, come to New York to open a studio, with little or no hair on her head but whatever she had deftly pulled back over a large forehead and held down in the back by combs. Her body had the thinness and exquisiteness of an Aubrey Beardsley portrait. She affected black tight-fitting dresses of material heavy enough to suggest that she might have worn other things beneath. (No one believed that she ever did.) She might have been an ebony naiad rising out of a midnight tarn with the dark waters pearled closely all over her body. Her long smoothly fashioned neck rose like the stem of a goblet out of her black bodice to hold the equally small gypsy-swarthy face with its long thin eyes, penciled nose, delicately petaled lips, naturally red.

Only her voice and her accent betrayed her Midwestern origin and the fact that she was solidly American. But the waving gesture with her ductile arms and fingers that came to points like willow leaves, suggested faraway music in rooms drowsy with perfume. One always expected her to be infinitely bored and to break into the languid affectedly annoyed speech of those who think themselves superior and never can prove it except by being annoyed. But if she spoke at all she spoke with enthusiasm, in quick jerky phrases as if she were afraid of losing the next word, the next word which would prove to be the best of all she had uttered. And people always said it was too bad that her voice was unmistakably nasal and that she rolled her "r's" with such emphasis. But more than this trait, her name completely and irrevocably seemed out of all keeping with the frail exoticism of her body and personality. Angel Smith could, however, be proud of her name, for it was the same name her father had, and her father was known for the millions he had amassed in new nitrate deposits in South America. She and Donato were to be the *pièces de resistance* of Selma's party.

She had come not with Borriner, who always came unattended to Selma's parties, but with a colossal Mr. Wildman whose face never appeared shaven so black and thick was his beard, with a voice that was even blacker and thicker than his beard and which he was forever trying to force into sentimental registers. He had started life a teacher of English in the city high schools, had written several plays of ponderous delicacy which had never got on the stage and was now rounding out his forty-fifth year by writing highly successful detective stories for children's magazines. He was always inordinately and effusively happy to meet you and immediately patronized you by telling you that you had missed your calling or had at least not given quite sufficient attention to the technical details to succeed. So he had told Angel repeatedly, so he had told Borriner, with more truth, so he was to tell Donato that night until he managed to irritate the young man into a prolonged and most painful defense of his method of carving in wood and throwing aside all established technicalities.

"What I want to do is to make faces talk . . . not just be patterns. Don't you see you have got to make them talk? I want a face to swear and be excited, stick its tongue out, puff up its cheeks, yell, spit, yes, spit at you. They're all patterns in the museum as if the faces never had moved a muscle since they were born. That's my idea. You have got to make them talk. . . ."

Selma had taken Donato shopping, had made a perfect selection of grey-blue flannel with a light stripe for his suit, got him a shirt and tie in harmony, with just enough color to heighten the brilliance of his sad grey eyes. Angel Smith had given him her hand at the full length of her arm and as he shook it, she left it in his, and opened wide her long narrow eyes.

"Why, he's a young god," she confided to Wildman at once.

Londin took him off to a corner immediately after his long argument with Wildman.

"Selma has talked a lot about you," he said in his unhurried voice. "I like the heads. You might arrange them in groups around an idea. You know what I mean. . . . I think you have genius . . . but you are very young. Don't get yourself involved too much in this sort of thing. . . ."

Donato had been quiet after that, pondering Londin's words. Angel patted Wildman on the knee, and said, "You sit here, you growler, while I go and talk to that exquisite god. . . ."

Her black dress clung to her like her skin and covered her to her feet so that she seemed to be moving like some creature peculiar to the night. She undulated her body into a sitting posture next to Donato, who, not knowing what to do, had not risen for her, nor moved to make room.

"Oh, you are a real god, sir, besides an artist. You won't even stir for a charming lady. . . ."

His white teeth flashed and his eyes took up their brightness as he turned to her. But she saw that he had been disturbed out of a reverie and said so.

"Yes, I was thinking. . . ."

"Ah, but you mustn't. It's positively forbidden at your age. . . ."

"Why?"

Selma had floated over to them, and as she heard his earnest *why* leaned over his shoulders, touching his head with her breasts.

"You must never question a young lady and you must never argue with one. That's lesson number one for tonight."

She kissed him playfully on the hair. "He's just a child. . . ." She laughed, stroked him on the cheek and left.

"You're a big boy, though," whispered Angel, putting her face close to his. "And I want to see you again. You'll come to my studio, won't you, and bring some more of your work. Maybe you could pose for me?"

Donato smiled and smiled. He could say nothing.

She coaxed him. "You will come."

Londin's words fresh in his mind, he hesitated, but she got him to nod a "yes" and then she said,

"I'll be waiting for you. Next Tuesday at four. My name's in the telephone book. . . ."

Selma at this point slipped in between them again and settled herself on the divan where they both had been sitting.

"And now while we have another drink, Donato, you must get up and perform for the company." She addressed the group. "He can do marvelous things with just two puppets. Watch him."

Donato arose and took from behind the divan a screen of white paper. He placed it on two chairs at one end of the room, attached a bulb to the electric fixture and lowered it down to a place behind the screen. He showed the company an Arlecchino he had made himself, a Pulcinello, and a Columbine.

"Three, not two," he informed the audience.

They hung from strings behind the screen. All the other lights were put out. On the screen the shadows of the puppets showed distinct in form and outline. Donato moved the screen forward, then back, then forward again. The shadows were finally framed perfectly within the area of the screen. With deft handling of strings he made the three puppets go through a series of dances exquisite in their buffoonery. Now they pursued each other in a circle, now they clambered on each other's backs, now they knelt and pleaded with upstretched hands, and now they fell face on the floor in utter despair. They went through a wide gamut of tricks.

Wildman actually applauded.

"That's good, you know. He could do wonders with it. He would have to get a larger screen, however, study the details of anatomy, put in a great deal of work."

The show was over. Wildman patted Donato on the back.

"That's good stuff, kid. Really. You made those heads too?"

The party broke up. Londin spoke to Selma.

"I like your friend."

-4-

As they left, Selma took Donato aside and whispered in his ear.

"Come back. Fifteen minutes."

Donato flushed wildly, could not say a word in the elevator, refused a lift in a taxi.

"Don't forget. Tuesday," he heard Angel call.

He ran, ran for half the block and then stood stock still. He felt all his body tremble, flame sweep over it, his mouth parch. Cars whirled past him, the lighted stores threw their plaques of light in front of him, the night air felt cool on his cheeks. But he seemed to want to brush them aside. He was seized with an overwhelming desire for strength, strength to press against a wall and with one desperate push cause the building to topple. Then he laughed to himself, but it was a laughter that was more like weeping. Londin's words rang in his ears. "Don't get yourself involved in this sort of thing." He was the oldest one there. His face seemed kind and understanding. There was no reason for him to have said what he did unless from an experience that must have been real. And yet there were the other words and the pressure on his hand. "Come back. Fifteen minutes."

He ran back. Selma opened the door. The lights had been dimmed. She took him in her arms and kissed him.

"You're staying here tonight."

XVII. THE FALL SESSION

THE RECAPTURE of a mood is the most difficult as it is the most disillusioning of all mental processes. This Amy found to be true on her first meeting with Donato after the opening of school. The shame of having exposed her feelings to him had left her numbed, and yet she had wanted to know again the sensation of delight in his presence. The coldness and the quietness with which she greeted him were genuine enough, but she realized that they were also a shell constructed out of her desire for protection against the very reaction of joy which she constantly had in Donato. And she was honest, too, in her thinking and could confess to herself that Crabbing had had something to do with this new feeling.

Crabbing had preceded her down the long corridor, only half-lighted by the white globes in the ceiling because sunk below the street level. He was holding open a swinging door into the church-like auditorium where the initial organization conference was being held. At the same time he was trying to bow in his courtliest fashion. He so held his face that the goatee and the puffy eyes seemed more comically than ever to justify the nickname of Nanny.

"Good morning," he said. "You look exceptional."

Somehow he had contrived to make the greeting sound like a reproach and the sight of the heads in the auditorium and the scattered talking to take on the character of a courtroom where she was to be tried.

"It's the half-light, Crabbing," she answered, distrustfully.

"Oh, you mustn't say that. . . ."

"You look exceptional, yourself," she added, emphasizing each word.

"Stayed right in town," he confided, advancing with her into the dim assembly hall. "Saw you accidentally several times — once in a drugstore with a young man — quite a dapper chap, I must say — was it Contini?"

The innuendo was unmistakable, and the mechanical laughter that accompanied it sly and suggestive. She was glad to be rescued by Miss Batten and to be drawn into the swirl of small talk and the accounts of summer doings.

She was made to feel altogether out of the picture. Having remained in New York showed the most incomprehensible lack of spirit. How foolish she felt for not having gone off as the others had done. Even taking a course at Oxford, or in a summer college in Vermont, smacked of something highly adventurous.

"Divine's the word — just divine, those old colonial homes. And Mr. Gaylord — he — oh, he was rapturous, just too rapturous!"

172

The waggly old head on the waggly old neck was for a moment lit with the fire of rapid superlatives.

"I had a quiet summer — down in Ohio with the family — after New York for a year, it's a haven, don't you know?"

From behind, Amy heard several of the younger girls in laughing whispers.

"From the first day out — pursued me all the way across the continent — got into the same airplane with me — What could I do? Of course, dear, and more! . . . We're marrying, Christmas. . . ."

Most of the teachers had merely gone here and there, remained with parents, studied, rushed around, anything for a change, anything to fill in the time. There were those who had been bolder than the others. The stories were never related in detail. But there were hints: hints of handsome foreign men and weekend expeditions to Corsica, to a Swiss chalet, a lodge in the Tyrol; hints of a bit of wildness in Montmartre, not without comic elements; hints of amours begun on board the boat and completed under clear night skies in Sorrento or Taormina. What had made her remain in New York? Was it the chance return of Philip? Was it the meetings she had hoped for with Donato?

If the first day without the students had proved to be a trying ordeal of clerical duties, the following Monday, when the thousands of students poured incessantly through the corridors, was like attempting to solve the most abstruse complications by setting up a desk in the middle of Times Square. Donato had opened the door of her room once or twice during the day, waved his hand to one or two of the boys, tried to catch her eye, and left in a hurry.

–2–

At the close of the day she was in her room. It seemed as good a place as any to stay. She just wanted to sit and sit, impervious to feeling, to thought, and never stir again. She looked out across the unending jumble of rooftops. In the distance rose a cloud-like huddle of trees, flashing languidly in the warm September sun. Puffs of white cloud rose into the unruffled expanses of sky. The noises of the street, many stories below, came muffled like the confused trials on horns and drums before the band bursts into the march. A hopeless, futile feeling it was — not so much of loneliness as of weariness.

"Amy," she said to herself. "This will never do. The first day back and you feel this way. . . ."

Very few of the teachers had dropped in to her room to say even "Hello." She had so little to say to them. In the restroom, she had sat outside of the animated circle of gossipers and talkers, full of their summer experiences. She had sat there as she sat now, withdrawn, unnoticed. There was a knock on her door.

Donato entered, smiling.

"Good afternoon, Miss Rollins," he said, quietly, having somehow sensed the atmosphere of the room.

"How are you, Donato?"

"I thought I'd come to see if you needed any help."

The boy did look like a Hermes. There was no mistaking it, thought Amy . . . the suppleness of his body, the flash of his movements!

But she said, "Thank you. I am through with all my work."

"You're lucky. Some teachers are still plugging away. . . . Are you walking up Broadway?"

"No, Donato. I am staying here a while. I think I shall stay here and prepare some plans."

"I thought we'd walk. . . ."

"I'm too busy. . . ."

"Well, I'll go down town. . . ."

"You're doing some work?"

"If I can get it. I pose a bit."

He had his hand on the knob and looked at her full face, his grey eyes saddening as they rested on her.

"I'm glad," she answered, stooping to pull out a drawer. And then as she placed a book on her desk, and drew out some pencils and paper, she added, "Maybe you will be seeing a good deal of artists and learning things, too. . . ."

"Yes."

"You see Selma?" she inquired casually, making a scraping noise with her chair as she moved closer to the desk.

"Selma? No. She's in Cuba and is going further south later."

"I know she will be pleased to hear you're back at school."

"Yes. I know."

There was a pause. Amy had begun to write.

"Oh, good afternoon," he said, and bolted out.

But the room was no longer quiet. The thud of the door as it closed re-echoed unceasingly. There was the sound of his voice too, and the sad light in his eyes, both playing like moving shadows in the silence.

She read, "Caesar built a bridge across the River Rhone."

"Will they know the word 'built'?" she asked herself. "I'll have to assign that word first. 'The girl placed the book on the table.' 'Placed'? Will they know 'placed'? I am sorry they are using this text this term. Why can't we have another text?"

She continued to write. The afternoon shadows deepened. A sweeper stuck his head into the room once or twice, and then left, allowing the door to thud again. Every time it closed it made the same sound. The sound re-echoed throughout the room, and there was a flashing of teeth and quiet grey eyes saddening.

She was conscious of these things as if they were distant happenings. In front of her lay a sheet of paper, and on it she had written a list of words for her students to study, the pages of the translations which they were to work out for the next several weeks.

"That's a good piece of work done. Tomorrow I will go to the florist's and get that exaltata. I do need that fern."

As she left her room, the thud of the door as it closed crowded into her thoughts. It kept making an echoing sound as if doors were perpetually to be shutting behind her for the rest of her life, and she must get herself accustomed to the noises they made. And with the sounds came a flash of light. If she strained, she could see the light was coming from two eyes resting on her and becoming sad.

The first days of school were always tiring. There were so many new faces, hundreds of new names, each a character apart and solid, in the mass interested, even mildly zealous, but as individuals distrustful, with no feelings for their studies, sometimes slightly cynical, often brazenly superior. There they sat in regular rows in the hot September sunlight, the glow of the vacation days still on their faces. Amy tried to pick out those who would make good students, those who would give trouble. Already she had been forced to raise her voice — always a painful experience to her. Already she had realized that on these shoulders the mantle of learning sat most lightly indeed; in those eyes the torch of culture cast but flickering gleams. Rather would they have an incident, no matter how trivial, to make them laugh, than an explanation, no matter how brilliant, to make them think.

Their compact silence seemed to hum, "What have you got for us? Show us if you can." It engendered a perpetual struggle in her mind: to teach the few and forget the many — a struggle which more than anything else brought misgivings of her usefulness. It fatigued her more than keeping so many resistant personalities subdued. It was only when the term got well under way, and her interest and enthusiasm for her subject, together with her sympathy and gentle unforced humor, had begun to permeate the class atmosphere that the pupils were aroused to activity. At such times she was not so worn out, the lonely afternoons seemed less unbearable.

She had just enough energy to talk to Bezo and to Mrs. Nilins, turn some plants to the sun, spend some time with the ferns she was attempting to rear despite the discouragement of her florist, mark several blooms for repotting. Then came supper with Mrs. Nilins in the big dusty room downstairs, and not long after bed. Miss Batten had promised to visit her but had not put in an appearance. The telephone bell never rang.

–3–

October had finally displaced September. November would be coming on, the long holidays in December, the close of the term, and then more new faces, the spring and the summer, and another school year. The thought lay on Amy like a cloth one has to keep on a swollen muscle although it weighs the part down and adds to the pain. She was hoping her Chinese sacred lily would blossom for Thanksgiving day, and she and Mrs. Nilins spent many anxious minutes inspecting it for ill effects of the variable weather. There were, too, her Roman hyacinths for Christmas. She knew they would flower. There was something she could look forward to every month. Dr. Polter had mentioned something about his wife doing a great deal with bulbs. She certainly would try to force at least one pot of her oxalis and have them ready for Mrs. Polter on Christmas. If only the myna she had ordered from that very nice old bird fancier several blocks up the avenue would arrive! Of course, she should have gone to one of the big stores. But the old fellow had promised her surely, and how his eyes had danced as they went through the catalogues together. He had heard of mynas — sure he had heard of them. An old sailor he knew, had one — tied to a gold chain and that tied to his wrist. They could learn any language.

The concerts would soon be starting. She would attend one every week with Miss Batten or go alone. For other evenings there were the Latin inscriptions she promised Dr. Filtray to translate for him. She intended gathering Latin and Greek poems about birds, both in the original and in translations. She would experiment with some versions of her own. The school library had several excellent books of English versification. She must surely see Miss Fichais about borrowing them for a long period.

She was glad that Donato had not called on her again. Possibly it had been a mistake to inquire about his progress in his classes. It made her happy that he was doing well, but she meant never again to wait in her room after the last gong in the hope that he would knock at the door. She still remembered how sad he looked as he left her the first afternoon of school, and she had often imagined how he must have stood on the steps outside the building waiting for her to come down. She could see him shrug his shoulders in his Italian fashion and then walk slowly down the long flight of stairs. It was better this way. Nor had Philip sent her one of his disturbing letters or telegrams. The days of her life were shaping themselves into quietness, and her interests were sufficiently challenging to keep her gently busy.

It had become a pleasant thing to sit in her room with Mrs. Nilins softly rocking in her mother's old chair. The sound of Bezo spasmodically pecking at his seeds, and the little thuds the chaff made as it dropped into the basin of the cage added ever the slightest charm to the tick of the clock and the movement of the rocker. And the new lamp: how reposeful was the light it cast, mellowing the bright colors of the flowers in the windowsill and giving the broad leaves of her Cocos Weddelliana a soft rich texture. The banging trolleys and the numerous disturbances from the street were effectively shut out. She could work at her translations in peace and comfort.

It was Miss Batten who carried to her the first stirrings of the gossip that was to break in upon her quiet like a series of stones thrown by little boys into one's windows. But it was Donato himself, and later an unending bombardment of letters and telegrams from Philip that shattered the serenity of her new loneliness, and finally drove her in desperation to Europe and to sickness. It was as if she had placed all her feelings into a crystal globe as one does a cherished plant, and some one had dashed it to the floor and it had broken into a dozen shards.

"Ever do that goat Crabbing for anything?" Miss Batten asked Amy one day.

They were standing in line in the teacher's cafeteria waiting for the others in front to move.

"I am talking aloud purposely, Miss Rollins. They'll hear me over the dishes if they have to."

Amy hurried with her salad and coffee and took a seat in her accustomed corner far from the rest. The lunch room was below the street level and only the newness of the curtains, yellow theatrical gauze with a hasty embroidery of green-yarn blossoms, permitted the light to filter through and on to the yellow oilcloth tables.

"What a nightmare in yellow," cried Miss Batten, almost slapping her tray on the table. It made enough noise to invite the attention of a dozen diners. "And whoever thought of yellow oilcloth? It's in keeping with the yellow streak in the profession."

She finally lowered herself to her chair, drew it up noisily and leaned over toward Amy, her 'broad shoulders efficaciously setting up a wall between Amy and the others.

"What's this I hear, Amy?" she asked. "Ever do anything to that idiot?"

"Crabbing?"

"Never knew of a man named better."

"Why, no. . . ."

"Been spreading ghastly stuff around the place. Mentions no names and makes sure to whisper something about his just hearing of it."

"Why, I haven't heard anything, Rita."

Rita Batten grunted as she poured spoonful after spoonful of sugar into her cup with such energy as to cause even that process to be noisy.

"That settles it in my mind. It's you he's aiming at. Guess what the old giboon's been barking? Seems one of the teachers and not too young a one . . . pretty, too, he said . . . been seen in speakeasies with one of the boys . . . well, not speakeasies . . . some sort of drinking place . . . very chummy too they were . . . a vicious sort of lad, in with the gangs in his district. . . ."

Talk such as Miss Batten related to Amy rarely formed the basis of any accusation against teachers. They enjoy all the immunities of persons veiled in the anonymity of crowds. Open scandals blazoned in the newspapers are a different thing. No man in authority will undertake, as is done in small towns, to investigate gratuitous and unidentified rumors and discover the modicum of truth at their center.

Amy understood only too well that what Miss Batten had told her was taking place in the school and that Crabbing must have instigated it. The letter that had not reached Donato flashed into her mind. But as she recalled the wording of it she could not in all reason be shaken with fear because of it. She was sensible enough to realize that no harm of any sort could attach itself to her, but nevertheless the moment she heard of the talk was a painful one, and the whole day and evening distressing. She could not get it out of her mind and kept wondering just what point Crabbing had in view. If it was to make her feel uncomfortable, he was succeeding admirably. There was nothing she could do and nothing she would do. One thing she did realize and that was that it would be utter folly to make too much of it. Even if Donato were to begin once more to renew his attentions, she was certain that she would not dismiss him.

-4-

It was several days after this episode that Donato did break in upon her, and that letters and telegrams from Philip began once more to arrive. Not a day passed now, as a matter of fact, that some missive did not come. The wording was always strange and the contents invariably bitter — even childish, as if a madman were attempting to put into coherent statement his complaint against the forces that make such as he possible in the world.

"I have cried for peace," one telegram ran, "and they give me a tomb."

"Three weeks in hospital with a lot of bums," read another, "and I know Christ must have been a gentleman. I'd like to be an executioner."

Still another said: "Vermin crawled over me in the boxcar all night: but, God, I ask you, don't even I have to live?"

They became so frequent that she threw several aside without opening them. Gradually she began to dread their coming. Even at school she opened a note addressed to her with trembling fingers and uneasy mind. She finally called down to Mrs. Nilins when the door bell jangled,

"If it's a telegram, don't bring it up."

The thought of another became a nightmare. It haunted her everywhere she went; it would pass in front of her vision as she taught her classes. Had she only known actually what had taken place in Philip's life, just where he was and what he was doing, she would not have been so completely overcome by the incessant flow of missives. He did not have much money. The few dollars he was receiving from the federal treasury could not suffice both to provide for his wants and for these telegrams. It was unbelievable that in the state of mind he must be in he could have found work and retained it for any period. She wrote to her sister, but Ann replied, as she had many times before, that she knew no more than Amy. She appealed to the telegraph companies but they had no way of identifying the sender and much less a way of knowing his whereabouts. The telegrams came from no one place two times running. They preyed on her mind, and possibly that was Philip's idea. A long letter practically explained it as such besides having the effect of rendering Amy almost nervewracked with fear and horror.

"*The dying,*" read one paragraph, "*used to be thought of as endowed with the prophetic curse. Amy, beware. I am dying. As I lie here in a vagrant's cell, unclean and* unshorn, my body torn with the lingering malice of war gas, I raise my finger, lean and trembling, and call down upon you the wrath of the ancient gods of Aeschylus. Like the matricide, Orestes, so shall you go through life pursued by the furies of vengeance. . . ."

"But this is fantastic," cried Amy. "He is insane. The poor boy . . . and no way to reach him. . . ."

She brooded over the letter until it became a kind of dream from which she could not escape day or night. Better to have had him with her looking after him as she had looked after her mother! Darkness again had fallen upon her moments of ease, and the privacy of the sweet evenings was now a storm of conjectures.

She had become jumpy enough to quiver with fright the next morning.

"Oh, Miss Rollins," she heard herself called just as she left the room where she had, like a factory hand — the thought always struck her — punched the hour of her arrival in the time clock. "Oh, Miss Rollins."

She knew it was the voice of her department head, and she turned around.

His slightly affected New England speech, with very little twang and very much Harvard, preceded his tall athletic figure with its top of waving white hair.

"You'll excuse me for calling out. But I did want to make sure you didn't go upstairs before I saw you."

He transferred his soft hat and the unfailing inevitable detective story magazine to the other hand while he dug with the first one into his trousers' pocket and fetched out a bunch of jingling keys.

"Won't you come to the office?" and stooping low and laughing nervously as if he dreaded the interview more than she, he showed her in. His pink face glowed with the effort of his bow, and the blue eyes sparkled under the silver of his eyebrows.

"Do take a seat, Miss Rollins. . . . Have you seen this new edition of Cicero?"

"Oh, was it only that?" asked Amy as she handled the big red book and furred the pages hastily. "It's good isn't it," she said, "full of good pictures."

"Slightly anachronistic and anticipatory of modern civilization," laughed Dr. Garitsen. "But, Miss Rollins, I was going to say," and he cleared his throat to the accompaniment of his jerky apologetic laugh. "I was just wondering, is there anything I can do for you? Honestly, my good lady, honestly. You seem in need of something. . . ."

"Why, Doctor," exclaimed Amy, straightening up, her own eyes flashing. "Isn't my work all right?"

"Of course, of course . . . capital, Miss Rollins, capital. . . . But you yourself. You seem out of sorts, unhappy, even sick, and I wondered are your classes heavy?"

"No . . . not at all . . . no, indeed. . . ."

"You have three preparations . . . Virgil, Cicero . . . and the beginners?"

"But it's all right, sir. They're no burden. I enjoy them in fact . . . they're a relief, one for the other. . . ."

Sounds of footsteps and the shouts of boys preluded the beginning of the day. There was a hand on the knob. Amy looked in the direction with a little show of concern.

"I didn't mean to interfere, Miss Rollins. But you have not looked well. You ought to have a longer rest. Have you thought of a sabbatical?"

"But there's nothing wrong, Doctor, nothing . . . I am managing nicely. . . ."

"Just friendship, you understand. . . . Very well — as you say. I was prepared to suggest it to Dr. Polter. . . ."

The door opened and they heard a quick "Excuse me" as it shut again.

"Thank you, Dr. Garitsen. . . . It is very sweet of you. . . ."

As he escorted her to the door, he bowed again and laughed in the same apologetic fashion. "All right, as you say . . . take it easy at any rate . . . don't let things bother you . . . we don't want another breakdown in the school. . . ."

The words pursued her as she hurried through the crowded halls. Boys jostled her without so much as "I beg your pardon." A boy running an unofficial marathon the whole length of the corridor collided with her. Her papers and book were trampled upon before she could recover them. A rubber heel had left the trademark *Untiring Heel Company* on the head of Scipio Africanus. Ordinarily, Amy would have laughed at the distortion of that dour and assertive warrior's countenance glaring under the dirt of the twentieth century footprint, but this time she did not even thank the boys who had helped her. She put the book back under her arm with rapid nervous fingers, her lips quivering, and her eyes bright with anger.

"Beat it, kid," she heard one of the boys exclaim.

"Yeah," came the answer. "She'll blame us."

She hurried up the steps without waiting for the elevator, taking the wrong staircase.

A boy catcalled after her. "The wrong staircase! Can't you read the signs?"

Her room was in an uproar. She caught herself screaming. She could hear her voice above the sound of the boys, like something that did not belong to her, thin, querulous, uncontrolled. She wanted to run away at the moment, far from the eyes of her class. Shame brought a flush to her cheeks and tears to her eyes.

"Hey, sit down there," a diminutive chap shouted. He jumped on a desk to repeat it. Amy took him by the collar and forced him back into his seat.

"I didn't ask you to help," she cried. And as he stared sidelong at her, crowding his head into his shoulders as if to avoid a blow, he could not realize how grateful she was to him, for he had provided the sufficiently dramatic episode to draw the attention of the rest of the class. They saw at once that Miss Rollins meant business and retreated to their seats — each in his own good time to be sure — but they did take their seats and keep quiet.

Miss Batten had run in between periods.

"What's up, Amy? The favorite cat die? Come on, perk up. You look all down on your uppers, young woman."

"Had a wretched night, Rita. . . ."

"Sleep it off this afternoon. By the way, what do you know about that Contini boy?"

Amy jumped.

"God, did I frighten you? I just wanted to know what to do with him. His work in trig's getting off. I thought you were his big sister or something. Polter mentioned it in conference last year."

There was a note on her desk after lunch.

"Are you looking after Donato Contini? He is slumping badly in American history."

"Is there going to be no nice note ever, ever?" She sat down, disconsolate.

–5–

The two classes after lunch proved stupid and noisy. No one seemed to have done a stroke of work at home. The mother of one boy had left him with the baby, and the baby had been taken sick. Another student had been compelled to run an errand for his father. Too much work in mathematics had made another boy's Latin take on the proportions of a year's construction job and he was not going to begin it at one o'clock a. m.

"I felt too tired, Miss Rollins, honest . . . I'm getting a cold and I felt too tired."

"I left my book in school. . . ."

"My pages are torn out want to see? Ah, why don't you want to believe me?"

She decided she would not teach the class. She ordered the boys to take their books and study. She sat at the desk and stared at them. The room sank into a dead silence. All Amy saw was bent heads, frightened heads, heads row on row, stretching forever and forever into space, out through the walls, out through the dirty tenements that lined the opposite street, out through the enormous apartment houses with their glitter and their display, and then she heard the class breathing softly and heard the turning of the pages and the scraping of the pencils, and imperceptibly the breathings and the turning pages and the scraping pencils joined into one confusion of sound. And the sound increased like stirring wind, then like the combined noises of all the muddled streets in New York. And yet the noises were separate sounds; they screeched and yawled, and battered and banged. She tried to drive them off with her hands. She placed her hands to her ears to shut them out. Deep in her mind, however, she still could hear them rumble and fall, rise and swell, and then finally they deadened into an intense vibrant hum like a far away storm over water.

She was conscious of a figure at her side, short and portly, with a drooping mustache like a viking's. The figure stooped close to her ears, but she kept her hands over them. She knew he was going to shriek at her and she must keep the sound away.

"I wouldn't just sit here doing nothing," Dr. Polter was saying. "Hadn't you better circulate about the room and be helping the students?"

She did not move. In a dim distant fashion she was aware that the figure was the principal on his tour of inspection. He left. She kept staring at the boys and marveled, marveled at their docility, at their silence, their application, and though she heard the infinitely reduplicated cadences of their breathing and their pages turning and their pencils scraping, she could hear her voice above it all, shouting at them angrily:

"What do you think it's all about? What are you studying for? What do you think you are going to get out of it all? Will you find happiness in those Latin prefixes and those gerundives and those absolutes? They're the embalmed carrion of rotting ideals, boys, rotting ideals. Don't you touch them. Let them alone. Jump out of your seats and make a bee line for the straightest road out of this burying ground. Get out there into the open. Run away from this. Can't you see? Can't you see there is no life here, no life here, no life here? What do you want? What do you want out of life?"

Bells were clanging. A thousand feet were running madly. There were shouts. The day was at an end, but the students' kept their seats in front of her, and she could hear herself crying aloud at them, her voice clear above the pandemonium of noises that billowed in from the hallways. She ran out of the room, forced her way through the crowds of boys. The teachers' room was momentarily empty. Everyone was attending to the dismissal of one's class. She hastened to the mirror. One look at her pale drawn face, and she stopped dead. All her muscles straightened and stiffened. She breathed heavily. Clammy cold beads clung to her temples and rolled to the corners of her lips. She went unsteadily to the couch and lay down until the final gongs had rung. She remained there while dozens of her colleagues rushed in, applied powder to their faces, adjusted their hats, shouted at each other and left. When all the noises of the emptying school had ceased, she washed her face, combed her soft yellow hair, pulled down her blouse, and returned to her room. She had been in it a few minutes before she discovered Donato standing at the window in back of the room gazing intently in her direction.

–6–

"Donato! You here?"

His face brightened with smiles, but the slight drooping of his finely molded lips did not escape her. She noted it with a little misgiving in her heart. He was in trouble and in one of his moods of depression. Creature of brilliant enthusiasms and sudden collapse of spirit he was, as Selma had told her. He was in need of her. In some way the dejection that had weighed down her own heart cleared away as if the light in Donato's eyes had been a bright sun drawing up the mists. A quick running of musical notes echoed in some remote region of her thoughts, and she sensed, as she heard it, the reawakening of her feelings, alert once more to the sun gleaming on the roofs, to the thousand disparate noises of the city jangling music in the air. She knew that the boy in front of her, with his sad hand-some features, with the look of a genius in his grey brilliant eyes, was, as it were, the fulfillment of all this sunlight, of all this activity. For his type were the city and nature in continual activity. The building in which she was had been erected for him. The verses in the book there on the table had been sung two thousand years ago to make sure of his coming. She and the hundreds of teachers throughout the length and breadth of the country had been instructed to be on the lookout for the emergence of just such a boy and to direct his energies and his longings and his dreamings until they should flower and bear fruit and add richness and beauty to the land. "Is this a wild fantastic thought?" she asked herself. "But is it?"

"I didn't want to come, Miss Rollins," she heard him say.

"What is it, Donato? You're not doing well in your subjects."

"I know."

She had feared that he would burst into an explanation that would be a charge against her for neglect and lack of interest. But after saying, "I know," he waited for her to speak.

"Why, Donato?"

"Too many parties, maybe."

"Parties?"

"It's all over now."

"Why, this sounds terribly exciting, and surprising too."

She pulled on the old felt hat she had worn on her trip to Eston. It fitted so close to her head that it revealed the fineness of its outlines and threw into sharp relief her commanding nose, the full lips beneath it, and the firm rounded chin.

"You would be hard to do in clay," she heard Donato say, admiration frankly glowing in his voice. "I've puttered around a good deal in Storel's studio and in Angel's too."

"Well, what with parties and with puttering around studios, how can you hope to keep up with your studies?"

"I will from now on."

"But you can't do all these things, boy, and pose too. You still pose?"

"Now and then only. A man doesn't get many calls."

They had walked down the stairs and were emerging into the street. Amy breathed deeply as if on the point of breaking into a series of gym-nastic exercises. Donato noticed it and laughed.

"God, I thought only the pupils felt that way after leaving school. It's how I feel. The place seems awfully dingy and without air like an old cave. . . ."

"Tell me about everything. . . ."

She liked the pressure of his fingers on her arm as he guided her across the street. But she made an effort to withdraw it, and as she did so Donato's arm dropped quickly to his side almost as if his hand had been slapped.

"Oh it's nothing really, but it's going to make a big difference, Angel Smith . . . you don't know about her. She has taken an interest in me and let me use her studio and got me posing jobs and all that. . . ."

"Parties, you mean. . . ."

"Yes, parties." He smiled as he looked at her, and the smile was ever the slightest bit too lacking in candor. It left a queer impression with her as if there were many things he would never tell her. As she listened to him the impression became stronger and stronger until finally it had vitiated all the sweet delight and the proud joy she had taken in him from the beginning of their meeting. The boy had changed into the man, and the man retained too much of the boy not to seem sullied like a fruit become so luscious and soft it breaks at the touch.

"Too many parties, Miss Rollins . . . not nice parties. . . ."

She wanted to scream, to command him to leave her and go his own way. She had heard and had known of boys come too suddenly into experiences who derived an additional satisfaction by relating them to girls and to older women — older women in particular. Stories had circulated about the school. She had always wondered how some of the women could laugh at the foul moonings of such boys, at the exaggerated tales they told with little stealthy leerings from half-shut eyes. Was this happening to her now, and was she allowing it to continue?

"It was always late before I got home and I couldn't do much work. But I tried to keep up with my sculpture. . . ."

She turned upon him.

"Why do you tell me this?" The sharp tone brought him to a complete standstill. He looked stunned, and for a minute she hesitated, felt stirred to a maternal softness of feeling and wanted to take him into her arms and with his head on her shoulder listen to his brave story of life and love. However, she looked at him sharply and with a steady coldness that offered Donato no choice.

"Oh, no reason, Miss Rollins. . . . I just wanted to see you really. We have been such good friends, and I owe so much to you. . . ."

"Is there anything I can do for you?"

"No. . . . I just wanted to see you. . . ."

"That's over now, isn't it? You have seen me. . . . I hope you'll find time for your school work. It's more important. . . ." The words sounded hollow and mean like a long laugh overheard in an insane ward. She recalled the hysteria of the afternoon in her classroom and the image of it was a blaze in her mind, a blaze that blotted out all other thoughts, all present sensations, and left her with parched mouth, flushed brow and torrid cheeks.

"Good afternoon," she said curtly and left.

XVIII. SABBATICAL LEAVE

AMY HERSELF recognized the need of a complete change. Letters had stopped coming from Philip. Donato had dropped out of her life. Both had become like distant sounds in a far-flung landscape, persistent items in the general scheme of thought and feeling, but lacking the needed immediacy that compels action. She felt herself to be a person moving away from a loved stopping place and hearing forever the receding sounds of its activity and its farewells too. And the farther away she moved, the more vacant and the more unmeaning seemed the space in which she had her habitation and her being. She did not, therefore, require either Mr. Garitsen's solicitude nor the constant suggestion of Miss Batten to apply for a sabbatical leave. Two incidents hastened her decision. In fact, but for one she would never have taken the step.

She had always regretted not having followed her original impulses to leave Mrs. Nilins' apartment and seek rooms in a modern building. The increased rent might not have been excessive expenditure for the gain in well-being, in ease, in spaciousness. To have a gold-laced flunkey bow her out and bow her in, to have the sight of broad lobbies, carpeted in oriental splendor, elevators within chutes of burnished steel, replicas of enormous Greek urns, Dianas holding nervous hands across their bosoms, corners fitted out as medieval shrines — Amy thought of it often with a kind of wistfulness, despise it in her heart as she might, for its garishness, its chromatic cheapness, its vulgar flamboyancy. And yet, she knew she would have been like a little girl at her first ball, flushed with the richness and bigness of it all. She would not have felt caught and imprisoned.

Ever since her parting from Donato the apartment in Mrs. Nilins' brownstone had dwindled into meanness. Do what she might with ferns and blooms, hang new curtains, and recover the lampshades, it still exhaled the fifty years of accumulated dust, the decay of a grandeur that was no more, the premonitions of lonely old age to come. At times she dreaded climbing the stairs laid with the rugs that had not been taken up for a generation. With every creaking sound was released a mocking voice that said, "And the days pass, and youth goes." It was like hearing the sound of the lugubrious bell in a Trappist monastery and the wearied voice of a monk, in the cracked treble of old age, shrilling unsteadily, "Pray for your souls, one more hour of your life is gone." And as Mrs. Nilins sat so contentedly rocking away the evening through, she seemed the incarnation of all this decomposition into dust and whispers of what was once robust and solid and hopeful.

-2-

A new high school had opened farther downtown. Clay modeling and other handicraft subjects were to be taught. Hundreds of boys, depressed with their academic routine, were jumping at the chance of a change. Among them was Donato. He had been duly transferred with the remainder of the group and had not bidden Miss Rollins goodbye.

On Amy the omission had the effect of a positive blow.

"Say, Amy," Miss Batten cried out to her across the table in the rest room, "that chap Contini, the one you big-sistered, has departed these shores. . . ."

"I knew he would go," is all Amy said.

"Better place for him. What's a boy with his looks and his genius want in a place like this?"

"Whose good looks?" A thin little woman piped. She had been lying on the lounge near the window, smoking incessantly, following the vagaries of the clouds over the Hudson. This was the first word she had spoken.

"Well, whose?" growled Miss Batten.

"I thought you were talking of one of the men." The voice floated as lazily as the smoke from her cigarette.

"And if I was?" retorted Miss Batten, swiveling around vigorously.

"I'd like to know him, that's all. I haven't seen one yet that wouldn't serve as a horrid lesson to all young girls. . . ."

"You'd jump at any one of them. . . ."

"Well, I at least would have the chance. . . ."

Miss Batten for answer turned her expansive back upon her, and something in its amplitudes constrained the young person into silence. But another one in the farther corner, penciling a whole batch of theme papers with a speed that expressed more annoyance than interest, cried out, "They are talking of that bronze god. . . ."

"Oh, he?"

"The one we saw pie-eyed at the Gorgon's Den."

"The Italian boy — you remember — with the slim girl in that gorgeous black. . . ." The young woman who spoke could not have been more than several months out of college.

Her shock of yellow hair flared out behind her as if a wind were perpetually blowing it. She sat on her chair with her legs crossed under her, managing to suggest that she might have been occupying a whole rug instead of the square foot of hard oak. Never once did she raise her eyes as she spoke nor once did she cease making indefinite quicksilver-like scrawls over the papers she was reading. Her voice bounced out of her mouth like an invisible rubber ball that hit the nearest obstruction and came to a dead stop. It was all frightfully annoying to Miss Batten, in fact to everyone in the room except the young lady smoking the cigarette at the window. Nothing could have modified her contralto monotone and her flowing, languid gestures. Occasionally she moved a small foot several inches into the air, and

from half-shut eyes leisurely surveyed its instep and toes and then gradually allowed it to fall back into place as if it were a precious blown-glass
ornament. Between them these young women had succeeded in causing
the older women to withdraw into defensive groups of twos and threes at
remote tables, backs turned to them, stiffened by smothered wrath.

"Of course I remember — the one that danced like a willow tree in pain.
I didn't know the boy was a student here. Why, I danced with him. . . ." and
she conducted a languorous scrutiny of her left instep.

"Oh, you're positively unclean," bounced out of the declined head of
the other.

"They shouldn't have such tempting gods around. . . ."

Amy could listen to no more of it. She tried to follow her text. But the
bedizened illustration of Caesar's bridge over the Rhone crawled with melting colors, and the Latin words on the opposite page squirmed and writhed
before her vision. Miss Batten's growling whispers did not drown the hateful
words; they served rather to sharpen and vivify them. She sat holding her
book with nervous fingers, her face paling, her eyes closing and opening.

"There's more to that boy than to all the teachers in this school rolled
into one. . . ."

"There certainly is. . . ."

"For looks. . . ."

"And dress. . . ."

"And savoir. Oh, he knows a thing or two. . . ."

"And for brains. . . ."

"*And for brains.* . . ." each word bounced out separately. Amy could
stand no more. She gathered her papers and left.

"What did I tell you?" The contralto voice careened across the room,
trailing a note of superior wisdom.

"You bet," came back the staccato affirmative.

–3–

"Why should I have minded all this?" Amy almost shouted at herself
as she ran down the steps. Her room was occupied by another class and she
had no place to retreat to, no place where she could be alone. Sounds of busy
classes crossed and crisscrossed her attention: high-pitched voices, laughter,
a boy sing-songing a poem, outside noises that stole up the staircase and
lingered like sounds one tries without success to muffle. Even the empty
corridors were filled with continuous syllabling as of distant chaffering. She
had such desperate need to be alone. She thought of the library. There at
least it would be silent. She took a seat at the teachers' desk — a long oaken
table running the length of two windows. She opened her book. Out of the
pages leaped the polychrome of Caesar's bridge, and with it she heard once
more the whole hateful conversation repeated, not in echoes in her memory,

but in actual shouts. She placed her fingers in her ears, closed her eyes, in agonized effort to keep them out. One of the teachers noticed the gesture. Pallor spread over her face. He was a ruddy-faced sand-haired man with a considerable potbelly and not much neck, who sniveled and sniffled at every other word — the last person in the world to offer sympathy.

"Can I do something for you?" He wheezed as he waited for the reply.

Miss Rollins got up, leaving her book on the desk, and hurried out.

"I'll be damned," he said quite audibly and then sniffled even louder as if he had condemned himself and his perpetual cold to damnation.

-4-

She hastened home at the close of school. A light snow had begun. The flakes crowded in front of prematurely lighted windows and then lost themselves in whole areas of dusk only to reappear as they floated down to the sidewalks. A light wind accompanied the flurry, a spasmodic movement of air that played tricks with the white confusion. At one corner it had caught up a swirl of loose paper and cycloned it gaily around an electrolier. The scraps dashed around the base for a second and then circled up in larger and larger whirls until they grasped some invisible portion of the wind and trailed, hanging for dear life, into the upper air. Amy stopped to watch.

A shred of the funny section of a newspaper gyrated so fast around the steel pole that its color became blended in one streak like a distant indistinct rainbow. It slowed up its movements as it rose higher, hung like a bird for the length of a breath on some unseen column of air, then darted down for several feet, skirled around the lamppost and once again began its ascent. Higher and higher it went. The snow came down faster and in increasing abundance. And so the colored scrap seemed to be forcing its way up against it, through the mass of flakes, shouldering them aside, cutting through their ranks, merrily asserting itself.

The whole spectacle took a few seconds, yet a long enough time for a small crowd to collect. Amy became aware of it and had a feeling that a phantom, dreaded for months in the mind, had finally assumed corporeal shape and reality. But what could she do? There were several colored men standing near her. One appeared to Amy to be even more interested than she was in the peregrinations of the paper scrap; for he looked in amazement at her and then he looked in greater amazement to the top of the electrolier, his eyes wide open, his mouth a stupid void. His intentness, evidently, availed him nothing. For he shrugged his shoulders, laughed a rich, silvery laugh, nudged his companion, and said, in a whisper from which the laughter had not gone, "She's off her nut." And so announcing his thoughts, he walked off, still laughing his rich silvery laughter.

It was only then that Amy realized what had happened to her. She had the queer sensation of all life within having stopped absolutely and for the time in which it ceased another entity, distinct and remote, had shaped itself out of her own body, her own thoughts, her own feelings. What had been she for years was not she any longer, yet the body was hers as before. She reasoned it out as she hastened home before the snow should cover the sidewalks. Evidently she had wanted to forget everything that had ever befallen her, be reborn, find delight in small things, in the casual, the useless, and in that delight discover a real motive for continuing to be. For, as she was now, she was an utter failure. Something that should have developed for her out of the hopes and the anxieties of a life time had not found material conformation. It was still but a shadowy seed dropped in the shadowy soil of her desires, ungerminated because unfed by living waters.

Somehow it had something to do with Stephen, with Crabbing, with Donato. If it could but bloom and be, it would do more than merely display its flower, like one of the plants she was so carefully tending at home. It would radiate color, it would burst info flame, and the flame would be warmth and fulfillment. In its radiance, teaching would acquire a new meaning. Those bold girls with their nonchalance and their sophistication would be understandable; they would be lovable. That funny red-faced man with his wheezings and his sniffles would have ample justification to be sympathetic. She would not be in a cage, like Bezo, imprisoned, denied all but a limited area in which to move and have her being.

The snow touched her cheeks with fleeting softness. It felt unusually cold. It seemed collected in mounds at her feet, mounds which she kicked away but which kept trailing after her. She felt shivery, and yet her cheeks were hot and flushed. She must hurry home. As soon as she got home, without even listening to Bezo's chirp, without going to the windows for an inspection of her flowers, she went to bed. Her eyes shut at once, and she sank into slumber devoid of sensation and dreams.

–5–

Never could she have believed that her school work could become as boring as it became in the next weeks. Never a day passed but she reached home tired, ready for bed. She found herself writing criticism on the children's work, which hours later screamed at her out of her memory, and pursued her for days at a time like gadflies — so sharp did they seem, even vicious. There were times when her voice seemed to detach itself from her body and assume the semblance of a winged creature that flew about the room alighting on this boy and that and pecking at his eyes, at his cheeks, maliciously, savagely. She stood aside and watched it — watched at least the ravage it made among the pupils. They looked up with scared eyes, bent their heads as if to avoid listening to her, sat dumbfounded with uneasy leers on their faces. One of the parents had come to complain that the half-term mark was unfair. Amy turned upon the mother — not one of the foreign women who took the teacher's harshness and strictures as necessary to the development of their children. She was a trim plump woman, with a velvet dress that flounced saucily above the ankles and a hat that sufficiently shadowed her eyes to give them a more than worldly look. She reported the incident to Mr. Polter and Mr. Polter saw fit to make an immediate visit to her room.

"But this is no way, Miss Rollins. . . . We are paid to teach children and to give their parents an account of them and their progress. We are not here to browbeat anyone. This is surprising, Miss Rollins, coming from you. . . ."

Amy listened, said nothing, continued with her work. And as the work appeared to grow heavier and heavier, and the pupils to become less and less interesting, she, too, seemed to feel heavier herself, worn down, desirous only of sleeping. And in consequence she had become even more withdrawn and aloof. She had already refused invitations to house parties of teachers, had not gone to the annual social affair of the school.

"Couldn't meet the wives of the men, and the married women won't bring their husbands."

She tried to be facetious with Miss Batten, but Miss Batten gathered Amy into the soft berth of a great arm, and whispered,

"You're in a wicked slump, girl. . . . Come out of it. . . ."

Even with Mrs. Nilins she was short, quick-tempered.

"Just don't rock as if you were happy," she shouted one night.

The topknot began to bob in anguished agitation as Mrs. Nilins faced Amy, tears in the corners of her eyes.

"Why, Amy!" is all she could say, as her fingers snapped back and forth between her lips.

But Amy had risen from her chair, and rushed into her room, and thrown herself on the bed.

"Don't come in . . . let me go to sleep, please, please. . . ."

Her voice had left her as she detected it doing in her classroom. The sounds it made hung in the air like winged creatures that hum viciously before they swoop and sting. She had heard the door dose behind Mrs. Nilins, followed the stair noises, as Mrs. Nilins slowly creaked her way downstairs, but above them all Amy could still hear her voice, sharp, mean, bitter. Fear seized her. Would she be uttering words over which she had no control? She put her fingers tight over lips and held them there as if by so doing she could prevent all utterance forever and forever.

She had gone to sleep early and awakened refreshed. Nevertheless, she had the sense of something in the distant reaches of her memory which needed to be recalled and made the basis of action. She stood before the mirror combing her hair out, watching the light of the morning run with little golden steps the length of the thin strands. She found satisfaction in the sight.

"Just what happened last night?"

The question bothered her. But when she went downstairs for her hasty breakfast with her old companion and housekeeper, the scene of the night before came back. She went immediately to Mrs. Nilins, put an arm about her waist and drew the thin body close to hers.

"I'm so sorry," she said. . . . "I don't know why I did it. Maybe it's because I am so tired . . . so tired. . . ."

"But you are, dear," whispered Mrs. Nilins, patting Amy's hand very, very slowly.

"You have been working too hard . . . and keeping too close at home. . . . You must get away. . . ."

Amy did something she had never done before. She stooped and kissed Mrs. Nilins on both cheeks.

"There! You're too good to me. You would die if I left . . . die of fright and loneliness. I would, if you left me. . . ."

"No, Amy. . . . It is I who would be alone, more than ever . . . you have been here so long now, and this last while we've become like mother and daughter. I often imagine what it would be like if my Jenipher were alive . . . and do you know that I imagine it would be just like this? . . ."

"And you expect me to leave you? I am staying right on and taking care of you. . . ."

From that day there seemed to be an improvement in her attitude. Memories of her walks with Donato came to her. There were pictures of him too, standing, as it were, apart from the whole world, a statue of ancient date, cold marble to everyone else, but quick with life when she gazed upon it or placed light fingers on its hair. These recollections and imaginings now left no after effects of excitement and nervousness; they had been like torments for weeks. She was happy again; she would not be compelled to put the thought of Donato completely out of her mind. And yet she knew too well that her whole system was jangled out of harmony. But she would have striven against it and not have decided to go off to Europe had it not been for an incident more tragic than she had thought possible.

–6–

She had been having considerable success with her plants. The ferns had massed themselves along her windowsills and crowded toward the panes. The red flowers of the crab cactus shone more vividly than usual against the solid green array.

With her birds, however, she had been having trouble. Bezo still led his contented busy existence but had become shyer and less vocal. The myna in the cage in the opposite corner had invaded the exclusive precincts of his reign. The long black-bodied bird, shimmering green and purple in the light, maintained a steady dignity whether he clung to the cage or slowly flew within its narrow confines. Proud of his white quill feathers, his golden-orange beak, his yellow legs, the bright yellow mantle of his head, he swung himself with a good deal of mock vigor in his square green enclosure, almost twice the size of Bezo's circular cell. He had been taught already to shout with fantastic shrillness, "I am Sir Donald." This he would say at the slightest provocation. If Bezo, tired with his brittly pecking at seeds, hopped on to his swing and raised his full-throated trill into the highest registers he was able to reach, Sir Donald, without warning, burst into the aria with "I am Sir Donald, I am Sir Donald, I am Sir Donald." Bezo, in desperation, would raise his song higher, but he soon found he was no match for the larger fellow, brought his song to an end, retired to a corner of his cage, and withdrew into himself. It was the same when Amy came home and cried, "Hello, everybody." Sir Donald had shrieked "Hello, everybody" three times over, and Bezo's little chirp was lost in the din.

"But oh, Bezo, you mustn't sit away over there and look so sad."

Amy put a finger into his cage and laughed at him. Bezo shook himself and flew gaily to the wires she was fingering. She held him on the tip of her fingers and whistled. Bezo broke into his customary song. It had long been a sort of ceremonial between them — a ceremonial that had brought smiles to her lips and laughter into his long-sustained bubbling warbles. But now, no sooner did Bezo's trill begin than there came the sharp, shrill announcement from the other side of the room: "I am Sir Donald, I am Sir Donald."

"Quiet there, Sir Donald."

And the answer came back: "Quiet there, Sir Donald."

"Well, hello then," cried Amy, laughing and going up to him.

"Well, hello then," came the response with just as much laughing and in exactly the same intonation. And Sir Donald stretched out his yellow-wattled head to await her coming.

Bezo grasped the wires of his cage angrily and began the same furious twittering he had always directed at Crabbing. But on these occasions the voice was shriller, angrier, more persistent.

"Hush, Bezo! hush, Bezo!" Amy would admonish him tenderly.

"Hush, Bezo! hush, Bezo!" Sir Donald would repeat.

Then Bezo became quiet, retired to a distant segment of his cage, puffed up his shoulder feathers and sank his head very low into them. From that moment he was silent for the rest of the afternoon and evening. He would not venture out as often as he used to do. If he did, he made wide circles about Sir Donald's cage in an unmistakable endeavor to avoid it.

"That bird's not happy now," whispered Mrs. Nilins to Amy many times.

"It would seem so."

"Resents him . . . more than he did Crabbing."

"It's the old story, Mrs. Nilins, native stock and immigrant. . . ."

Mrs. Nilins did not find the remark funny. She merely shook her head, "Well, he isn't happy. . . ."

"Oh, he'll get used to it."

But Amy was too sanguine. No matter how many months went by, Bezo did not show any greater acceptance of Sir Donald. In fact, his adventurings around the room had become fewer and fewer. Like an old acrobat attempting too dangerous a stunt he performed his table trick with slow and feeble movements. His singing lost its spontaneity and fervor. He pecked at his seeds with less energy, and as the chaff fell into the basin there was no longer the same bright metallic thud. Sir Donald, in the meanwhile, had grown sleeker and entirely adapted to his new surroundings. He proved so apt in learning new words that Amy had even taught him to repeat several of her favorite Latin lines. He had learned one that he would repeat to himself even without the necessary cue.

> "*Nunc est bibendum,*
> *Nunc pede libero. . . ."*

The words issued clear and forceful, and the gay revelry of the lines echoed in the rhythm.

–7–

At such times Bezo clung desperately to the wires of his cage and, forcing out his bill, twittered madly in a frantic effort to outdo Sir Donald. But even this he gave up doing, as Sir Donald became more proficient and, in consequence, more vigorous. And then the time came when he barely chirped. He became listless, forlorn and altogether quiet. Amy brought him to the birdman — the birdman whose face was as tender looking as a girl's despite the deep hollows in his cheeks, the bent nose, the long upper lip that hung over his lower one. He was completely bald, and the wrinkles ran from his thin neck up to the top of his head and down again until they met the deep cleft immediately over his nose.

The old man held Bezo close to his ear, took the bird's bill into his mouth, offered it little seeds from his hand.

"There's nothing wrong, Miss Rollins. He has a good heart . . . listen to it."

He placed the little yellow fluff close to Amy's ear. There was no mistaking the rhythmic flowing of the blood. It was like a little whispered tick, ever so far away, ever so lost in a confusion of sounds. Something clutched at her heart as she listened.

"It seems so sad."

"No, it's normal enough," answered the fancier in his slow reedy voice.

"But he is sad . . . because of that myna, you know. . . ."

Amy decided she must return Sir Donald, or sell him. One day she placed an advertisement in one of the papers. She was happy that at least that much toward getting Bezo back into his cheerful state had been done. On her way home she meditated the words she would address him. "Shall we rusticate Sir Donald, young sinner? We'll put him by himself in the big bedroom. You shall have the great fine parlor all to yourself. And you know I love you, don't you, now? Sing for me! You'll do the circuit too, won't you?

Hop! Hop!" She anticipated Bezo's happiness and quickened her steps.

Mrs. Nilins was at the door awaiting her return. "Strange," thought Amy. "It's so cold and raw!"

"What are you doing here?" she asked scoldingly.

Every movement of Mrs. Nilins' face seemed to have been long thought out before, so deliberate, so steady was it.

"Amy, Amy," she whispered, and her fingers snapped back and forth, back and forth between her lips.

"Is it Philip. . . ? What is it?"

"Amy, Bezo died this morning. . . ."

"Died?"

As if her presence would restore life to the dead bird, Amy pushed past Mrs. Nilins and ran the whole two flights of stairs. Mrs. Nilins had wrapped Bezo in a silk handkerchief and placed him among the ferns on the windowsill.

"I thought he would like it there, Amy."

> "*Nunc est bibendum*
> *Nunc pede libero,*"

clicked Sir Donald's voice in merry rhythm.

Amy had no heart to cry to Sir Donald to stop it. She removed Bezo from the silk shroud, and held him tenderly in her hand. . . .

"Bezo," she called softly. "Big brute . . . won't you do your pretty circuit? Bezo . . . don't play possum, Bezo . . . up . . . hop . . . hop . . . hop . . . ."

Amy stared at her lifeless pet, her eyes wide open, her lips twitching. . . .

"Hop . . . hop . . ." she kept crying, louder and louder till by a natural gradation the word turned into a series of sobs that shook her frame. Her voice caught, the sobs choked in her chest. She fell to her knees near a chair and placing her head on the cushioned seat she wept bitterly . . . Mrs. Nilins kneeled down beside her and put a hand on Amy's shoulder. . . .

"No, Amy, no . . . don't . . . don't . . . not like this!"

–8–

Amy fell into a bout of hysteria, but not an hysteria of agitation and sudden explosive desires.[1] Rather was it more like a shock that leaves one numbed and cold, capable of following one's ordinary routine of tasks and feelings, but without the sensitiveness that makes possible thought and

---

[1] In the original published text of *Miss Rollins in Love*, the first sentence of subchapter 8 above contained a printing error and read as follows: "'Bezo,' she called softly. 'Big brute . . . won't you do hysteria following her mother's burial, but not an hysteria of agitation and sudden explosive desires.'" Since there is no other known draft of *Miss Rollins in Love* to consult, I rewrote the first part of this sentence in order to reflect what I assume was its intended meaning.

comment, glad acceptance and expressed rebellion. Life fell into a static pattern with a suddenness that allowed of neither protest nor amen. She tended to her flowers, carried on casual but unanimated conversations with Sir Donald, tolerated Mrs. Nilins with her continual rocking. But she was no more keenly aware of plant, bird, or woman than if they had been shadows that flitted in and out of her life and demanded attention if manifest only in raised lids or a turn of the head. Sir Donald, indeed, himself began to feel the absence of Bezo in the diminished heartiness of Amy's interest. His lusty and imperious shout of "I am Sir Donald" evidently had required the cue of Bezo's inspired cadenzas. It was not heard now except on the rare occasions when Amy provoked him into reiterated statements. The plants, however, continued to bloom on their appointed days as if no vicissitude of sorrow or accession of delight could tempt them to droop unduly or to raise their colorful arms in sudden happiness.

School meant less and less to Amy. She had not even the feeling that it was slipping out of her consciousness as the main stay of her life. Her energies had fallen to a state much too low to permit of the reaction. Had she been capable of sensing it, it would have been painful and would have prodded her into such an immediate outburst of energy as to have returned school to its place of central significance and left her in the end far more exhausted than actually happened.

"For God's sake, Amy girl," Miss Batten cried one morning, "you'll become a trial to yourself if you keep on this way. Get another canary! There must be thousands in the city. Every canary looks alike to me."

"But I'm all right, Rita," she answered. "It isn't the canary. Sir Donald's twice as much fun . . . . Oh, Rita, Rita," she cried, taking hold of Miss Batten's hands and clasping them in a tight nervous grip that made her friend open startled eyes. . . .

"Child . . . why child . . ." whispered Miss Batten, thoroughly alarmed at the pale face with its open twitching lips. "Come in here and sit down. . . ."

They went into an empty classroom. The combined effect of drawn shades and a grey rainy morning had thrown the room into a depressing gloom.

"Let me pull up the shades," Miss Batten said.

"No, Rita. . . . Oh, I am so sorry. Just let me rest a minute. . . . There. . . ." Amy drew a long breath and smiled. . . .

"Are you going to Europe next term?" she asked, at length, laughing like a person exhausted after a long exertion that has nevertheless been fun.

"Who's going to stop me?"

"I'm coming along then, Rita . . . I have got to get away . . . make a fresh start. . . ."

"You bet you have to, old girl," Miss Batten cried with unmistakable pleasure. "And if you hadn't promised me this morning, I was going to have Polter and Garittsen order you. You need it . . . nothing like Europe . . . in two weeks you forget you were a school teacher — in three months you forget you were Amy Rollins — in six you're the equal of Mary Garden."

XIX. MORTIMER

AMY ROLLINS was the only person on board the *Martin Van Buren* whose homecoming the fog in New York did not spoil. In the sultry September night, they appeared steaming into a colossal bath, the walls of which were hidden in an indefinite distance. The fabled skyline had to be left to the imagination or referred to the scattered memories of trips on the Staten Island Ferry. The immediate prospect offered no stimulation either to optic nerve or patriotic emotion.

To Amy's frayed and jumpy system, however, it was a charmed emulsion, a soft ooze of liquid, medicinal and easing. Like an amphibian she lay stretched out in her steamer chair, delighting in the damp feel of the fog, in the blurred restrictions of the view. "Delighting," however, was not the word she herself would have used for a state of body utterly devoid of mental control — the inertness of an animal too sick to move. For she did not care whether the ship steered into interminable fogland to be brought up finally on a shoal of mud and gravel. And should it strike against piled rocks and then catapult back to sink softly like a sandbag, she knew she would retain her reclined posture, her hands dangling, her eyes open but unperceiving, while the waters gurgled and closed over her with soundless finality.

Recovering from her nervous breakdown in Italy, she had determined upon getting back to the States and to her work. She did not need the doctors to assure her that the determination was the initial symptom of renewed well-being. But she knew better than the doctors the hollow interiors of her soul from which drifted the mists that folded themselves over her nerves, her heart, her senses, rendering her impervious to the inflow of desire, the magic of the days. She kept saying to herself, standing off as it were impersonally, shaking a quiet finger as if there were not enough energy left for a more vigorous gesture,

"Amy, you really don't desire death. It's just that you have not learned how to live . . . and you're thirty-one. You had a chance with Stephen. You fled from it. You went abroad. Remember how you used to yearn for a trip? What did you get out of it? Why, just now you almost slapped that Mortimer boy, that whippersnapper of a Jew, for offering you a cocktail. What's the matter with a cocktail? Amy, Amy you're a fool. What's the matter with that boy, Mortimer? He's the only one that's noticed you. . . . Why not take what you can? But you sit there . . . like a turtle in mud. . . ."

She was aware of the voice as if it belonged to another person, heard it come to her out of the hollowness that was herself, and yet detach itself and swing in midair like a bird on a twig cocking its head to one side saucily, angrily. Not even the hoarse gargle of a foghorn suppressed it. It jumped into a higher register and continued:

"And that young Italian boy with his blonde hair and blue eyes. . . . So much like Donato. Amy, you're a prude. You know you longed to stroke his hair, pull back his head, and . . . jump if you must . . . kiss him . . . not to mention the other picture that came to you — his lithe body naked, standing on a rock, a Hermes perched for flight. . . . The grandeur that was Greece! The glory that was Rome! They were in that boy . . . in the romantic mooning, yes, mooning of the lad . . . the voice like a flute behind azaleas perfuming the night . . . you turned from it . . . then what? There before you lay stretched out your youth, like an ancient moor in the darkness covered with ruins. Ruins, Amy, ruins . . . not of the marvels of old but of your child-hood with its structures of dreams and ambitions and hopes. . . ."

The multiplicity of fog-signals, the padded scurrying sounds in the dimness, the shadows rushing past her — she knew the trip was at an end. The casual companions of the trip would be shouting their goodbyes. She must avoid them . . . get to her cabin and wait.

The voice pursued her as she made her way to her stateroom.

"Why are you hurrying? Go into the dining room. The crowd's having a last drink all round. Mortimer has something to say to you. . . ."

She stood before the mirror, nervously slipping the wisps of straying hair under her hat. Her picture in the bathroom two years previous flew back into her vision like a bird that has swept into a copse and risen out of it again. She smiled. She remembered the Narcissus episode. She recalled the drive to Eston, the shabby lodge in the well of pines sibilant with the young winds of April the drowsy days with Stephen, his unpressed soft ways . . . the night on the cliff. . . . She both shuddered and stiffened at the thoughts that tramped like a besieging host into her mind, coming at the command of the voice that kept talking to her, that had talked to her since she left the hospital in Como and started her return trip. "What have you gained? What would you have lost? What can you lose now? You have led a useful life . . . symbol of the serviceable, you are. . . . What of it? Work again in a few days? What do they care about Cicero . . . ? Cicero . . . noble periods . . . pimpled-nose orator of the majestic brow — grand old Roman — bah . . . Amy, you're a fool . . . *Carpe . . . carpe diem . . . nunc est bibendum.* . . . No, Amy you're not in for another break . . . but you're back again to where you were with Stephen . . . he's married now . . . but call him up . . . the day is only Thursday . . . several hours at the school tomorrow . . . the weekend's yours . . . damn the scruples . . . going to sit in your rooms all the three days . . . sit . . . all . . . the . . . time? . . . Alone, too, now — entirely! Not even Philip — insane now — hardly a chance of recovery — alone — Amy — alone."

Amy ran out of her stateroom into the diner. But she recoiled. The lights had become shabby. The whole salon seemed neglected — like a dance hall allowed to remain unswept and untidied for weeks. There was no one in the place. The tables held several glasses. One was rolling on its side, back and forth, back and forth, incapable of progress either way, acknowledging the mastery of the slight swell in the Hudson.

Amy laughed aloud, and she heard her laughter, as detached as the voice, a laughter like the sound of a xylophone struck by padded hammers. And she looked around the room as if she disbelieved the witness of her eyes. Her shoulders sagged with her drooping form. A short laugh escaped her. . . . "The world moves from incident to incident. Each incident is small, is big, is stupid, is gay. It merges into the next and the next gets torn from it and has a life of its own. There was a gay party here but several minutes ago. They had forgotten in brief hilarity the procession of duties that forms a whole life, and now they are watching the liner docking. The mist evidently is lifting . . . lifting sufficiently to allow it. Everybody is eager to be off. Where will they all go? To another gay party. Anything is an excuse for a party. What did they save and scrimp for? To provide occasions for another party, and still another party . . . sit around with glasses in their hands . . . wise cracking ('Amy, you're slangy,' laughed the voice) complaining even while they're making merry . . . finding a way to forget . . . to . . . forget. . . ."

"Caught you in the act. . . ."

-2-

Mortimer was talking over her shoulder into her ear.

His voice was like a trickle of foam over moss, and the pressure of his body on hers like the feel of a water-soaked log. She drew in the outlines of her body as if by an act of contraction she could reduce it speedily enough to lose the sensation of outward contact.

"You're too late, Amy . . . the shouting and the tumult's dead . . . the captains and the kings departed. . . ."

She shrank further, like one who stoops to avoid a blow. And as she did so, she felt the excitement of his hands about to press palms, nervous fingers, heat upon the whole length of her arms. The slight shudder that went through her she realized was not altogether unpleasurable, like tepid lather before the swift water of a shower. Simultaneous creaking of ropes as the tugs pulled at the liner, raucous horns blasting through the fog, a babble of voices alternately muffled and lifted . . . she heard them all, she knew the moment to be leaving was at hand, and her unswept rooms careened into her vision. She saw the dusty Axminster, the old four-poster, the dog-eared mirror, heard the bated whispers of Mrs. Nilins. And the interminable loneliness of the night, the procession of the innumerable days, the afternoons alone, the evenings alone, the weekends alone. . . .

"You care a bit for me. . . ."

She tried to turn around to lift her hand and strike him.

"You've been trying to avoid it," Mortimer continued, "but I have been pursuing you. You've got nobody waiting for you and no one is waiting for me. Three's company, two's a treat. We'll leave the ship together. . . ."

She was surprised at herself as she turned around and faced him without hesitation, smiling almost gratefully. In the half-brightness the close-packed ringlets on his head gave his soft features an almost cherubic look, and his eyes flashed with a kind of sympathy that further disarmed her. And this was despite the lurking threats of an interest, manifest in his slitted eyes, not entirely devoid of a desperate desire now or never to achieve a grand moment. She read correctly the marks of disappointment stamped upon a countenance meant to be sprightly, constantly visited with anticipations of furtive joys stolen from a denying world, and she fell quickly into a melancholy as she perceived that this slim young man had realized her loneliness, her sense of failure, of having been left behind by the hordes that knew their destination. Not only had he realized all this, but he had understood with the canniness of one who himself has suffered in like measure, that an initial boldness might win her attention, and that the events to follow might not be without their poetry. He was hiding nothing, and she was grateful for it. She smiled inwardly at the full-blown hopes that danced in his eyes like a slow garden that has responded vigorously to the first warmths of May.

But she was not completely surprised at herself, only somewhat amused as she answered his question.

"Yes. Let's make a night of it. . . ."

–3–

New York was a roar encased in a blanket of fog. The humidity hung like a cloud over the entire city, and the street vehicles and the crowds had not yet withdrawn into the thousand compartments designed for the few hours they spent in rest. Like their ship, the taxi they had taken could make but slow progress. They saw its lights and the lights of other taxis and street cars rainbow and halo through the gray filter of near-rain. Amy looked out in silence and thought, "Better this than the stuffy rooms."

"Wouldn't be half so pleasant in your apartment alone. . . ."

Mortimer made the remark as if it were a necessary accompaniment of the trip. She felt she must turn and talk to him. She tried to be gay and careless.

"Anything's better than an apartment in New York. . . ."

"Even a compartment on board a ship. . . ."

"Even . . . or a taxi. . . ."

"Wait until you get to the speakeasy I have in mind. . . ."

"Oh, are we going to a speakeasy? . . ."

"A loaf of bread, a jug of wine, you know. . . ."

"I need both. . . ."

"Refreshment after toil, ease after pain. . . ."

"You quote perpetually. . . ."

"What are my thoughts, Amy? I may call you Amy, no? What's in a name? I was saying, what are my thoughts? Those of poets dead and gone, but the poets can put them in many a golden phrase, and I can't . . . sometimes, you know, I feel as if experiences themselves ought to be available in the same fashion as the records of them. Open a cupboard and there's a cruise around Cape Horn. Open another and there's a love affair. . . . You can't get them in books . . . like you . . . like me. . . ."

His utterance was soft like the ooze of a thick liquid over an uneven surface but melodic and cadenced as if he were reading poetry. She gave no thought to what he was saying, not sure that it amused her. But she recognized a quality in him as he spoke which duplicated the image she had of herself, a soul easily bruised, meant for a nunnery. His books, his poetry, the numerous quotations that interlarded his speech, they were recesses into which he ran for hiding. The intensities at the dead center of his personality he dared not reveal — they would be laughed at, possibly trampled upon, and he withdrew them into the shell of his habits as a snail does its body.

They had sat opposite each other for an hour. Mortimer had ordered an elaborate Italian dinner. The antipasto, brought out on a serving table of rustic logs, danced with innumerable colors. Beets against green capers, the soft striped pink of Italian ham against the pale lengths of celery, the poppy-red of the pimento against the clustered knobs of pickled cauliflower — she welcomed the array, repelled as she had been by the dinginess of the room, the low ceiling, the rough planking on the floors, the garish crude splotches on the walls they called scenes from Venice. In the other room a radio brayed and hummed, the clatter of dishes punctuating the indefinite combination of meaningless sounds. The humidity had weltered in and hung over the scene, a real presence, but amorphous and Protean. It clung around the incandescent bulbs that glittered inside the paper globes, fantastic in tints. It stuck to the knives and the chairs so that no matter what one touched or what one sat upon it worked its way between. She listened to Mortimer, tried to be pleasant and bright, to smile at his wit, and to enter into the intense debates he started on the value of freedom, the importance of an income, the need for social reforms, the conventions, war, crockery collecting as opposed to book collecting, anything, everything. Besides the cocktails he had had on board the Martin Van Buren, he had several others. She too had had one, but Mortimer had poured in additions now and then. Why did not the liquor bubble about in her brains, releasing the cables that tied down her thoughts, bringing the flush of animation to her cheeks? Why did it subdue her rather, tie her tongue, suffuse her eyes with a film that shut out the light? She heard Mortimer, talking, talking, as he labored with the meat on his plate, shoving it to one side and then to another, hacking at it, or turning it over a corner with an exploratory fork, delicately, as if he were performing an operation on living flesh.

"My race is supposed to be a voluble one, Amy, but I am not really voluble . . . you hear me, but what am I telling you? Do you know anything of me except that I spotted you on board the ship and liked you from the very beginning? Is she mortal maid, said I to myself, this seeming goddess with golden hair? . . . The march of the human mind is slow . . . that's not really true . . . the march of the mind is a gallop . . . it always is ahead of the body . . . the body is like the heavy artillery . . . it slows up the whole movement . . . take you and me, possessed of the human face divine, you of one more divine than mine . . . a face in which do meet sweet records, promises as sweet. . . ."

Her head had become one with the humidity. Was this making a night of it? What was he droning, droning, with the queer rise now and then of his inflection, the upturning of all his features, eyes, eyebrows, lips, even his nostrils, and his waiting to see the effect of his speech? Making a night of it? She laughed . . . a trill that escaped her without knowing it. She heard it ascend and diffuse itself through the room, drop into Mortimer's eyes like a shaft of light, and touch into animation the heads of the other diners. They jerked about to look at her. Making a night of it! Her laughter became infectious. . . . There was Mortimer. He was leaning over the table, taking her hand in his and laughing too, the same trill-like notes. His hand felt warm and wet as it lay on hers, and when he pressed her fingers a nervousness, an eagerness communicated itself to her. She looked up to see Mortimer's eyebrows raised at their extreme points.

"You're like Mephistopheles," she heard herself saying.

"You're like . . . what does it matter, Amy? You're like. . . ." He held her hand and laughed. The diners at the nearby table looked at him and they laughed too. One was a woman of great bulk, with a hat that sat uneasily upon her head, thin puckered eyes behind heavy glasses. She simpered constantly. When she heard Mortimer laugh she raised a fat-creased hand heavy with rings and bracelets and let it come down slowly upon the table. The glasses and dishes clattered. And when that had been accomplished she raised her simper into a squeaky little laugh that aroused Mortimer so forcibly that he dropped Amy's hand to look at her.

"See her husband there, Amy," he spoke in a stealthy whisper. "He's fatter than she is and drunker. . . . Beaded wine winking at the brim — the blushful Hippocrene — it can make devils out of angels, Amy, Christians out of Jews, Jews out of Popes, and . . . drink some more," he said, straightening up, "Drink, drink, drink . . . for tomorrow . . . but everybody knows that."

Amy drank fast, with no stop, looking at Mortimer over the rim of her glass.

"There," she cried gaily, and placed the glass down as if asking for approval.

"We'll make a night of it yet," he laughed.

"You bet." She tossed her head like a dancer.

He tossed his head too, and raised his hands above it in the manner of a tangoist, and clicked his fingers like castanets.

"You're not bad looking, young man," she told him, laughing. "Your nose is too pointed and your eyes are too slitty . . . but there's poetry in your face. . . ."

"And in my soul, Amy. . . ."

"Let us drink another?" she asked.

"Five others. . . ."

The emaciated little waiter poured the next glass, winking at Amy. They drank in silence.

"The sweet poison of misused wine. . . ." Mortimer raised his glass.

"Another quotation?" asked Amy, archly but by way of reproof lifting a finger.

"Just a trick I got from T. S. Eliot. . . ."

"You're up on all the modern poets. . . ."

"No, Amy, down on them — they beat me to it. . . ."

"You wanted to be a poet?" asked Amy, tenderly, holding a fresh glass to her lips, and making a soft sucking noise.

"I'm the ashes of one, but still in their ashes burn the wonted fires. Another hogshead of gin, and Homer had better look to his fame. But, you know, Amy," he said as if imparting a secret, "I can never drink a hogshead of gin and so I can only quote. Damn it all, damn it all," (he made deprecating noises with his mouth) "why can't I drink a hogshead of gin?"

"But why can't you?" Amy questioned, bending toward him as if with the tenderest of affection.

"Because I haven't enough sorrows to drown. . . ."

For a second Amy looked at him in the greatest sadness, genuinely moved by the remark. But she brightened up quickly, and said, "What, not enough sorrow in your life?"

"Only two sorrows, Amy . . . shall I explain. . . ."

Her laughter was such a compound of astonishment and amusement that Mortimer looked pained.

"Oh, Mortimer," she hastened to add, placing a hand on his, "do tell me. But be careful. I think you're making me like you. What are your two sorrows?"

"For one thing, I was born a Jew . . . for another, I'm a school teacher."

"That's a common enough combination," exclaimed Amy, laughing.

"But too much for me. Every Jew despises himself for having only dreams, and every teacher crawls under the debris of once glittering hopes. . . . They ought to hang Dante's inscription over hell over the portals of every school house — for pupils and teachers alike. It's filled with men who would and couldn't and with women who could and wouldn't. . . ."

Amy cried, "Poor disappointed lad. . . ."

But Mortimer only smiled and did not allow the interruption to be more than the merest pause. He leaned over the table, thrusting his head forward and whispered as if for the first time in his life he were making a complete confession.

"Amy, I chucked the Talmudical school . . . went unshaved until my nineteenth year . . . *inberbe puer* . . . true son of Abraham . . . and then one night, suddenly, for no reason, I said 'tomorrow for the Gentile university' . . . and I went . . . professors all atheists and pacifists, internationalists and cynics . . . dispensing occidental culture by the mouthful . . . got filled up with it and incapacitated for useful living, like selling shoestrings or running a pickle factory . . . and so into teaching I go and there, what do I find? Pinheads self-magnified, time-servers with no love for books or children, smug as mechanics with fat jobs . . . reiterating the imbecilities and the puerilities of the ages and calling it wisdom. . . ."

"But you stick to it. . . ."

"And shall until death do us part. . . ."

"But why, but why? Go out into the world . . . you have talent. . . ."

"When I consider, Amy, how my life is spent . . . . Oh, what's the use? Why, I'm fit for nothing . . . not even lovemaking. . . . Here am I jabbering away . . . making a night of it . . . a mess of it . . . of everything. . . . Damn it, damn it, why can't I drink a hogshead of gin? . . . Baudelaire was right. 'Get drunk,' he said . . . 'Get drunk. . . .' but I can't do even that . . . Amy, I watched you from the first day out of Bordeaux. . . . 'I'll make her,' I said . . . you looked unhappy and alone . . . I was too . . . and here I am with you and. . . ." he laughed. "Look you, Amy, what a paragon of virtue is man . . . I am drunk and don't know it. . . . I am afraid to be drunk . . . afraid, Amy, for if I were drunk I should throw my arms about you. . . . Amy, for God's sake, say something . . . you're not helping me at all . . . you sit there and drink. . . ."

Amy, however, was not drinking. Her hand was around a glass as she listened to him. The soft trickle of his voice was like water running over pebbles in the night, making a quiet music but a sad music that rises above the stir of leaves and the infinite murmurs of the darkness. The garish, dirty room had been transformed as he talked. Her own dreams, imprisoned in the routine of years, had loosened themselves and wandered about like illuminated phantoms, and she followed them about, the movements of her eyes pausing when they paused under the tinted paper globes, in the dark corners, at the side of the fat woman now so drunk that she incessantly simpered as she raised and reraised her fat-padded hands. She saw his sadness in the unrealized quality of her own dreams, and like him she wanted to find a refuge in talk and would have talked, but it was not her habit. All she could do was to sense the futility of her life, having dared and not accomplished, having sought and not found.

"Bright boys come to me, Amy," she heard Mortimer resume, "and say, 'What shall I do?' Do . . . what shall anybody do? No wonder Eliot quotes. It's a good habit. It's vicarious achievement. What can I tell the kids? . . . the hungry mouths look up and are not fed . . . not by me . . . I am not fed myself. . . . I'm living on prison fare . . . a trip to Europe . . . remakes me for a few months. . . ."

Amy laughed as she recalled the words of Miss Batten.

"Of course, you laugh, and then back to prison. . . . I had a bright youngster in the senior class last term . . . forced out of his school for something or other . . . and sent to us on a transfer . . . a sculptor. . . ."

"A sculptor," asked Amy quickly, her blue eyes casting out the slight film of her drinking.

"If ever there was one . . . a veritable genius . . . and wrote the most astounding themes. . . . One began, 'The days curdle about me . . .' not a pleasant image, but a boy to say that! I questioned him . . . an Italian boy. . . ."

"Donato!" Amy almost shouted it. "Did you know him?"

"For several months . . . and then I don't know what happened . . . got into trouble with the law and was placed in a penitentiary or something. . . ."

Mortimer saw the flushed cheeks of Amy go pale, and her eyes brighten preternaturally. He ascribed it to the influence of the liquor and was about to continue with his narration when she placed her hand on his and said very earnestly,

"Do you mind paying the check? I want to go."

"All right," he blurted almost as if he had said "Damn it."

"I'm sorry. . . ."

"Do you live far?"

"Uptown. . . ."

"Baggage all taken care of?"

"Yes . . . let's go. . . ."

"Messed it again," he exclaimed, whistling for the waiter.

The mist of the early evening had condensed into a heavy moisture. The lights of the streets and the stores gleamed from behind it as if from behind a semi-transparent drapery hung the whole length of the city. The sounds, though muffled, were redoubled and thudded back and forth in the cab. Whatever of mirth and gayety had been in their mood drooped now despite, or possibly because of, the alcoholic prodding.

"Amy," whispered Mortimer.

She looked at him.

"You cannot think what I had hoped out of this. . . ."

"Oh, yes, I can," she said. "I don't have to think twice. . . ."

"Oh, but I thought there would be romance . . . when the lips have spoken. . . ."

There was only the noise of the car for answer. Amy's thoughts were not with his. He sensed the division between them, but not being able to account for it ventured on placing an arm about her shoulder, and saying,

"We still can make a night of it?"

She did not reply, nor remove his hand. He continued quietly.

"From the moment I saw you, Amy, there was something. There still is. You attract me immensely . . . you are in search of something . . . just as I am. . . ."

–4–

She hoped to detain Mortimer long enough to get all the necessary details of Donato's plight. The young man had hoped a great deal from her words, "Let's make a night of it." His hopes soared when he actually found himself climbing the creaking stairs of the old house in the wake of the woman he had already compared to a goddess fair and gracious. His head swam, not with the liquor, but with the sharp thrill of being allowed to put his arm about her and lift a dreamy eager face to his. All the muscles of her body quivered slightly, and he drew her close to him, nibbling excitedly at her chin, her neck, her ears, making little sucking noises in his throat. But he could not have divined that the agitation that he believed he had communicated to her was but the effect of thoughts in no way connected with him. Slightly uncontrolled as his gestures were — the wine and the cocktails had been delightfully stirring — he was, nevertheless, aware that he was stroking her cheeks, and at the same time turning her around toward him. The vision of her breasts, partially hinted at by the slight exposure of her disordered blouse, had become an acute longing; his imagination leaped with flame. His mouth sought the lower reaches of her neck.

Amy was making no protest. She had turned on the light and, almost as if the material full-bodied Mortimer she felt and heard at her side were but a figure in a dream, it was rather the boarded floor, the faded Axminster, the chipped mahogany coffee table, of which she was unpleasantly conscious. They gathered in themselves all the memories of her loneliness and became stark, ugly symbols. She wanted to brush them out of her sight as one might articles from a table until they fall to the floor irreparably shattered. At the same time, she was conscious, too, of Donato, and asking herself a hundred questions about him. Outside the mist had become rain, rain that fell steadily, whistling noisily in the yards, dashing in long sighs against the walls of the houses and then withdrawing in little troubled shouts. In the darkness, windows like scared eyes, blinked unsteadily. She was aware of it all, as if Mortimer's hands upon her endowed her with a multiple perceptivity. . . . Then all these various items, distinct and separate, and her many memories became indistinguishable. They had become a roseate mist that spiraled in stranded whorls, whorls that ascended finally into onyx columns supporting an unseen roof, and then filigreed off into the distance, floating iridescent gossamers. . . .

Mortimer had drawn her to the couch, and had gently laid her head on the massed pillows and stretched out her body its full length. The first shock of the news about Donato had sobered her momentarily, but now the close air of her room had revived, not her as it were but her intoxication. She had fallen into a soft yielding drowsiness that was not altogether sleep, but a state in which all sensations were singly sweeter and yet subdued. Laughter rippled through her and a fire threaded its way from many points to all the extremities of her body, a fire that made her nerves

tremble and quiver and then settle into a vibration so delicate that it was
not movement but a sound.

In her ear was a broken voice, the embodied quality of dream turned
to pleasant music. . . .

"So beautiful — even the tips of your ears delicate shells. . . ."

There was on her breasts a shadowy pressure of the gentlest hands.

"And your breasts, Amy . . . they are beautiful too . . . like firm suc-
culent fruit . . . your nipples . . . strawberries half-drowned in cream. . . ."

Walls and curtains, the ferns on the windowsills, detached themselves
from their moorings like the lightest of shallops and glided away and returned on long receding billows. And above them all floated tinted clouds
forever massing and forever dividing into myriads of petals that fell and
fell and fell. . . .

"But this is dream and sleep and waking. . . ."

"Oh, Amy, not in dire forgetfulness, but trailing clouds of glory. . . ."

She heard her own voice distant as the sounds of bells on water. . . .
There was laughter in it and a spirit of joy untroubled, serene and clear.

"Oh, Mortimer, why will you always quote . . . ?"

"No more from now on . . . for this, Amy, is a whole poem in itself . . .
this body of yours . . . these white arms — these lips opening to sigh. . . ."

A cool wet wind had entered the room. She could feel it pass over
her cheeks like imponderable fingers, press upon her forehead, and then
move off. And she felt with it the pressure of Mortimer's lips and then of
his arm inserted under her waist and raising her body, and the pressure
of the cool wet wind was all over her, and yet it mingled with a steadier
eager pressure of his body, warm, quivering. . . .

"You marvelous beauty," she heard. "You marvelous beauty. . . ."

The voice was thick and hot, uneasy, broken. It flooded her like a
warm ooze that fired her skin and yet left her cool and shivering at the
center of her being.

"Mortimer," she whispered, "Mortimer . . . you must tell me all . . . tell
me all. . . ."

The same amused ripple of laughter as before was in her voice, calm,
clear. . . .

"Yes . . . yes. . . ."

She repeated "You must tell me all" over and over again, trying dimly
through a fog to understand why she said it. She heard a vague ringing
of bells in the most backward recesses of her mind, but in the foreground
kept rising the same soft roseate vapors that billowed into columns and
then filigreed away, and across them rang joyous bells and a sweet urgent
voice told her of delectable things.

Then she took Mortimer's head in her hands and looked into the lighted hazel eyes and saw the flames mount in them. She pushed his head back
and laughing softly, happily; she studied his slightly negroid lips, the round
face like a cherub's, the mass of small black ringlets packed close over his

scalp. She fingered ringlet after ringlet. Each one gleamed jet in the misting rose of the air, and as she let it fall it was like a feather dropping through space illuminated with shifting lights. Smiles of pleasure spread over her face, sparkled in her eyes, settled in the moist corners of her mouth.

"What rings!" she said. "Rings . . . they're like the hair on the heads of Greek gods. You know Praxiteles. . . ."

Something troubling and unbalancing passed over her eyes. She let Mortimer's head fall. Stirred with passion and rendered less sensitive to subtle turns of mood by the still lingering effects of the liquor he had drunk, he thought she was yielding completely. She had dropped her arms, relaxed her head, and with mouth partly open, eyes closing, she lay motionless under the full length of his body. He heard her whisper to him, whisper without bringing her lips together as if, he thought, she were afraid the effort would shatter the sweetness of her mood.

"All, Mortimer, you must tell me all. . . ."

The words meant nothing to him. He pressed kiss after kiss upon her cheeks, her neck, upon her exposed breasts. The hope that had been a flicker flamed into vivid reality. He had removed her skirt, and as he walked with it, unsteady on his legs, to place it on a chair he heard her murmur,

"But all, Mortimer, but all. . . ."

Intoxicated as he was, he knew that Amy, too, unaccustomed to drinking, was now under the complete influence of the cocktails she had consumed. He stood in the middle of the floor, the back of his hand over his face, looking at her through dancing eyes, hesitating. But it was only a second. He stumbled toward the couch, and pressed himself upon the lovely body. . . .

Whether it was the impact of his gesture, or the gust of fresh wind that blew from the window, or something inside her, which had been hitherto only on the outskirts of her consciousness but now had beaten its way to the center of her mind, she rose suddenly to a sitting posture, throwing Mortimer to one side with a gesture not so much violent as decisive. She saw at a glance that she was undressed but she made no attempt to cover herself nor did she manifest any abrupt shame. Mortimer had been stunned by the quick change in the situation, and he, too, sat as motionless as she. Only for a second, however, for he placed an arm about her bare shoulders and pressed her close to him. . . .

"Amy," he pleaded, "Amy. . . ."

Amy merely stared into space, seeking for images and thoughts in the distance. She patted the hand on her shoulder, sweetly but without spirit.

"Poor Donato . . ." she said. "You must tell me all. . . ."

"Donato?" inquired Mortimer . . . "Donato?"

"You told me about him . . . you must tell me all. . . ."

"But there is time for that, Amy . . . tomorrow, the next day . . . . This is our moment now . . . the moment I saw you thinking about on the boat . . . the moment that leaped to my mind the first sight I had of you. . . .

Everything else can wait. . . ."

Amy leaned toward him as he lowered her head and kissed her on her chin, her neck, her bosom. . . .

"You are a sweet boy, Mortimer," she murmured, "But you must tell me . . . tell me all . . . Everything else must wait. You will understand . . ."

She extricated herself gently from his embrace, and as if she and Mortimer had lived together for years, she rose, put on her blouse and skirt, hastily arranged her hair.

Mortimer too rose to his feet, gazing at her as if he had lost the power of motion and of speech. She asked him to sit down as she herself took a seat.

"Tell me about Donato. . . ."

"Well, I'll be damned . . . I'll be Goddamned," was all the answer she obtained. Mortimer was staring at her in unabashed amusement as well as violent annoyance and frustration. "What do I care about Donato? What is he, anyhow? Why did you bring me up here? . . ."

"Mortimer," she whispered, "I know what you think of me . . . it can't be any other way now . . . . Please tell me all . . . the poor boy . . . you can't know . . . . He's alone . . . he needs someone. . . ."

"Not this minute. Suppose he does. What can you do for him now. . . ?"

"Do tell me what you know. How can I explain . . ? Where is he, in prison?"

In the end Mortimer related what he knew. Donato had been committed to a reformatory. It must have been six months ago at least. He had assaulted someone or other in a speakeasy. There had been a general free-for-all fight. Police had broken in and only he and the man he had floored with a chair or something had been found in the place. . . .

"I'm sorry, Mortimer . . ." she said as he left.

–5–

Several days after she had learned from Mortimer that Donato had been committed to a reformatory, was in fact still within its walls, Amy sat quietly at her window, satisfied that in a short time Donato would be released. There was in her face the gentle reflection of a thought which glowed like a lamp within her. Downstairs the room in which Donato was to live and have his sculptor's studio had already been cleared of its furniture, a half century old. She had seen the stuffed black mohair chairs carried downstairs to the junkman's cart, the rugs piled up and carted away, the massive oaken bed with its heavy carvings of lions and lion cubs taken apart and removed. A little shadow of sadness fell upon her musings, however, as she recollected with what a trembling of the head and unhappy eyes Mrs. Nilins had watched the disassembling of her old bedroom, so long untouched and so long cherished.

"No," she had said to Amy, when the plan had first been broached to her, but it was a startled "No" in which new and old affections clashed. "I have only you now, Amy. It was a sweet room in its time, and I never thought to use it again. You do what you want with it, dear. . . ."

Amy had never seen Mrs. Nilins's fingers snap so slowly and so thoughtfully between her two lips. She saw, for the first time as a vivid scene, the slight young girl followed by the portly gentleman with his dashing waistcoat, mounting gaily and proudly the old brownstone stoop. And for a minute she hesitated. She would not have the room dismantled. But there was Donato now, homeless, penniless!

Could she move? That would make Mrs. Nilins even more unhappy and deprive her of some rent money, too, little though she needed it. Amy, besides, could not have afforded to seek quarters elsewhere. There was nothing else she could get so cheap, so convenient, with a Mrs. Nilins to help with the cleaning and the meals.

It had been her first thought when Mortimer revealed the tragedy that had befallen Donato, and no other line of conduct suggested itself to her.

"I must get him out, and he must come to live with me."

There was no question in her mind about the propriety of the move. Donato was in prison, a young genius, of extraordinary personal charm and great promise. He had need of direction, constant sympathy, understanding, leisure, and the love that flowing in and through all the events of one's days brings the serenity and the quiet joy without which the heart and mind can never fully develop. The school had failed to reach him. In fact, those at its head had failed even to recognize his potential greatness. Because of his unfortunate brother, indeed, he had been considered a potential criminal. Against such indifference and such positive distrust he had to contend alone. She, herself, had been as guilty as the rest, guiltier even. She who knew the difficulties of his home life, the poverty, the narrowness which — despite the dream at its center and the tradition of an art form of old world loveliness — broke sturdy spirits; she who knew of his ambitions and his capacity, she who knew of the sweetness and the beauty of his personality, she had abandoned him in his greatest need. Both as teacher and friend she had fallen short of the obvious demands of the situation, allowed him to drift alone at an impressionable age, seek unnecessary adventure, neglect his abilities which in themselves could have been, and must be, his salvation.

But there was no feeling of expiation in her decision. It was to her the simplest and therefore the only thing to do. And only once, and then more like a passing light that one never quite makes out as it loses itself in darkness, only once did she have an image of Donato, slim and tall, poised like a Hermes, his bronze features glowing, the essence and the substance of a dream. And in the same fashion and for only a twinkling moment was she aware that Stephen and Crabbing and Mortimer now lacked bulk and form, were nothings in a distant world that had suddenly become shadow. Life had simplified itself for her. It had fallen into a pattern, a pattern that satisfied and soothed.

As she sat by her window, now and then touching the points of her ferns, or running her fingers through them as if they had been a loved one's hair, she smiled with pleasure at the outlook of having Donato in his room downstairs. She had just come in from interviewing the painter who was to do it over. She had already ordered the large daybed Donato would need. She had assembled chairs and dresser, simple things, unpainted wood, suitable articles for a studio. Donato himself would have to decide on the other items. It had cost a good deal. It was to cost a good deal more. But of what use was her money to her? Her requirements were simple. She had always made her clothes do for several seasons. . . . Her calculations left her contented. Without the actual spending they contained all the elements of a sacrifice that was at one and the same time rendering her and another person happy. And as she thought of the numerous ways in which her salary was going to be useful, school became more and more a significant item. She could now face uninspired classes. They would be more than a challenge. . . .

Not even the letter from the government sanitarium in which Philip was confined disturbed the bright serenity of her mood. Reports had come to her from time to time in Europe. She had written to him even in her periods of greatest distress. He could not read her letters, but the doctors had declared that the despondency that overwhelmed him would lift some day. He needed rest and comfort, the prolonged hope of quiet days and balanced food and sleep. The present report was not too reassuring. It spoke of a precipitous relapse into despair, loss of weight, periods of insomnia that brought fits of wild and fanciful sermonizing to the entire universe. She wrote him a letter, pleading with him, declaring her love for him, holding out the prospect of being reunited. It was a letter full of gentle words and brightened here and there with bits of her arch humor. Donato had sweetened her life already, sweetened it even before he had come to live under the same roof with her. The ecstasy of it, the settled and placid moods that followed the ecstasy — how they all merged into a feeling of stepping on roads that led to definite places where there would be comfort and ease and even delight. All this filtered gently into her letter to Philip and she knew it must bring to him light and peace and lead him back into normal ways. . . .

XX. THE REFORMATORY

-1-

DESPITE THE liquor and scene with Mortimer, Amy's singleness of purpose had filled her with a direct and driving energy. She had fallen into a
drugged sleep, more like a stupor than slumber, through which a glittering thread of motivation ran taut and straight. After her bath and hasty
breakfast, she could put her arms around the excited Mrs. Nilins, kiss her
pale withered lips, and exclaim a hundred little nothings.

"Oh, you dear, you dear!" Mrs. Nilins kept whispering, "I'm so happy,
so happy. . . . And you were in last night, and I didn't know . . . you dear,
you dear!" And she kept patting Amy's hand and holding on to her returned friend as if she would never again let Amy go.

Neither sleepiness nor fatigue restricted Amy's activity. As soon as
she could comfortably escape the group of teachers who crowded around
her, she went to the public telephone.

"This is Amy, Stephen, Amy Rollins." And without giving him an opportunity to express surprise, she added, "You must see me today. At any-
time . . . at your convenience. . . ."

Stephen's office was, like himself, spacious and leisurely: a large mahogany desk in the center of a thick plush rug, several massive chairs with
comfortable arms and deep seats, long rows of legal books behind glass
doors, a number of efficient metal lamps, and one large window through
which the light would have streamed, stark and brilliant, but for heavy
brown drapes. He had grown stouter and his hair thinner; the muscles of
his face had softened under the eyes, at the corner of his lips, under the
chin — a man who had always taken life as it came, easy, unperturbed,
and toward himself most indulgently well disposed.

"*Salve, salve,*" he laughed, "It is Amy . . . never thought to see you
again . . . never. . . . You're looking fine."

He drew his chair and paunch nearer, and took one of Amy's hands in
both of his — heavy hands, padded with knobs of fat. "Looking perfectly fine."

He would not believe she had suffered a nervous breakdown.

"My God, no! Impossible! Why, your skin . . . it's so clear! You don't
look frightened . . . you used to, Amy, you know. . . . And you didn't get
your work done in Italy? I have been scanning the book reviews for a title
from you. . . . But what's on your mind?"

"You're married, Stephen. . . ."

Amy felt she must say something personal, but the thought upper-
most in her mind seemed almost to be shouting itself out.

"All of a year. . . ."

Then the question she came to ask jumped out of her as if it were something over which she had no control.

"Stephen, can you get a boy out of prison?"

"Prison, Amy?"

"It's Donato. . . . I must have told you about him. . . ."

"But, Amy, you just don't go and get people out of prison. . . ."

For a second, the troubled Amy of a year ago sat back, staring at the lawyer.

"I thought you could help," she murmured, smiling as she saw him smiling. It was obvious that she did not have the proper understanding of the rigors of the law.

"Well," said Stephen, "I might help. . . . Tell me the whole story." He leaned forward, sympathetic and interested.

Since Amy could not give a complete account of what had happened, Stephen made the suggestion that they visit Donato and learn the details at first hand.

"But I don't know where he is, Stephen. . . ."

A series of telephone calls brought the desired information. Donato had been committed to the City Reformatory for Delinquent Boys.

"Have you time, Amy? We could arrange to go immediately to the reformatory itself . . . this afternoon. . . ."

–2–

Mr. Kilbourne, the warden, had delayed his supper to see Amy and Stephen. The man was massive. Not a portion of him but was inordinately huge and heavy from big head to enormous feet. With ponderous hands, covered with a mesh of fine reddish hairs, he kept waving Stephen and Amy into his large bare office with its spool-backed benches, plain varnished chairs, and walls painted a terracotta red. He had not spoken a word. Not only had he waved them into the room but he had also waved them just as quietly into their seats. Amy had gotten to the state where she feared to have him talk at all, for she expected him to bellow at her when he did. But his large blue eyes were soft, and the smooth face was pink and unwrinkled like a child's. And though his voice was the heaviest bass, it was slow and modulated as if he were always talking to frightened sick children whom he was anxious to soothe. Amy fell immediately into a relaxed position as if she were herself a child reassured into acceptance of a harsh world.

"Always glad, Mr. Bennett, to let people in at any time if they can do anything for the boys . . ." he said, as he subsided into his seat. "It's you who are interested in Donato Contini, Miss Rollins? A fine boy that . . . an artist, Mr. Bennett. He's teaching our boys . . . and we give him every chance . . . made a head of me. . . ."

Mr. Kilbourne chuckled meditatively as if the head had been a sort of joke. . . .

"We'll fetch him for you, at once. . . . You know, I am glad you came. He's doing well here, behaves and all that . . . ready for parole this month in fact . . . but he's got to stay here . . . there's no place to which he can go . . . father died . . . he hasn't a relative. . . ."

He leaned forward and waved his hand for them to draw their chairs nearer. There was a tone of serious secretiveness in his behavior. His blue eyes saddened a trifle, and the flickering smile that constantly quivered on his lips faded away.

"You know, Mrs. Kilbourne and I have taken him into our family. No good letting him mingle with the others. Lots of those boys are rough specimens. What they don't know isn't worth worrying about. Their idea of a hero is a man that's jackknifed or plugged a cop. . . . You know the boy well, don't you, Miss Rollins?"

Amy had been listening attentively, leaning forward so as not to miss a single word. But in her eyes had appeared shadows of anxiety and lights of joy at the same time. By her manner she might have been a mother, and yet there was that in the play of interest in her countenance and posture that denoted feelings not so single nor so simple. She knew that Mr. Kilbourne's inquiry had been inspired by her expression of more than commonplace concern. . . .

"I was a teacher of his, and he confided in me a good deal. . . ."

"Told you his whole story, didn't he?"

"Yes . . . very few knew it. . . ."

"Only I . . . his lawyer doesn't know it to this day. He does odds and ends of jobs around my private residence on this island . . . everyone of the boys has to do something . . . and that keeps him from the really vicious crowd . . . Mrs. Kilbourne thinks the world of him . . . and I told you he has a class in clay modeling and drawing. You must see the display in the library . . . You know him too, Mr. Bennett?"

"Not at all, sir," answered Stephen. "He might have wasted away in a dungeon for all I knew of the case. . . ."

"It is an instance, Mr. Bennett, where the application of the law — I say it with your permission?" (Bennett nodded) " — is justified in theory but not in practice. The effects are more dangerous than the error the law seeks to punish, or, at best, correct. . . ."

"You know, Mr. Kilbourne," interposed Amy, "I just learned by accident that he was in a reformatory . . . and I have no idea — no clear idea — of just what he did. It's too dreadful to think about. Imagine keeping a boy like that shut up here with criminals. . . ."

"It is not so bad, Miss Rollins, not so bad. Many of them will settle down — a few, well, they ought to have different treatment from this . . . Donato will amount to something . . . he has great talent. . . ."

"What was the charge, Mr. Kilbourne?" asked Bennett.

"Assault. . . . Ran amuck in a speakeasy — seems to have got in with some arty girls that guzzled like fish. He was very fond of one of them . . . they had drunk a good deal. . . . Some one or another in the crowd — a man — had offered the girl an insult: flicked her under the chin, called her something like 'Cutie' . . . suggested making a date . . . they were all pretty well lit up. . . . A fight ensued. The man was at the point of death for weeks. Donato had struck others too . . . the judge thought it the wisest thing to commit him here . . . he would give no account of himself . . . would not talk . . . . They located his father finally, but they found the old man starving. Perhaps you know, Miss Rollins . . . he manufactured and exhibited marionettes. Well, the room was piled up with them and the old man lay on the floor surrounded by them . . . he died the next day. . . ."

Amy stared at Mr. Kilbourne with motionless lids, her mouth alone showing her emotion in the slight twitches, like shadows, at the corners. She sat upright, incapable of movement. . . . Only when Stephen asked, "What can we do for him, Mr. Kilbourne?" did she relax, but only long enough to turn to the questioner.

"He has served eight months . . . his record is excellent . . . he could leave almost at once. But where will he go? He is still a minor under the law, and must have a guardian. . . . The magistrate committed him with that understanding."

"He will live with me, Mr. Kilbourne," Amy said without hesitation. Her manner indicated that there should never have been the faintest doubt of the arrangement.

"I suspected some such hitch," Stephen added, "and had explained it to Miss Rollins. She understands, of course, that she would be required to adopt him. . . ."

"It would be splendid," commented Mr. Kilbourne, dropping his voice to a whisper which mingled surprise, admiration, and satisfaction at a problem solved. "It would be splendid. He will repay you in the fine work that he will do. . . . Are there any legal obstacles, Mr. Bennett?"

"For one thing, sir, the boy himself, would have to express his consent. . . ."

"But he will," cried Amy. Stephen could not help but turn to her, and as he did so, for the first time since he had known her, realized the essential quality of her character. Love to Amy, he reflected, must be an outpouring of tenderness and sympathy. He had satisfied his own mind that her interest in Donato sprang from sources deeper in her instincts than the diffused and superficial philanthropy of the school teacher. Man of the world he was in sufficient measure to allow him to ascribe to it a tinge of something less fine — but only a tinge. He would have been the first to defend the genuineness and the purity of her motive without at the same time denying the danger of the arrangement. For the time being, his feelings for her were all intense admiration; for, despite what he termed the danger of the guardianship she had suggested, he foresaw the elements of sacrifice in it and the practically inevitable separation that must ensue once the difference in age became acutely vivid to them both. For a while, as these thoughts flashed into focus, he was filled with the gentlest pity for her and expressed in his own heart the wish that the years of devotion to another's life which she was planning for herself would not leave her altogether broken and unhappy. He was glad when the door opened and a boy entered to announce that Donato was coming.

–3–

Donato had not fared badly in spite of his imprisonment. Definite tasks and regular hours with such favorable opportunities to work at his sculpture, as related by Kilbourne, had added color to his olive cheeks, filled out his slimness to proportions that made his body appear rounder and softer, and had even caused him to grow sufficiently taller to render his height striking. But neither the wholesome diet and his regular occupation nor the kindly and loving regard for him shown by the warden and his wife had been able to supply the touch of happy alertness to his features that is the symbol of freedom. And the sadness evident at the depths of his brilliant grey eyes, instead of being softened, had grown more persistent and unmistakable. One would hesitate to take the young man's hand in sympathy, no matter how much moved to it, once those sadness-filled eyes fixed themselves upon one. They looked out from under the long brown lashes with a steadiness that seemed to belie the evident fear that had been built up within him. He still smiled with all his teeth, but it was a smile that contradicted its own sweetness when the extremities of the lips puckered ever so slightly and, immediately, drooped. The god was there in the finely molded body, the beautiful head with its covering of glistening chestnut ringlets, the chiseled nose and the almond-shaped eyes. But suffering had placed its stamp upon him, and one hesitated whether to offer love or to leave him alone with his sorrow.

"You know these people, Donato?" asked Mr. Kilbourne, stretching out his hand to take hold of the boy's arm.

Donato had not been informed that he was being summoned to the office to meet his friend and teacher. When he saw Amy, he stopped short, hesitated, smiled in an embarrassed, hurt way, as if he had been discovered performing a shameful deed, and made the movement of extending his arm. There were tears in Amy's eyes despite the smile on her lips. Donato saw the tears and tears came to his eyes too.

"Oh thank you, Miss Rollins," is all he said.

"Donato," Amy cried and went up to him, taking both his hands in hers, but relinquishing them at once in an evident effort not to draw him into her arms. "Donato, I'm sorry . . . for everything. . . ."

Donato returned her full, bright gaze. His eyes sparkled with the unshed tears that had gathered in them. It was as if the feelings in her had thrown their blaze into the depths of his.

"I'm glad you came to see me," he said, trying hard to smile.

"It's his first visit," explained Kilbourne to Stephen.

"That's right," Donato asserted, succeeding this time in bringing a smile of real pleasure to his lips.

"Donato," interrupted Mr. Kilbourne, placing his immense hand upon the boy's shoulder. "Would you like to leave this place?"

Donato turned wondering eyes to the warden, but the pleasure on his face, after a momentary deepening, faded completely.

"But where'll I go?" he asked, as though he believed that the warden had been amusing himself.

"Well," laughed Mr. Kilbourne, patting Donato's cheek, "how would you like to be the ward of Miss Rollins, hey?"

"You could live with me." Amy added. "Mrs. Nilins has many rooms. We'll clear one for you . . . you could have a studio, too."

She spoke in low tones as if she were stroking his hand while he lay sick in bed. There was also a pleading quality in her voice, but she had not intended it. She was sharply aware of it, and a flush overspread her features, deepening the blue of her eyes, so that they dominated her expression. Donato could not withdraw his gaze from her; in fact, he seemed not to be listening to her words at all but rather attempting to find in the depths of her glowing eyes a reason for the bewildering and disconcerting plan which she was proposing.

"Mr. Kilbourne has been nice," I know. . . . But you can't stay here. . . . There is so much ahead of you, Donato . . . and you need leisure and a home. . . ."

Donato's unwavering gaze, his posture devoid of all restlessness, as if her speech had charmed him into immobility, had evidently entered into her consciousness like something critical, distrusting, questioning. She feared to stop talking. Donato must not put into words the full force of the thoughts now only dimly revealed in his attitude. . . .

"You see you must come with me. . . . It is the only solution. Mr. Kilbourne and Mr. Bennett — he's a lawyer, Donato — agree. It is the best thing."

Her eyes had sought Donato's with the eager intensity of her whole heart, and for a second she had seen the unbelieving, puzzled look diminish and retreat into dim interiors behind soft restless mists. Tears had once again gathered in them and like light mountain rain had obscured their steady brilliance. A silence fell upon the two, a silence which isolated them from the rest of the group and, by a like token, rendered each clearer to the other not only in outline but in spirit. They stood poised and still, far away and yet near, desirous of touching and yet withdrawing farther and farther. They might have remained thus for an eternity, conscious once again of a bond between them, but incapable either of severing it at once and for all time, or of strengthening it until they should be at one in heart and feeling. It was Mr. Kilbourne who broke in upon the mood and caused them both to fall back into a reality that was sharp and painful, for both now realized the danger and the difficulties of the arrangement.

"I could not have worked out a better plan for you, Donato," he said.

Donato spoke for the first time.

"But how can I, Mr. Kilbourne? I haven't any money and I haven't a position. Don't they say I have got to have a job first?"

"That's the least of our worries, boy," said the warden, putting an arm about Donato's shoulders and patting him with each finger separately. "This is the point. Miss Rollins will adopt you. . . ."

Donato looked his amazement, and in doing so made them all sense what had been so keen a feeling only between him and Amy. Hesitation and awkwardness gave Kilbourne's next remark a tentative quality which weakened its full strength.

"As a teacher, occupying a respected position in the community, Miss Rollins will be accepted by the courts as a most fitting guardian. . . ."

"But, Mr. Kilbourne. . . ."

"It's the only solution, Donato. . . . Do you want to stay here three years longer? . . ."

"It's only a legal form," interposed Mr. Bennett who had by this time been acutely aware of the cause of Donato's distress. "It will gain you your freedom. What happens after that — you will be on parole — depends altogether upon you. Miss Rollins is offering you a home. You can find work and pay your way. It is natural for you to want to do it. We all appreciate that. Your hesitation does you credit. But it is not altogether a wise attitude for you to take."

"Oh, this is too painful," suddenly cried Amy . . . "I had no idea it would all be so difficult. Donato must decide for himself, and he must decide to come with me. There can be no question about it. You understand, Donato . . . look at it in the right way. How can you, how can you stay here another day in these ugly buildings, among all these boys? You owe it to your father's memory and your brother's, Giulio's. . . . Leave this place, come with me, develop your talents. Whenever you want to, you can go away. It's only so you can get out of here . . . soon . . . before it kills the spirit in you. . . . Say you will, Donato, say you will. . . ."

"Why, yes . . why, yes. . . ." Donato replied in an undertone, like a youngster intimidated by his teacher . . . "I was thinking of you . . . why should you do this? It's too much for you. . . ."

She took his hand in hers and turned toward Mr. Kilbourne and Stephen.

"How soon can the necessary papers be signed?"

XXI. TRANSFIGURATION

A CHANGE had come over Amy. Everybody at school realized it. Everybody commented upon it. They had learned of her nervous breakdown in Europe, had contributed to the monthly sum to send her trifles of sweets and knick-knacks, and then had proceeded to forget all about her.

The composition of the faculty was always a temporary affair. Teachers came, left a brief impression of themselves on one or two colleagues and several pupils. Before one knew it, they had gone: the red-haired French teacher with her dramatic part and still more dramatic bun; the young man who affected 1890 sideboards and talked perpetually of conditions in Sumatra; the daughter of the great Western educator who had had the temerity to rise in conference and criticize the dispensation that ordains fixed seats, fixed blackboards, fixed rooms, fixed programs of study. Over their going no one had made a fuss. They were gone and that was all.

So had it been with Amy. The stately, slightly overdignified blonde, who kept aloof from everyone and yet seemed forever anxious to be friends — she was gone too. The pupils as well as the teachers had forgotten her. All she was now was a name for the payroll clerk to wonder about.

"Say, Timmie. This Miss Rollins now . . . what is she, on sabbatical or maternity. . . ?"

"Don't make me laugh, Sadie. On maternity! Why, she'd freeze a man to death!"

"I don't know about that. What's this boy they talked about?"

On her return to school, however, the change in her had loosened many tongues. . . .

"Hey, what!" Miss Batten exclaimed, "Nervous breakdown or not, Europe's the place for rejuvenation. Look at me — lost ten pounds and had the refusal of ten proposals. I'll wager you a new caddy — and I need one — she'll be sporting a husband before the year's up. . . ."

"Well, if it will make her less scared looking, she can sport two of them, and good luck to her," piped an angular bony woman with exposed teeth, and spectacles that maintained a precarious perch on her thin bridge. "She has never seemed satisfied either with herself or the world. People like her need an incubator of cotton wool and hourly doses of smelling salts . . . ."

"It isn't all of us can make your perfect adjustment, Miss Stevenson. You never wanted for much and never missed it."

The plump person who spoke, with her hair done in an indecisive pompadour, kept her red pencil zigzagging noisily over her composition papers, as if she could not possibly have been listening to the conversation, certainly not talking.

"Miss Rollins, poor thing, either aimed too high or didn't know what to aim at." She continued. "College makes us all more or less like that. But if I had had her looks or her figure I should have had five husbands, or as many men, before I suffered a breakdown. . . ."

"Tosh, Miss Berlmer," exploded Miss Batten. "You talk as if men are a *sine qua non.* Amy could have had her pick of a dozen, but she seems to have done as well for herself with six months in a sanitarium. I'd advise you all to do the same if you're going to lose any sleep over the trousered contraptions."

Widespread as was the impression Amy had produced on her return from her leave, the impression she made as the new term progressed was even more pronounced. Few of the teachers could have known the cause. Miss Batten, who was a frequent visitor, did not lack the requisite shrewdness to perceive that some connection existed between Donato's release from prison, his residence in the Nilins brownstone, and Amy's exceptional growth in beauty, in poise, in her work as a teacher. But Miss Batten had fed on the milk of human kindness and could not have come to conclusions such as Crabbing was beginning to spread in the form of subtle but persistent innuendos.

–2–

Donato had not only been released from the reformatory; he was now an established resident of Mrs. Nilins's. Thanks to the efforts of Selma Kreymdorf he had obtained employment as a stylist in crockery at one of the large department stores. Several days after her interview with Mr. Kilbourne, Amy was startled by a visit from Selma. Miss Kreymdorf had panted into the room with outstretched hands and had exhaled the weariest sigh.

"My dear," she said, elongating the vowels dramatically, "my dear," and she actually persuaded Amy to stretch out her hands too and let them be taken by Selma's and appropriately held and squeezed. "My dear, imagine. You are a wonder — you must let me express myself — just a wonder. Imagine!"

She sat down with exquisite languor, removing the blue foxes from her neck, and patting with the gentlest movements the outblown clouds of her fluffy hair. Amy sat down too, all attention, her body straight and taut. There was no mistaking the impatience in her posture nor the suggestion of enmity in her steady gaze. But neither her posture nor her continued silence perturbed Selma.

"Miss Rollins," she said, "we all owe you so much — the friends of Donato, I mean. Mr. Londin and I, for instance, oh, and many others. Imagine, we never knew a thing. I was in South America, and Mr. Londin was out of town too. . . . Why, we heard only yesterday by the merest accident. Mr. Bennett does occasional legal work for Mr. Londin's firm. Well, they got discussing this and that, and before you knew it . . . well, it shocked me horribly. Eight months in that place! Imagine, and you, you had the good sense, the great heart. . . ."

Amy's face remained as hard as it had been at the beginning. She had allowed Selma to go on, and Selma would have continued indefinitely had not Amy at last interposed a word.

"It is not quite certain that we can get him out yet."

"No!" Selma leaned forward. "Oh, I wonder, can I help?"

"Yes, I think. He refuses to go back to school, and he must have a steady occupation. Can you get him some interesting employment?"

"Oh," exclaimed Selma, drawing back, and finding it necessary to remove her scarves entirely. "Oh, that's so difficult these days . . . oh, it must be interesting and it must be decent, don't you know. Something light?"

"Oh, anything, Miss Kreymdorf . . . work of some sort. Mr. Londin maybe. . . . ?"

"Why, of course, of course. . . ."

Amy rose, and Selma stretched out her hand and seizing Amy's, pulled Amy to her. "You mustn't think harshly of me." The lines of her face broke into a warm pleading smile. There was something in the light of it which was franker than Amy supposed a woman dared be to another. And as she returned the smile, she was at no pains to conceal the suspicions she had had for a long time.

Selma rose this time, still grasping Amy's hands.

"We all of us like him a great deal . . . all of us . . . not even you can have a warmer interest in him, Miss Rollins. We must do all we can for him."

Amy perceived that her visitor had disclaimed nothing and had not made any attempt at defending herself unless the counter thrust was a form of defense. The tight-fitting tailored dress with its short smart jacket made a becoming background for the replaced scarves. Amy acknowledged the superior attractiveness in the hurried glance she gave Selma's clothes and, although she had no desire to say it, was moved to comment, "Donato will be having so little time. If he works by day and goes to art classes or models at home evenings. . . ."

"Oh, I suppose. . . . There's so much to him. Oh, you must keep him at his work. We may come sometimes, may we not, Miss Rollins, Mr. Londin and I?"

"Donato will have his own studio. . . ."

"Well, isn't that just marvelous! Imagine!"

Amy did not miss the undercurrent of rebuke in the laughter upon which the last words had rolled. It was so marked that she began to fear that she had ruined Donato's chances of getting a position. She both amused and startled Selma by her next remark.

"Donato will be his own master, Miss Kreymdorf . . . but he must have employment. You understand?"

Selma encircled Amy's waist and laughed.

"Oh, you dear, you dear. You mustn't be frightened. Mr. Londin will get him work. . . ."

–3–

Simple and wearisome tasks may be made to sound grand by being given a name touched with poetry. Donato was not averse to work but something forthright in his nature made him smile wryly at the pretentious title he held in *Maurice's Fifth Avenue*. Assistant stylist! His name appeared in a large gilt frame with a velvet interior, done in neat white enameled letters — *Donato Contini — Assistant stylist. Crockery.* There were other names in the same velvet plaque — the names of the president of the firm, all the other officials, and the name of the general stylist in charge of all the assistants.

The general stylist was a huge Russian by a French mother as was suggested by the enclosure of yellowish bronze skin in which his sparkling steel-blue eyes were set. A masterful nose, the septum of which departed at right angles from the face immediately below the forehead and then stood out as a definite straight line for its full length, overshadowed the small febrile mouth with its thin moist lips. Conceit and fear mingled in the expression. He had struggled for years to establish his reputation as a leading modernist sculptor. He still remembered the exiguous meals of herring and borsht in the dingy sawdust-sprinkled restaurants in the Lower East Side, the half dollars he had borrowed from everyone to whom he was introduced and which he still owed, the occasions when he had sneaked into a small curio shop and sold for as little as a quarter a mask or a triangular head on which he had lavished his genius. It was Selma who had discovered him and had shown him about, and it was through Mr. Londin — whose relation to Selma Pierre Orgulowich thoroughly understood — that he obtained his start as an ultra-fashionable stylist. The real designation of his position should have been window dresser. He did sketch designs for boxes, for wrappers, suggested and executed forms and frames for carrying various items of merchandise. But it was on the windows that he poured the full flood of his efforts. There was no denying the fact that the window dressing was done with considerable skill in the placement of shadows and angles, silver disks and corniced gold, cloud-like formations of gauze and squares of burnished steel. A hat against such a background achieved the distinction of an artistic masterpiece, and a suit of pajamas seemed suitable only for imperial limbs. Mr. Orgulowich had reason to be conceited. The fear was of subtler origin.

After all credit had been assigned him for the beauty of the window displays, the work was, at the best, ephemeral and narrowly utilitarian. He had no illusions about it. He sensed in it none of the grandeur he felt when he had completed a figurine composed entirely of small enamel blocks with the shoulders merged into the abdomen and the legs elevated at acrobatic angles to the torso. The hybrid soul had been poured into the hybrid mold. The startling quality in the composition arrested the attention and elicited the word of praise, bewildered and hesitating though it was. But the satisfaction that he now enjoyed was in the comfortable check at the end of the month. He watched in vain the passersby for a sign of delight in the scenic drops and structures behind the merchandise. He had done his task too well. The socks and the handbags, the shirts and the shoes claimed the admiration of those who stopped to look. The soul of Orgulowich was lost in the inanities of the theatrical sets behind the articles on sale. And he naturally doubted their value and wondered how long it would be before the management realized the stupidity of it and decided that the check was a waste of funds. That would mean a return to the precariousness of the former years, for he now lived splendidly and managed to save only a slight amount. Moreover, he had practically abandoned his other plastic efforts and dreaded that he had lost the requisite soul state that brought them forth.

Londin had asked him to employ Donato, and Orgulowich could not refuse. He soon learned that in Donato he had to do with a person of definite and undeniable talents. One glance at the heads which Londin had shown the general stylist had been a convincing argument.

"Oh, most naturally, Mr. Londin, we could not afford to refuse him the employment." His steel blue eyes glittered. "This head is the most remarkable." He pronounced remarkable with the accent on the last "a." "Most remarkable. Oh, I can give you the assurance, Mr. Londin. Mr. Maurice will like it. . . ."

At the beginning Orgulowich had assigned light jobs to Donato and had sent him home early.

"You're the lucky, but the lucky artist, Donato. You have the time allowed to you and the place for you to make the money and learn too and still be your own master — your own soul master, Donato. You will show me your work when you have completed it?"

Amy was always glad to see Donato arrive home early and immediately go to his rooms. He had bought himself a set of sculptor's tools, considerable amounts of clay, had constructed workbenches out of old boxes, and spent a long time in the construction of frames for heads, torsos and figures. She tidied the studio in the morning before she left for school, never once letting Donato know that the small amount of money he was paying for rent would not suffice for the meals supplied him and a maid, too, to do the work of cleaning up. It was work, however, only in that it consumed time and effort. In reality the pleasure she derived far outbalanced the fatigue it cost her. To catch a sight of a head in the process of its creation, to watch it grow day by day into a form that denoted character and purpose, was delight and ecstasy. The teachers might note the glow of health in her cheeks, the face rounding, the eyes alert and almost gay.

They could never divine the strands of joy out of which were built her new spirit and her new vitality.

At first, between her and Donato the meetings had been more or less of a casual nature. They both realized that behind the exterior of interest and friendship there were feelings which they did not dare express. But they contrived without conscious design to be companions without intimacy, friends without emotion. They met at supper. Donato invariably told of his day's work.

"Today I moved huge Greek jars from one corner of the stock room to the other. There were fifteen of them. All of them were manufactured somewhere in Connecticut but they have been made to look ancient. They are going to use one in each window and hang socks from the brims."

"Not from the brims!" Mrs. Nilins exclaimed in great excitement.

"But Mr. Orgulowich wouldn't do a thing like that," added Amy.

"I suppose not. But the marble and the crockery and the metal that he uses just to display underwear and things. . . . I wish I had half of the material."

"Why, haven't you enough, Donato?"

"Oh, plenty. But it seems such a fool waste of stuff. . . ."

"The windows do look beautiful!"

"They do."

"Have you finished the head of the anti-Christ?"

"In a way, Amy." (Amy had insisted after several weeks that he must use her first name.)

"Can't you?"

Donato rose and went over to the windowsills. Even in the huge dining room that formed Mrs. Nilins' own living quarters Amy had placed groups of plants. Donato had learned to care for them and every evening he spent some time looking over the leaves, fingering the soil, asking questions. Amy followed him and they both stooped over the Chinese fan palm that had successfully withstood the early cold and the more injurious steam heat.

"It's doing very well, isn't it, Donato?"

"Yes," he answered as he ran his hand over the large leaves.

"You're getting a bit out of sorts, young man," suddenly exclaimed Amy in a voice meant to be sharp and laughing at the same time.

"Oh, I haven't been able to finish anything the last few days. I need a model."

"That's easy. Couldn't I do, and Mrs. Nilins?"

"It's an idea!" His eyes beamed. "Let's try."

Several nights they hurried their supper and hastened to the "studio" upstairs. The large room was poorly lighted so that the mantelpiece with its array of heads, masques, and figures looked more like an assembling place for fantastic odds and ends. The platform Donato had built was directly under the one chandelier with its two bulbs but even in that situation did not have enough light to reveal the necessary details of the model sitting on it. Amy's face was lost in the half light; Donato struggled with it nevertheless. They had both laughed and joked a good deal before Amy was seated in the exact position Donato desired. But once he had begun to work, he worked steadily, without smiling, as if the rapture of the moment might be lost by a word not in harmony with the spirit in him.

"I am afraid I shall never get you," he confided to her one night. "I don't know why. Maybe the light. Maybe I get too tired these days. Orgulowich is working me terribly hard. You know, I showed him those heads — the anti-Christ with the business man and the artist around the broken cross. I could see he liked it. But he frowned and told me to stick to more conventional stuff. 'You'll never sell this stuff, I give you my assurance.' That's all he said. Then he gave me the toughest job in the place. He has made huge steel slabs and placed heavy mirrors to the side of them — projections like, you know. Well, I had to move those myself. . . . He wouldn't give me any help either. Almost broke my back."

"Well, that's only once. . . ."

"No, it's every day now. I asked him once, 'Can I get a chance at fixing up the crockery window myself?' He frowned and then he smiled, and walked away. . . ."

-4-

One night both Amy and Donato had felt too tired to continue with the bust he was making of her. The next evening Donato was compelled to work overtime. When he arrived home, he went immediately to bed. The Christmas season was approaching and the stores were demanding that all their employees work later hours. But, except for the night when he had gone to sleep early, Donato insisted upon spending some time in the studio. Amy remonstrated with him, but he had assured her that he was not tired any longer.

"Got my second wind, Amy. I could keep going all night."

But she had been sufficiently worried to welcome a visit from Selma and Londin. They sat in the studio and talked. On another occasion Selma had called up. She felt constrained to ask Amy whether Donato might go out.

"Well, why not?" asked Amy laughing. "It's for him to say. I'm not his mother, after all. . . . Here's Donato, he'll talk to you."

Donato lifted an appealing face to Amy.

"May I?" he asked in his turn, smiling to suggest that he appreciated the fiction of her being his mother.

"Why, of course, Donato. It will do you good. You have been working so hard."

But when he had left, she went at once to the plants and busied herself with them in uneasy, random fashion. The loneliness that had been before Donato had come to stay with her and Mrs. Nilins returned with the suddenness of water that has burst through an accidental aperture. It flowed all around and about her. It filled the corners of the rooms. She did not dare look into the dark studio. She feared even to go to her bed. And, although she finally did, she did not sleep. She waited for the sound of the door opening and for footsteps on the stairs.

"Oh, ho, Amy," she at last heard the low whispered call of Donato.

"Oh, ho," she answered. "Back early, aren't you?"

"You bet, oh," he sang out.

"Tired?" she called out.

"Oh, ye-es. . . ."

"Right to bed then. . . ."

"Ye-es."

She heard his door shut. She listened for sounds of his stirring about. She fell slowly into a sleep, troubled sleep. But she was awakened from it by the noise of something falling. She slipped on a robe and went to her door. Under Donato's door was a light.

"Donato," she called. "Donato."

There was no answer. She felt uneasy. She wanted to go down, open the door, and walk in. But she dreaded that too. She had never once entered the room after he had shut the door for the night. She called again, and again there was no answer. She tiptoed downstairs and knocked on the door.

"Donato."

"He must be asleep," she thought, "and left the light burning." She opened the door and walked in. There he was at a stand, molding a figure with his fingers. She stood still for a minute, marveling at his concentration. But at the same time she recalled how tired he was looking, how hard he was working at the store, and that he had been out. She was about to call his name but thought better of it. She walked up to him and placed her hand on his shoulder. Only then he turned around, startled.

"Oh, you scared me," he gasped.

"But it's so late, Donato."

They looked at each other. Amy was now in the habit of braiding her hair at night, and the two braids of gold fell down over her shoulders and down her bosom. The uncertain light traveled along them, flickering as it touched the knotted strands. It was natural for Donato to see them and to follow their lengths until they stopped over her full breasts, partly exposed by the loose robe.

"You shouldn't be up so late, young man," she said, placing a hand on his cheek. But instead of answering in words, she saw him raise his eyes to her, eyes in which a queer light had pooled. And then she recalled that he had been out with Selma and that he had been kissed by Selma, and . . . she dared not carry her thoughts beyond. She shuddered but managed to smile again as she stroked Donato's cheek once more and said,

"Get right to bed now. Don't forget I am your guardian and must give an accounting of you. There's going to be no tired, sick boy around here."

He laughed, too, but she noted the same strange brilliance in his eyes as he said, "All right."

–5–

That night Amy lay awake until the first grey of the winter morning. Through her window she saw the dark shadows of unlighted warehouses. She heard the noise of cars in the nearby garage. The trolleys clanged, and the horses of the milkmen beat a slow, steady clatter. The images of the night dropped away from her: Donato's eyes, her own flushed face as she had hurried under her covers. The feelings that had coursed through her body like rivulets of flame subsided and all her limbs quivered with shaken nerves. Then as she sank into a slow tired sleep the images returned. But she averted her head from Donato's gaze, drew the blankets about her in sudden fear and lost all consciousness.

From that time on a note of constraint entered into their meetings. But they continued as before, having their evening meal together, talking of this and that, interested in his sculpture. She feared, however, that he was showing the effects not only of his application by night but also of his exertions by day.

"Donato," she reminded him one evening. "You know you have not done a bit of studying. Remember that you promised Mr. Kilbourne. . . ."

"My God," he answered, putting his hands to his head in mock seriousness. "Study! What do you call reading up on the lives of the artists and going through Borriner's books? Isn't that study? . . ."

"Of course . . . but let's read some Latin together. You always liked it."

"Do you want to, Amy, really, or do you think I need it?"

"Oh, goose . . . of course, I want to. . . ."

They tried that on different occasions. Amy even suggested the theater.

"But, Amy," he protested. "You say yourself *ars longa vita brevis*. . . ."

"I know. But we must have some relaxation. . . . Let's. . . ."

It was a lark. They walked the twenty blocks to the play. They shared the jokes, looking at each other when one was made, and laughing together. On the way back, they stopped for hot chocolate and crackers, standing up at the counter of a crowded drugstore, repeating the bright passages of the play, discussing its merits. It was snowing when they got out, but they decided to walk home.

"This is fun," she said, taking his arm, and pressing close to him. "Watch the flakes sparkling as they pass the lights. They're like white starlings."

"It's coming down fast."

"It's all over your coat." She brushed off the accumulation. "You need a heavier one."

"Got to get that block of marble first. . . ."

"Let me buy you the coat. . . ."

"No. This is all right. . . ."

"Oh look," he exclaimed after a short silence, as they stopped under a light to allow a car to pass. "You're all covered over. You're like a white image. Look . . . stand over there . . . yes, you are. . . ."

She laughed as he looked at her through two circled fingers.

"You're like a Galatea. . . ."

"Oh you certainly learned your myths. . . ."

She again put her arm under his, pressed close to him, and walked briskly alongside. On the stoop they helped each other brush off the snow from their clothing. Sprays of it fell on their cheeks.

"Stop throwing it down my neck, silly."

"I am not. . . ."

"But you are. . . ."

They looked at each other like school boys and laughed. "Good night, silly boy," she cried once they got inside and hurried up the stairs.

"Oh, I can catch you," he shouted, and ran in pursuit.

But she had got to her room and was looking out from a chink in the door, which she held slightly ajar. "Good night," she whispered, laughing.

XXII. FULFILLMENT

-1-

"THERE IS not the room for the pure art," Orgulowich was expounding as he turned over in his fingers the small head of Amy, which Donato had brought for his inspection. "There is not the room for the art that will not fit into the general order. We want the art that tells the story of business. . . ."

This was not the first time that the general stylist had carefully explained, without direct application to be sure, that Donato's efforts were doomed to failure. This discouragement which Orgulowich was at such great pains to administer affected Donato in spirit only. He did keep asking himself whether his labor and his ambitions would be of any real value in the scheme of things, but no matter how despondent the doubts might render him, he found it impossible not to retreat to his studio in the evening, sometimes all day Sunday, and apply himself to the definite systematic program he had outlined for himself.

As he saw one head after another emerge from clay or stone, he had the sensation of seeing distinct blurred flames, that had existed only in his mind, transformed into concrete and tangible realities, realities which finally usurped the entire space of the visible universe. They seemed the only verities. Even Amy moved off into dim regions beyond the immediate ken. Selma, Orgulowich, the people he met in his work, the apartment houses that flanked the streets, the concourse of cars moving like molten lava between the perpendicular walls of buildings, the flash of sunlight on windows, infinitely duplicated, the sight of mounded snow in the parks, glistening with straying lights — all fell back to a remote periphery and left, living and eternal, these heads and these groups, smiling lips and teeth clashing in anger, eyes that like gimlets worked themselves into one's consciousness.

This had become the real world, and the actuality only a shadowy and indefinable void. And as the sensation grew, he argued less and less with Orgulowich and he worked harder and harder at his sculpturing. But he could not help realizing that the farther he withdrew himself from the influence which Orgulowich desired to exert upon him, the more Orgulowich's attitude of friendliness changed and the more he drove the younger man.

"Make out the boss ain't riding the kid," he heard one of the girls confiding to her friend.

"He sure is."

"Yeah — that's what I say. He's too stuck up though, and you gotta do something to bring a kid like that off his perch. . . ."

"You sure have to. . . ."

"Yes — that's what I say. . . ."

Donato, however, knew better. With a sure instinct, born of the creative urge, he had begun to suspect that in Orgulowich's attitude there was not a little of jealousy, resentment rather. The older artist, transformed now into one of the minions of utility, was rationalizing his conduct, and, in the process, becoming vehement in his opposition to the young boy who persisted in placing "the pure art" above all other considerations. His anger was fanned by the continued refusal on Donato's part not only to discuss the theories Orgulowich was developing but also to acknowledge that they had any merit whatsoever. And so he used his position to impose the heaviest tasks on the boy, to keep him working long hours, and at times to lecture him sharply on slight errors or lack of industry. At first, Donato had spoken of this treatment to Amy, but in order not to cause her any further anxiety he had stopped doing so.

Nor did he feel he should report it to Selma. To give up the position and seek another was impossible. Not only would it have to be explained to the parole officer with the consequence that it might redound to his discredit, but it might also smack of ingratitude to those who had helped him. Despite the fatigue, despite the indignities he was at times made to endure, he performed his tasks cheerfully. But the strain of maintaining this attitude and the work itself, together with his labors at night, began to tell upon him. Amy was urging him to take a rest, not work at night for a while, get to sleep early, walk, read.

"After the exhibition, Amy."

The exhibition of the New Artists was finally announced. Through Londin and Selma, he managed to obtain a place for a half dozen of his pieces. He had put modest prices on each and had hoped to sell them all. The proceeds would permit him to drop his work at Maurice's and devote all his time to his art.

He had already formed a project in his mind which he was anxious to carry out. An old peasant woman, with a face completely covered with a mesh of the finest wrinkles, was to pose for him. Her head was to become the central piece in a group to be entitled "The Fruit of the Womb." But the old woman was too old to walk the long distance from her home in the Italian section to his studio, certainly after dark. He needed, too, a large block of marble. He had gone to a stone yard and selected a large plinth. It would cost a great deal to move it. Amy had promised to defray the expenses of it, however. For weeks before the exhibition he had worked far into the night. Orgulowich had got wind of the matter and began pushing Donato harder and harder. By the time the exhibition had opened, he had, despite his youth, every sign of illness and fatigue. But his hopes proved medicinal.

"I'll get purchasers," he insisted. "You'll see, Amy. They're great heads. The bust of the child will sell for sure. You wait and see. . . ."

The six pieces did sell. He rushed home with the news. Amy had never seen the gay spirit of the Italian in him reach such heights. He threw his arms about her, embraced Mrs. Nilins, talked to the plants, sang at the top of his voice. The next day, however, he discovered that the buyers had been Londin and Selma. And his depression was complete. He sat down at Amy's desk, and called her to him.

"Watch," he said, as she stood at his shoulder.

He took a pen and wrote:

"Dear Selma:

How sweet of you to like my stuff and even buy it! But why didn't you say you wanted it before I exhibited? You could have had it then. Now I can only do the next best thing. I am returning the check the committee sent, and asking you to keep the heads for my sake.

Donato. . . ."

–2–

No remonstrance on Amy's part could cause him thus to change his mind. And out of loyalty to him, she refused to accept the checks Londin and Selma offered her as a kind of reserve for Donato. The blow was a severer one than Amy or Donato himself realized. He dreaded to tell the real facts to Orgulowich, but in the end he did.

"I think you are right, Mr. Orgulowich," he said one morning.

"Right, Donato? Right about what?"

"Pure art, sir."

"But you sold your pieces . . . that is the proof . . . the sale price — ah! that makes the art."

"No . . . I didn't sell them. Some friends of mine bought them out of pity. . . ."

Donato looked his superior squarely in the eyes, but he could not keep back the alternate flush and pallor on his face, nor the tears that came to his eyes.

"Sorry, old man, oh, but so sorry," cried Orgulowich, taking Donato's hand.

That evening Donato went to bed sick. For days he lay inert and cold. Then he fell into a coma, and one night, unable to keep on his bedclothes he contracted a serious cold. The cold developed into pleurisy.

The task of nursing him fell on Amy and Mrs. Nilins. The routine of rising hastily, attending to Donato, snatching a bite, hurrying to school, returning anxiously, spending the afternoon and the evening in the sick room, attentive to every detail of the treatment, managing the household — it returned like a memory she had lost. But instead of depressing her, it wrought an unusual effect. The teachers were astounded at her great happiness. Her work at school became so noteworthy that Mr. Polter got into the habit of sending to her the visiting teachers.

Crabbing alone had in some measure divined the cause.

"I say, Rita," he said to Miss Batten, "Amy's looking fitter than ever."

"Well, suppose she is. Do you have to smile so maliciously?"

"She's got that boy all to herself, now he is sick. . . ."

"Crabbing," Miss Batten answered, staring in his face, "some day you are going to be generous and going to die from the exertion of it."

If the six weeks of his illness had shut Donato within the closet of her affection and given her the illusion of his being entirely hers, the days of his convalescence brought him nearer to her in a real way. While he lay in bed ill, even when he had been operated upon, he had seemed less a person than just someone to assist. Had she been a nurse in a hospital and had he been one of her charges, she could not have acted differently, nor could he have distinguished her from any other nurse. He suffered too much, he was happy to have her ministrations, he looked with wide scared eyes as she sat next to him or passed his bed, he let his hand be held without returning a pressure. Even when she bent over him and placed her lips to his ears so that her voice might not be too great a strain on him, he had lain quiet, motionless, as if she had been the merest effigy of herself in shadow.

The weeks that followed were blessed weeks. Donato's eyes brightened even at the sound of her footsteps. Although the muscles of his chest pained him if he talked or even smiled — except slowly, with gentle effort — he called her name, and his face lighted with pleasure as she came near. The exertion of a conversation was too great, but he held her fingers and, turning his head, would say:

"Has it been ten years? . . ."

"Hush, goose, it's been only a month. . . ."

"Seems years. . . ."

"We'll have you up soon. . . ."

"Shall we go out into the wind and the sun?"

"And where there's grass. . . ."

"That will be nice. . ."

"We'll be all alone . . . no doctor even. . . ."

Donato lifted his long lashes and the grey eyes beneath shone weakly. The question in them was real, and it went to Amy's heart at once. "Is she Amy, my Miss Rollins?" For the teacher had dropped away, the years between them had become as nothing. Gathered in her eyes, in the softness of her words, the anxiety of her manner, were the impulses, the desires that he had seen in other women. No longer was she the pedestaled, the withdrawn — she was like Selma, like Angel, a child of love.

Then came the long walks together. She had spent a considerable amount of money on doctor's bills, and Donato refused to be sent to the country.

"We'll go to the parks, and take the buses. . . ."

They met after school and sat under the trees, watched the children play, noted the arrival of new birds, the young leaves on the branches, the flower beds unfolding from color to color. For several weeks on their return home they had an early dinner, and Donato went to bed. They had both learned to laugh meaninglessly but joyously at everything — bad puns, a spoon falling, a mouthful of soup that proved too hot, getting too tired and having to rest unexpectedly. They talked at great length about his sculpture, her work at school. He became interested in her difficult problems of discipline and instruction. She believed that some of his comments were particularly shrewd and acted upon them.

"He's only showing off, that boy — give him the hard lines to read."

"Why, Donato, he'd only hold the book up to his nose and giggle into it."

"He's a tough case all right. . . ."

"I'm going to give him easy lines and then maybe he will think he's bright. . . ."

"That's an idea . . . and put him in charge of the class."

They had scrutinized every statue in Central Park.

"If I see another one, I'll have a relapse. . . ." Donato said one day.

"Don't be conceited. . . ."

"Oh, I know, but don't you rub it in. . . ."

She put her arm about his waist. "Silly, don't take it so seriously. Wait until you start on Mam-ma 'Chele." (Mam-ma 'Chele was the old Italian peasant woman who was going to pose for him.)

-3-

Amy was happy, and yet she was aware of a restlessness in both herself and Donato which checked the full coursing of her spirits in mid-career and left her bewildered, uncertain. Her body ached with tension; her breath left her and returned suddenly; her cheeks reddened and grew cold. Action and dream were merged in a speechless confessional of excitement.

At such times, however, she found simple ways of slipping out of her mood and returning at once into the lighted path of her new life. A snatch of song, a whistled tune, a quick run to her flowers — she was happy again! How she wished for another Bezo, another Sir Donald! She would go to them and pour out her confessions, and they would sit up, head cocked to one side, blinking sagely, even roguishly. And when she ceased, they would break into their song or chatter, and how she would laugh then, herself gay as the birds, as carefree, as assured! She contented herself with placing her hand behind a verbena leaf and letting her restlessness flow out and pool in the subdued ecstasy of her love for its delicately mingled colors. Or she stooped low over her oxalis blooms, her mouth close to their brilliant petals, and stood so, unmoving, without thought, sensing only the presence of a divinity of beauty and order and peace. . . .

She found another solace in letters to her brother. Philip was reported to be making a recovery. He would have days of complete lucidity, and on those days the first wish he would express would be for his sister's letters. She filled them with details of her school life, accounts of her own doings, descriptions of Donato's work. . . . They had become tonic to the fevered life-beaten Philip. The doctors urged her to continue them. And she did. His letters were not what they used to be, melancholy, fantastic jeremiads. She treasured one in particular.

"Discovery, darling Amy, is greater than invention. Imagine never having come upon a wild flower in your whole life, unexpectedly, among grasses, near a stone; nor having penetrated into a woods and found a lovely pool, glimmering with sea green shadows. That sort of thing would give me the most rapturous feeling even when I had had no sleep, no food, no rest for days. I could weep at the sight of a meadow lily, an Indian pipe! . . .

"Is meeting people filled with equivalent joy? Your letters answer yes, yes, yes — like music. . . ."

Philip, then, understood what Donato had become in her life. The poet in him had penetrated at once beneath the texture of her words to the steady glowing of her feelings. Dear Philip! In his few normal hours, he had been presented with the burden of her own problems. The well and the adjusted had sought encouragement and approval from the sick and the disordered. He who needed her had become a sweet support, distant though he was in time and space. Not that she had confessed in explicit words this love that was giving point to her life. But the unuttered truth of her passion suffused her words with colors like those on the surface of some stones which seem then not to be opaque and cold but translucent and warm. Philip had divined and blessed. Nor had he complained. He who might have justly claimed her love was glad she had found a love that quickened and revitalized. . . . Dear Philip! When he was well again, he must return. The three of them and Mrs. Nilins . . . they could be happy. . . . She dared not allow her thoughts to dwell too long upon it! . . .

–4–

June with its bursts of heat came upon them. Donato sat in the park or on the stoop of the house — drawing. His mind was occupied with vast aims. Projects for lifesize groups flashed across his mind and found momentary fixation in hasty pencil sketches. He mingled realistic heads with fantastic images unknown except in his own dreams. Now that the days were longer, they could sit at the window looking out on the boxed-in yards with their little gardens. Their own house plants were blooming. There they studied his sketches, Amy making few comments, allowing Donato to do all the talking. She was fascinated by the fervor and the earnestness which lighted his features as if they were but the crystal exterior of a lamp that glowed within. His face had become thin and pale and the grey eyes shone still as if with fever.

But when he explained his drawings, spoke of the lines of the faces he meant to depict, the emaciated cheeks, the troubled pupils achieved a natural intensity as if he were all spirit. After some minutes of rapid ecstasy, in words that caught, as though they might be stone, the essence of his visions, he stopped instantly. A fixed look in her eyes, a wonder passing like shadow over her features, arrested him. Then they could not withdraw their gaze, break the tenseness with speech or smile. Flame leaped between them and the space about them was darkness. And when at last the taut feelings snapped neither could continue. There had come between them that which was stronger than art, that which was more vivid than dream, that which erased the reality of the moment and merged them into the unending motion of the tides and the stars flowing with the flowing of their blood.

Amy had no illusion about her feelings, and she understood those of Donato. Nor had he failed to sense the new force that was stirring within them both. It frightened him as it frightened her. But it had become intenser with each passing day. It had found its way into his nights. At times it tore through his flesh like a torrent of fire. His vision of Amy at such moments was without detail of lineament or bulk. Rather was it the focal point toward which converged all feeling, all thought, all desire. And despite his nights with Selma, despite the casual intimacies that had occurred during his brief residence among what Mr. Kilbourne had called "arty girls," it never occurred to Donato that his reactions toward Amy were physical. There came back into his consciousness the memories of several afternoons when a look from her eyes had been like a light flooding dark places and had made him feel less bitter toward a world that had cost him such pain at an early age. Education had acquired new meanings, his ambitions had become significant, the days as they passed rolled into coherent purpose.

"I must get back to my work," he announced one day.

He had no doubt of himself nor had he any doubt of the high quality of the calling he had chosen.

When Amy smiled indulgently, he replied,

"I don't mean the store."

"You must not go back to that. . . ."

"Oh, yes," he said. "Just so soon as I can. But I did mean my sculpture."

"You are not strong enough, Donato. . . ."

"Next week, then. . . ."

"Next week . . . very well . . . let's go hear music in the meanwhile."

The night was hot. All of New York had poured itself out into the streets. They climbed a knoll in the park, found a place on the grass, and listened to the band below. All about them sat men and women, straining for the sounds that floated through the darkness. Children, unimpressed with the music, ran after each other, screamed and laughed. Adults in their turn scolded and yelled for them to stop. Couples climbed the near-by stone steps, hand in hand, arms about each other's waists, shuffling their feet, guffawing. Like a steady pressure the heat weighed down on everything. The trees drooped, motionless, opaque shadows. The lights of the houses in the distance gleamed dull and steady as if the curtains or the shades on the windows had never stirred, would never stir. The tubas blared and the drums rolled, beating themselves against the confusion, and, out of the chaos of sound, occasionally came a silence upon which hung poised, on wings that vibrated so rapidly that they seemed without movement, the thin silver notes of flutes — notes that imperceptibly lost themselves in the slowly rising wailing of the clarinets.

"I thought it would be beautiful," said Amy, clutching Donato's arm.

"It's like the statues," replied Donato, looking up at her and laughing. She laughed too and stroked his cheek.

"Don't be mean. They're artists too. What can they do about this?" And she made a gesture to embrace the noise, the inattention, the fatigued bodies drugged with the heat, stretched out in sleep under stars that seemed to sputter sullenly in the heavy sky.

Donato rose. "Let's go. I can't stand this."

–5–

They mingled with the crowds sauntering on the walks. They too attempted to fall into the slow rhythms of the passersby and like them find a quiet content in being out of doors, despite the heat, the jostling, the confusion. Amy had taken Donato's arm and could occasionally pat his hand.

"You're restless," she said.

"I just can't stand this, can you?"

"Let's go back to the apartment. We can throw up all the doors and the windows. If there's a breeze it will come through. We'll put out all the lights. . . ."

Donato turned his head to her. His eyes rested uneasily on hers. There was an instantaneous arrestation of all their movements — they stopped walking, stopped talking, they seemed to have stopped breathing. They were lost in a flame that billowed and rolled between them, about them.

"Let's go to the movies," Donato suggested.

But it was too late for the picture.

"I should have enjoyed it," laughed Donato.

"And I too . . . we haven't been ever . . . only to the play. . . ."

"I know what," suddenly cried Donato. "Let's have a shadow marionette show. I fished out a Columbine and a Pierrot and a Don Quixote on his horse. . . ."

"A show just for us?"

"Well, let's invite the block," he answered.

They laughed and hurried their steps. On the way home they discussed a hundred details of the show they had planned. One little bulb behind the screen would be sufficient. Amy would be the audience.

"Don Quixote is going to reconcile the lovers, Amy," announced Donato. "They have quarreled over the bad bean soup Columbine has prepared. Pierrot has thumped on the table and the soup has bounced up like a lot of geysers and spoiled the cloth, her dress, and even scalded her a bit. But Pierrot rises in wrath. She rises in fury. . . ."

His studio room was in darkness. He took her hand and led her across the threshold. Their figures were slightly darker shadows outlined against the confused light that filtered in from the street and the backyards. As he shut the door he said, jestingly,

"Oh, but I'm afraid . . . it's dark and I'm trembling. . . ."

"I'm trembling too," whispered Amy, but her words were not jest.

He drew her to him, and he could see her eyes leap with fire — the same eyes with which Selma had said, "Come back. In fifteen minutes"; the same eyes with which Angel had said, "You will come to see me?"; the same eyes with which the girl in the speakeasy had spoken to him — dreaming and vibrant, still flames, unsteady, bewildering.

His eyes caught the radiance and leaped with the reflection. His whole body quivered, not only with the motion of his own nerves but with the steady pressure of Amy's feelings. Smiles that brought pain pulled at the sensitive muscles of their lips, and anguish that became laughter filled the pauses of their breathing. Speech that is relaxing came not to them and their bodies faced each other tense, taut, motionless. Now the flaming that had become symbol of these moments was a rushing billowing of fire that swept over them, burned the darkness away, passed on and beyond, and left them standing, incapable of action. But it subsided and they looked at each other and gentle laughter echoed between them and they called each other by name and they put their arms about each other and they were lost in a darkness that was pain and music and dreams.

XXIII. CHANGE

–1–

MRS. NILINS had aged rapidly the past year. There had been days when she was unable to leave her bed. Amy took over the preparing of dinner, the care of the house, and numerous other duties usually performed by the sick woman. No matter how hard she worked, however, Amy showed no trace of fatigue, of being driven, nor the slightest sign of the nervousness and the jumpiness that had characterized her for years. Stephen Bennett had on several occasions invited himself and his wife for an evening visit.

"What have you done to Amy, Donato?" he had asked at one time.

Amy answered for him. "He has proved that the law is all wrong. Have you seen his latest group? Let us all go to the studio."

Donato, like Amy, had developed too. He never actually lacked poise and self-sufficiency; his two years with Amy, however, had resulted in defining the maturity of his carriage, the assurance of his thoughts, and the self-confidence in his art which is the insignia of the artist.

"This is meant to represent the germination of all things," he was explaining to Mrs. Bennett while Amy and Stephen were examining some small figures on the mantelpiece. Mrs. Bennett's jerky exclamations of wonder and delight formed the sharpest contrast to a figure whose plumpness suggested lethargy and somnolence. The bobbed hair that cut a straight pattern down the sides of her round face by itself would have denied the possession by her of any real feeling for the delicate and the lovely. But her brown eyes gathered the lights in other people's and revealed easy sympathies and understanding, which are more than a substitute for trained appreciations.

"It's wonderful, Donato," she piped. "Just wonderful! That's clouds, isn't it, piled up about the legs of these phantoms, as you call them. . . ."

"*Clouds* will do," laughed Donato. "I did think it might be the breath of the eternal and rising out of it are snakes and souls, vicious heads and the sweet faces of babies. . . ."

"Wonderful, Donato, just wonderful!"

Donato and Amy were happy together. Their lives had grown into complements that fulfilled and rounded each of them. Donato had not been able to get back his position at Maurice's nor had he been able to procure employment elsewhere. He had been discouraged, had fallen into a period of depression out of which neither Amy's unfailing kindness nor the moments of sweet and quiet love with her had been able to raise him. But she had held up the necessity of his continuing with his sculpture. She had bought blocks of granite, of marble, quantities of clay — all small, to be sure, as was made imperative by the size of the studio — and had paid for the casting in bronze of some of his diminutive modelings. Without his knowledge too, she had gone from art dealer to art dealer in an effort to dispose of some of his work. She had had sufficient success to use it as a plea for him to reconcile himself to staying at home and devoting himself entirely to the cultivation of his genius. Gradually he had been won over to the plan and worked all the harder out of a realization of the efforts Amy had made. And as he grew in mastery over his material, as he began to sense the growth of a technique which more and more seemed a capable instrument for the expression of his thoughts, the longer the hours he applied himself, the greater the exertions he made. If Amy was pleased, he was happy, and if he was happy, Amy was even happier.

Selma and Londin paid visits too but rare ones. In their presence Amy was not altogether herself, and the realization of that made Donato uneasy too. But their visits, though few, resulted in criticisms which fired Donato with new energy.

"Londin doesn't get my meaning. Why can't bizarre states of the soul be expressed in regulation anatomy? Orgulowich's contortionists seem like baby stuff alongside of Rodin, Epstein . . . . I'll show them, Amy. I'll go back to Michelangelo and express the present too. . . ."

Amy would sit on the edge of the platform, her arms clasped about her knees, gazing up at the astounding boy as if she were the child and he the older of the two. She recalled the trust that his father had had in him, and on these occasions wished that his father might be present. Don Emanuele was never mentioned between them in any sentimental way. They had attempted to recover his marionettes, many of which had been stolen while Donato was in prison. Many of the figures they had stored away in the cellar, several they had hung in the studio, a number had been stood up in the hallways, and one or two made corner pieces in her own rooms.

"They give me the creepiest sensations, those monsters," Miss Batten complained. "They're like what I used to see when the lights went out in my room when I was a child. A smile that never stops is worse than a dead man's stare!"

But Miss Batten did not really complain. She came frequently, and took for granted the new arrangements. She had understood without being told and had said immediately:

"Common sense reveals itself in many ways. I'd like to knock that thought into a hundred fool craniums I can mention in one breath. . . ."

Occasionally Donato gave one of his shadow shows. On such evenings Londin, Selma, Miss Batten, and Borriner formed the audience. Amy had a number of times invited several of the boys in her classes and one or two of the teachers. They were jolly occasions — particularly for Mrs. Nilins. She had entered from the first into Amy's spirit and made one with her in rejoicing over Donato.

But despite these contacts, Amy and Donato had for more than a year lived entirely unto themselves. They had a vocabulary for each other never used in the presence of a third person. Their privacies were singularly complete. They might have gone on for many years in this way whether or not Donato had achieved any success, whether or not they had had friends. At least so Amy thought, and so Donato managed to suggest by his utter acceptance of the life that had developed between them.

Her one sadness was Philip. There had been some talk of his leaving the Federal Sanitarium and taking up his living with her. The letters from him had become more and more normal, his behavior had been reported as falling once more into the customary patterns, and his health had definitely improved. But almost on the eve of his departure he had sunk again into the blackest despondency and despair. The latest reports seemed to indicate the onset of an incurable depressive mania. But although she continued to write to him, still hoping that he would eventually recover his mind, the letters were fewer, and her thoughts about him sadder. Fortunately, the love for Donato sustained her, and she knew thereby that she was twice blessed. In fact, she was afraid she was too happy, and more than once in her heart there surged vague rumors from a world that had once been — a world of loneliness and of long days, and of a spirit that yearned with the excitement of hope and was never appeased. But the rumors were only vague echoes and they soon merged and were lost in the steady harmony of her new sweet life. . . .

–2–

The young artist, however, had been nursing dreams. The narrow circle of his admirers, more or less unanimous in their opinions of his work, had fired him with beliefs about his powers. He had begun to expect a vast and immediate success. He was approaching the age of twenty-one, and twenty-one to him seemed the ultimate limit of his apprenticeship. He had worked intermittently on the group he had entitled *The Fruit of the Womb*. It was to be the *pièce de resistance* of his display when, having arrived at the age of maturity, he would startle the world with his offerings. He would have a personal exhibition. There would follow headlines. He would become the idol of the hour. The newspapers would carry full page illustrations. The several tentative showings in group exhibitions had not been so decisively successful as both he and Amy anticipated, but some few things had been favorably commented upon — they kept the clippings in a brand new scrap book which Amy had bought.

But more than the three lines of praise in the critical columns, they treasured the memories of a visit which had been as exciting as it was unexpected and brief. The door bell had rung, and a chauffeur in uniform had inquired whether Donato lived there. Then there floated into his studio a woman, Amazonian in size, but the central force as it were of a cloud of silk and brocade and feathery wraps subtly interwoven with color and mingling with faint hints of a perfume too subtle to be distinguished. She batoned delicately with her lorgnette and maintained her sharp master-ful nose at a certain elevation, possibly to allow the resonant notes of her voice to achieve their invariable effect of falling softly and trailing away into spaces beyond and above the immediate. And over the glitter of her eyes palpitated, like butterfly wings, long effective black lashes.

"You are Mr. Contini?" She said it as if she were going to question the affirmative answer. Amy she ignored entirely.

"You exhibited some children's heads recently?"

"Yes. . . ."

"At Paulino's?"

"Yes!" Donato was uncertain whether he should not have answered in the negative. But she was looking over his head.

"That's a marionette in the fireplace? How odd and how effective! Well, sir, the heads were all bought — three of them, and I wanted one. Can you send me another?"

Donato had taken the head to the address. Some vague thoughts that he might be entertained for the evening had colored his errand, but evidently he was taken for a delivery boy, the box was accepted, and a check arrived in due time.

"Fifty dollars, fifty dollars! Why, that is as much as the others combined. . . ."

"Maybe we can get away this summer, Amy, to that artist colony. . . ."

They discussed the plan at length and looked forward to a full summer in the country.

"There'll be mountains, Donato. . . ."

"Isn't it funny, I have never seen mountains. . . ."

"And forests. . . ."

"And I have never seen forests. . . ."

"Your education has been neglected. . . ."

"But I know the dates of Sennecharib and the Battle of Tilsit."

A difficulty arose in Mrs. Nilins. She had not been well, and toward the close of the spring term, she had been more often in bed than out of it. The doctor thought it might be feasible to take her to the country too. But Mrs. Nilins shook her head. It still retained the little brave topknot that seemed always on the point of teetering off its eminence, but the thin face had become thinner; the eyes had sunken into sockets that were almost fleshless, and blinked out sadly.

"No, Amy . . . you're good . . . both of you . . . but I have not stirred from this place for forty-four years. . . ."

"Never too late, Mrs. Nilins," Donato had said.

But no amount of pleading availed.

"You both go. I can manage here. . . ."

Amy, however, would not hear of her staying alone.

"Why, then, we shall all stay right here together," Donato decided.

"No, Donato. You go," said Amy. "It will be an experience for you."

In the end, he consented, saying, "I'll take up the bust of Mam-ma 'Chele and complete it there."

His letters were long and sweet and detailed. In the beginning he mentioned all the persons he met. Donato was not a hero worshipper, but his remarks about some of the well-known painters and sculptors who had cottages in Woodston came perilously near to adoration. But it was not because of their art, rather because of a quality of insouciance in their talk, an aloofness without false dignity, an assertiveness without conceit, and withal easy manners without familiarity.

In one letter he had said: "Some of the people here say the woods and the forests and the skies at night make one feel very small. But those who say so have done nothing and can do nothing. Storel doesn't mention them, nor does Falkinson. They seem capable of putting an arm about a mountain in comradeship. Falkinson was doing a landscape and I was modeling a clump of trees — isn't it queer, Amy, sculptors don't model trees? — when he turned to me and said, 'You know, Contini, I sometimes expect the mountains to frisk about like lambs.'"

His letters told of the poets who came and read their verses.

"*Remember how we read Juvenal together and what fun he pokes at the poets who insisted on spouting their iambics? Well, two thousand years have not changed them much. The ones who write tripe don't need to be coaxed; in fact, we have got to coax them to keep quiet. There is one up here teaches in one of the high schools. The only thing poetic about him is his hair. Every time he reads a line you would think he was quoting from Shakespeare and honoring that gentleman in so doing. But Forster, the New England poet, was here the other night. It was not until two in the morning that he consented to read — my only dissipation, Amy, really. Remington, the dean of the poets up here, rules the place with an iron hand and it's usually an early command to bed from him. You ought to have heard him read — each word was a note by itself and merged with the others without strain. No tossing back of the head, no dramatic gestures; just soft modulations, a pleasing smile, soft twinkling grey eyes, and something in his manner that said, 'It's an experience I have put into the words I know. Now, if you like it, it would be sweet. . . .' And you can see the birches swinging and the colt running in his poems about them. I never knew there was such poetry in the world today. Don't the teachers at school know about it?*"

–3–

Amy had not had any real notion of what pain loneliness can be. The years before Donato had been solitary ones. She had dreaded the long afternoons, feared the nights when she would wake up suddenly with a desire to touch some one, to hear someone, and find only vacancy, silence, darkness.

Terror had possessed her upon her return from Europe. For her was the sure knowledge that at the termination of her trip there would be empty rooms, a lonely routine without point, a perpetual round of days alone, alone.

But at that time there had been nothing else. Every step on the creaking stairs had not been a stopping place for her and Donato to hold hands, to laugh. The little vestibule on top of the landing had not been consecrated to dear memories of long, blinding embraces. The flowerpots on the windowsills had not been the tender occupation of two pairs of hands, of two interested hearts. She and Donato had not lain on the couch close to the window and witnessed the slow drifting of the stars far above the dense shadows of the warehouses. They had not then together transformed, by the mere wishing of it, the irregular roof lines into magic mountain ranges, the warehouses into spectral galleons, the uncoordinated rumblings of the city into the cries of gods rising with the sun and standing poised on the stars. Into those days, so far back now, had not come a young god out of his imprisonment and by the touch of long, gentle figures filled her rooms with what had never been on land or sea, the consecration and the poet's dream.

She had been glad to see him go, for she knew that he had been living too close to her, immured within the narrowing walls of the city. Her heart, nevertheless had filled with misgivings. The two years with him had been too magical. She had been too happy, happy as she had longed to be throughout her whole childhood and adolescence, too happy for it to have the finality and the permanence of truth. There had never entered into her mind any doubts as to the beauty and the wisdom of her companionship with Donato. It had matured him and had fulfilled her own life.

But Amy never once had justified it on a basis even so intangibly utilitarian. It had been because the clouds were, and waters flowed, and children were taught in school. It would have been impossible for her to imagine her life without it nor would she have agreed that it could have and should have been avoided — not even now in her moments of anguish. She bathed Mrs. Nilins' forehead tenderly, held up the old woman's head so she might sip the tea Amy had prepared. But her thoughts were miles away with Donato. She followed him everywhere. She saw, with a clarity that was blindness, that he was admired, that there must be Angel Smiths and Selmas about him. She did not shut out the scene, nor did she regret what she had done. Hers had been the happiness; hers should be the sorrow.

She was now thirty-one and Donato ten years younger. For him there would be numerous temptations, for her there should have been preparing the settled round of an existence devoted to loved ones. She could welcome it. She could continue forever with Donato and Mrs. Nilins. But the lonely days and the lonely nights, the lonely studio and the lonely chairs were now like torches in unexpected places, and revealed what, in the fullness of her first love for Donato, she could not have anticipated. Now, as she saw the fine wrinkles in the corners of her eyes, the flesh drawing on her hands, the neck that had been smooth and firm imperceptibly softening, she did not hesitate to face the vague events that were shaping themselves for the future. It was only a question of how long it would be.

Her habit of talking to herself returned during those two months of living without Donato. She had hoped that he too would become lonely and that he would return some day unexpectedly, burst into her room, take her into his arms, and allow her to place her head on his shoulders and half-weeping and half-laughing listen to her anguished but happy "Donato, my Donato!" But he had not come back nor had he written that he was lonely.

"Don't be silly, Amy," she said to herself in the mirror, shaking a finger meant to be humorous. "He is a young boy, and he has never had such an experience before — meeting all these marvelous people, being in sight of woods and mountains and open sky. Doesn't he write to you every day — almost every day — have it as you will! Where else would he go? This is his home — he must come back here."

Toward the end of the summer a letter came which caused her her first real distress. That night she woke up with a start, the words of the letter flamed across the dark room like a grotesque advertisement sign. *"Angel Smith in person."* Donato had intended them to be funny. *"You never saw such slenderness and how she can wear black in summer and make you feel it to be her own sleek smooth skin — well, it's the marvel of the place. Of course, by day she dresses, or rather undresses like all the others here. She looks like Atalanta — the swift runner of Calydon. Her slim legs speed from her under her girdled tunic and end in the lightest of sandals. And her filleted black hair! She has become the sensation of Woodston."*

Amy got up from her bed and walked the floor. Mrs. Nilins was sleeping in the sitting room to which Amy had had her bed removed.

"Is that you, Amy?" Mrs. Nilins asked.

"Yes . . . I thought you called."

"No. I'm all right." Her feeble whisper was lost in the stillness.

Tears came to Amy's eyes.

"But he could not do that — he could not do that." Her heart shouted the words. "But, silly, silly, what has he done? Admired a girl? He will be back soon. . . ."

Several days before he was scheduled to return, he wrote:

"You won't mind, Amy darling, will you, should I stay here a week longer? I have finished the head of Mam-ma 'Chele — and what an utter symbol of old age she looks: travail and hopes, sufferings and joys all melted into a composite mass of flesh that crawls with wrinkles. You see that I have set my own stamp of approval on it and I do not care what others may say. I want you to see it soon, but I must complete the figure of the matrix out of which the old head is to emerge, and Angel has promised to pose for me. Her figure is so slim that size can be made to embrace the old withered head between her legs and arms without dominating the group, and besides, I can have her toss back her own head and give it ever the slightest serpent-like look."

Her interest in his work was too keen and genuine for her not to see in the letter only the eagerness of the artist. She sat back and shut her eyes. Following his descriptions she tried to construct a picture of the group as he was planning it. She realized how suitable for the model of what Donato termed "the matrix" the body of Angel was. Her straight reed-like form, supple and bending, with its suggestion of quivering vitality so intense that it could flow only through the thin conduits of her legs and arms and torso! Angel Smith stood before her as a mere image. "It's fortunate for Donato to have got her to pose for him. . . ." But the words were no sooner spoken than she laid the letter on the desk and dropped her head between her arms. She wept, quietly, without bitterness, without reproach.

"It must be so, Amy. . . . They're both young . . . and see what she can give him . . . wealth and a thousand contacts . . . what am I?"

As Amy raised her head, and looked around the roam, on the windowsills with their ferns, on the floor where the exaltata and the cactus palms sat, she shook her finger in a gentle rebuking fashion.

"So, Amy, you dared think of a lifetime like this. You poor, naughty woman! Crabbing could have told you, and Mr. Sidon and even Stephen. Can't you see the lids slip back behind Crabbing's eyes and can't you hear his goat-like laugh — the surprise intended to be sympathy, and the cry of malice in his own soul?"

She realized that the perception of the possibilities that filled her with fear signified a change — a change not only in herself but in Donato, too. From now on she was prepared for a modification of their habits. She dreaded the evenings when he would want to go out. He had not gone out without her since the first day of their love. But he would want to now. That much, she knew it in her heart, would happen. She sensed too that there would be others who would share with her the first sight of his work as each piece was completed. Their comments would be more valuable. Hers were all delight and wonder; theirs would be discriminating, based on training and knowledge. Praise from them would be significant.

–4–

Amy had the misfortune of proving herself right in her intuitions, much as she had hoped that the fearful things might not happen. But she had not been prepared for the shock of Donato's first remarks. He had telegraphed that he would be coming in the evening. With trembling lips and eyes she waited for him as he ran up the stairs — three steps at once. How they creaked with his weight! Creaked? No — how they sang, sang, "Donato, Donato is back!" Even Mrs. Nilins was sitting up in bed, her face drawn with feeble smiles.

But as he held her in his arms — she had not had the time to look at him — all the old happiness came back, came back in a flood like sunshine over leaves. She felt her whole body flushing. Slight tremors ran like music throughout the length of her legs, her arms, her neck. Then they gathered in her lips, and her lips trembled as she kissed him. She stood him off at a distance, took him by the hand, and led him to a window.

"Stand there — don't say a word — don't move — I want to see you, what you look like . . . Donato, how you have grown! You are taller by an inch, I swear it, and slimmer. And look at the bronze of your skin, and your hair. It's not chestnut. It's become almost gold, dean washed gold! Let me see — rise on tiptoe — raise your hand — ever so high — no smiling, there, no laughing! That's it. You are posing for me . . . hold the position Donato, you are, you are Hermes come back to earth. . . ."

"Oh, you silly," he cried and seized her once more in his arms. She pressed close to him, but not as she used to, before he had gone to Woodston — with real abandon now, as if she were a young girl and he a full grown man, hesitant too, and eager, with eyes turned up to his, smiling uncertainly, and laughing a soft gay laugh deep in her heart. . . .

"I am so happy, Donato, so happy. You know I feared you would never come back. . . ."

"But I am here, and here I shall always be. . . ."

Affectionately, she slapped him on his cheeks with both hands. Then, pinching him with some vigor, she kissed him full on the lips.

"There, you young god . . . see how mortal maid can love. . . ."

He put her arm around his waist, and his around hers, and walked over to the couch.

"Oh, listen," he said. "You don't know what luck I had in Woodston. That's the place to go — for an artist, I mean. You have to meet others in your own work. . . . You remember Storel? He liked my *Fruit of the Womb* — raved about it. But he said what's the use of it in miniature. You've got to do it lifesize to make it mean anything. And then he said that if I needed a larger studio to finish it I could have his. He's going off to Europe for a year. . . . Of course, I can't hire it, you know. But Angel's paying the rent and I'm to use it. . . . Isn't that great?"

The silence that fell on Amy brought his words to an abrupt end. He placed his hands on both her shoulders and turned her toward him.

"What's the matter?" he asked, genuinely moved. "Aren't you glad?"

"Why, of course, goose," and she laughed and stroked his chin. "It's going to be great for you. . . ."

She had emphasized the "you" just a trifle, so that he raised his eyebrows, puzzled.

"Not for me only, Amy . . . for you, too."

"I know it, boy," she assured him. "Come now and say hello to Mrs. Nilins."

XXIV. ANGEL

DONATO INSISTED that he could take care of Mrs. Nilins while Amy was at school.

"Why, I would not hear of it, silly boy," Amy exclaimed. "You have got your work. . . ."

"Oh, I'm not ready to go downtown yet. Storel is still here, and the marble hasn't arrived. . . ."

"Nevertheless and in spite of and because," Amy in her turn insisted, placing two fingers on his lips, "You are not going to take care of Mrs. Nilins. She would not like a young god at her bedside anyhow. . . ."

"What shall I do here all day? I'm restless now as it is. . . ."

No matter how he tried, Donato could not work. Amy had perceived all too clearly that the two months at Woodston had unsettled him — the changes she had dreaded in their relationship were coming about. She dared not press him too closely with questions as to what he had done all day.

"Oh, it's wicked, Amy. . . . I must have worked too hard in Woodston. All I want to do is sleep — if I read, the words all seem stupid."

The practical nurse was dismissed for the evening and the care of Mrs. Nilins devolved upon Amy. But there was little to do. The old woman was suffering from the cumulative effects of an exhaustion which she had never found time to allay. She rebelled at having to stay in bed, but when she did get up and walk about the room for several minutes, the nurse was compelled to lead her back, raise the old woman in her arms, and place her in bed as one would a baby.

Mrs. Nilins had never complained. She did not complain now. All she would say would be:

"Fancy that, nurse, and I have walked up and down this house for over forty years."

She kept looking for Amy's coming in the afternoons. Amy's step on the stair was the surest medicine. Smiles came to her lips, her little eyes brightened, and she brought her fingers to her lips in an effort to move them up and down. In the evening, before she fell asleep, she expected Amy to sit at the bedside and talk to her. She had asked that Amy read to her.

"I always liked *John Halifax, Gentleman*," she told Amy, "and I've read it over and over. It was Mr. Nilins's favorite book too. Would you mind, Amy?"

Donato had sat in the other room reading too, or he had waited in the studio until Mrs. Nilins would go to sleep for the night. The whole house felt the influence of the sickness. The creaking sounds seemed to have multiplied, the faded rugs looked hopelessly threadbare, the old wall paper gave out an unmistakable odor of mustiness. Several of the neighboring brownstone houses were in the process of being wrecked to make room for one of the sumptuous modern buildings. The dust from the crumbling walls, sifted by the winds and the continual pounding of machinery, rose into the air, hung over everything in fine invisible layers, and at night, when the atmosphere had cleared, floated high and far, filtered into the open windows, through the screens. It lay on the ferns and the palms, shining silver in the half darkness. And with it there came a scent of faded, worn-out things, and a silence too, that was like the cessation of all noise. For by day the wreckers hammered and banged, shouted and called. Machines clacked and sputtered, trucks ground their gears and the traffic in the street became so heavy that the curses of impatient drivers floated in through the windows. But at night there came an end to all this, and the contrast left an impress of utter and irretrievable sorrow, as if a whole busy village had been engulfed in an instantaneous earthquake and where had been life was only leveled dust stretching all about and losing itself in the sky. Not only Donato but Amy too felt the penetrating influence of it and shivered slightly as though they might have been shown in a concrete illustration the truth of a sermon upon subsidence, decadence, and evanescence.

But Mrs. Nilins said, "Isn't it lovely and quiet? It has always been lovely and quiet in this street. Mr. Nilins chose it for that."

Amy had urged Donato to go out for a walk, go downtown. She had even suggested that he pay Selma a visit.

"No, I'll wait. . . ."

"But you know how long it will be. If I stop reading and think she is asleep, she will pat my hand and say, 'Are you tired, dear?' and I haven't the heart to stop."

"All right, Amy," he said one night. "I'm going downtown."

She had waited for his return, sleeping uneasily, rising in bed, going to the window. All the sounds of an old house seemed to have combined into a conspiracy to wake her at the oddest moments. She saw the moon streaming in and resting like a spotlight on her bed. There appeared to be something the silver ray sought to show her. She moved her hands across it, and as she did so an echo somewhere in the house seemed suddenly to have found a voice, and the voice said, "Hollow, all hollow." Amy jumped out of bed and hurried down to the studio. The clock said three but Donato had not returned. She lifted the covers and crept in. She did not know how long after it was, that the lights were turned on and Donato stood in front of her.

He dared not look at her. He had lowered his head.

"I am sorry," he whispered.

"Sit down by me," she asked him. "Where have you been, little goose?"

"Downtown," he answered as she stroked his cheeks, and ran her fingers through his hair.

"With Angel?"

"Yes, Amy. . . ."

She placed a finger under his chin and lifted up his head. It was the first time that he had turned his eyes to hers. They gazed steadily at each other.

"Kiss me," said Amy, "and tell me all about it. . . ."

"We were looking over the studio with Storel, changing things around, people dropped in, there was a kind of improvised party . . . that's all."

She kissed him rapidly and ran upstairs.

Most of Donato's time from now on was spent in the studio downtown.

"You must come and see it, Amy. I am going to make the group in clay first. . . . and the marble will come next . . . I'll need workmen to assist. . . ."

"I can spare some money," said Amy, sitting close to him, and laying an arm on his shoulders. "There's no reason why you shouldn't have mine. . . ."

Donato hung his head, and was silent.

"Don't you need it?"

"Why, of course," he whispered.

"Then, you shall have it. . . ."

"But I couldn't, Amy. . . . I'll peddle some busts and make a few dollars. . . ."

"What nonsense, you big goose! Or is Angel going to lay it out?"

Donato looked up, something between injury and dismay portrayed in his features.

"Amy!" is all he said.

"You can always pay it back. . . ."

"All right, Amy," he blurted. . . . "I'll take it . . . as a loan. . . ."

"Angel shall not have all the credit for you!" she cried, brightening up and laughing gaily as if she had been made unexpectedly happy. "She is still posing for you . . . . ?"

"Oh, yes. I couldn't do anything without her. . . ."

The final blow fell upon Amy with unexpected suddenness. Had it not come so, it would have hurt her more. As it was, she had been seriously worried by Mrs. Nilins's condition. The doctor had expressed the fear that the old woman might go at any minute.

"You know, Miss Rollins," he said, one foot on the running board of his car, his bag in his hand, a look of the greatest impatience on his face, "I never have seen a more perfect case of a body just running itself down — no pain, no illness, no nervous condition. Well, keep well yourself, young lady." He waved his free hand, made his way into the car, and as she started to walk, she heard the self-starter growl, the gears grind, the car pant and a streak of wheels and glistening paint had shot past her.

"*Sic transit*," exclaimed Amy.

When she arrived at school she found a letter in her box summoning her to Mr. Polter's office before she met her classes.

That fat little gentleman with his Viking mustache greeted her effusively, beckoned her to a seat and then shut the doors of the office.

"Miss Rollins," he began, in his blunt fashion, "I have an anonymous letter in my desk. I am going to ask you to read it. And I do so only to inform you that such letters do get written. It's only for your own information. I have made up my mind already and you may rest assured that I am forgetting everything. . . ."

The typewritten unsigned letter said:

"Allow me as a citizen to take the liberty of informing you that a certain Miss Amy Rollins, a teacher of Latin in your school, is guilty of conduct unbecoming a teacher. I naturally make no suggestion, but presume that you will know best what to do. Miss Rollins is at present living in intimate relationship with a young man who was once a pupil in your school. It has been brought to my attention that the students and the teachers at the school are aware of the situation and that it is distinctly a matter for your investigation and action."

Amy read it slowly without apparent emotion. Although the color mounted into her cheeks, she handed the letter to Dr. Polter as if it had been something casual and said, "Thank you, sir, for letting me see it."

She gathered her things, rose, and said goodbye. She heard Doctor Polter tearing the letter. "That's that," she said to herself. "All the earmarks of Crabbing's work. . . ." It might have been a common incident judging from the cool manner in which she reacted. But she was not able to complete her day at school. When she reached her home, she discovered that the nurse had been trying to get her on the telephone.

"She's very feeble, Miss Rollins. I don't see how she will last the day."

Mrs. Nilins, however, lingered for days without saying a word, without movement, without even smiling. The only awareness she showed was at times when Amy raised her head and placed the water glass to her lips. Donato came home every evening for his dinner and now that Amy had informed him that Mrs. Nilins was very low and could not hold out much longer, stayed with her.

"It's a sad place, isn't it, Donato, after your hard work in the studio?"

"I am working hard, but you are, too."

"You are sweet, little goose," she said, and patted his hand.

They attempted to resume their reading together. They spent hours in the studio, she reading and looking up furtively at him while he quietly drew sketches of contemplated groups and figures. As in the spring, they began again making bad puns and laughing at them, ridiculing each other's intonations and laughing at that. Though there seemed to have passed out of their relationship a certain rapture and joy that had filled it in the beginning, their evenings together were the sweetest they had had.

"How happy I am Donato! Just imagine — you are a grown sculptor. In three months you will be exhibiting really mature work — work that is technically good and touched with poetry too. . . ."

"But it's not my exhibit really," asserted Donato, "and that's why you're so thrilled. It's yours, Amy — it's all the poetry you taught me out of Virgil and Horace and Juvenal . . . it's all the poetry you gave me out of your own life . . . don't you remember the first term I was at school . . . what a little scared fellow I was and how I came to your room, and how you smiled at me and patted me on the head and said, 'This boy knows a thing or two, and he's going far. . . .' Remember? I had brought in a drawing of a Roman soldier and his armor and his shield. . . ."

"You were a sweet child, my goose . . . but you are now. . . ."

One night Donato had returned late, looking fatigued and depressed.

"Good God," he cried, "are they going to be riveting at night too. . . ?"

–2–

The apartments that were going up next to Mrs. Nilins' brownstone were a skeleton of beams against dark skies. It was obvious that the contractor feared too punctual snows and was anxious to have the frame work completed so that the bricks might be laid before a really cold snap and heavy weather set in.

"It's maddening, Amy . . . it isn't the noise even . . . it's the rhythm . . . a horrid cadenza . . . Whitman ought to hear this — how even he could get more than a headache out of it. . . ! How's Mrs. Nilins?"

Amy hovered about him, more concerned about his dispirited attitude, the unmistakable signs of dejection in him, than the prolonged illness of the old woman upstairs.

"Something wrong, Donato?"

"Oh, I don't know . . . I feel flattened out . . . there's no life in my fingers. . . . Maybe the inspiration is gone. . . ."

"You poor boy. But I thought you never needed inspiration. . . ."

"Well, then, it's because I just can't work. . . ."

Amy put her arms about him. "Something wrong? Tell me. . . . How far have you got with the group. . . ?"

The rat-ta-ta of the rivets broke in upon them. Donato removed Amy's hands from his shoulders, rose abruptly and left the room. She heard him go to the studio but was too shocked by his strange action to do more than stand gazing at the door. And then a kind of darkness fell in front of her eyes, and she felt her knees trembling with excitement. Slowly, as if by an appropriate pressure on her hair, she could soothe herself into composure and calm, she placed both her palms close to her temples, her fingers on the unruly yellow strands. The rivets pierced her ears like hot spikes, and as the noise and the pain of them died away, the resultant quiet was a signal for her emotions to break into turbulence. Do what she could to stem them, they rushed about her like waters in a whirlpool, as noisy, as agitated, as infinitely dark and terrifying.

"Amy," she heard the voice that spoke to her in periods of distress, the voice of her loneliness and of her search for happiness, "you are not far wrong this time. You made a bold play for good fortune, and when you thought you had won you find that you have lost. And don't blame Donato — you sought him out. You sought him out for his own good, but his good was your joy. You have been selfish. You were not content with the casual offering of Stephen, the affection of Crabbing, the passion of Mortimer. You had to have all those and more. You had them all in too great abundance . . . and now it's coming to an end . . . to an end. . . ."

She heard Mrs. Nilins call, but it was like the voice of one too far away to reach in a short time. She must see Donato first and assure herself of the suspicions that tore through her quiet.

She opened the door of the studio. Donato was chiseling at a head with a vigor that belied the eagerness it connoted.

"Donato. . . ."

He turned abruptly and faced her.

"You must tell me all," she exclaimed. She spoke like one in great fright, driven by desperation to a final critical burst of energy. "I want to know everything . . . now . . . now. . . . Do not stand there, Donato, as if you had lost your speech. I command you to speak at once — and to tell me everything — now — do you hear me? now. . . ."

Her voice had become a shriek, her whole body trembled, her eyes pleaded with sad, wild lights.

The voice of Mrs. Nilins, like a faint echo of Amy's cries, filled in the pause before the calm that followed.

"Come, Amy. . . ."

Donato had paled. He changed the chisel he had been using from one hand to the other and back again. He followed with his eyes the various steps of the transfer as if it were important that it trace certain scheduled and proper arcs. Once he tossed the tool several inches in the air. It twirled, somersaulted, and fell back into his hand. That seemed to be a cause for smiling, and he did smile; and then only did he look up at Amy and heard at the same time the calling of the sick woman upstairs.

"Amy," he said, "do go upstairs. . . ."

"Yes, Donato, I must go upstairs. . . ."

Amy's steps seemed to synchronize with the rhythmic barbaric tapping of the rivets. Donato listened, and as if the noise he heard were a cause for amusement, his face broke into smiles, but the smiles pulled down the corners of his mouth, and his whole countenance sagged in sorrow. And as if the rivets had been all the strain he could withstand, he did not hear nor did he see Amy enter again. Only when she stood close to him was he aware of her presence.

"She's fast asleep . . . just called out in her sleep. . . ."

They exchanged quick sad glances, smiles came to their eyes. Then, as if driven by sudden winds, they fell into each other's arms, and in their kiss lost sight of the heavens, and the changes that move and have their being under the stars.

They lay on the daybed, laughing.

"Oh, you can be savage, Donato. . . ."

Donato merely stroked her cheek, and said:

"It was madness, Amy, madness. . . ."

"You're not getting serious again, little goose? You pulled too long a face when you first came in. You frightened me so! You left me trembling! I wondered what had happened. And do you know? . . ." (she twisted the flesh of his cheeks between her fingers) ". . . I had an idea that you were leaving me, going away, never coming back again. . . ."

With the inexperience of youth, arrogant with its own successes, incapable of understanding pain, except such as withers its own hopes, he seized her hands, and holding them tight between his fingers, he cried, "How could you know?"

She spoke quietly, "Then I was right?"

Donato answered "Yes" without taking his eyes away from her.

"You were going to leave me. . . .?"

"No, not really. . . ."

"But you wanted to. . . ."

"Yes . . . but not because I wanted to leave you, Amy, not ever, not ever. . . ."

"It's Angel?"

The question drifted with a smile to her lips.

"Yes. . . ."

"Donato, my little goose," she said softly, pressing one hand on his shoulder, and stroking his cheeks, his hair, his eyes with the other; "don't you know that you must not think of me too much? You must not let me hold you back from your work, or even from someone else — if you love her. You do love Angel?"

She took his face in both her hands as she said this, and so hard did she bring her hands together that he tried to escape from her, draw his head back, even throw her off with one push of his strength against her. Wry smiles contorted his lips, jerked at the corners of his eyes, filled hopelessly the scared, empty pupils. Words he could not frame, nor could he free himself from the tight hold she had of him.

"You know that, don't you, boy?" she asked again and again. "Don't let my life clog up yours, drag you down? You hear me, don't you? What's the use of sacrifice? It tears your heart open, but you alone witness the blood spurting from every artery. Nobody else cares, nobody else pities you. Don't sacrifice yourself for me, Donato. . . . don't throw up your young life out of foolish loyalty . . . you owe me nothing . . . nothing . . . nothing . . . my little goose boy. . . ."

Her hands dropped and her lips fell quivering. All she could do was to present him a face with tears trickling slowly down her nose, down her cheeks until they reached her mouth. There they pooled in the corners and caught the uneven light of the dusk. She was exhausted — that much he could see. The daily round of duties at school and on behalf of the sick woman had been too much for her. She might have gone on indefinitely could she but have counted on his love, or at least on their companionship with its moments of play and its intenser periods of passion. That over, everything else was meaningless and like all meaningless things weighed upon her and the horror of it became an emptiness out of which she had need to escape. He was sorry for her, but in no spirit of pity. He was sorry because he realized with a keenness that was more than understanding that Amy had built a whole structure of dreams upon their union. As the days between them passed, they left with him a steadily increasing rest-lessness; with her, a steadily increasing contentment. It was something which had happened, as it were, out of nothing and developed into a shape over whose molding he had had little or no control. The collapse of the edifice thundered about them — and on both it left a sorrow that was the perception of the inevitable.

"Amy. . . ." was the only word he could find.

"You must go at once to Angel," suddenly exclaimed Amy. "At once, Donato. . . . I would like to say I release you — release you, Donato. Do you hear? But I have never bound you . . . you are free. . . ."

"But she is going away . . . leaving New York. . . ."

"Go with her . . ."

"You don't understand, Amy," he informed her with some irritation. "One doesn't turn a thing like this on and off like a spigot. Angel has some notion about all this between you and me . . . and so she is going away . . . leaving me with you. . . ."

Amy rose with a start to her feet. She pressed the knuckles of her fists into her cheeks and cried: "Really — she too — she is making a sacrifice . . . for me . . . giving you up to me. . . ."

Amy burst into laughter, laughter that began deep in her chest, and swelled gradually into hysteria, spasmodic, varying constantly in pitch, running the whole gamut of excitement, amusement, despair. It ended on a clear bell-like note as if she were prepared to prove that his remark was too comical indeed for further comment.

"No, Donato . . . you go back to Angel . . . you tell Angel you are not a fixture of mine . . . use those words to her . . . you go now . . . Mrs. Nilins is calling me . . . she will live a long while yet . . . I shall always have her. . . ."

And once more, as if the exertion of her talk and the outpouring of her feelings had completely overwhelmed her spirits and her body, she took a seat on the couch, buried her head in her hands, and sat down quietly, sat like a stone that has rolled for several feet and come to a stop. She even allowed Donato to put his arms about her, gently and apologetically, with no open show of kindness, for that he realized would have been too much to bear. They remained so for several seconds and then through the open door came the sound of Mrs. Nilins's voice. The uproar of the riveting had ceased, and there was no other unusual noise except the passing of cars, and an occasional drifting in of people's voices.

"Amy . . ." the feeble call was clear and pleading.

Amy patted Donato's hands and got up.

"You go to Angel, little goose," she said, and ran up the steps.

Donato sat in his place on the couch, his chin propped up by his hands, thinking. Every item of the room, without his looking up to see it, flashed before his mind. There was the mantelpiece with its array of heads and torsos, and there was the platform upon which Amy had often sat while he attempted to mold a portrait of her. There, in their gay attires, were the marionettes: Clorinda and Brandimarte, Columbine and Pulcinello. He saw the bench with the spatulas and the chisels and the sponges. And there was the stool upon which Mam-ma 'Chele had posed for hours on end, her wrinkled hands folded in her lap, her old black shawl tightened under her chin, the face with its infinite corrugations and its pinpoints of eyes lost in the deep caverns of the sockets. . . . He shrugged his shoulders — that trait of the Italian he was not likely to lose. Then he rose and went to the door. Everything was quiet upstairs. He put on his hat and coat, and walked out. . . . Even he had the sensation of leaving vague shadowlands into which he had by accident drifted on some faraway day, time out of mind.

–3–

An unexpected return of energy had permitted Mrs. Nilins to rise to a sitting posture. When Amy came into the room, the old woman waved a hand of welcome as if she were a little girl greeting a school friend. The face, with its hollows and its wrinkles all closing in on the mouth as if in an effort to close up life once and for all, was lighted up by the brilliance of her eyes, unmistakably shining with fever. She had always insisted on having the little hair which she had left done up in the meager topknot that had occupied the pinnacle of her person for so many years. There it was now, tied with a black ribbon, attempting to maintain its precarious position. Two fingers of her hand were snapping back and forth between her lips and there was a look in her eyes somewhat roguish, as if she were up to some mischief or were going to relate a bit of ridiculous gossip.

Amy hurried to the bedside at once, and raising her finger in a scolding manner, said, "Naughty, to be sitting up this way . . . Get right down between your sheets at once. . . ."

But Mrs. Nilins merely moved her fingers back and forth with increased speed and winked at Amy with a decisively mischievous twinkle of her eyes.

"No . . . Amy . . ." she whispered, and it seemed to Amy that the old woman had acquired sudden vitality and might at any moment have been able to get up from her bed and putter around the room.

"No . . . Amy . . . listen. . . . I must tell you now. . . . when you were in Europe. . . ."

Amy leaned over the bed and drew the old woman gently back into the hollows of the pillows.

"No, Amy," she said, and it seemed to Amy angrily. . . . "You sit down and listen to me. Is that the door? Maybe it's Donato coming in. You know, Amy, everything seems so clear to me today. I can hear the slightest noise. There was a child crying across the way. Neighbors with a child, just moved in. Been no children here for a long time. . . . Did you hear it crying? It must be sick. Listen now and you can hear it too . . . ever the tiniest infant . . . can just barely sit up. . . . That was the door, Amy. . . . Do you suppose it's Mr. Crabbing coming in?"

She waved her hand for Amy to be at ease and keep her seat.

"It ought to be Mr. Crabbing. He said he would return some day. . . . When you were in Europe, he came here constantly. . . ."

Mrs. Nilins had turned to Amy as if she had never been ill and was now as strong and as vigorous as the younger woman.

"Came to see me every day. . . ." and once more Mrs. Nilins winked and her eyes gleamed in a bright, saucy way.

"Pumped me about you . . . how much money you had . . . what you saved every month . . . and then he began. . . ." Mrs. Nilins laughed quietly in the back of her throat, and her fingers moved rapidly between her lips.

"You must not talk this way, dear," cried Amy . . . "You must lie down . . . go to sleep . . . it's time. . . ."

"I know, Amy dear, I know. . . . I do hear the child crying . . . it's ever the tiniest infant . . . don't you hear it?"

"Yes . . . it will keep quiet soon . . . you rest. . . ."

Tears came to Amy's eyes; there was no child crying. She had heard it said that sometimes the dying, in the few minutes left them, relive the scenes and moments which they have most cherished. And she knew too that in cases of prolonged enfeeblement such as this, a person will have confused memories seeking for expression. She wondered. Could the old woman be dying? She was alone with Mrs. Nilins. What would she do?

"Listen, Amy . . . about Crabbing . . . he began making love to me . . . would I marry him, he asked. He showed me his bank books, Amy . . . he had saved a great deal . . . a great deal . . . he could make me happy. . . ."

Mrs. Nilins' fingers achieved a rapidity of movement that was becoming more and more unbearable to Amy, and into her eyes there crept at more frequent intervals the roguish look that had been in them when Amy first went upstairs. Filled with her own recent sorrow, Amy could not listen to her dying friend without shuddering, wanting to put her fingers into her ears, her hands over her eyes, see nothing, hear nothing — nothing until all sound should cease, and she should raise her head and see the pale wrinkles fixed in death. But she knew she must be kind — who could resist this revived childishness in the dying woman — this attempt at playful gossip, with its hints of the ridiculous and the grotesque?

"He could make me happy . . . so he said . . . pool our resources. . . ." Mrs. Nilins winked again. "And, listen, listen, Amy . . . I took him to my closet downstairs . . . and I said, 'Mr. Crabbing, may I present you with some waistcoats and a beaver hat. . . ?'" (Mrs. Nilins laughed ruminatively, chuckling to herself, snapping her fingers between her lips). "'What for?' he asked me . . . and . . ." "Amy darling," she suddenly cried, her fingers resuming their movements with ever accelerating speed . . . "Amy darling . . . I answered . . . is that child still crying? Can't you hear it? . . . I answered Mr. Crabbing . . . can't you hear the child too, Amy? . . . I answered Mr. Crabbing, 'You could never carry it off in that beaver and those waistcoats, could you, Mr. Crabbing?'"

Mrs. Nilins turned her small, wrinkled face to Amy, and gazed at her with laughing eyes. Between her lips snapped her fingers, and all over her face there were the quick movements of amusement registering themselves. It seemed as if all her wrinkles had achieved an instantaneous and separate animation, and each had become the courier of joy to the other. For all the muscles of her cheeks, those around the mouth, and the puckers at the corners of the eyes, quivered with unfeigned merriment. And she looked at Amy, her pupils having suddenly become clear and glowing, as clear and as glowing as a young girl's who has heard sweet laughter and is about to take it up and laugh just as wholeheartedly.

"That was funny, Mrs. Nilins," said Amy, bending over the bed and trying to assist the old woman to relax and slide back on the pillow. But Mrs. Nilins waved her away again, this time feebly. She was about to open her lips. Her fingers rose to the height of her mouth, waved slowly down, made the upward movement with even greater slowness, fell as if they had an eternity to trace the arc of the descent, and then her whole hand dropped swiftly like a weight, and the room filled with the echo of its muffled thud on the counterpane. A gentle ruminative chuckle sounded in the depths of her throat. Her eyes sparkled once more. The topknot on her head teetered imperceptibly and then as the head jerked forward sharply the topknot loosened and a hank of hair, silvery black, dangled directly across the old woman's eyes. One more spasmodic movement, her head pulled up, and sank back on the pillow. . . .

Amy took hold of the cold hand and patted it.

-4-

"I haven't met your Angel," Amy was saying to Donato a week after the funeral. "When shall I see her?"

Amy's voice was cheerful, and despite the fact that her face showed

signs of the fatigue and the distress attendant upon the burial of Mrs. Nilins, she was animated. One might have said that for the first time was
now lifted from her life a burden of sorrow too subtle to have been apparent to the casual eye. And the lifting of the sorrow had not only released
new energies but had given spring and elasticity to her muscles. Only in
their sweetest moments together had Donato seen Amy so full of delight
and so buoyant in carriage and looks as now. He could not have penetrated beneath the brilliant surface of her acting. He was too young for
that, and though sorrow had smitten him and had drawn over his eyes
the film that magnifies the objects in their view, he was now too filled with
the elixir of success to sense sharply the anguish in Amy. For the anguish
was of the quality that seeks to hide itself from the gaze of even those who
have loved us. Were it visible it would not remain long, and to Amy from
now on the only self-sufficiency was to be this knowledge that although
she had been broken on the wheel, no one — not even Donato — had seen
her muscles contract in pain.

"Yes, indeed, Donato, you must bring Angel to see me."

She was busy with her small watering can.

"The steam heat has been drying up the soil quite fast," she said. "Especially this last week. I had so much to attend to . . . I hope I won't lose
the oxalis. . . ."

Donato followed her with his eyes, puzzled as he had never been before.

"She has gone back to her home," he said.

"In Kansas?"

"Yes. . . ."

"You'll marry from there?"

"Yes. . . ."

Amy turned around to face him. "Well, now," she said, "and are you
never, never coming back east?"

"Oh, yes, on our way to Europe. . . ."

"Right after the wedding?"

"Yes. . . ."

"Oh, come, little goose," she said and drew up Donato's head with a
movement of her hand. "Speak in sentences. Remember at school how we
had always to make you and the rest of the children speak in sentences. . . . We
still have to. . . . All of them, Donato . . . there's an Italian boy just like you . . .
grey eyes too . . . and all he can say is 'Yes, teacher,' 'No, teacher,' and hang his
head. . . . He's adorable, Donato . . . but he has no talent. . . . I don't suppose he
will ever pass his tests this term. . . ."

"You're going to keep on teaching?"

"Why not, young man. . . .?"

"Oh, I thought you might do something else. . . . You know I always
think the good teachers ought to be doing something else. . . . they seem
so out of place in school. . . ."

"And so," said Amy, laughing, "I'm not going to see Angel?"

"But you will be in New York?"

"Why, surely. . . ."

"We'll stop on our way to Europe. . . . Where shall it be?"

"At the Massachusetts . . . in the lobby. . . . I'll be waiting for you. . . ."

For a moment Donato thought that he had seen the passing of pain across her face. Certainly her eyes did dim for a second, and a pallor crept into her features. She stretched out her hand. Donato took it. It was cold and trembled.

"Why, Amy. . . ."

"It's nothing Donato . . . the steam heat, maybe . . . do open a window. . . ."

She made her way alone to the couch and sat on the edge of it, supporting herself on one hand.

"That feels good, goose boy," she said while a slow wan smile flickered about her lips. . . . "Oh, I thought I should faint. . . . the air is so good . . . don't shut the window, dear. . . ."

He sat down near her and was about to take her hand again.

"No, Donato . . . don't do that. . . . No. . . . I'll be all right. Get your hat. . . . We had better go out to eat . . ."

XXV. THE CACTUS BLOOMS

-1-

THE LOBBY of the Massachusetts hotel glittered and echoed. Amy had come in timidly and just as timidly had taken a seat on one of the long shining velour couches. Several men had glanced at her and then sat down nearby. She had opened the large expanse of fur collar on her loose-fitting blue coat and shaken off the snowflakes it had gathered. As she exposed the full, well-molded neck and the eager face above it, she might easily have been taken for a woman with nothing to do, waiting for a chance encounter. One of the men leaned forward with an air of perfect casualness and spoke. Her eyes sparkled with vigor uncommon to her, and her teeth flashed with a frank smile.

"No, you couldn't be the person I was to meet here?" asked the stranger.

"No, I'm not," she answered without any suggestion of anger; in fact, she continued to smile with sufficient warmth to invite another remark.

"I'm expecting someone on the late train. . . ."

"So am I. . . ."

She regarded him long enough to want to laugh at the broad-striped black and red scarf folded about his neck like the top of a toga. She did reveal her amusement, however, as she noted the incongruous spats and the thick gold-handled cane which he had sent out exploratory movements ahead of him. . . .

Nothing daunted, the man continued, "How about the grill? We could wait over a sandwich."

There was something distinctly pleasant about this, thought Amy. It would not be altogether stupid to enjoy the warmth and luxury of this spacious lobby — more like a Roman atrium than anything else she had seen in New York — and if the occasion arose, take the proffered invitation and await developments. But she smiled sweetly, and said, "No, thank you . . . the train will be in any minute. . . ."

His next remark she did not answer, and so she finally saw him pick himself up, straighten his scarf, swing out his cane and march farther down to await the incoming train. She was seated close to one of the huge palms that raised their broad leaves like fans into the air, and she moved closer to it so as to allow its shadow to fall over her. A drowsiness had come over, the drowsiness that came over her almost every night now. At last she had understood the meaning of her fainting spell on the evening when she had parted from Donato. Her muscles softened, became languid, her eyes

259

filled with heaviness, her whole body was overcome with lethargy. She was seized with a desire — not so overpowering as insistent — to move away from people, even from herself, to stretch herself somewhere and fall into a slumber, a slumber that would seal her spirits completely, allow no past and no future in fantastic jumble to crowd into her dreams. The bright lights, the colorful drapery, the heat of the room, the subdued but uninterrupted confusion as of thousands of feet tramping on thick grass that permitted no echo, the restrained hurry of the bellboys, the burring of distant bells, laughter not given full scope, names called, deadened echoes of dishes clattering in some far region — how the muted, muffled pandemonium of sound and movement, like a warm billow without force or momentum, rolled over her, and with even gentle pressure bore her down, down. How she wanted to lean her head back and sleep . . . forget . . . and not be disturbed. . . .

It was a curious sensation, to be awaiting someone and yet not daring to think about her. A whole month had elapsed since she and Donato had parted. She had feared that it would be insupportable agony. But, aside from the great loneliness of the empty house, become like a sound one cannot quite make out in the darkness of the night there was nothing but peace in her heart — even a note of gladness. She saw the future clearly and realized that it would be complete. There would be Philip to provide for, and the child that would soon be born. Donato had come into her life like the wind into empty space and having gone had left the imprint of his being, a shadow echoing in silence. Angel had not even acquired outline in Amy's mind. At first her lissome form, her exotic costumes, the bright ambitions that had brought her to New York — these things played about in Amy's thoughts tantalizing in their uncertainties of line and substance. Amy had longed keenly for a sight of her but only for a day or two. No sooner had she divined the presence of life within her body, than she ceased to think of anyone else. Donato himself seemed to lose bulk and contour. And Angel retreated into that region just beyond reality where the mind stores the longed-for and the unseen. . . .

And yet now she must not miss Angel and Donato. She had come purposely to meet them as they hurried through New York on their way to Italy. The newspapers, as he had predicted by the vehemence of his own hopes, for more than a week had been hailing the advent of the new sculptor. They vied with each other in presenting the fairy story of his life: his magical emergence from obscurity into the dazzle of the headlines, the Arabian Nights splendor of his wedding to Angel Smith, fabulous heiress of the fabulous millionaire of the west. Not a detail had they missed — except his life with Amy. She had followed the stories with terrifying misgivings . . . and yet she had not actually suffered from fear. What things she might have told them!

But of his child she could not tell them, the child which she was bearing — of the child which she would never permit him to see or know about. She could not tell them of their sweet days together, of the part she had played in his awakening. That must all be kept quiet . . . for everybody's sake . . . for the child's too. . . .

Time was passing. She knew she could not have slept. She looked at her watch. It was at least ten minutes past the time when they should have come. Could she have missed them? But trains are late . . . and it was snowing.

She leaned her head back and shut her eyes. It was so restful to shut them so. It kept out the glare and curiously enough too the noise. Surely, they would soon be coming. . . .

There was a tap on her knee. She woke with a start. A man bowed very low, and whispered, "I am sorry, madam . . . did I disturb you?" He hurried on without waiting for her reply.

She rose quickly. Could it be? The large clock said eleven. More than an hour after the appointed time. She went to the telephone booth.

"The Western Limited, sir . . . has it come in?"

"Oh, yes . . ." came the reply.

"On time?"

"Yes, indeed, madam. . . ."

Amy rushed to the clerk's desk.

"Has there been a message for me?"

The sharp-faced brown little man did not look up. "The name please?"

"Amy Rollins. . . ."

He looked through a stack of letters. "No," he answered.

"No telegram, sir?"

"No, I am sorry, madam . . . anything else I can do for you?"

This time he looked up and saw her face. The note of unbelievable disappointment amounting almost to anguish had been too unmistakable.

"Pardon me," said the clerk. "Aren't you the Miss Rollins that taught me Latin?"

"I wouldn't be surprised," she answered.

"Think of that meeting you here. . . . You know it seems impossible Somehow we kids all think teachers are sort of school fixtures. We never expect to see them when we get out. . . ."

–2–

The taxi jerked and stopped, jerked and stopped, as it made its way through the snow drifts. The lights from the stores threw chromatic fan-shaped rays through the welter of dense flakes, and here and there blocked out the windows with borders of rainbow. All sound and movement seemed padded. Even the grinding of the gears, by the time it reached Amy's ears, had become deadened into a soft roaring sound. Amy sat back in the car and looked out. The snow had blanketed one of the windows and through that she barely discerned rapidly retreating shadows.

Through the other window she beheld lighted homes, tier on tier, stationary, complete. Other taxis passed filled with passengers, passengers like
herself whirling one knew not where.

A moving picture crowd was cautiously picking its way across the
street. The snow fell in heavier and heavier masses. Now and then a sudden wind caught and spiraled it with momentary truculence, and finally,
in brusque deviltry, whirled it into the eyes and the mouths of the pedes-
trians. They stopped, unable to move, and the taxi honked its horn.

Amy looked out, interested in each single detail of the scene. She was
eager to catch every change of item or contour avid for a correct knowledge of what street they had already reached, wondered what it had cost
her so far. But despite her interest, in reality nothing made an impression
upon her. It was as if she were an infant before whose eyes are dangled a
host of commonplace objects for no other reason than to keep it quiet. She
had a dread, in fact, that the swift changes of scene were bound to come to
an end. Through her mind flashed the thought that she ought to direct the
taxi driver to keep on riding as long as the gas would last, and then to fill
up the tank again and continue. . . .

But the ride came to its conclusion. She hurried up the steps, and for
fear that the driver might suspect that she was frightened at going into the
empty house, inserted the key into the hole with great decisiveness, threw
open the door and ran, ran upstairs through the dark. She found her bed
and sank upon it. The drowsiness had come back with the first sensing of
the heavy heat in the apartment. As she sank upon the bed she knew that
she was not going to weep but drift into the deep slumbers that she had
been having for the last month.

She had not been asleep long before she heard a queer sound. She
fought against hearing it. She moved out her hands in the darkness as if
to drive it away. But there was the continual burring. She rose as if in a
stupor. The telephone!

"TELEGRAM FOR MISS AMY ROLLINS. DATED BOSTON FEBRUARY
10. . . . AVOIDING PUBLICITY SAILING FROM BOSTON WILL SEE YOU
ON OUR RETURN TRIP. SIGNED DONATO AND ANGEL."

She slowly crushed her fists. She heard paper crunch between her
fingers as if she had had the missive in her hand. And only then, for the
first time since Mrs. Nilins's death, tears came to her eyes. These were tears
without sobs, quiet and gentle, like water coursing down the side of a leaf.
Her lips trembled; she tried to bite them shut. No sound escaped them,
however, and no memory, no thought moved in her mind. She retraced
her steps to her bed like an automaton the movements of which are slow
and easy and sure. And only when she had lain for several seconds in
her bed did the sorrow in her find an outlet in sound. But it was only in
soft, short sobs . . . and as she sobbed she looked out upon the darkness
and saw the white curtain of the snow hanging between her gaze and the
illimitable spaces without.

–3–

Miss Batten had vowed that she would discover Amy Rollins. Some months after the death of Mrs. Nilins the old brownstone house in which Amy had lived was thrown down. Upon it, even before the leaves were green on the trees, there had risen a new apartment house. Almost as if Amy had been buried under it or had formed part of the cement that went into its building, Amy was not to be found.

She had come to school one morning, gone into the principal's office, and informed Dr. Polter that she had already sent in her resignation. There were no articles which she cared to take. She said she would continue living in the same place for several months. Letters would reach her there and anybody who cared to call would find her at home.

Miss Batten had gone the same day, but it was too late. Amy had left.

Rumors of Miss Rollins's resignation had spread at once, and a dozen tongues offered a dozen explanations. It was known that Mrs. Nilins had died and Crabbing had suggested time and again that the old woman had a penny or two salted down. . . .

"A wise old woman that — saved every cent. I suppose she left it all to Amy. Fifty thousand the building alone was worth . . . fifty thousand. . . ." His goat-like eyes glittered and his goatee bobbed furiously up and down. "And who can tell how much cash? She is a lucky woman — Amy Rollins."

–4–

The years had passed, however, and no one had reported having seen or heard from Amy. An opulent car, shining black like a seal just out of water, had rolled in front of the school, and a young man, his trousers creased with rectilinear exactness, had mounted the steps and walked rapidly into the office.

"Dr. Polter?" He bowed low.

"Yes, sir. . . . What can I do for you?"

Dr. Polter had grown more rotund, his face more flaccid, his mustache drooped with less of the Viking strength it once had had.

"I am Donato Contini, sir. . . ."

"Who?" His blue eyes, lost in the soft meshes of fat about the sockets, beaded with good-natured inquiry.

"Donato Contini. . . ."

Donato smiled as was his wont, with all his face, his teeth flashing, his grey eyes alive with interest.

"Oh yes . . . oh yes. . . ." answered the principal somewhat ambiguously. . . . "So many boys leave us, you know . . . and they come back and we have to be excused if we don't know one from the other. . . . And what are you doing with yourself, young man?"

Donato, who was now twenty-nine, laughed sheepishly, and transferred his cane to the other hand. He looked around the office and noted that the carpet that had once been green and shining was now threadbare, that the Alma Tadema Amy had so admired now faintly glimmered behind a layer of dust, that the mahogany tables with their glass tops were nicked in the corners and along the edges of the legs. A musty smell pervaded the room, and he wondered where it came from. Could souls exude musty smells? But there was a question that Dr. Polter had asked him. That must be answered first.

"I'm a sculptor, sir. . . ."

"A sculptor! Well, that's too bad. We should have steered you away from that — art doesn't pay . . . into a small position, in business, in the professions, with an assured little income — that's the ticket!"

Again Donato smiled. Evidently Dr. Polter had not heard of his series of brilliant successes: *The Pioneer Grandmother, The Immigrants at Ellis Island, The Marionette Director,* and the monuments to the old explorers, the hundreds of heads of infants bought up by the wealthy almost as if they had been doughnuts . . . and paid for richly . . . his cheapest stuff at that. . . .

He smiled indulgently, and again shifted his cane.

"Dr. Polter," he said. "I remember a number of the teachers. There was a Miss Rollins . . . she taught Latin . . . would you know how I could get in touch with her, sir?"

"Miss Rollins?" Again Dr. Polter's blue eyes beaded with inquiry. "Oh, yes, oh, yes . . . we did have a teacher by that name . . . some years ago . . . resigned I think. . . ."

"I did want to see her, sir. . . . I have written her on several occasions and never had an answer. In fact, my letters were always returned. . . ."

Dr. Polter sat up in his swivel chair and grasped its arm with more than uncommon vigor. For a second, Donato's eyes danced with embarrassment. Dr. Polter had leaned forward ever so slightly as his custom was with students whom he was examining. Interest gave a sharp momentary glitter to his eyes.

"I seem to remember," he said, speaking in a soft measured tone, "that there developed a considerable amount of talk. . . ."

He looked up quickly and stopped short, however, as Donato raised his cane abruptly to transfer it to his other hand.

"I beg your pardon, Mr. Contini. . . . I do want to assist you. . . . I was saying, considerable talk had developed about Miss Rollins. She went off — like that!" He made a sudden upward movement with upraised palm and loose fingers. . . . "People wondered a good deal. . . . She seemed to be trying to cover a mystery and instead created one. . . ."

"We were good friends, sir, and I have wanted ever so much to locate her. When I called at the old house. . . ."

"It had been torn down?" All of Dr. Polter's face muscles were called into play to ask the simple question and to follow it up. . . . "Nothing remains long in this city. . . . The new generation smashes left and right. . . ."

"I found the house torn down. . . . Has no one seen her since?" Donato politely pushed his questions to the front. . . .

"No we lose sight of people very soon. . . ."

Donato displayed his increasing disappointment, amounting now almost to irritation. Dr. Polter in answer drew his chair close to his large mahogany desk, made a vigorous show of fumbling through important documents, coughed somewhat pompously, and said:

"I am afraid I can't help you, sir. . . ."

"Well," cried Donato, laughing in a kind of standardized cheeriness, "I did want to see her . . . so much, sir. . . ."

Evidently he could not maintain the conventional offhandedness of his first words. Some note of unabashed sincerity in the "so much, sir" struck Dr. Polter as unusual. He looked up.

"I'm sorry," he said, and rose from his chair in a gesture of sympathy. . . . Donato, however, bowed very low, passed his cane to the other hand, and walked rapidly out of the office. He stood for a few seconds at the door of his car, having beckoned to the chauffeur not to move. With his cane he tapped the edges of his shoes, and then as if he had come to the conclusion of a serious deliberation, with some energy he opened the door. In a second the car was lost in the confusion of the traffic.

–5–

Miss Batten had laid a solemn injunction upon herself and was bent on fulfilling it.

"Sixteen years are left before my pension starts," she informed Miss Stevenson one day, lanky Miss Stevenson grown now more lanky, more angular, more withered, possibly by way of contrast to her friend. "And before I gain another ton, I tell you, Dorothy, I shall know about Amy. . . ."

It was that summer that Miss Batten had made good her boast. She had renounced her old allegiance to Europe and for some time had become a panegyrist for the therapeutic values of a trip through the States. There mingled with her attitude the determination that she must discover Amy and she knew that Amy would not be in Europe. But the rejuvenation which she was seeking seemed to flee her as she approached it and yet never quite to escape. For at the conclusion of every summer she returned as energetic as ever and as demonstratively unconcerned with the agitations and the regrets of those who yearned and of those who never found.

The level sands of New Mexico's desert she had only recently learned were stretches of pure serenity. They were the latest regions she was exploring for the elixir she had missed in the radiant routine of settled love and purpose. In reality she had abandoned all hope of finding it despite the gayety and vigor of her utterances. And yet it seemed resident in the unfailing determined gentleness of these dazzling sands. How their expanses traveled on and on until they reached the foot of distant mountains, coral and purple shadows that were unfolded quietly within the blue calmness of the sky. The placid movement of these interminable expanses toward a definite horizon, however, gathering colors as the shadows of cloud and wind chanced upon their surfaces, suggested that all turmoil could cease, that all action is in vain, that to seek and not to find is as sweet as to clutch the coveted article of one's dream.

"And that," said Miss Batten in her heart, "is sense."

Her Mexican chauffeur was whirling her with intrepid speed to the ranch she had chosen for her summer stay. She had distrusted the flamboyant claims made in the advertisements and was even now being confirmed in her belief by the pretentious old car in which she sat.

"What are those mountains?" she shouted.

"Las Hermosas, Senora," flashed back the driver.

"Anybody live there?"

"Mexicanos — some Americanos too — artists. They have flower show . . . everyone go. . . ."

At the Hotel, she heard further accounts. There was a rumor that an American lady had distinguished herself by offering several new specimens of cactus plants. These plants had hitherto not been known to blossom. But the miraculous had happened; the American lady had endowed them with flowers. Extraordinary blooms they were — as true creations, almost, as if the gardener had sculptured them out of the frail and invisible materials of an inward life that could be expressed in no other form.

Miss Batten had herself transported to the remarkable gardener's cottage. The small adobe buildings, painted a pale coral, flashed in the late afternoon sun. Above them, flanked in clever masses, or speeding off in narrow trails only to flow out again into broad beds of bloom, cactus grew in all forms and sizes. It seemed incredible that spikes and burrs, mean-looking devices to catch the unwary, as Miss Batten put it, should have assumed so many varieties of green shells, or should have shot into the air such gorgeous jets and pillars of color.

Amy recognized Rita at once.

"It's so good to see you," she said as she held out her hand. "I am glad it was you found me out. But really I did not escape. . . . I came where I seem to belong — all of us — listen!"

She turned around.

"Donato," she called.

A voice answered. "Wait a while, mother. I'm wrestling with Uncle Philip — almost got him on his back. . . ."

"Well," smiled Amy. "You will meet him later. You must stay for the night and meet us all. . . ."

Miss Batten placed an ample arm around her former colleague.

"Amy," she said, "you must tell me. However did you grow such a garden?"

STEVEN J. BELLUSCIO

Steven J. Belluscio is a professor of English at Borough of Manhattan Community College/City University of New York, where he teaches composition, American literature, and Italian-American literature. He lives in the Poconos with his wife and children.

VIA Folios

A refereed book series dedicated to the culture of Italians and Italian Americans.

NATALIA COSTA-ZALESSOW, ed; JOAN E. BORRELLI, trans., *Voice of a Virtuosa and Courtesan. Selected Poems of Margherita Costa,* Vol. 116, Poetry: Bilingual Edition, $24

NICOLE SANTALUCIA, *Because I Did Not Die,* Vol. 115, Poetry, $14

MARIO MIGNONE, *The Story of My People: From Rual Southern Italy to Mainstream America,* Vol. 111, Italian-American Memoir, $17

GEORE GUIDA, *The Sleeping Gulf,* Vol. 110, Poetry, $14

JOEY NICOLETTI, *Reverse Graffiti,* Vol. 109, Poetry, $12

LEWIS TURCO, *The Hero Enkidu,* Vol. 107, Poetry, $14

ALBERT TACCONELLI, *Perhaps Fly,* Vol. 106, Poetry, $14

RACHEL GUIDO DEVRIES, *A Woman Unknown in Her Bones,* Vol. 105, Poetry, $11

BERNARD J. BRUNO, *A Tear and a Tear in My Heart,* Vol. 104, Non-Fiction/Memoir, $20

FELIX STEFANILE, *Songs of the Sparrow,* Vol. 103, Poetry, $30

FRANK POLIZZI, *A New Life with Bianca,* Vol. 102, Poetry, $10

GIL FAGIANI, *Stone Walls,* Vol. 101, Poetry, $14

LOUISE DESALVO, *Casting Off,* Vol. 100, Fiction, $22

MARY JO BONA, *I Stop Waiting for You,* Vol. 99, Italian/American Poetry, $12

RACHEL GUIDO DEVRIES, *Stati Zitta, Josie,* Vol. 98, Children's Literature, $8

GRACE CAVALIERI, *The Mandate of Heaven,* Vol 97, Italian American Poetry, $11

MARISA FRASCA, *Via Incanto: Poems from the Darkroom,* Vol. 96, Italian American Poetry, $12

DOUGLAS GLADSTONE, *Carving a Niche for Himself: The Untold Story of Luigi Del Bianco and Mount Rushmore,* Vol. 95, Italian American History, $12

MARIA TERRONE, *Eye to Eye,* Vol. 94, Poetry, $15

CONSTANCE SANCETTA, *Here in Cerchio: Letters to an Italian Immigrant,* Vol. 93, Italian/American Studies, $15

MARIA MAZZIOTTI GILLAN, *Ancestors' Song,* Vol. 92, Poetry, $14

MICHAEL PARENTI, *Waiting for Yesterday: Pages from a Street Kid's Life,* Vol. 90, Memoir, $15

ANNIE RACHELE LANZILLOTTO, *Schistsong,* Vol. 89, Poetry/Gay Studies/Women Authors, $15

EMANUEL DI PASQUALE, *Love Lines,* Vol. 88, Poetry and Italian American Studies, $10

JOSEPH ANTHONY LOGIUDICE AND MICHAEL CAROSONE, *Our Naked Lives: Essays from Gay Italian American Men,* Vol. 87, Gay Studies and Italian American Studies, $15

JAMES J. PERICONI, *Strangers in a Strange Land: A Survey of Italian-language American Books (1830–1945),* Vol. 86, Italian American Studies, $24

DANIELA GIOSEFFI, *Pioneering Italian American Culture: Escaping La Vita Cucina,* Vol. 85, Cultural Studies/ Women's Studies/Literary Arts, $22

MARIA FAMÀ, *Mystics in the Family,* Vol. 84, Poetry, $10

ROSSANA DEL ZIO, *From Bread and Tomatoes to Zuppa di Pesce "Ciambotto,"* Vol. 83, Italian American Studies, $15

LORENZO DELBOCA, *Polentoni,* Vol. 82, Italian Studies, $20

SAMUEL GHELLI, *A Reference Grammar,* Vol. 81, Italian American Studies, $20

ROSS TALARICO, *Sled Run,* Vol. 80, Fiction, $15

FRED MISURELLA, *Only Sons,* Vol. 79, Fiction, $17

Published by Bordighera, Inc., an independently owned, not-for-profit, scholarly organization that has no legal affiliation with the University of Central Florida and the John D. Calandra Italian American Institute, Queens College/CUNY.

VIA Folios

A refereed book series dedicated to the culture of Italians and Italian Americans.

FRANK LENTRICCHIA, *The Portable Lentricchia,* Vol. 78, Fiction, $17

RICHARD VETERE, *The Other Colors in a Snow Storm,* Vol. 77, Poetry, $10

GARIBALDI LAPOLLA, *Fire in the Flesh,* Vol. 76, Fiction, $25

GEORGE GUIDA, *The Pope Stories,* Vol. 75, Fiction, $15

ROBERT VISCUSI, *Ellis Island,* Vol. 74, Poetry, $28

ELENA GIANINI BELOTI, *The Bitter Taste of Strangers Bread,* Vol. 73, Fiction, $24

PINO APRILE, *Terroni,* Vol. 72, Italian American Studies, $20

EMANUEL DI PASQUALE, *Harvest,* Vol. 71, Poetry, $10

ROBERT ZWEIG, *Return to Naples,* Vol. 70, Memoir, $16

AIROS & CAPPELLI, *Guido,* Vol. 69, Italian American Studies, $12

FRED GARDAPHÉ, *Moustache Pete is Dead! Long Live Moustache Pete!,* Vol. 67, Literature/Oral History, $12

PAOLO RUFFILLI, *Dark Room/Camera oscura,* Vol. 66, Poetry, $11

HELEN BAROLINI, *Crossing the Alps,* Vol. 65, Fiction, $14

COSMO FERRARA, *Profiles of Italian Americans,* Vol. 64, Italian American, $16

GIL FAGIANI, *Chianti in Connecticut,* Vol. 63, Poetry, $10

BASSETTI & D'ACQUINO, *Italic Lessons,* Vol. 62, Italian American Studies, $10

CAVALIERI & PASCARELLI, eds., *The Poet's Cookbook,* Vol. 61, Poetry/Recipes, $12

EMANUEL DI PASQUALE, *Siciliana,* Vol. 60, Poetry, $8

NATALIA COSTA, ed., *Bufalini,* Vol. 59, Poetry

RICHARD VETERE, *Baroque,* Vol. 58, Fiction

LEWIS TURCO, *La Famiglia/The Family,* Vol. 57, Memoir, $15

NICK JAMES MILETI, *The Unscrupulous,* Vol. 56, Humanities, $20

BASSETTI, ACCOLLA, D'AQUINO, *Italici: An Encounter with Piero Bassetti,* Vol. 55, Italian Studies, $8

GIOSE RIMANELLI, *The Three-legged One,* Vol. 54, Fiction, $15

CHARLES KLOPP, *Bele Antiche Stòrie,* Vol. 53, Criticism, $25

JOSEPH RICAPITO, *Second Wave,* Vol. 52, Poetry, $12

GARY MORMINO, *Italians in Florida,* Vol. 51, History, $15

GIANFRANCO ANGELUCCI, *Federico F.,* Vol. 50, Fiction, $15

ANTHONY VALERIO, *The Little Sailor,* Vol. 49, Memoir, $9

ROSS TALARICO, *The Reptilian Interludes,* Vol. 48, Poetry, $15

RACHEL GUIDO DE VRIES, *Teeny Tiny Tino's Fishing Story,* Vol. 47, Children's Lit, $6

EMANUEL DI PASQUALE, *Writing Anew,* Vol. 46, Poetry, $15

MARIA FAMÀ, *Looking For Cover,* Vol. 45, Poetry, $12

ANTHONY VALERIO, *Toni Cade Bambara's One Sicilian Night,* Vol. 44, Poetry, $10

EMANUEL CARNEVALI, Dennis Barone, ed., *Furnished Rooms,* Vol. 43, Poetry, $14

BRENT ADKINS, et al., ed., *Shifting Borders, Negotiating Places,* Vol. 42, Proceedings, $18

GEORGE GUIDA, *Low Italian,* Vol. 41, Poetry, $11

GARDAPHÈ, GIORDANO, TAMBURRI, *Introducing Italian Americana,* Vol. 40, Italian American Studies, $10

Published by Bordighera, Inc., an independently owned, not-for-profit, scholarly organization that has no legal affiliation with the University of Central Florida and the John D. Calandra Italian American Institute, Queens College/CUNY.

VIA FOLIOS
A refereed book series dedicated to the culture of Italians and Italian Americans.

DANIELA GIOSEFFI, *Blood Autumn/Autunno di sangue,* Vol. 39, Poetry, $15/$25
FRED MISURELLA, *Lies to Live by,* Vol. 38, Stories, $15
STEVEN BELLUSCIO, *Constructing a Bibliography,* Vol. 37, Italian Americana, $15
ANTHONY J. TAMBURRI, ed., *Italian Cultural Studies 2002,* Vol. 36, Essays, $18
BEA TUSIANI, *con amore,* Vol. 35, Memoir, $19
FLAVIA BRIZIO-SKOV, ed., *Reconstructing Societies in the Aftermath of War,* Vol. 34, History, $30
TAMBURRI, et al., eds., *Italian Cultural Studies 2001,* Vol. 33, Essays, $18
ELIZABETH G. MESSINA, ed., *In Our Own Voices,* Vol. 32, Italian American Studies, $25
STANISLAO G. PUGLIESE, *Desperate Inscriptions,* Vol. 31, History, $12
HOSTERT & TAMBURRI, eds., *Screening Ethnicity,* Vol. 30, Italian American Culture, $25
G. PARATI & B. LAWTON, eds., *Italian Cultural Studies,* Vol. 29, Essays, $18
HELEN BAROLINI, *More Italian Hours,* Vol. 28, Fiction, $16
FRANCO NASI, ed., *Intorno alla Via Emilia,* Vol. 27, Culture, $16
ARTHUR L. CLEMENTS, *The Book of Madness & Love,* Vol. 26, Poetry, $10
JOHN CASEY, et al., *Imagining Humanity,* Vol. 25, Interdisciplinary Studies, $18
ROBERT LIMA, *Sardinia/Sardegna,* Vol. 24, Poetry, $10
DANIELA GIOSEFFI, *Going On,* Vol. 23, Poetry, $10
ROSS TALARICO, *The Journey Home,* Vol. 22, Poetry, $12
EMANUEL DI PASQUALE, *The Silver Lake Love Poems,* Vol. 21, Poetry, $7
JOSEPH TUSIANI, *Ethnicity,* Vol. 20, Poetry, $12
JENNIFER LAGIER, *Second Class Citizen,* Vol. 19, Poetry, $8
FELIX STEFANILE, *The Country of Absence,* Vol. 18, Poetry, $9
PHILIP CANNISTRARO, *Blackshirts,* Vol. 17, History, $12
LUIGI RUSTICHELLI, ed., *Seminario sul racconto,* Vol. 16, Narrative, $10
LEWIS TURCO, *Shaking the Family Tree,* Vol. 15, Memoirs, $9
LUIGI RUSTICHELLI, ed., *Seminario sulla drammaturgia,* Vol. 14, Theater/Essays, $10
FRED GARDAPHÈ, *Moustache Pete is Dead! Long Live Moustache Pete!,* Vol. 13, Oral Literature, $10
JONE GAILLARD CORSI, *Il libretto d'autore, 1860–1930,* Vol. 12, Criticism, $17
HELEN BAROLINI, *Chiaroscuro: Essays of Identity,* Vol. 11, Essays, $15
PICARAZZI & FEINSTEIN, eds., *An African Harlequin in Milan,* Vol. 10, Theater/Essays, $15
JOSEPH RICAPITO, *Florentine Streets & Other Poems,* Vol. 9, Poetry, $9
FRED MISURELLA, *Short Time,* Vol. 8, Novella, $7
NED CONDINI, *Quartettsatz,* Vol. 7, Poetry, $7
ANTHONY TAMBURRI, ed., *Fuori: Essays by Italian/American Lesbians and Gays,* Vol. 6, Essays, $10
ANTONIO GRAMSCI, P. Verdicchio, Trans. & Intro., *The Southern Question,* Vol. 5, Social Criticism, $5
DANIELA GIOSEFFI, *Word Wounds & Water Flowers,* Vol. 4, Poetry, $8
WILEY FEINSTEIN, *Humility's Deceit: Calvino Reading Ariosto Reading Calvino,* Vol. 3, Criticism, $10
PAOLO GIORDANO, ed., *Joseph Tusiani: Poet, Translator, Humanist,* Vol. 2, Criticism, $25
ROBERT VISCUSI, *Oration Upon the Most Recent Death of Christopher Columbus,* Vol. 1, Poetry, $3

Published by Bordighera, Inc., an independently owned, not-for-profit, scholarly organization that has no legal affiliation with the University of Central Florida and the John D. Calandra Italian American Institute, Queens College/CUNY.